THE GIFT OF BATTLE

(BOOK #17 IN THE SORCERER'S RING)

MORGAN RICE

D1329409

Morgan Rice is the #1 bestselling and USA Today bestselling author of the epic fantasy series THE SORCERER'S RING, comprising seventeen books; of the #1 bestselling series THE VAMPIRE JOURNALS, comprising eleven books (and counting); of the #1 bestselling series THE SURVIVAL TRILOGY, a post-apocalyptic thriller comprising two books (and counting); and of the new epic fantasy series KINGS AND SORCERERS, comprising six books. Morgan's books are available in audio and print editions, and translations are available in over 25 languages.

TURNED (Book #1 in the Vampire Journals), ARENA ONE (Book #1 of the Survival Trilogy) and A QUEST OF HEROES (Book #1 in the Sorcerer's Ring) and RISE OF THE DRAGONS (Kings and Sorcerers—Book #1) are each available as a free download!

Morgan loves to hear from you, so please feel free to visit www.morganricebooks.com to join the email list, receive a free book, receive free giveaways, download the free app, get the latest exclusive news, connect on Facebook and Twitter, and stay in touch!

"THE SORCERER'S RING has all the ingredients for an instant success: plots, counterplots, mystery, valiant knights, and blossoming relationships replete with broken hearts, deception and betrayal. It will keep you entertained for hours, and will satisfy all ages. Recommended for the permanent library of all fantasy readers."
--Books and Movie Reviews, Roberto Mattos

"[An] entertaining epic fantasy."
—Kirkus Reviews

"The beginnings of something remarkable are there."
--San Francisco Book Review

"Action-packed …. Rice's writing is solid and the premise intriguing."
--Publishers Weekly

"A spirited fantasy ….Only the beginning of what promises to be an epic young adult series."
--Midwest Book Review

KINGS AND SORCERERS

RISE OF THE DRAGONS (Book #1)
RISE OF THE VALIANT (Book #2)
THE WEIGHT OF HONOR (Book #3)
A FORGE OF VALOR (Book #4)
A REALM OF SHADOWS (Book #5)
NIGHT OF THE BOLD (Book #6)

THE SORCERER'S RING

A QUEST OF HEROES (Book #1)
A MARCH OF KINGS (Book #2)
A FATE OF DRAGONS (Book #3)
A CRY OF HONOR (Book #4)
A VOW OF GLORY (Book #5)
A CHARGE OF VALOR (Book #6)
A RITE OF SWORDS (Book #7)
A GRANT OF ARMS (Book #8)
A SKY OF SPELLS (Book #9)
A SEA OF SHIELDS (Book #10)
A REIGN OF STEEL (Book #11)
A LAND OF FIRE (Book #12)
A RULE OF QUEENS (Book #13)
AN OATH OF BROTHERS (Book #14)
A DREAM OF MORTALS (Book #15)
A JOUST OF KNIGHTS (Book #16)
THE GIFT OF BATTLE (Book #17)

THE SURVIVAL TRILOGY

ARENA ONE: SLAVERSUNNERS (Book #1)
ARENA TWO (Book #2)

THE VAMPIRE JOURNALS

TURNED (Book #1)
LOVED (Book #2)
BETRAYED (Book #3)
DESTINED (Book #4)
DESIRED (Book #5)
BETROTHED (Book #6)
VOWED (Book #7)

For Jake Maynard.

A true warrior.

"You come to me with a sword, a spear, and a javelin—
but I come to you with the Name of the Lord, Master of Legions, God
of the battalions."

--David to Goliath
I Samuel, 17:45

CHAPTER ONE

Thorgrin, standing on the violently rocking ship, looked out before him and slowly, in horror, began to realize what he had just done. He looked down in shock at his own hand, still gripping the Sword of the Dead, then looked up to see, but inches away, the face of his best friend, Reece, staring back at him, eyes wide open in pain and betrayal. Thor's hands shook violently as he realized he had just stabbed his best friend in the chest and was watching him die before his eyes.

Thor could not understand what had happened. As the ship tossed and turned, the currents continued to pull them through the Straits of Madness, until finally, they emerged out the other side. The currents calmed, the ship leveled out, and the thick clouds began to lift as with one final burst, they exited into calm, still waters.

As they did, the fog that had enveloped Thor's mind lifted, and he began to feel his old self, to see the world with clarity once again. He looked at Reece in front of him, and his heart broke as he realized it was not the face of an enemy, but of his best friend. He slowly realized what he had done, realized that he had been in the grips of something greater than himself, a spirit of madness he could not control, which had forced him to perform this horrible act.

"NO!" Thorgrin shouted, his voice broken with anguish.

Thor extracted the Sword of the Dead from his best friend's chest, and as he did, Reece gasped and began to collapse. Thor chucked the sword away, not wanting to lay eyes upon it, and it landed with a hollow thud on the deck, as Thor sank to his knees and caught Reece, holding him in his arms, determined to save him.

"Reece!" he called out, crushed by guilt.

Thor reached out and pressed his palm against the wound, trying to stop the bleeding. But he could feel the hot blood running through his fingers, could feel Reece's life force ebbing out of him as he held him in his arms.

Elden, Matus, Indra, and Angel rushed forward, they, too, finally free from the grips of their madness, and they crowded around. Thor

1

closed his eyes and prayed with all he had that his friend come back to him, that he, Thor, be given one chance to rectify his error.

Thor heard footsteps, and he looked up to see Selese rush forward, her skin more pale than he'd ever seen, her eyes aglow with a light that was other-worldly. She dropped to her knees before Reece, took him in her arms, and as she did, Thor let him go, seeing the glow surrounding her and remembering her powers as a healer.

Selese looked up at Thor, her eyes burning with intensity.

"Only you can save him," she said urgently. "Place your hand on his wound now!" she commanded.

Thor reached out and placed a palm on Reece's chest, and as he did, Selese laid her hand over his. He could feel the heat and power coursing through her palm, over his hand, and into Reece's wound.

She closed her eyes and began to hum, and Thor felt a wave of heat rise up in his friend's body. Thor prayed with all he had that his friend come back to him, that he be forgiven for whatever madness had driven him to do this.

To Thor's great relief, Reece slowly opened his eyes. He blinked and looked up at the sky, and then slowly sat up.

Thor watched, amazed, as Reece blinked several times and looked down at his wound: it was entirely healed. Thor was speechless, overcome, in awe of Selese's powers.

"My brother!" Thorgrin cried out.

He reached out and hugged him, and Reece, disoriented, slowly hugged him back as Thor helped him to his feet.

"You are alive!" Thor exclaimed, hardly daring to believe it, clasping his shoulder. Thor thought of all the battles they had been in together, all the adventures, and he could not have tolerated the idea of losing him.

"And why would I not be?" Reece blinked, confused. He looked all around at the wondering faces of the Legion, and he seemed puzzled. The others each stepped forward and embraced him, one by one.

As the others stepped forward, Thor looked around and took stock, and he suddenly realized, with horror, that someone was missing: O'Connor.

Thor rushed to the side rail and frantically searched the waters, remembering O'Connor, at the height of his madness, had leapt off the ship into the raging currents.

"O'Connor!" he yelled.

The others rushed up beside him and searched the waters, too. Thor stared down and craned his neck to look back at the Straits, at the raging red waters, thick with blood—and as he did, he saw O'Connor, flailing, being sucked in right at the border of the Straits.

Thor wasted no time; he reacted instinctively and leapt up onto the rail and then dove headfirst over the edge, into sea.

Submerged, startled by the heat of it, Thor felt how thick this water was, as if he were swimming through blood. The water, so hot, was like swimming in mud.

It took all of Thor's strength to swim through the viscous waters, back up to the surface. He set his sights on O'Connor, who was beginning to sink, and he could see the panic in his eyes. He could also see, as O'Connor crossed the border into the open sea, the madness beginning to leave him.

Still, as he flailed, he was beginning to sink, and Thor knew that if he didn't reach him soon, he would soon sink to the bottom of the Straits and never be found again.

Thor redoubled his efforts, swimming with all he had, swimming through the intense pain and exhaustion he felt in his shoulders. And yet, just as he neared, O'Connor began to sink down into the water.

Thor felt an injection of adrenaline as he watched his friend sink beneath the surface, knowing it was now or never. He burst forward, dove down underwater, and gave a great kick. He swam underwater, straining to open his eyes and see through the thick liquid; he could not. They stung too much.

Thor closed his eyes and drew upon his instincts. He summoned some deep part of himself that could see without seeing.

With another desperate kick, Thor reached out, groping the waters before him, and felt something: a sleeve.

Elated, he grabbed O'Connor and held on tight, amazed at the weight of him as he sank.

Thor yanked, as he turned and with all his might aimed back up for the surface. He was in agony, every muscle in his body protesting, as he kicked and swam for freedom. The waters were so thick, held so much pressure, his lungs felt as if they might burst. With each stroke of his hand, he felt as if he were pulling the world.

Just when he thought he would never make it, would sink back down to the depths with O'Connor and die here in this awful place, Thor suddenly broke the surface of the water. Gasping for air, he turned and looked all around and saw, with relief, that they had emerged on the other side of the Straits of Madness, in the open waters. He watched O'Connor's head pop up beside him, saw him, too, gasping for air, and his sense of relief was complete.

Thor watched as the madness left his friend and the lucidity slowly returned to his eyes.

O'Connor blinked several times, coughing and gasping out the water, then looked to Thor, questioningly.

"What are we doing here?" he asked, confused. "Where are we?"

"Thorgrin!" called a voice.

Thor heard a splash in the water and he turned and saw a heavy rope land in the water beside him. He looked up and saw Angel standing up there, joined by the others at the rail of the ship, which had sailed back to meet them.

Thor grabbed it, grabbing O'Connor with his other hand, and as he did the rope moved, Elden reaching down with his great strength and yanking them both up the side of the hull. The other Legion joined in and pulled, one yank at a time, until Thor felt himself rising through the air and, finally, over the rail. They both landed on the deck of the ship with a thud.

Thor, exhausted, out of breath, still coughing up sea water, sprawled on the deck beside O'Connor; O'Connor turned and looked at him, equally exhausted, and Thor could see the gratitude in his eyes. He could see O'Connor thanking him. No words need be said—Thor understood. They had a silent code. They were Legion brothers. Sacrificing for each other was what they did. It was what they lived for.

Suddenly, O'Connor started laughing.

At first Thor was worried, wondering if the madness was still upon him, but then he realized that O'Connor was fine. He was just back to his old self. He was laughing from relief, laughing from joy at being alive.

4

Thor began to laugh, too, the stress behind him, and the others all joined in. They were alive; despite all odds, they were alive.

The other Legion stepped forward and grabbed O'Connor and Thor and yanked them back to their feet. They all clasped hands, embraced joyfully, their ship, finally, entering waters with smooth sailing ahead.

Thor looked out and saw with relief that they were sailing further and further from the Straits, and lucidity was descending over all of them. They had made it; they had passed through the Straits, albeit with a heavy price. Thor did not think they could survive a trip through it again.

"There!" called out Matus.

Thor turned with the others and followed his finger as he pointed—and he was stunned by the sight before them. He saw a whole new vista spread before them on the horizon, a new landscape in this Land of Blood. It was a landscape thick with gloom, dark clouds lingering low on the horizon, the water still thick with blood—and yet now, the outline of the shore was closer, more visible. It was black, devoid of trees or life, looking like ash and mud.

Thor's heartbeat quickened as beyond it, in the distance, he spotted a black castle, made of what appeared to be earth and ash and mud, rising up from the ground as if it were one with it. Thor could feel the evil emanating off of it.

Leading to the castle was a narrow canal, its waterways lined with torches, blocked by a drawbridge. Thor saw torches burning in the windows of the castle, and he felt a sudden sense of certainty: with all his heart, he knew that Guwayne was inside that castle, waiting for him.

"Full sails!" Thor cried out, feeling back in control again, feeling a renewed sense of purpose.

His brothers jumped into action, hoisting the sails as they caught the strong breeze that picked up from behind and propelled them forward. For the first time since entering this Land of Blood, Thor felt a sense of optimism, a sense that they could really find his son and rescue him from here.

"I'm glad you're alive," came a voice.

Thor turned and looked down to see Angel smiling up at him, tugging on his shirt. He smiled, knelt down beside her, and hugged her.

"As I am you," he replied.

5

"I don't understand what happened," she said. "One minute I was myself, and the next…it was like I did not know myself."

Thor slowly shook his head, trying to forget.

"Madness is the worst foe of all," he replied. "We, ourselves, are the one enemy we cannot overcome."

She frowned, concerned.

"Will it ever happen again?" she asked. "Is there anything else in this place like that?" she asked, fear in her voice as she studied the horizon.

Thor studied it too, wondering the very same thing himself—when all too soon, to his dread, the answer came rushing out at them.

There came a tremendous splash, like the sound of a whale surfacing, and Thor was amazed to see the most hideous creature he'd ever seen emerging before him. It looked like a monster squid, fifty feet high, bright red, the color of blood, and it loomed over the ship as it shot up out of the waters, its endless tentacles thirty feet long, dozens of them spreading out in every direction. Its beady yellow eyes scowled down at them, filled with fury, as its huge mouth, lined with sharp yellow fangs, opened up with a sickening sound. The creature blotted out whatever light the gloomy skies had allowed, and it shrieked an unearthly sound as it began to descend right for them, its tentacles spread out, ready to consume the entire ship.

Thor watched it with dread, caught up in its shadow with all the others, and he knew they had gone from one certain death to the next.

CHAPTER TWO

The Empire commander lashed his zerta again and again as he galloped through the Great Waste, following the trail, as he had been for days, across the desert floor. Behind him, his men rode on, gasping, on the verge of collapsing, as he had not given them a moment to rest the entire time they had been riding—even throughout the night. He knew how to drive zertas into the ground—and he knew how to drive men, too.

He had no mercy on himself, and he certainly had none for his men. He wanted them to be impervious to exhaustion and heat and cold—especially when they were on a mission as sacred as this. After all, if this trail actually led to where he hoped it might—to the legendary Ridge itself—it could change the entire fate of the Empire.

The commander dug his heels into the zerta's back until it shrieked, forcing it ever faster, until it was nearly tripping over itself. He squinted into the sun, scrutinizing the trail as they went. He had followed many trails in his life, and had killed many people at the end of them—yet he had never followed a trail as enthralling as this one. He could feel how close he was to the greatest discovery in the history of the Empire. His name would be memorialized, sung of for generations.

They ascended a ridge in the desert, and he began to hear a faint noise growing, like a storm brewing in the desert; he looked out as they crested it, expecting to see a sandstorm coming their way, and he was shocked, instead, to spot a stationary wall of sand a hundred yards away, rising straight up from the ground into the sky, swirling and churning, like a tornado in place.

He stopped, his men beside him, and watched, curious, as it did not seem to move. He could not understand it. It was a wall of raging sand, but it did not come any closer. He wondered what lay on the other side. Somehow, he sensed, it was the Ridge.

"Your trail ends," one of his soldiers said derisively.

"We cannot pass through that wall," said another.

7

"You have led us to nothing but more sand," said another.

The commander slowly shook his head, scowling back with conviction.

"And what if there lies a land on the other side of that sand?" he retorted.

"The other side?" a soldier asked. "You are mad. It is nothing but a cloud of sand, an endless waste, like the rest of this desert."

"Admit your failure," said another soldier. "Turn back now—or if not, we shall turn back without you."

The commander turned and faced his soldiers, shocked at their insolence—and saw contempt and rebellion in their eyes. He knew he had to act quickly if he were to quash it.

In a fit of sudden rage, the commander reached down, grabbed a dagger from his belt, and swung it backwards in one quick motion, lodging it in the soldier's throat. The soldier gasped, then fell backwards off his zerta and hit the ground, a fresh pool of blood collecting on the desert floor. Within moments, a swarm of insects appeared out of nowhere, covering his body and eating it.

The other soldiers now looked to their commander in fear.

"Is there anyone else who wishes to defy my command?" he asked.

The men stared back nervously, but this time said nothing.

"Either the desert will kill you," he said, "or I will. It's your choice."

The commander charged forward, lowering his head, and cried a great battle cry as he galloped right for the sand wall, knowing it might mean his death. He knew his men would follow, and a moment later he heard the sound of their zertas, and smiled in satisfaction. Sometimes they just had to be kept in line.

He shrieked as he entered the tornado of sand. It felt like a million pounds of sand weighing down on him, chafing his skin from every direction as he charged deeper and deeper into it. It was so loud, sounding like a thousand hornets in his ears, and yet still he charged, kicking his zerta, forcing it, even as it protested, deeper and deeper inside. He could feel the sand scraping his head and eyes and face, and he felt as if he might be torn to bits.

Yet still he rode on.

Just as he was wondering if his men were right, if this wall led to nothing, if they would all die here in this place, suddenly, to the commander's great relief, he burst out of the sand and back into daylight, no more sand chafing him, no more noise in his ears, nothing but open sky and air—which he had never been so happy to see.

All around him, his men burst out, too, all of them chafed and bleeding like he, along with their zertas, all looking more dead than alive—yet all of them alive.

And as he looked up and out before him, the commander's heart suddenly beat faster as he came to a sudden stop at the startling sight. He could not breathe as he took in the vista, and slowly but surely, he felt his heart swell with a sudden sense of victory, of triumph. Majestic peaks rose straight up into the sky, forming a circle. A place that could only be one thing:

The Ridge.

There it sat on the horizon, shooting up into the air, magnificent, vast, stretching out of sight on either side. And there, at the top, gleaming in the sunlight, he was amazed to see thousands of soldiers in shining armor, patrolling.

He had found it. He, and he alone, had found it.

His men came to an abrupt stop beside him, and he could see them, too, looking up at it in awe and wonder, their mouths agape, all of them thinking the same thing he did: this moment was history. They would all be heroes, known for generations in Empire lore.

With a broad smile, the commander turned and faced his men, who now looked at him with deference; he then yanked on his zerta and turned it back around, preparing to ride back through the sand wall— and all the way, without stopping, until he reached the Empire base and reported to the Knights of the Seven what he personally had discovered. Within days, he knew, the entire force of the Empire would descend upon this place, the weight of a million men bent on destruction. They would pass through this sand wall, scale the Ridge, and crush those knights, taking over the final remaining free territory of the Empire.

"Men," he said, "our time has come. Prepare to have your names etched in eternity."

CHAPTER THREE

Kendrick, Brandt, Atme, Koldo, and Ludvig trekked through the Great Waste, into the rising suns of the desert dawn, marching on foot, as they had been all night, determined to rescue young Kaden. They marched somberly, falling into a silent rhythm, each with hands on their weapons, all peering down and following the trail of the Sand Walkers. The hundreds of footprints led them deeper and deeper into this landscape of desolation.

Kendrick began to wonder if it would ever end. He marveled that he had found himself back in this position, back in this Waste he had sworn he would never step foot in again—especially on foot, with no horses, no provisions, and no way of getting back. They had put their faith in the other knights of the Ridge that they would return for them with the horses—but if not, they had bought themselves a one-way ticket into a quest of no return.

But that was what valor meant, Kendrick knew. Kaden, a fine young warrior with a big heart, had nobly stood watch, had ventured bravely into the desert to prove himself while standing guard, and he had been kidnapped by these savage beasts. Koldo and Ludvig could not turn their back on their younger brother, however grim the chance—and Kendrick, Brandt, and Atme could not turn their backs on all of them; their sense of duty and honor compelled them otherwise. These fine knights of the Ridge had taken them in with hospitality and grace when they had needed them most—and now it was time to repay the favor—whatever the cost. Death meant little to him—but honor meant everything.

"Tell me about Kaden," Kendrick said, turning to Koldo, wanting to break the monotony of silence.

Koldo looked up, startled from the deep silence, and sighed.

"He is one of the finest young warriors you will ever meet," he said. "His heart is always bigger than his age. He wanted to be a man before he was even a boy, wanted to wield a sword before he could even hold one."

10

He shook his head.

"It surprises me not that he venture too deep, would be the first one on a patrol to be taken. He backed down from nothing—especially if it meant watching over others."

Ludvig chimed in.

"If any of us had been taken," he said, "our little brother would be the first to volunteer. He is the youngest of us, and he represents what is best in us."

Kendrick had assumed as much from what he'd seen when talking to Kaden. He had recognized the warrior spirit within him, even at his young age. Kendrick knew, as he always had, that age had nothing to do with being a warrior: the warrior spirit resided in someone, or it did not. The spirit could not lie.

They continued marching for a long time, falling back into their steady silence as the suns rose higher, until finally Brandt cleared his throat.

"And what of these Sand Walkers?" Brandt asked Koldo.

Koldo turned to him as they marched.

"A vicious group of nomads," he replied. "More beast than man. They are known to patrol the periphery of the Sand Wall."

"Scavengers," Ludvig chimed in. "They have been known to drag their victims deep into the desert."

"To where?" Atme asked.

Koldo and Ludvig exchanged an ominous look.

"To wherever it is they are gathering—where they perform a ritual and tear them to pieces."

Kendrick flinched as he thought of Kaden, and the fate that awaited him.

"Then there is little time to waste," Kendrick said. "Let us run, shall we?"

They all looked at each other, knowing the vastness of this place and what a long run they'd have before them—especially in the rising heat and with their armor. They all knew how risky it would be not to pace themselves in this unforgiving landscape.

Yet they did not hesitate; they broke into a jog together. They ran into nothingness, sweat soon pouring down their faces, knowing if they did not find Kaden soon, this desert would kill them all.

11

*

Kendrick gasped as he ran, the second sun now high overhead, its light blinding, its heat stifling, and yet he and the others continued to jog, all gasping, their armor clanking as they ran. Sweat poured down Kendrick's face and stung his eyes so badly, he could barely see. As his lungs nearly burst, he had never known how badly he could crave oxygen. Kendrick had never experienced anything like the heat of these suns, so intense, feeling like it would burn the skin right off his body.

They would not make it much further in this heat, at this pace, Kendrick knew; soon enough, they would all die out here, collapse, become nothing but food for insects. Indeed, as they ran, Kendrick heard a distant screech, and he looked up to see the vultures circling, as they had been for hours, getting lower. They were always the smart ones: they knew when a fresh death was imminent.

As Kendrick peered out at the footprints of the Sand Walkers, still trailing off into the horizon, he could not comprehend how they had covered so much ground so quickly. He only prayed that Kaden was still alive, that all of this was not for nothing. Yet he could not, despite himself, help but wonder if they would ever reach him at all. It was like following footprints out into a receding ocean.

Kendrick glanced around him and saw the others slumped over, too, all stumbling more than running, all barely on their feet—yet all determined, like he, not to stop. Kendrick knew—they all knew—that as soon as they stopped moving, they would all be dead.

Kendrick wanted to break the monotony of the silence, yet he was too tired to talk to the others now, and he forced his legs onward, feeling as if they weighed a million pounds. He dared not even use the energy to look up into the horizon, knowing he would see nothing, knowing that he was doomed to die here after all. Instead, he looked down to ground, watching the trail, preserving whatever precious energy he had left.

Kendrick heard a noise, and at first he was sure it was his imagination; yet it came again, a distant sound, like the humming of bees, and this time he forced himself to look up, knowing it was stupid, that nothing could be there, and afraid to be hopeful.

Yet this time, the sight before him made his heart pound with excitement. There, before them, perhaps a hundred yards away, was a gathering of Sand Walkers.

Kendrick jabbed the others, and they each looked up, too, snapped out of their reverie, and they each saw it with a shock. Battle had arrived.

Kendrick reached down and grabbed his weapon, as the others did, too, and felt the familiar rush of adrenaline.

The Sand Walkers, dozens of them, turned and spotted them, and they, too, prepared, facing them. They shrieked and burst into a run.

Kendrick raised his sword high and let out a great battle cry, ready, at last, to kill his foes—or die trying.

CHAPTER FOUR

Gwendolyn walked solemnly through the capital of the Ridge, Krohn at her side, Steffen trailing behind her, her mind reeling as she pondered Argon's words. On the one hand, she was elated that he had recovered, was back to himself—yet his fateful prophecy rang inside her head like a curse, like a bell tolling her death. From his dire, cryptic statements, it sounded as if she were not meant to be together with Thor forever.

Gwen fought back tears as she walked quickly, with purpose, heading for the tower. She tried to block out his words, refusing to allow prophecies to run her life. That was the way she had always been, and that was what she needed to remains strong. The future might be written, and yet she felt it could also be changed. Destiny, she felt, was malleable. One only had to want it badly enough, be willing to give up enough—whatever the cost.

This was one of those times. Gwen absolutely refused to allow Thorgrin and Guwayne to slip away from her, and she felt a rising sense of determination. She would defy her destiny, no matter what it took, sacrifice whatever the universe demanded of her. Under no circumstance would she go through life without seeing Thor or Guwayne again.

As if hearing her thoughts, Krohn whined at her leg, rubbing up against it as she marched through the streets. Snapped out of her thoughts, Gwen looked up and saw the looming tower before her, red, circular, rising up right in the center of the capital, and she remembered: the cult. She had vowed to the King that she would enter the tower and try to rescue his son and daughter from the grips of this cult, to confront its leader about the ancient books, the secret they were hiding that could save the Ridge from destruction.

Gwen's heart pounded as she approached the tower,; anticipating the confrontation before her. She wanted to help the King, and the Ridge, but most of all, she wanted to be out there, searching for Thor, for Guwayne, before it was too late for them. If only, she wished, she

14

had a dragon at her side, as she used to; if only Ralibar could come back to her and take her far across the world, away from here, far from the problems of the Empire and back to the other side of the world, to Thorgrin and Guwayne once again. If only they could all return to the Ring and live life as they once did.

Yet she knew those were childish dreams. The Ring was destroyed, and the Ridge was all she had left. She had to face her current reality and do what she could to help save this place.

"My lady, may I accompany you inside the tower?"

Gwen turned at the voice, snapping out of her reverie, and she was relieved to see her old friend Steffen by her side, one hand on his sword, walking protectively beside her, eager, as always, to watch over her. He was the most loyal advisor she had, she knew, as she reflected back on how long he had been with her, and felt a rush of gratitude.

As Gwen stopped before the drawbridge before them, leading to the tower, he peered out at it suspiciously.

"I don't trust this place," he said.

She laid a comforting hand on his wrist.

"You are a true and loyal friend, Steffen," she replied. "I value your friendship, and your loyalty, but this is a step I must take alone. I must find out what I can, and having you there will put them on guard. Besides," she added, as Krohn whined, "I will have Krohn."

Gwen looked down, saw Krohn looking up at her expectantly, and she nodded back.

Steffen nodded.

"I shall wait for you here," he said, "and if there's any trouble within, I shall come for you."

"If I don't find what I need within that tower," she replied, "I am afraid there will be much greater trouble coming for all of us."

*

Gwen walked slowly over the drawbridge, Krohn at her side, her footsteps echoing on the wood, crossing over the gently rippling waters beneath her. All along the bridge were lined up dozens of monks, standing at perfect attention, silent, wearing scarlet robes, hands hidden inside them, with their eyes closed. They were a strange lot of guards, unarmed, incredibly obedient, standing guard here for Gwen didn't know how long. Gwen marveled at their intense loyalty and devotion to

15

their leader, and she realized it was as the King said: they all revered him as a god. She wondered what she was getting into.

As she neared, Gwen looked up at the huge, arched doorways looming before her, made of ancient oak, carved with symbols she did not understand, and she watched in wonder as several monks stepped forward and pulled them open. They creaked, disclosing a gloomy interior lit only by torches, and a cool draft met her, smelling faintly of incense. Krohn stiffened beside her, growling, and Gwen walked inside and heard it slam behind her.

The sound echoed inside, and it took a moment for Gwen to get her bearings. It was dark in here, the walls lit only by torches and by the filtered sunlight which poured in through stained glass high above. The air in here felt sacred, silent, and she felt as if she had entered a church.

Gwen looked up and saw the tower spiraled ever higher, with gradual, circular ramps leading up the floors. There were no windows, and the walls echoed with the faint sound of chanting. The incense hung heavy in the air here, and monks appeared and disappeared throughout, walking as in a trance in and out of the chambers. Some waved incense and some chanted, while others were silent, lost in reflection, and Gwen wondered more about the nature of this cult.

"Did my father send you?" echoed a voice.

Gwen, startled, wheeled to see a man standing a few feet away, wearing a long, scarlet robe, smiling back at her good-naturedly. She could hardly believe how much he resembled his father, the King.

"I knew he would send someone sooner or later," Kristof said. "His efforts to bring me back into his fold are endless. Please, come," he beckoned, turning aside and gesturing with his hand.

Gwen fell in beside him as they walked down a stone, arched corridor, heading gradually up the ramp in circles to the higher levels of the tower. Gwen found herself caught off guard; she had expected a crazed monk, a religious fanatic, and was surprised to find someone affable and good-natured, and clearly in his right mind. Kristof did not seem like the lost, crazy person his father had made him out to be.

"Your father asks for you," she finally said, breaking the silence after they passed a monk walking down the ramp the opposite way, never lifting his eyes from the floor. "He wants me to bring you back home."

Kristof shook his head.

"That's the thing about my father," he said. "He thinks he has found the only true home in the world. But I have learned something," he added, facing her. "There are many true homes in this world."

He sighed as they continued walking, Gwen wanting to give him his space, not wanting to press too hard.

"My father would never accept who I am," he finally added. "He will never learn. He remains stuck in his old, limited beliefs—and he wants to impose them on me. But I am not him—and he will never accept that."

"Do you not miss your family?" Gwen asked, surprised that he would commit his life to this tower.

"I do," he replied frankly, surprising her. "Very much. My family means everything to me—but my spiritual calling means more. My home is here now," he said, turning down a corridor as Gwen followed. "I serve Eldof now. He is my sun. If you knew him," he said, turning and staring at Gwen with an intensity that frightened her, "he would be yours, too."

Gwen looked away, not liking the look of fanaticism in his eyes.

"I serve no one but myself," she replied.

He smiled at her.

"Perhaps that is the source of all your earthly worries," he replied. "No one can live in a world where they do not serve someone else. Right now, you are serving someone else."

Gwen stared back suspiciously.

"How so?" she asked.

"Even if you think you serve yourself," he replied, "you are deceived. The person you are serving is not *you*, but rather the person your parents molded. It is your *parents* you serve—and all of their old beliefs, passed down by their parents. When will you be bold enough to cast off their beliefs and serve you?"

Gwen frowned, not buying his philosophy.

"And take on whose beliefs instead?" she asked. "Eldof's?"

He shook his head.

"Eldof is merely a conduit," he replied. "He helps cast off who you were. He helps you find your true self, all you were meant to be. That is

17

whom you must serve. That is who you will never discover until your false self is set free. That is what Eldof does: he sets us all free."

Gwendolyn looked back at his shining eyes, and she could see how devoted he was—and that devotion scared her. She could tell right away that he was beyond reason, that he would never leave this place.

It was scary, the web that this Eldof had spun to lure all these people in and trap them here—some cheap philosophy, with a logic all to itself. Gwen did not want to hear any more; it was a web she was determined to avoid.

Gwen turned and continued walking, shaking it off with a shudder, and continued up the ramp, circling the tower, gradually going up higher and higher, wherever it was leading them. Kristof fell in beside her.

"I have not come to argue the merits of your cult," Gwen said. "I cannot convince you to return to your father. I promised to ask, and I have done so. If you do not value your family, I cannot teach you to value it."

Kristof looked back at her gravely.

"And do you think my father values family?" he asked.

"Very much," she replied. "At least from what I can see."

Kristof shook his head.

"Let me show you something."

Kristof took her elbow and led her down another corridor to the left, then up a long flight of steps, stopping before a thick oak door. He looked at her meaningfully, then pulled it open, revealing a set of iron bars.

Gwen stood there, curious, nervous to see whatever he wanted to show her—then she stepped up and stared through the bars. She was horrified to see a young, beautiful girl sitting alone in a cell, staring out the window, her long hair hanging on her face. Though her eyes were wide open, she did not seem to take notice of their presence.

"This is how my father cares for family," Kristof said.

Gwen looked back at him, curious.

"His family?" Gwen asked, stunned.

Kristof nodded.

"Kathryn. His other daughter. The one he hides from the world. She has been relegated here, to this cell. Why? Because she is touched. Because she's not perfect, like him. Because he's ashamed of her."

Gwen fell silent, feeling a pit in her stomach as she looked at the girl sadly, wanting to help her. She started to wonder about the King, and started to wonder if Kristof had any truth to his words.

"Eldof values family," Kristof continued. "He would never abandon one of his own. He values our *true* selves. No one here is turned away out of shame. That is the blight of pride. And those who are touched are closest to their true selves."

Kristof sighed.

"When you meet Eldof," he said, "you will understand. There is no one like him, nor will there ever be."

Gwen could see the fanaticism in his eyes, could see how lost he was in this place, this cult, and she knew he was too far lost to ever return to the King. She looked over and saw the King's daughter sitting there, and she felt overwhelmed with sadness for her, for this entire place, for their shattered family. Her picture-perfect view of the Ridge, of the perfect royal family, was crumbling. This place, like every other, had its own dark underbelly. There was a silent battle raging here, and it was a battle of beliefs.

It was a battle Gwen knew she could not win. Nor did she have time to. Gwen thought of her own abandoned family, and she felt the pressing urgency to rescue her husband and her son. Her head was spinning in this place, with the incense thick in the air and lack of windows disorienting her, and she wanted to get what she needed and leave. She tried to remember why she'd even come here, then it came back to her: to save the Ridge, as she had vowed to the King.

"Your father believes that this tower holds a secret," Gwen said, getting to the point, "a secret that could save the Ridge, could save your people."

Kristof smiled and crossed his fingers.

"My father and his beliefs," he replied.

Gwen furrowed her brow.

"Are you saying it is not true?" she asked. "That there is no ancient book?"

He paused, looked away, then sighed deeply and fell silent for a long time. Finally, he continued.

"What should be revealed to you, and when," he said, "is beyond me. Only Eldof can answer your questions."

Gwen felt a sense of urgency rising within her.

"Can you bring me to him?"

Kristof smiled, turned, and began to walk down the corridor.

"As surely," he said, walking quickly, already distant, "as a moth to a flame."

CHAPTER FIVE

Stara stood on the precarious platform, trying not to look down as she was pulled higher and higher in the sky, seeing the vista expand with each yank of the rope. The platform rose higher and higher along the edge of the Ridge, and Stara stood there, her heart pounding, in disguise, the hood pulled low over her face, and sweat trickling down her back as she felt the desert heat rising. It was stifling this high up, and the day had barely broken. All about her were the ever-present sounds of ropes and pulleys, wheels squeaking, as the soldiers yanked and yanked, none realizing who she was.

Soon, it stopped, and all was still as she was standing at the peak of the Ridge—the only sound that of the howl of the wind. The view was staggering, making her feel as if she were standing at the very top of the world.

It brought back memories. Stara recalled the time she'd first arrived at the Ridge, fresh from the Great Waste, with Gwendolyn and Kendrick and all the other stragglers, most of them more dead than alive. She knew she was lucky to have survived, and at first, the sight of the Ridge had been a great gift, had been a sight of salvation.

And yet now here she was, prepared to leave, to descend the Ridge once again on its far side, to head back out into the Great Waste, back out into what could be a sure death. Beside her, her horse pranced, its shoes clicking the hollow platform. She reached out and stroked its mane reassuringly. This horse would be her salvation, her ticket out of this place; it would make her passage back across the Great Waste a very different scenario than it had been.

"I don't recall orders from our commander about this visit," came the commanding voice of a soldier.

Stara stood very still, knowing they were talking about her.

"Then I shall take that up with your commander himself—and with my cousin, the King," Fithe replied confidently, standing next to her, sounding as convincing as ever.

Stara knew he was lying, and she knew what he was risking for her—and she was forever grateful to him for it. Fithe had surprised her by being good to his word, by doing everything in his power, as he had promised, to help her leave the Ridge, to help her have a chance to go out there and find Reece, the man she loved.

Reece. Stara's heart ached at the thought of him. She would leave this place, however safe it was, would cross the Great Waste, cross oceans, cross the world, just for one chance to tell him how much she loved him.

As much as Stara hated to put Fithe in jeopardy, she needed this. She needed to risk it all to find the one she loved. She could not sit safely in the Ridge, no matter how glorious and rich and safe, until she was reunited with Reece.

The iron gates to the platform creaked open, and Fithe took her arm, accompanying her, as she wore her hood low, her disguise working. They stepped off the wooden platform and onto the hard stone plateau atop the Ridge. A howling wind passed through, strong enough to nearly knock her off balance, and she clutched the horse's mane, her heart pounding as she looked up and saw the vast expanse, the craziness of what she was about to do.

"Keep your head down and your hood lowered," Fithe whispered urgently. "If they see you, that you are a girl, they will know you're not meant to be up here. They will send you back. Wait until we reach the far end of the ridge. There's another platform waiting to bring you down the other side. It will take you—and you alone."

Stara's breath quickened as the two of them crossed the wide stone plateau, passing knights, walking quickly, Stara keeping her head down, away from the prying eyes of soldiers.

Finally, they stopped, and he whispered:

"Okay. Look up."

Stara pulled back her hood, her hair covered in sweat, and as she did, she was dazed by the sight: two huge, beautiful suns, still red, rose up in the glorious desert morning, the sky covered in a million shades of pinks and purples. It seemed as if it were the dawn of the world.

As she looked out, she saw the entire Great Waste spread out before her, seeming to stretch to the end of the world. In the distance there was the raging Sand Wall, and despite herself, she looked straight down.

She reeled from her fear of heights, and she immediately wished she hadn't.

Down below, she saw the steep drop, all the way down to the base of the Ridge. And before her, she saw a lone platform, empty, waiting for her.

Stara turned and looked up at Fithe, staring back at her meaningfully.

"Are you sure?" he asked softly. She could see the fear for her in his eyes.

Stara felt a streak of apprehension rush through her, but she then thought of Reece, and she nodded without hesitation.

He nodded back at her kindly.

"Thank you," she said. "I don't know how I can ever repay you."

He smiled back.

"Find the man you love," he replied. "If it cannot be me, at least it can be someone else."

He took her hand, kissed it, bowed, and turned and walked away. Stara watched him go, her heart filled with appreciation for him. If she hadn't loved Reece the way she had, perhaps he would be a man she would love.

Stara turned, steeling herself, held the horse's mane, and took the first fateful step onto the platform. She tried not to look out at the Great Waste, at the journey before her that would almost certainly mean her death. But she did.

The ropes creaked, the platform swayed, and as the soldiers lowered the ropes, one foot at a time, she began her descent, all alone, into nothingness.

Reece, she thought, *I might die. But I will cross the world for you.*

CHAPTER SIX

Erec stood at the bow of the ship, Alistair and Strom beside him, and peered down at the teeming waters of the Empire river below. He watched as the raging current forked the ship left, away from the channel that would have led them to Volusia, to Gwendolyn and the others—and he felt torn. He wanted to rescue Gwendolyn, of course; and yet also had to fulfill his sacred vow to those freed villagers, to free their neighboring village and wipe out the Empire garrison nearby. After all, if he did not, then the Empire soldiers would soon kill the freed men, and all of Erec's efforts to free them would have been for naught, leaving their village back in the hands of the Empire once again.

Erec looked up and studied the horizon, very conscious of the fact that every passing moment, every gale of wind, each stroke of the oar, was taking them farther away from Gwendolyn, from his original mission; and yet sometimes, he knew, one had to divert from the mission in order to do what was most honorable and right. Sometimes the mission, he realized, was not always what you thought it was. Sometimes it was ever-changing; sometimes it was a side journey along the way that ended up becoming the *real* mission.

Still, Erec resolved inwardly to vanquish the Empire garrison as quickly as possible and fork back upriver toward Volusia, to save Gwendolyn before it was too late.

"Sir!" yelled a voice.

Erec looked up to see one of his soldiers, high on the mast, pointing to the horizon. He turned to see, and as their ship passed a bend in the river and the currents picked up, Erec's blood quickened to see an Empire fort, teeming with soldiers, perched at the edge of the river. It was a drab, square building, built of stone, low to the ground, Empire taskmasters lined up all around it—yet none watching the river. Instead, they were all watching the slave village below, packed with villagers, all under the whip and rod of Empire taskmasters. The soldiers mercilessly lashed the villagers, torturing them on the streets under hard labor, while the soldiers above looked down and laughed at the scene.

Erec reddened with indignation, seething at the injustice of it all. He felt justified in forking his men this way up the river, and determined to set wrongs right and make them pay. It might just be a drop in the bucket of the travesty of the Empire, and yet one could never underestimate, Erec knew, what freedom meant to even a few people.

Erec saw the shores lined with Empire ships, guarded casually, none of them suspecting an attack. Of course, they would not: there were no hostile forces in the Empire, none that the vast Empire army could fear.

None, that is, but Erec's.

Erec knew that while he and his men were outnumbered, still, they had the advantage of surprise. If they could strike quickly enough, perhaps they could take them all out.

Erec turned to his men and saw Strom standing there beside him, eagerly awaiting his command.

"Take command of the ship beside me," Erec commanded his younger brother—and no sooner had he uttered the words than his brother burst into action. He ran across the deck, leapt off the rail and onto the ship sailing beside them, where he quickly headed to the bow and took command.

Erec turned to his soldiers crowding around him on his ship, waiting his direction.

"I don't want them alerted to our presence," he said. "We must get as close as we can. Archers—at the ready!" he cried. "And all of you, grab your spears and kneel down!"

The soldiers all took positions, squatting low all along the rail, rows and rows of Erec's soldiers lined up, all holding spears and bows, all well-disciplined, patiently awaiting his command. The currents picked up, Erec saw the Empire forces looming close, and he felt the familiar rush in his veins: battle was in the air.

They got closer and closer, now but a hundred yards away, and Erec's heart was pounding, hoping they were not detected, feeling the impatience of all his men around him, waiting to attack. They just had to get in range, and every lap of the water, every foot they gained, he knew, was invaluable. They only had one chance with their spears and arrows, and they could not miss.

Come on, Erec thought. *Just a little bit closer.*

Erec's heart sank as an Empire soldier suddenly turned casually and examined the waters—and then squinted in confusion. He was about to spot them—and it was too soon. They were not in range yet.

Alistair, beside him, saw it, too. Before Erec could give the command to start the battle early, she suddenly stood, and with a serene, confident expression, raised her right palm. A yellow ball appeared in it, and she pulled her arm back and then hurled it forward.

Erec watched in wonder as the orb of light floated up in the air above them and came down, like a rainbow, and descended over them. Soon a mist appeared, obscuring their view, protecting them from Empire eyes.

The Empire soldier now peered into the mist, confused, seeing nothing. Erec turned and smiled at Alistair knowing that, once again, they would be lost without her.

Erec's fleet continued to sail, now all perfectly hidden, and Erec looked over at Alistair in gratitude.

"Your palm is stronger than my sword, my lady," he said with a bow.

She smiled back.

"It is still your battle to win," she replied.

The winds carried them closer, the mist staying with them, and Erec could see all of his men itching to fire their arrows, to hurl their spears. He understood; his spear itched in his palm, too.

"Not yet," he whispered to his men.

As they parted the mist, Erec began to catch glimpses of the Empire soldiers. They stood on the ramparts, their muscled backs glistening, raising whips high and lashing villagers, the crack of their whips audible even from here. Other soldiers stood peering into the river, clearly summoned by the man on watch, and they all peered suspiciously into the mist, as if suspecting something.

Erec was so close now, his ships hardly thirty yards away, his heart pounding in his ears. Alistair's mist began to clear, and he knew the time had come.

"Archers!" Erec commanded. "Fire!"

Dozens of his archers, all up and down his fleet, stood, took aim, and fired.

The sky filled with the sound of arrows leaving string, sailing through the air—and the sky darkened with the cloud of deadly arrowtips, flying high in an arc, then turning down for the Empire shore.

A moment later cries rang through the air, as the cloud of deadly arrows descended upon the Empire soldiers teeming in the fort. The battle had begun.

Horns sounded everywhere, as the Empire garrison was alerted and rallied to defend.

"SPEARS!" Erec cried.

Strom was first to stand and hurl his spear, a beautiful silver spear, whistling through the air as it flew with tremendous speed then found a place in the stunned Empire commander's heart.

Erec hurled his on his heels, joining in as he threw his golden spear and took out an Empire commander on the far side of the fort. All up and down his fleet his ranks of men joined in, hurling their spears and taking out startled Empire soldiers who barely had time to rally.

Dozens of them fell, and Erec knew his first volley had been a success; yet still hundreds of soldiers remained, and as Erec's ship came to a stop, roughly touching down on shore, he knew the time had come for hand-to-hand battle.

"CHARGE!" he yelled.

Erec drew his sword, leapt up onto the rail, and jumped through the air, falling a good fifteen feet before landing on the sandy shores of the Empire. All around him his men followed, hundreds strong, all charging across the beach, dodging Empire arrows and spears as they burst out of the mist and across the open sand for the Empire fort. The Empire soldiers rallied, too, rushing out to meet them.

Erec braced himself as a hulking Empire soldier came charging right for him, shrieking, lifting his ax and swinging it sideways for Erec's head. Erec ducked, stabbed him in the gut, and hurried on. Erec, his battle reflexes kicking in, stabbed another soldier in the heart, sidestepped an ax blow from another, then spun around and slashed him across the chest. Another charged him from behind, and without turning, he elbowed him in the kidney, dropping him to his knees.

Erec ran through the ranks of soldiers, quicker and faster and stronger than anyone on the field, leading his men as one at a time, they cut down the Empire soldiers, making their way toward the fort. The fighting grew thick, hand-to-hand, and these Empire soldiers, nearly twice their size, were fierce opponents. Erec was heartbroken to see many of his men fall around him.

But Erec, determined, moved like lightning, Strom beside him, and he outmaneuvered them left and right. He tore through the beach like a demon released from hell.

Soon enough, the business was done. All was still on the sand, as the beach, turned to red, was filled with corpses, most of them the bodies of Empire soldiers. Too many of them, though, were the bodies of his own men.

Erec, filled with fury, charged the fort, still teeming with soldiers. He took the stone steps along its edge, all his men following, and met a soldier who came running down for him. He stabbed him in the heart, right before he could lower a double-handed hammer on his head. Erec stepped aside and the soldier, dead, came tumbling down the steps beside him. Another soldier appeared, slashing at Erec before he could react—and Strom stepped forward, and with a great clang and a shower of sparks, blocked the blow before it could reach his brother and elbowed the soldier with the hilt of his sword, knocking him off the edge and sending him shrieking to his death.

Erec continued charging, taking four steps at a time until he reached the upper level of the stone fort. The dozens of Empire soldiers who remained on the upper level were now terrified, seeing all their brothers dead—and at the sight of Erec and his men reaching the upper levels, they turned and began to flee. They raced down the far side of the fort, into the village streets—and as they did, they were met by a surprise: the villagers were now emboldened. Their fearful expressions morphed to one of rage, and as one, they rose up. They turned on their Empire captors, snatching whips from their hands, and began to lash the fleeing soldiers as they ran the other way.

The Empire soldiers were not expecting it, and one by one, they fell under the whips of the slaves. The slaves continued to whip them as they lay on the ground, again and again and again, until finally, they stopped moving. Justice had been served.

Erec stood there, atop the fort, breathing hard, his men beside him, and took stock in the silence. The battle was over. Down below, it took a minute for the dazed villagers to process what had happened, but soon enough they did.

One at a time, they began to cheer, and a great cheer rose up in the sky, louder and louder, as their faces filled with pure joy. It was a cheer of freedom. This, Erec knew, made it all worth it. This, he knew, was what valor meant.

CHAPTER SEVEN

Godfrey sat on the stone floor in the underground chamber of Silis' palace, Akorth, Fulton, Ario, and Merek beside him, Dray at his feet, and Silis and her men across from them. They all sat gloomily, heads lowered, hands across their knees, all knowing they were on a death watch. The chamber trembled with the thumping of war up above, of the invasion of Volusia, the sound of their city being sacked reverberating in their ears. They all sat there, waiting, as the Knights of the Seven tore Volusia to pieces above their heads.

Godfrey took another long drink from his sack of wine, the last sack left in the city, trying to numb the pain, the certainty of his looming death at the hands of the Empire. He stared at his feet, wondering how it all could have come to this. Moons ago, he was safe and secure inside the Ring, drinking his life away, with no other worries but what tavern and what brothel to visit on any given night. Now here he was, across the sea, in the Empire, trapped underground in a city under ruin, having walled himself into his own coffin.

His head buzzed, and he tried to clear his mind, to focus. He sensed what his friends were thinking, could feel it in the contempt of their glares: they never should have listened to him; they should have all escaped when they'd had the chance. If they had not come back for Silis, they could have reached the harbor, boarded a ship, and now been far from Volusia.

Godfrey tried to take solace in the fact that he had, at least, repaid a favor and had saved this woman's life. If he had not reached her in time to warn her to descend, she would certainly be up above and dead by now. That had to be worth something, even if it was unlike him.

"And now?" Akorth asked.

Godfrey turned and saw him looking back at him with an accusatory look, voicing the question that was clearly burning in all of their minds.

Godfrey looked around and scanned the small, dim chamber, torches flickering, nearly out. Their measly provisions and a sack of ale were all they had, sitting in one corner. It was a death vigil. He could still hear the sound of the war up above, even through these thick walls, and he wondered how long they could ride out this invasion. Hours? Days? How long would it be until the Knights of the Seven conquered Volusia? Would they go away?

"It's not us they're after," Godfrey observed. "It's Empire fighting Empire. They have a vendetta against Volusia. They have no issue with us."

Silis shook her head.

"They will occupy this place," she said somberly, her strong voice cutting through the silence. "The Knights of the Seven never retreat."

They all fell silent.

"Then how long can we live down here?" Merek asked.

Silis shook her head as she glanced at their provisions.

"A week, perhaps," she replied.

There suddenly came a tremendous rumble up above, and Godfrey flinched as he felt the ground shaking beneath him.

Silis jumped to her feet, agitated, pacing, studying the ceiling as dust began to filter down, showering over all of them. It sounded like an avalanche of stone above them, and she examined it as a concerned homeowner.

"They have breached my castle," she said, more to herself than to them.

Godfrey saw a pained look in her face, and he recognized it as the look of someone losing everything she had.

She turned and looked at Godfrey gratefully.

"I would be up there now if it weren't for you. You saved our lives."

Godfrey sighed.

"And for what?" he asked, upset. "What good did it do? So that we can all die down here?"

Silis looked glum.

"If we remain here," Merek asked, "will we all die?"

Silis turned to him and nodded sadly.

"Yes," she answered flatly. "Not today or tomorrow, but within a few days, yes. They cannot get down here—but we cannot go up there. Soon enough our provisions will run out."

31

"So what then?" Ario asked, facing her. "Do you plan to die down here? Because I, for one, do not."

Silis paced, her brow furrowed, and Godfrey could see her thinking long and hard.

Then, finally, she stopped.

"There is a chance," she said. "It is risky. But it just might work."

She turned and faced them, and Godfrey held his breath in hope and anticipation.

"In my father's time, there was an underground passage beneath the castle," she said. "It leads through the castle walls. We could find it, if it still exists, and leave at night, under the cover of darkness. We can try to make our way through the city, to the harbor. We can take one of my ships, if there are any left, and sail from this place."

A long, uncertain silence fell over the room.

"Risky," Merek finally said, his voice grave. "The city will be teeming with Empire. How are we to cross it without getting killed?"

Silis shrugged.

"True," she replied. "If they catch us, we will be killed. But if we emerge when it is dark enough, and we kill anyone who stands in our way, perhaps we will reach the harbor."

"And what if we find this passageway and reach the harbor, and your ships aren't there?" Ario asked.

She faced him.

"No plan is certain," she said. "We may very well die out there— and we may very well die down here."

"Death comes for us all," Godfrey chimed in, feeling a new sense of purpose as he stood and faced the others, feeling a sense of resolve as he overcame his fears. "It is a question of how we wish to die: down here, cowering as rats? Or up there, aiming for our freedom?"

Slowly, one at a time, the others all stood. They faced him and all nodded solemnly back.

He knew, at that moment, a plan had been formed. Tonight, they would escape.

CHAPTER EIGHT

Loti and Loc walked side by side beneath the burning desert sun, the two of them shackled to each other, as they were whipped by the Empire taskmasters behind them. They trekked through the wasteland and as they did, Loti wondered once again why her brother had volunteered them for this dangerous, backbreaking job. Had he gone mad?

"What were you thinking?" she whispered to him. They were prodded from behind and as Loc lost his balance and stumbled forward, Loti caught him by his good arm before he fell.

"Why would you volunteer us?" she added.

"Look ahead," he said, regaining his balance. "What do you see?"

Loti looked ahead and saw nothing but the monotonous desert stretched out before them, filled with slaves, the ground hard with rocks; beyond that, she saw a slope to a ridge, atop which labored a dozen more slaves. Everywhere were taskmasters, the sound of whips heavy in the air.

"I see nothing," she replied, impatient, "but more of the same: slaves being worked to their deaths by taskmasters."

Loti suddenly felt a searing pain across her back, as if her skin were being torn off, and she cried out as she was lashed across her back, the whip slicing her skin.

She turned to see the scowling face of a taskmaster behind her.

"Keep silent!" he commanded.

Loti felt like crying from the intense pain, but she held her tongue and continued to walk beside Loc, her shackles rattling under the sun. She vowed to kill all of these Empire as soon as she could.

They continued marching in silence, the only sound that of their boots crunching beneath the rock. Finally, Loc inched closer beside her.

"It's not what you see," he whispered, "but what you *don't* see. Look closely. Up there, on the ridge."

She studied the landscape, but saw nothing.

"There is but one taskmaster up there. One. For two dozen slaves. Look back, over the valley, and see how many there are."

Loti glanced furtively back over her shoulder, and in the valley spread out below, she saw dozens of taskmasters overseeing slaves, who broke rock and tilled the land. She turned and looked back up at the ridge, and she understood for the first time what her brother had in mind. Not only was there only one taskmaster, but even better, there was a zerta beside him. A means of escape.

She was impressed.

He nodded in understanding.

"The ridgetop is the most dangerous job post," he whispered. "The hottest, the least desired, by slave and taskmaster alike. But that, my sister, is an opportunity."

Loti was suddenly kicked in the back, and she stumbled forward along with Loc. The two of them righted themselves and continued up the ridge, Loti gasping for air, trying to catch her breath beneath the rising heat as they ascended. But this time, when she looked back up, her heart swelled with optimism, beating faster in her throat: finally, they had a plan.

Loti had never considered her brother to be bold, so willing to take such risk, to confront the Empire. But now as she looked at him, she could see the desperation in his eyes, could see that he was finally thinking as she was. She saw him in a new light, and she admired him greatly for it. It was exactly the type of plan she would have come up with herself.

"And what of our shackles?" she whispered back, as she made sure the taskmasters were not looking.

Loc gestured with his head.

"His saddle," Loc replied. "Look closely."

Loti looked and saw the long sword dangling in it; she realized they could use it to cut the shackles. They could make a break from there.

Feeling a sense of optimism for the first time since being captured, Loti perused the other slaves atop the peak. They were all broken men and women, hunched mindlessly over their tasks, none with any defiance left in their eyes; she knew at once that none of them would be of any help to their cause. That was fine by her—they did not need their help. They needed but one chance, and for all these other slaves to serve as a distraction.

Loti felt one final hard kick in the small of her back, and she stumbled forward and landed face-first in the dirt as they reached the peak of the ridge. She felt rough hands drag her back up to her feet, and she turned to see the taskmaster shove her roughly before turning and heading back down the ridge, leaving them there.

"Get in line!" yelled a new taskmaster, the sole one atop the ridge.

Loti felt his calloused hands grab the back of her neck and shove her; her chains rattled as she hurried forward, stumbling into the work field of slaves. She was handed a long hoe with an iron end, then given one last shove as the Empire taskmaster expected her to start tilling with all the others.

Loti turned, saw Loc give her a meaningful nod, and she felt the fire burning in her veins; she knew it was now or never.

Loti let out a cry, raised the hoe, swung it around, and with all her might brought it down. She was shocked to feel the thud, to see it lodged into the back of the taskmaster's head.

Loti had swung around so quickly, so decisively, clearly he had never expected it. He had not even time to react. Clearly no slave here, surrounded by all these taskmasters and with nowhere to run, would ever dare such a move.

Loti felt the buzz of the hoe throughout her hands and arms, and she watched in shock, then satisfaction, as the guard stumbled forward and fell. With her back still burning from the lashes, it felt like vindication.

Her brother stepped forward, raised his own hoe high, and as the taskmaster began to writhe, he brought it straight down on the back of his head.

Finally, the taskmaster lay still.

Breathing hard, covered in sweat, her heart still pounding, Loti dropped the hoe in disbelief, sprayed with the man's blood, and exchanged a glance with her brother. They had done it.

Loti could feel the curious stares of all the other slaves around her, and she turned and saw that they were all watching, mouths agape. They all leaned on their hoes, stopping work, and gave them a horrified look of disbelief.

Loti knew she had no time to waste. She ran, Loc beside her, shackled together, to the zerta, lifted the longsword from its saddle with both hands, raising it high, and turned.

"Watch out!" she yelled to Loc.

He braced himself as she lowered it with all her might and slashed their chains. It sparked, and she felt the satisfying freedom of their chains being severed.

She turned to go when she heard a shout.

"And what of us!?" shouted a voice.

Loti turned to see the other slaves come running over, holding out their shackles. She turned and saw the waiting zerta, and she knew time was precious. She wanted to head east as soon as she could, to head to Volusia, the last place she had knew Darius was heading. Perhaps she would find him there. Yet at the same time, she could not stand to see her brothers and sisters shackled.

Loti raced forward, through the crowd of slaves, slashing shackles left and right, until all of them were free. She did not know where they would go now that they were—but at least freedom was theirs to do with as they wished.

Loti turned, mounted the zerta, and held out a hand for Loc. He gave her his one good hand and she pulled him up—then gave the zerta a fierce kick in its ribs.

As they took off, Loti exhilarated at her freedom, in the distance, she could already hear the shouts of the Empire taskmasters, all spotting her. But she did not wait. She turned and directed the zerta down the ridge, down the opposite slope, she and her brother bursting out into the desert, away from the taskmasters—and on the other side of freedom.

CHAPTER NINE

Darius looked up in shock, staring back at the eyes of the mysterious man kneeling over him.

His father.

As Darius stared into the man's eyes, all sense of time and space fell away, his entire life freezing in that moment. It all suddenly fell into place: that feeling Darius had had from the moment he had laid eyes upon him. That familiar look, that certain something that had been tugging away at his consciousness, that had been bothering him ever since they'd met.

His *father*.

The word did not even seem real.

There he was, kneeling over him, having just saved Darius's life, having blocked a deadly blow from the Empire soldier, one which surely would have killed Darius. He had risked his life to venture out here, alone, into the arena, at the moment Darius had been about to die.

He had risked it all for him. His son. But why?

"Father," Darius said back, more of a whisper, in awe.

Darius felt a rush of pride to realize he was related to this man, this fine warrior, the finest warrior he had ever met. It made him feel that perhaps he could be a great warrior, too.

His father reached down and grabbed Darius's hand, and it was a firm, muscular grip. He yanked Darius to his feet, and as he did, Darius felt renewed. He felt as if he had a reason to fight, a reason to go on.

Darius immediately reached down, grabbed his dropped sword off the floor, then turned, together with his father, and they faced the oncoming horde of Empire soldiers together. With those hideous creatures now dead, his father having killed them all, horns had sounded, and the Empire had sent out a fresh wave of soldiers.

The crowd roared, and Darius looked out at the hideous faces of the Empire soldiers bearing down on them, wielding long spears. Darius focused, and he felt the world slowing as he prepared to fight for his life.

A soldier charged and threw a spear at his face, and Darius dodged right before it hit his eye; he then swung around and as the soldier neared to tackle him, Darius smashed him on his temple with the hilt of his sword, knocking him to the ground. Darius ducked as another soldier swung a sword at his head, then lunged forward and stabbed him in the gut.

Another soldier charged from the side, his spear aiming for Darius's ribs, moving too fast for Darius to react; yet he heard the sound of wood smashing metal, and he turned gratefully to see his father appear and use his staff to block the spear before it hit Darius. He then stepped forward and jabbed the staff between the soldier's eyes, knocking him to the ground.

His father spun with his staff and faced the group of attackers, the click-clack of his staff filling the air as he swatted away one spear thrust after the next. His father danced between the soldiers, like a gazelle weaving through men, and he wielded his staff like a thing of beauty, spinning and striking soldiers expertly, with well-placed jabs in the throat, between the eyes, in the diaphragm, felling men in every direction. He was like lightning.

Darius, inspired, fought like a man possessed beside his father, drawing energy off of him; he slashed and ducked and jabbed, his sword clanging against other soldiers' swords, sparks flying as he advanced fearlessly into the group of soldiers. They were larger than he, but Darius had more spirit, and he, unlike they, was fighting for his life—and for his father. He deflected more than one blow meant for his father, saving him from an unforeseen death. Darius dropped soldiers left and right.

The last Empire soldier rushed for Darius, raising a sword high overhead with both hands—and as he did, Darius lunged forward and stabbed him in the heart. The man's eyes opened wide, as he slowly froze and fell to the ground, dead.

Darius stood beside his father, the two of them back to back, breathing hard, surveying their handiwork. All around them, Empire soldiers lay dead. They had been victorious.

Darius felt that here, beside his father, he could face whatever the world threw at him; he felt that together, they were an unstoppable force. And it felt surreal to actually be fighting at his father's side. His father, whom he had always dreamt was a great warrior. His father was not, after all, just any ordinary person.

There came a chorus of horns, and the crowd cheered. At first Darius hoped they were cheering for his victory, but then huge iron doors opened at the far side of the arena, and he knew that the worst of it was just beginning.

There came the sound of a trumpet, louder than any Darius had ever heard, and it took him a moment to realize it was not the trumpet of a man—but rather, of an elephant. As he watched the gate, his heart pounding with anticipation, there suddenly appeared, to his shock, two elephants, all black, with long gleaming white tusks, faces contorted with rage as they leaned back and trumpeted.

The noise shook the very air. They lifted their front legs then brought them down with a crash, stamping the ground so hard that it shook, throwing Darius and his father off balance. Atop them rode Empire soldiers, wielding spears and swords, dressed head to toe in armor.

As Darius surveyed them, looking up at these beasts, larger than anything he had encountered in his life, he knew there was no way he and his father could win. He turned and saw his father standing there, fearlessly, not backing down as he stoically stared death in the face. It gave Darius strength.

"We cannot win, Father," Darius said, stating the obvious as the elephants began their charge.

"We already have, my son," his father said. "By standing here and facing them, by not turning and running, we have defeated them. Our bodies might die here today, but our memory lives on—and it shall be one of valor!"

Without another word, his father let out a cry and began to charge, and Darius, inspired, cried out and charged beside him. The two of them raced out to meet the elephants, running as fast as they could, not even hesitating to meet death in the face.

The moment of impact was not what Darius expected. He dodged a spear as the soldier, atop the elephant, threw it straight down at him, then he raised his sword and slashed at the elephant's foot as it charged right for him. Darius did not know how to strike an elephant, or if the blow would even have any impact.

It did not. Darius's blow barely scratched its skin. The massive beast, enraged, lowered its trunk and swung it sideways, smashing Darius in the ribs.

Darius went flying thirty feet through the air, feeling the wind knocked out of him, and landed on his back, rolling in the dust. He rolled and rolled, trying to catch his breath as he heard the muted shout of the crowd.

He turned and tried to catch a glimpse of his father, concerned for him, and out of the corner he saw him hurling his spear straight up, aiming for one of the elephant's huge eyes, then rolling out of the way as the elephant charged for him.

It was a perfect strike. It lodged firmly in its eye and as it did the elephant shrieked and trumpeted, its knees buckling as it tumbled to the ground and rolled, taking out the other elephant with it in a huge cloud of dust.

Darius scrambled to his feet, inspired and determined, and he set his sights on one of the Empire soldiers, who had fallen and was rolling on the ground. The soldier gained his knees, then turned and, still clutching his spear, took aim for Darius's father's back. His father stood there, unsuspecting, and Darius knew in a moment he would be dead.

Darius burst into action. He charged the soldier, raised his sword, and slashed the spear from his hand—then swung around and decapitated him.

The crowd cheered.

But Darius had little time to revel in his triumph: he heard a great rumbling, and he turned to see the other elephant had regained its feet—and its rider—and was bearing down on him. With no time to run out of the way, Darius lay on his back, took the spear, and held it straight up, as the elephant's foot came down. He waited until the last moment, then rolled out of the way as the elephant went to stomp him into the earth.

Darius felt a great wind as the elephant's foot rushed past him, missing him by inches, then heard a shriek and the sound of spear impacting flesh as he turned to see the elephant stepping on the spear. The spear rose straight up, all the way through its flesh and out the other side.

The elephant bucked and shrieked, running in circles, and as it did, the Empire soldier riding it lost his balance and fell, a good fifty feet, shrieking as he landed to his death, crushed by the fall.

The elephant, still mad with rage, swung the other way and smacked Darius with his trunk and sent him flying once again, tumbling in the other direction, Darius feeling as if all his ribs were breaking.

As Darius crawled on his hands and knees, trying to catch his breath, he looked up to see his father fighting valiantly with several Empire soldiers, who had been released from the gates to assist the others. He spun and slashed and jabbed with his staff, felling several of them in every direction.

The first elephant that had fallen, the spear still in its eye, regained its feet, whipped back up by another Empire soldier who jumped on its back. Under his direction, the elephant bucked, then charged right for Darius's father who, unsuspecting, continued to fight the soldiers.

Darius watched it happening and he stood there, helpless, his father too far away from him and he unable to get there in time. Time slowed as he saw the elephant turn right for him.

"NO!" Darius shrieked.

Darius watched in horror as the elephant rushed forward, right for his unsuspecting father. Darius raced across the battlefield, rushing to save him in time. Yet, he knew, even as he ran, that it was futile. It was like watching his world fall apart in slow motion.

The elephant lowered its tusks, charged forward, and impaled his father through the back.

His father cried out, blood pouring from his mouth, as the elephant raised him high in the air.

Darius felt his own heart close up as he saw his father, the bravest warrior he had ever seen, high in the air, impaled by the tusk, struggling to break free even as he was dying.

"FATHER!" Darius shrieked.

CHAPTER TEN

Thorgrin stood at the bow of the ship, tightened his grip on the hilt of his sword, and looked up in shock and horror at the massive sea monster emerging from the depths of the water. It was the same color as the blood sea below, and as it rose higher and higher, it cast a shadow over what little light there was in this Land of Blood. It opened its massive jaws, revealing dozens of rows of fangs, and it released its tentacles in every direction, some of them longer than the ship, as if a creature from the very depths of hell were reaching out to give them a hug.

Then it plunged down for the ship, ready to engulf them all.

Beside Thorgrin, Reece, Selese, O'Connor, Indra, Matus, Elden, and Angel all stood holding their weapons, standing their ground fearlessly in the face of this beast. Thor strengthened his resolve as he felt the Sword of the Dead vibrating in his hand, and he knew he had to take action. He had to protect Angel and the others, and he knew he could not wait for the beast to come to them.

Thorgrin leapt forward to meet it, up high onto the rail, raised his sword high overhead, and as one of the tentacles came swinging sideways for him, he swung around and chopped it off. The huge tentacle, severed, fell to the ship with a hollow sound, shaking the boat, then slid alongside the deck until it smashed into the rail.

The others did not hesitate either. O'Connor let loose a volley of arrows for the beast's eyes, while Reece chopped off another tentacle descending for Selese's waist. Indra threw her spear, piercing its chest, Matus swung his flail, severing another tentacle, and Elden used his ax, chopping off two in one stroke. As one, the Legion descended on this beast, attacking it like a finely tuned machine.

The beast shrieked in rage, having lost several of its tentacles, pierced by arrows and spears, clearly caught off guard by the coordinated attack. Its first attack halted, it shrieked even louder in frustration, shot up high into the air, and then just as quickly plunged beneath the surface, creating great waves and leaving the ship rocking in its wake.

Thor stared out at the sudden silence, puzzled, and for a second he thought that maybe it had retreated, that they had defeated it, especially as he saw the beast's blood pooling at the surface. But then he had a sinking feeling that all went too quiet, too quickly.

And then, too late, he realized what the beast was about to do.

"HANG ON!" Thor yelled to the others.

Thor had barely uttered the words when he felt their ship rise up unsteadily from the waters, higher and higher, until it was in the air, in the tentacles of the beast. Thor looked down and saw the beast beneath it, its tentacles wrapped all over the ship from bow to stern. He braced himself for the crash to come.

The beast hurled the ship and it went flying like a toy through the air, all of them trying to hold on for dear life, until it finally landed back in the ocean, rocking violently.

Thor and the others lost their grip and went sliding across the deck every which way, smashing into the wood as the ship tossed and turned. Thor spotted Angel sliding across the deck, heading for the rail, soon to go over the edge, and he reached out and grabbed her small hand, holding her tight as she looked back at him with panic.

Finally, the ship righted itself. Thor scrambled to his feet, as did the others, bracing for the next attack, and as soon as he did, he saw the beast swimming toward them at full speed, its tentacles flailing. It gripped the ship from all sides, its tentacles creeping over the edge, over the deck, and coming right at them.

Thor heard a cry and he looked out and saw Selese, a tentacle wrapped around her ankle, sliding across the deck, being yanked overboard. Reece swung around and chopped off the tentacle, but just as quickly another tentacle grabbed Reece's arm. More and more tentacles crept over the ship, and as Thor felt one on his own thigh, he looked around and saw all of his Legion brothers swinging wildly, chopping off tentacles. For each one they chopped off, two more appeared.

The entire ship was covered, and Thor knew that if he did not do something soon, they would all be sucked under for good. He heard a screech, high in the sky, and as he looked up, he saw one of the demon creatures released from hell, flying high overhead, looking down with a mocking gaze as it flew away.

Thor closed his eyes, knowing this was one of his tests, one of the monumental moments in his life. He tried to blot out the world, to focus inwardly. On his training. On Argon. On his mother. On his powers. He was stronger than the universe, he knew that. There were powers deep within him, powers above the physical world. This creature was of this earth—yet Thor's powers were greater. He could summon the powers of nature, the very powers that had created this beast, and send it back to the hell it had come from.

Thor felt the world slow all around him. He felt a heat rising within his palms, spreading through his arms, his shoulders, and back again, prickling, right down to his fingertips. Feeling invincible, Thor opened his eyes. He felt an incredible power shining through them, the power of the universe.

Thor reached out and placed his palm on the tentacle of the beast, and as he did, he seared it. The beast withdrew it immediately from his thigh, as if being burnt.

Thor stood, a new man. He turned and saw the beast's head rearing itself up along the edge of the ship, opening its jaws, preparing to swallow them all. He saw his Legion brothers and sisters sliding, about to be dragged over the edge.

Thor let out a great battle cry and charged the beast. He dove for it before it could reach the others, forgoing his sword and instead reaching out with his burning palms. He grabbed hold of the beast's face and laid his palms on it, and as he did, he felt them sear the beast's face.

Thor held on tight as the beast shrieked and writhed, trying to break free from his grasp. Slowly, one tentacle at a time, the beast began to release its grip on the boat, and as it did, Thor felt his power rising within him. He grabbed hold of the beast firmly and raised both of his palms, and as he did, he felt the weight of the beast, rising higher and higher into the air. Soon it hovered above Thor's palms, the power within Thor keeping it afloat.

Then, when the beast was a good thirty feet overhead, Thor turned and cast his hands forward.

The beast went flying forward, above the ship, shrieking, tumbling end over end. It sailed through the air a good hundred feet, until finally it went limp. It dropped down into the sea with a great splash, then sank beneath the surface.

Dead.

Thor stood there in the silence, his entire body still warm, and slowly, one at a time, the others regrouped, gaining their feet and coming up beside him. Thor stood there, breathing hard, dazed, looking out at the sea of blood. Beyond it, on the horizon, his eyes fixed on the black castle, looming over this land, the place that, he knew, held his son.

The time had come. There was nothing stopping him now, and it was time, finally, to retrieve his son.

CHAPTER ELEVEN

Volusia stood before her many advisors in the streets of the Empire capital, staring at the looking glass in her hand with shock. She examined her new face from every angle—half of it still beautiful, and the other half disfigured, melted away—and she felt a wave of disgust. The fact that half of her beauty still remained somehow made it all worse. It would have been easier, she realized, if her entire face had been disfigured—then she could remember nothing of her former looks.

Volusia recalled her stunning good looks, the root of her power, which had carried her through every event in life, which had allowed her to manipulate men and women alike, to bring men to their knees with a single glance. Now, all that was gone. Now, she was just another seventeen-year-old girl—and worse, half-monster. She could not stand the sight of her own face.

In a burst of rage and desperation, Volusia flung the looking glass down and watched as it smashed to pieces on the pristine streets of the capital. All of her advisors stood there, silent, looking away, all knowing better than to talk to her at this moment. It was also clear to her, as she surveyed their faces, that none of them wanted to look at her, to see the horror that was now her face.

Volusia looked around for the Volks, eager to tear them apart—but they were already gone, having disappeared as soon as they had cast that awful spell on her. She'd been warned not to join forces with them, and now she realized all the warnings had been right. She had paid the price dearly for it. A price that could never be turned back.

Volusia wanted to let her rage out on someone, and her eyes fell on Brin, her new commander, a statuesque warrior just a few years older than her, who had been courting her for moons. Young, tall, muscular, he had stunning good looks and had lusted after her the entire time she had known him. Yet now, to her fury, he would not even meet her gaze.

"You," Volusia hissed at him, barely able to contain herself. "Will you now not even look at me?"

Volusia flushed as he looked up but would not meet her eyes. This was her destiny now, for the rest of her life, she knew, to be viewed as a freak.

"Am I disgusting to you now?" she asked, her voice breaking in desperation.

He hung his head low, but did not respond.

"Very well," she said finally, after a long silence, determined to exact vengeance on someone, "then I *command* you: you will gaze at the face which you hate the most. You will prove to me that I am beautiful. You will sleep with me."

The commander looked up and met her eyes for the first time, fear and horror in his expression.

"Goddess?" he asked, his voice cracking, terrified, knowing he would face death if he defied her command.

Volusia smiled wide, happy for the first time, realizing that would be the perfect revenge: to sleep with the man who found her most loathsome.

"After you," she said, stepping aside and gesturing toward her chamber.

*

Volusia stood before the tall arched, open-air window on the top floor of the palace of the Empire capital, and as the early morning suns rose, the drapes billowing in her face, she cried quietly. She could feel her teardrops trickling down the good side of her face but not the other, the side melted away. It was numb.

A light snoring punctuated the air, and Volusia glanced over her shoulder to see Brin lying there, still asleep, his face bunched up in an expression of disgust, even in sleep. He had hated every moment he had lain with her, she knew, and that had brought her some small revenge. Yet still she did not feel satisfied. She could not let it out on the Volks, and she still felt a need for vengeance.

It was a weak bit of vengeance, hardly the one she craved. The Volks, after all, had disappeared, while here she was, the next morning, still alive, still stuck with herself, as she would have to be for the rest of her life. Stuck with these looks, this disfigured face, which even she could not bear.

Volusia wiped back the tears and looked out, beyond the city line, beyond the capital walls, deep on the horizon. As the suns rose, she began to see the faintest trace of the armies of the Knights of the Seven, their black banners lining the horizon. They were camped out there, and their armies were mounting. They were encircling her slowly, gathering millions from all corners of the Empire, all preparing to invade. To crush her.

She welcomed the confrontation. She did not need the Volks, she knew. She did not need any of her men. She could kill them on her own. She was, after all, a goddess. She had left the realm of mortals long ago, and now she was a legend, a legend that no one, and no army, in the world could stop. She would greet them on her own, and she would kill them all, for all time.

Then, finally, there would be no one left to confront her. Then, her powers would be supreme.

Volusia heard a rustling behind her and out of the corner of her eye, she detected motion. She saw Brin rise from bed, casting off his sheets and beginning to dress. She saw him slinking around, careful to be quiet, and she realized he meant to slip out from the room before she saw him—so that he would never have to look upon her face again. It added insult to injury.

"Oh, Commander," she called out casually.

She saw him freeze in his tracks in fear; he turned and looked over at her reluctantly, and as he did, she smiled back, torturing him with the grotesqueness of her melted lips.

"Come here, Commander," she said. "Before you leave, there is something I want to show you."

He slowly turned and walked, crossing the room until he reached her side, and he stood there, looking out, looking anywhere but at her face.

"Have you not one sweet parting kiss for your Goddess?" she asked.

She could see him flinch ever so slightly, and she felt fresh anger burning within her.

"Never mind," she added, her expression darkening. "But there is, at least, something I want to show you. Have a look. Do you see out there, on the horizon? Look closely. Tell me what you see down there."

He stepped forward and she laid a hand on his shoulder. He leaned forward and examined the skyline, and as he did, she watched his brow furrow in confusion.

"I see nothing, Goddess. Nothing out of the ordinary."

Volusia smiled wide, feeling the old sense of vindictiveness rise up within her, feeling the old need for violence, for cruelty.

"Look more closely, Commander," she said.

He leaned forward, just a bit more, and in one quick motion, Volusia grabbed his shirt from behind, and with all her might, threw him face first out the window.

Brin shrieked as he flailed and flew through the air, dropping down all the way, a hundred feet, until finally he landed face first, instantly dead, on the streets below. The thud reverberated in the otherwise quiet streets.

Volusia smiled wide, examining his body, finally feeling a sense of vengeance.

"It is yourself you see," she replied. "Who is the less grotesque of us now?"

CHAPTER TWELVE

Gwendolyn walked through the dim corridors of the tower of the Light Seekers, Krohn at her side, walking slowly up the circular ramp along the sides of the building. The path was lined with torches and cult worshipers, standing silently at attention, hands hidden in their robes, and Gwen's curiosity deepened as she continued to ascend one level after another. The King's son, Kristof, had led her halfway up after their meeting, then had turned and descended, instructing her that she would have to complete the journey alone to see Eldof, that she alone could face him. The way they all spoke about him, it was as if he were a god.

Soft chanting filled the air heavy with incense, as Gwen walked up the very gradual ramp, and wondered: What secret was Eldof guarding? Would he give her the knowledge she needed to save the King and save the Ridge? Would she ever be able to retrieve the King's family from this place?

As Gwen turned a corner, the tower suddenly opened up, and she gasped at the sight. She entered a soaring chamber with a hundred-foot ceiling, its walls lined with floor to ceiling stained glass windows. A muted light flooded through, filled with scarlets, purples, and pinks, lending the chamber an ethereal quality. And what made it all most surreal of all was to see one man sitting alone in this vast place, in the center of the room, the shafts of light coming down on him as if to illuminate him and him alone.

Eldof.

Gwen's heart pounded as she saw him sitting there at the far end of the chamber, like a god who had dropped down from the sky. He sat there, hands folded in his shining golden cloak, his head stark bald, on a huge and magnificent throne carved of ivory, torches on either side of it and on the ramp leading to it, obliquely lighting the room. This chamber, that throne, the ramp leading to it—it was more awe-inspiring than approaching a King. She realized at once why the King felt threatened by his presence, his cult, this tower. It was all designed to inspire awe and subservience.

He did not beckon her, or even acknowledge her presence, and Gwen, not knowing what else to do, began to ascend the long, golden walkway leading to his throne. As she went she saw he wasn't alone in here after all, for obscured in the shadows were rows of worshipers all lined up, eyes closed, hands tucked in their cloaks, lining the ramp. She wondered how many thousands of followers he had.

She finally stopped a few feet before his throne and looked up.

He looked back down with eyes that seemed ancient, ice-blue, glowing, and while he smiled down at her, his eyes held no warmth. They were hypnotizing. It reminded her of being in Argon's presence.

She did not know what to say as he stared down; it felt as if he were staring into her soul. She stood there in the silence, waiting until he was ready, and beside her, she could feel Krohn stiffening, equally on edge.

"Gwendolyn of the Western Kingdom of the Ring, daughter of King MacGil, last hope for the savior of her people—and ours," he pronounced slowly, as if reading from some ancient script, his voice deeper than any she'd ever heard, sounding as if it had resonated from the stone itself. His eyes bore into hers, and his voice was hypnotic. As she stared into them, it made her lose all sense of space and time and place, and already, Gwen could feel herself getting sucked in by his cult of personality. She felt entranced, as if she could look nowhere else, even if she tried. She immediately felt as if he were the center of her world, and she understood at once how all of these people had come to worship and follow him.

Gwen stared back, momentarily at a loss for words, something that had rarely happened to her. She had never felt so star-struck—she, who had been before many Kings and Queens; she, who was Queen herself; she, the daughter of a King. This man had a quality to him, something she could not quite describe; for a moment, she even forgot why she had come here.

Finally, she cleared her mind long enough to be able to speak.

"I have come," she began, "because—"

He laughed, interrupting her, a short, deep sound.

"I know why you have come," he said. "I knew before *you* even did. I knew of your arrival in this place—indeed, I knew even before you

51

crossed the Great Waste. I knew of your departure from the Ring, your travel to the Upper Isles, and of your travels across the sea. I know of your husband, Thorgrin, and of your son, Guwayne. I have watched you with great interest, Gwendolyn. For centuries, I have watched you."

Gwen felt a chill at his words, at the familiarity of this person she didn't know. She felt a tingling in her arms, up her spine, wondering how he knew all this. She felt that once she was in his orbit, she could not escape if she tried.

"How do you know all this?" she asked.

He smiled.

"I am Eldof. I am both the beginning and the end of knowledge."

He stood, and she was shocked to see he was twice as tall as any man she'd met. He took a step closer, down the ramp, and with his eyes so mesmerizing, Gwen felt as if she could not move in his presence. It was so hard to concentrate before him, to think an independent thought for herself.

Gwen forced herself to clear her mind, to focus on the business at hand.

"Your King needs you," she said. "The Ridge needs you."

He laughed.

"*My* King?" he echoed with disdain.

Gwen forced herself to press on.

"He believes you know how to save the Ridge. He believes you are holding a secret from him, one that could save this place and all of these people."

"I am," he replied flatly.

Gwen was taken aback at his immediate, frank reply, and hardly knew what to say. She had expected him to deny it.

"You *are?*" she asked, flabbergasted.

He smiled but said nothing.

"But why?" she asked. "Why won't you share this secret?"

"And why should I do that?" he asked

"*Why?*" she asked, stumped. "Of course, to save this kingdom, to save his people."

"And why would I want to do that?" he pressed.

Gwen narrowed her eyes, confused; she had no idea how to respond. Finally, he sighed.

"Your problem," he said, "is that you believe everyone is meant to be saved. But that is where you are wrong. You look at time in the lens of mere decades; I view it in terms of centuries. You look at people as indispensable; I view them as mere cogs in the great wheel of destiny and time."

He took a step closer, his eyes searing.

"Some people, Gwendolyn, are *meant* to die. Some people *need* to die."

"*Need* to die?" she asked, horrified.

"Some must die to set others free," he said. "Some must fall so that others may rise. What makes one person more important than another? One place more important than another?"

She pondered his words, increasingly confused.

"Without destruction, without waste, growth could not follow. Without the empty sands of the desert, there can be no foundation on which to build the great cities. What matters more: the destruction, or the growth to follow? Don't you understand? What is destruction but a foundation?"

Gwen, confused, tried to understand, but his words only deepened her confusion.

"Then are you going to stand by and let the Ridge and its people die?" she asked. "Why? How would that benefit you?"

He laughed.

"Why should everything always be for a benefit?" he asked. "I won't save them because they are not *meant* to be saved," he said emphatically. "This place, this Ridge, it is not meant to survive. It is meant to be destroyed. This King is meant to be destroyed. All these people are meant to be destroyed. And it is not for me to stand in the way of destiny. I have been granted the gift to see the future—but that is a gift I shall not abuse. I shall not change what I see. Who am I to stand in the way of destiny?"

Gwendolyn could not help but think of Thorgrin, of Guwayne.

Eldof smiled wide.

"Ah yes," he said, looking right at her. "Your husband. Your son."

Gwen looked back, shocked, wondering how he'd read her mind.

"You want to help them so badly," he added, then shook his head. "But sometimes you cannot change destiny."

She reddened and shook off his words, determined.

"I *will* change destiny," she said emphatically. "Whatever it takes. Even if I have to give up my very own soul."

Eldof looked at her long and hard, studying her.

"Yes," he said. "You will, won't you? I can see that strength in you. A warrior's spirit."

He examined her, and for the first time she saw a bit of certainty in his expression.

"I did not expect to find this within you," he continued, his voice humbled. "There are a select few, like yourself, who do have the power to change destiny. But the price you will pay is very great."

He sighed, as if shaking off a vision.

"In any case," he continued, "you will not change destiny here—not in the Ridge. Death is coming here. What they need is not a rescue— but an exodus. They need a new leader, to lead them across the Great Waste. I think you already know that you are that leader."

Gwen felt a chill at his words. She could not imagine herself having the strength to go through it all again.

"How can I lead them?" she asked, exhausted at the thought. "And where is there left to go? We are in the midst of nowhere."

He turned away, falling silent, and as he began to walk away, Gwen felt a sudden burning desire to know more.

"Tell me," she said, rushing out and grabbing his arm.

He turned and looked at her hand, as if a snake were touching him, until finally she removed it. Several of his monks rushed forth out of the shadows and hovered close by, looking at her angrily—until finally Eldof nodded at them, and they retreated.

"Tell me," he said to her, "I will answer you once. Just once. What is it that you wish to know?"

Gwen took a deep breath, desperate.

"Guwayne," she said, breathless. "My son. How do I get him back? How do I change destiny?"

He looked at her long and hard.

"The answer has been before you all along, and yet you don't see."

Gwen racked her brain, desperate to know, and yet she could not understand what it was.

"Argon," he added. "There remains one secret he has feared to tell you. That is where your answer lies."

Gwen was shocked.

"Argon?" she asked. "Does Argon know?"

Eldof shook his head.

"He does not. But his master does."

Gwen's mind reeled.

"His *master*?" she asked.

Gwen had never considered Argon having a master.

Eldof nodded.

"Demand that he bring you to him," he said, a finality in his voice. "The answers you receive will startle even you."

CHAPTER THIRTEEN

Mardig strutted down the castle corridors with determination, his heart pounding as he contemplated in his mind's eye what he was about to do. He reached down and with a sweaty palm clutched the dagger deep hidden in his waist. He walked the same path he had a million times before—on his way to see his father.

The King's chamber was not far now, and Mardig twisted and turned down the familiar corridors, past all the guards who bowed reverentially at the sight of the King's son. Mardig knew he had little to fear from them. No one had any idea what he was about to do, and no one would know what had happened until long after the deed was done—and the kingdom was his.

Mardig felt a whirlwind of conflicting emotions as he forced himself to put one foot in front of the other, his knees trembling, forced himself to stay resolved as he prepared to do the deed he had contemplated his entire life. His father had always been an oppressor to him, had always disapproved of him, while he had approved of his other, warrior, sons. He even approved of his daughter more than he. All because he, Mardig, had chosen not to participate in this culture of chivalry; all because he preferred to drink wine and chase women—instead of killing other men.

In his father's eyes, that made him a failure. His father had frowned upon everything Mardig did, his disapproving eyes following him at every corner, and Mardig had always dreamt of a day of reckoning. And at the same time, Mardig could seize power for himself. Everyone had expected the kingship to fall to one of his brothers, to the eldest, Koldo, or if not he, then to Mardig's twin, Ludvig. But Mardig had other plans.

As Mardig turned the corner, the soldiers guarding it reverentially bowed, and they turned to open it for him without even asking him why.

But suddenly, one of them stopped, unexpectedly, and turned to look at him.

56

"My lord," he said, "the King did not make us aware of any visitors this morning."

Mardig's heart started pounding, but he forced himself to appear bold and confident; he turned and stared back at the soldier, a stare of entitlement, until finally he could see the soldier looking unsure of himself.

"And am I a mere visitor?" Mardig answered coldly, doing his best to seem unafraid.

The guard slowly backed away quickly and Mardig marched through the open door, the guards closing it behind him.

Mardig strutted into the room, and as he did, he saw the surprised eyes of his father, who had been standing at the window and looking out looking pensively at his kingdom. He faced him, confused.

"Mardig," his father said, "to what do I owe the privilege? I did not summon you. Nor have you bothered to visit me any of these past moons—unless there was something you want."

Mardig's heart slammed in his chest.

"I've not come to ask anything of you, Father," he replied. "I have come to take."

His father looked confused.

"To take?" he asked.

"To take what is mine," Mardig replied.

Mardig took a few long strides across the chamber, steeling himself, as his father looked back at him, baffled.

"What is it that is yours?" he asked.

Mardig felt his palms sweating, the dagger in his hand, and did not know if he could go through with it.

"Why, the kingdom," he said.

Mardig slowly released the dagger in his palm, wanting his father to see it before he stabbed him, wanting his father to see firsthand how much he hated him. He wanted to see his father's expression of fear, of shock, of rage.

But as his father looked down, it was not the moment Mardig had expected. He had expected his father to resist, to fight back; but instead he looked up at him with sadness and compassion.

"My boy," he said. "You are still my son, despite all, and I love you. I know, deep in your heart, you don't mean this."

Mardig narrowed his eyes, confused.

"I am sick, my son," the King continued. "Soon enough, I will be dead. When I am, the Kingdom will pass to your brothers, not you. Even if you were to kill me now, you would gain nothing from it. You would still be third in line. So put down your weapon and embrace me. I still love you, as any father would."

Mardig, in a sudden rush of rage, hands shaking, leapt forward and plunged the dagger deep into his father's heart.

His father stood there, eyes bulging in disbelief, as Mardig held him tight and looked into his eyes.

"Your sickness has made you weak, Father," he said. "Five years ago I could never have done this. And a kingdom does not deserve a weak king. I know you will die soon—but that is not soon enough for me."

His father finally collapsed to the floor, motionless.

Dead.

Mardig looked down, breathing hard, still in shock at what he had just done. He wiped his hand on his robe, threw down the knife, and it landed with a clang on the floor.

Mardig scowled down at his father.

"Don't you worry about my brothers, Father," he added. "I have a plan for them, too."

Mardig stepped over his father's corpse, approached the window, and looked down at the capital city below. His city.

Now it was all *his*.

CHAPTER FOURTEEN

Kendrick raised his sword and blocked the blow as a Sand Walker brought its razor-sharp claw down for his face. It stopped it with a clang, sparks flying out, and Kendrick dodged out of the way, as the creature slid its claws down off the blade and swiped for his head.

Kendrick spun around and slashed, but the creature was surprisingly quick. It backed away, Kendrick's sword just missing. It then lunged forward, leaping high into the air and coming straight down for Kendrick—and this time, he was prepared. He had underestimated its speed, but would not do so a second time. Kendrick squatted down low and raised his sword high—and he let the beast impale itself, falling right through the blade.

Kendrick rose to his knees and swung his sword low, slashing off the legs of two Sand Walkers as they came for him. He then turned and thrust his sword backwards, stabbing one in the gut right before it landed on his back.

The beasts descended on him from all directions, and Kendrick found himself in the midst of a heated battle, Brandt and Atme by his side and Koldo and Ludvig by his other. The five of them instinctually backed up to each other, forming a tight circle, back to back, slashing and jabbing and kicking, keeping the creatures at bay as they watched each other's backs.

They fought and fought and fought beneath the blazing suns, with nowhere to retreat to in the vast, open space. Kendrick's shoulders ached, and he was up to his elbows in blood, exhausted from his long trek, from the endless battle. They had no reserves, and nowhere to go, and they all fought for their lives. The enraged screeches of these beasts filled the air, as they dropped left and right. Kendrick knew that they had to be careful; it was a long trek back, and if any of them were wounded, it would be a dire situation.

As he fought, in the distance, Kendrick caught a glimpse of the boy, Kaden, and he was relieved to see he was still alive. He struggled, his hands and arms bound behind his back and held back by several

59

creatures. The sight of him motivated Kendrick, reminded him why he had come out here to begin with. He fought furiously, doubling his efforts, trying to cut through all these beasts and make his way to the boy. He did not like the way they were handling him, and he knew he had to reach him before these creatures did anything rash.

Kendrick groaned in pain as he suddenly felt a slash across his arm. He turned to see a creature swinging again, coming down with his razor-sharp claws, right for his face. He could not react in time, and he braced himself for the blow, expecting it to tear his face in two—when suddenly Brandt lunged forward and pierced the creature through its chest with his sword, saving Kendrick at the last moment.

At the same time, Atme stepped forward and slashed a creature right before it could sink its fangs into Brandt's throat.

Kendrick then spun, slashing two creatures before they descended on Atme.

Around and around he went, spinning and slashing, fighting each and every creature to the last. The creatures fell at their feet, piling on the sand, and the sand turned red with blood.

Kendrick spotted, out of the corner of his eye, several creatures grabbing Kaden and beginning to run off with him. Kendrick's heart pounded; he knew it was a dire situation. If he lost sight of them, they would disappear in the desert and they'd never find Kaden again.

Kendrick knew he had to make a run for it. He broke free from the fight, elbowing several creatures out of his way, and chased after the boy, leaving the others to fight the creatures. Several creatures pursued him, and Kendrick turned, kicking and slashing to deter them as he went. Kendrick felt himself scratched on all sides, but no matter what, he didn't stop. He had to reach Kaden in time.

Kendrick, spotting Kaden, knew he had to stop him; he knew he only had one shot at this.

Kendrick reached into his waist, grabbed a knife, and threw it. It landed on a creature's neck, killing it right before it could sink its claws into Kaden's throat. Kendrick burst through the crowd, closing the gap, running all the way to Kaden and stabbing another right before it could finish him off.

Kendrick took a defensive position over Kaden, who lay on the ground, bound, as Kendrick killed off his captors. As more creatures closed in on him, Kendrick blocked their claws in each direction. He found himself surrounded, slashing in every direction, but determined to save Kaden. The others, he could see, were too immersed in battle to rush to Kaden's side.

Kendrick raised his sword high and slashed the boy's ropes, freeing him.

"Take my sword!" Kendrick implored.

Kaden grabbed the extra short sword from Kendrick's scabbard, and spun and faced the rest of the creatures, at Kendrick's side. Although he was young, Kendrick could see the boy was quick and brave and bold, and Kendrick was pleased to have him by his side, fighting the creatures.

They fought well together, felling creatures left and right. But, fight as they did, there were just too many of them, and Kendrick and Kaden were soon completely surrounded.

Kendrick was losing strength, his shoulders tiring, when suddenly, he saw the creatures begin to fall and heard a great battle cry from behind them. Kendrick was elated to see Koldo, Ludvig, Brandt, and Atme break through the lines, killing creatures in every direction. Encouraged, Kendrick fought back, making one last push, Kaden by his side. The six of them, fighting together, were unstoppable, felling all of the creatures.

Kendrick stood there in the silence, breathing hard on the desert sand, taking stock; he could hardly believe what they had just done. All around them were the piled up carcasses of the beasts, sprawled out in various directions, the sand red with blood. He and the others were covered in wounds, scratched up—but they all stood there, alive. And Kaden, grinning from ear to ear, was free.

Kaden reached out and embraced each one of them, one by one, starting with Kendrick, looking at him meaningfully. He saved his final embrace for Koldo, his eldest brother, and Koldo hugged him back, his black skin rippling in the sky.

"I can't believe you came for me," Kaden said.

"You're my brother," Koldo said. "Where else would I be?"

Kendrick heard a sound and looked over and saw the six horses these creatures had kidnapped, all tied to a rope together—and he and the others exchanged knowing glances.

As one, they all rushed over and mounted the beasts, each barely seated before they dug in their heels and prodded the beasts onward, back into the Waste, all heading back to the Ridge, back, finally, to home.

CHAPTER FIFTEEN

Erec stood at the stern of his ship, taking up the rear of his fleet, and checked back over his shoulder once again with anxiety. On the one hand, he was relieved that they had managed to wipe out that Empire village, to fork back up the river toward Volusia, toward Gwendolyn; on the other hand, he had paid a dear price, not just in lost men, but in lost time—he had wiped out whatever lead they'd had on the remainder of the Empire fleet. As he glanced back, he saw them following, way too close, snaking their way upriver, but a few hundred yards away, sailing the black and gold banners of the Empire. He had lost his day's lead on them, and they now followed him furiously, like a hornet chasing its prey, their superior ships, better manned, getting ever closer with each gust of wind.

Erec turned back and checked the horizon. He knew from his scouts that Volusia lay just beyond the bend somewhere—yet, at the rate at which the Empire was closing the gap, he wondered if his small fleet would reach it in time. He was starting to realize that if they did not make it in time, they would have to turn around and make a stand—and that was a stand, so vastly outnumbered, they could not win.

Erec heard a sound that raised the hairs on the back of his neck, and he turned and looked up to see a sight which left him with a cold dread: a wave of Empire arrows had been unleashed, and they now sailed through the air, blackening the sky, heading, in a high arc, for his fleet. Erec braced himself and watched with relief as the first volley landed in the water all around him, perhaps twenty yards from his ship, the sound of arrows hitting water sounding like heavy raindrops.

"ARROWS!" Erec yelled, warning his men to take cover.

Most of them did, and not a moment too soon. Another volley soon followed, these shot by crossbows with a further range, and Erec watched, horrified, as one reached the deck of his ship and one of his soldiers yelled out. Erec turned to see it sticking through his leg, pierced by a random arrow, the only one with a range just far enough to hit.

Erec felt a flush of indignation—and of urgency. The Empire was within range; too soon they would be overtaken, and with the Empire's fleet of thousands of ships, there was simply no way Erec's men could outfight them. Erec knew he had to think quickly.

"Shall we turn and fight, my brother?" asked Strom, coming up beside him.

Alistair looked back, too, standing calmly beside him.

"You will prevail, my love," she said. "I have seen it."

Erec felt encouraged by her words, as always, and as he stared and studied the landscape, an idea came to him.

"Sometimes," he said, "we must sacrifice to achieve something greater."

Erec turned to his brother, confident.

"Board the ship beside us. Evacuate it, then take up the rear," he commanded. He then took Strom's arm and looked him in the eye.

"When you're done," he added, "set that ship aflame, and sail it right for their fleet. You will jump on my ship before the flames overtake it."

Strom's eyes widened in appreciation for the plan. He jumped into action, running and leaping from the deck to the ship beside him, executing his brother's orders. He began barking orders, and the men fell in all around him, jumping into action and beginning to abandon ship, jumping onto the deck of Erec's ship. Erec could feel the weight of his ship growing heavier.

"More oars!" Erec cried, feeling them slowing.

He doubled the number of oarsmen on board, and they all pulled, heaving, as Erec's ship began to pick up speed.

"Spread out!" Erec commanded, realizing his ship was going too slow. "Jump to the other ships!"

His men did as commanded, jumping from his ship to several others in his fleet, distributing their weight evenly amongst the ships. Finally, Erec's ship righted and gained speed.

Erec turned to watch the last of the men jump from Strom's ship. Strom raised a torch and ran up and down the ship, setting flame to everything, then threw it with all his might. The torch landed on the mast, lighting it, setting the whole ship in a huge conflagration, and Strom turned, leapt back onto his brother's ship, and stood there, watching, as the ghost ship, aflame, drifted down current—right for the Empire fleet.

"Row!" Erec yelled, wanting to gain more distance from the flaming ship, from the Empire.

They gained more and more distance, speeding upriver.

The Empire fleet tried to turn out of the way—but there was nowhere to navigate in the tiny river. The flaming ship caused chaos. They attacked it, not realizing it was unmanned, wasting precious arrows and spears. The ship was pummeled from all directions—but nothing could stop the flow of it.

Within moments, the ship, a burning wreck, floated right to the center of the Empire fleet, parting it down the middle. And they had no way to stop it.

The ship struck the others, and as men shrieked and jumped out of the way, flames began to lick, spreading left and right, causing chaos in this Empire fleet. Soon, several other ships were on fire, with their soldiers scrambling to put them out.

"SIR!" Erec heard someone call out.

Erec turned to see one of his men pointing, and as he looked back upriver, he was struck by an awe-inspiring sight: a majestic city that could be no other than Volusia.

"Volusia," Alistair said, confidence in her voice, and Erec felt it to be so.

He glanced back, saw they had gained precious time—perhaps hours—and he knew they had a chance, albeit slim, to enter the city and get out before the Empire could catch them.

He turned and nodded to his men.

"Full sail ahead," he commanded.

*

Erec's fleet, sailing steadily upriver for most of the day, finally reached a turn in the bend, the current picking up, and as they did, Erec looked out, in awe at the sight. Spreading out before them was what could only be Volusia. A magnificent city, the most luxurious he had ever laid eyes upon, it was built of gold, shining even from here, its buildings and streets more orderly and meticulous than anything he had ever seen. Everywhere were statues, shaped as a woman who appeared to be a goddess, dazzling in the sun, and he could not help but wonder

65

who she was, and what cult worshipped her. Most of all, Erec was taken aback by its glistening harbor, filled with every manner of ship and vessel, many golden, sparkling in the sun, so bright he nearly had to look away. The ocean crashed on its shores, and Erec could see right away that this was a city of tremendous wealth and strength.

As he studied it, Erec was also surprised by something else he saw: black plumes of smoke. They wafted over the city, covering it like a blanket in every direction. He could not understand why. Was the city on fire? In the midst of an uprising? Under attack?

It was baffling to him. How could such a city, such a bastion of strength, be under attack? What force was there in the Empire strong enough to attack an Empire city?

And what concerned him most of all: was Gwendolyn involved?

Erec squinted, wondering if he were seeing things; but as they neared, as he heard the distinct sound of men crying out their death cries, he realized he was correct. And as he looked closer, he blinked in confusion. It appeared that Empire was attacking Empire. But why?

Everywhere, men were falling, thousands of soldiers pouring through the streets, through the open gates to the city, sacking it. These invaders wore the armor of the Empire, but it was a different color—all black. He saw they also flew a distinctive banner, and as he looked closer, he recognized it from his history books:

The Knights of the Seven.

Erec was even more perplexed. The Knights of the Seven, if he recalled, represented the entire Empire horns and spikes, all the provinces. What were they doing here? Why were they attacking an Empire city? Was a civil war breaking out?

Or worse, he pondered with dread: were they all here to kill Gwendolyn?

As they neared, Erec felt a sense of relief, but also of dread. Relief, because he knew the soldiers of Volusia would be distracted, would have their hands full, and that they would have no time to mount a defense as he entered their harbor. Yet he also felt dread as he sized up the strength and breadth of the invaders, wondering if he would have to fight them, too.

Either way, he would have to prepare for war.

Erec checked back over his shoulder and saw the remainder of the Empire fleet, having rebounded from his burning ship, beginning to close the gap again. There was not much time; if he was going to invade Volusia, to find Gwendolyn, he had to do it now—civil war raging or not.

"Are we walking into somebody else's fight?" Strom asked, looking out, beside him.

Erec examined the horizon, wondering.

"Only one way to find out," he replied.

His men, he could see, were all equally confused by the sight and all looked to him for direction.

"ROW!" Erec yelled out to his men. "FASTER!"

They gained speed, and as they neared the docks, Erec spotted something that made his blood cold: iron bars, as thick as trees, blocked the harbor, their spikes lowered down and disappearing into the waters. This iron portcullis, in the water, was a gate to the city's waterways, perhaps built to keep out invaders in times of trouble. But there was no other way in. If they did not find a way through it, Erec realized at once, they would be trapped—and at the mercy of the approaching Empire.

"Can we ram it?" Strom asked.

Erec shook his head.

"Our ships would shatter," he replied.

Erec stood there examining it, looking for some way out—when suddenly, he saw a curious sight, one which made him furrow his brow as he peered into the sun. It was an overweight man, running, heaving through the streets, looking very out of shape; beside him were several companions, looking as bad off as he. They all appeared to be drunk, and did not fit in here. They were clearly not soldiers. And from their dress, they did not appear to be from here.

And as Erec stared more closely, he realized with a shock that he recognized the man: the King's son. Godfrey.

Erec's confusion deepened. Godfrey? What was he doing here, in the midst of a civil war, running for his life toward the harbor, his big beer belly leading the way?

Yet as Erec watched him approach, squinting into the sun, he knew it was true. Godfrey was here. He had seen many strange things in his lifetime—but none as strange as this.

*

Godfrey stumbled and ran for the harbor, gasping and heaving, not knowing his body could move this fast. He trailed the others, Merek and Ario, and Silis and her men, gasping, wondering how they could run that fast. The only ones slower than he were Akorth and Fulton—and that didn't mean much. As sweat poured down his eyes, down his back, Godfrey cursed himself once again for drinking too many mugs of ale. If he ever survived this ordeal, he vowed to get back into shape.

Godfrey heard a shout behind him, and he turned and looked back to see the Volusian soldiers getting hacked to death by the invading armies of the Knights of the Seven. He gulped as he turned back and looked forward, in the distance, at the gleaming harbor of Volusia, feeling like a million miles away. He did not know if he could make it.

His lungs burned so badly that he finally had to stop, gasping. Immediately, Silis turned back and looked at him.

"Go without me!" he heaved. "I cannot run so fast."

But Silis stopped and turned.

"No," she insisted. "You once came back for me, and I shall for you."

She ran to him, draped an arm over his shoulder, joined by her men, who also went back for Akorth and Fulton, and began dragging him. His ribs ached as they ran with him through the streets, all of them hobbling along toward the harbor of Volusia.

Godfrey heard a rush of footsteps behind him, and suddenly she let go of him, turned, and drew her dagger.

There came a shout, and Godfrey turned to see she had stabbed a soldier in the throat, right before he could stab Godfrey in the back. He looked at her in awe; she had saved his life.

"I owe you," he said to her, in gratitude.

She smiled back.

"No you don't," she replied.

They continued to run, sprinting across the wide open courtyard, through all the chaos, always keeping their eyes on the harbor before them, packed with glistening ships.

68

As they neared it, there came another shout, and Godfrey turned to see a side gate collapse in the courtyard, and watched as hundreds more Knight of the Seven burst through. Volusian soldiers fell as their city was overrun, the Knights cruel and merciless, attacking and murdering all who stood in their path—even defenseless slaves. They raised torches and set everything to fire, and Godfrey realized they would not stop until they had razed this city to the ground. He did not understand why, but clearly they had some vendetta against Volusia herself.

Godfrey turned away from the sight, looking back to the harbor—and he was suddenly filled with dread. The boats they were heading for were all suddenly set aflame by the Knights.

Silis stopped, too, along with all her men, and stared in shock. For the first time since Godfrey had met her, she seemed to be at a loss.

They all stood there, breathing hard, hands on their hips, watching their future burn away. Godfrey realized they were now trapped, and would soon all be dead. There was no way out.

"Now what?" Ario asked, turning to Silis.

"How are we going to get out of here?" Merek asked.

Silis looked everywhere, scanning the harbor, eyes filled with panic—and he saw from her gaze that it was over—there was no way out.

Godfrey, heart pounding, scanned the harbor himself, looking for any sign of hope—just one empty ship. There were none.

But as Godfrey scanned the horizon, he saw something that caught his eyes in the distance. He blinked, wondering if he were seeing things. There seemed to be a small fleet of ships snaking its way upriver, sailing into the harbor. Those banners...he seemed to recognize them. But he knew it could not be.

Could it?

As the ships sailed closer, Godfrey squinted into the sun and saw that they were indeed ones he recognized: the banners of the Southern Isles. Erec. The greatest knight of the Silver.

But what was he doing here, in Volusia?

Godfrey's heart skipped a beat as it swelled with joy and hope. Erec. Their greatest knight. Alive. Here. Sailing into Volusia. His throat went dry with excitement. Godfrey felt a sudden surge of confidence, felt for the first time that they might actually make it out of here—when suddenly he realized that Erec was sailing into a dead end. He saw the iron gate up ahead, and he realized at once that Erec was in danger.

Godfrey, heart racing, surveyed the harbor and saw the huge iron crank beside the gate—and he knew at once that if he did not raise it, Erec and his men, pursued as they were by the huge Empire fleet behind them, would all soon be trapped. Dead.

And then something crazy happened: Godfrey no longer felt fear for himself. It was replaced by a burning urgency to save his friend. Without thinking, he began to run, through all the chaos, right for the harbor, and for that crank.

"Where are you going?" Silis called out, horrified.

"To save a brother!" Godfrey yelled back over his shoulder as he sprinted.

Godfrey ran and ran, breathing hard but this time not slowing. He knew that by running like this in the open courtyard he was exposed, and would likely get killed. For some strange reason, he no longer cared. Instead, he kept his eyes fixated on Erec's ships, on that crank, and remained determined to save them.

Godfrey was surprised to hear footsteps, and he turned to see the others running up beside him, catching up with him.

Merek smiled back, equally throwing caution to the wind.

"You better know what you're doing," he called out.

Godfrey pointed straight ahead.

"Those ships," he called out. "Those are Erec's. We must lift that gate!"

Godfrey looked out and saw the Empire fleet closing in on them and he ran faster than all the others, surprising himself, gasping in one last sprint until he reached the crank.

He jumped up, grabbed its huge handle, and pulled with all his might.

But it didn't budge.

The others caught up, and as one they all joined in, Silis and her men, Merek, Ario, and even Akorth and Fulton, all of them leaning on the massive iron crank and pulling with all their might. Godfrey strained and groaned beneath its weight, desperate to free Erec.

Come on, he prayed.

Slowly, the crank, with a great creaking noise, began to budge. It groaned and protested, but slowly it moved, and as it did, Godfrey saw the iron gate raise an inch.

They all let go of their grip, exhausted by the effort.

"It's going too slow," Ario observed. "We'll never open it in time."

Godfrey looked over and realized they were right—the crank was just too massive.

Suddenly, there came a barking, and Godfrey looked down to see Dray at his feet, a rope in his mouth, barking frantically. He realized that Dray was trying to tell him something, and he looked over to see a carriage and several horses, abandoned, a few feet away. His eyes lit up.

"You're a genius, Dray," Godfrey said.

Godfrey burst into action, looping one end of the rope over the crank, then running over and looping the other over the carriage. He then grabbed the whip off the back and whipped the group of horses again and again.

"RIDE!" Godfrey yelled.

The massive war horses neighed, then reared and took off with all their strength.

Suddenly, the crank began to move, again and again, faster and faster, as the horses ran farther and farther away.

Godfrey turned at the sound of groaning metal and was elated to watch the iron gate opening wide beneath the water. He was thrilled to see Erec's ships continuing on, sailing right for it, and finally slipping through the opening, just wide enough, and into the harbor.

"STAND BACK!" Godfrey yelled.

Godfrey drew his sword, rushed forward, and hacked the rope.

The crank wound furiously the other way, and the iron gate began to shut on itself again, sealing the harbor just as the last of Erec's ships passed through.

There soon came the sound of ships crunching and breaking, and Godfrey watched in awe as several Empire ships, right behind Erec, smashed into the iron gates and cracked into a million pieces. Hundreds of Empire soldiers cried out as their ships were impaled, falling overboard and into the harbor.

Godfrey saw the joy on the faces of Erec and his men as their fleet sailed into the harbor, safely inside. There came a shout of triumph, and of joy, and Godfrey knew he had saved them. He felt elated. Finally, for once, he had done something worthy.

*

Erec sailed through the gates, into the Volusian harbor, and his eyes opened wide in disbelief to look over and see it was Godfrey turning the crank, a dog at his heels, cutting the rope, opening those gates and saving their lives. As he severed the rope, the iron gates slammed close, cutting off the rest of the Empire fleet and leaving Erec and the others free inside the harbor and waterways of Volusia. He and all his men let out a cheer, as the Empire ships cracked and splintered behind them.

As Erec looked over at Godfrey, beaming, he saw him flanked by a group of people he did not recognize, and he felt a renewed sense of optimism. If Gwendolyn's brother was here, perhaps she was, too.

Erec studied the city with a professional soldier's eye, and he was confused to see battle everywhere, a city immersed in chaos, the Knights of the Seven flooding through the gates and invading what remained of the city, killing the last vestige of Volusian soldiers, who finally turned and fled. They had been completely routed. But why? Why would Empire turn on Empire?

With the Volusians killed and the city vanquished, horns sounded throughout the city, and Erec watched the Seven begin to depart en masse, leaving the city gates as quickly as they had rolled in. The vast army of the Knights of the Seven was already leaving, heading back out into the desert and leaving behind but a small force of perhaps a thousand men to kill and loot what remained of the Volusians. Clearly, Erec realized, this war had never been about occupying Volusia—but rather about a vendetta. Erec studied city streets, the open courtyards, and amid the thousands of Volusian corpses, he counted perhaps several hundred Knights remaining—about the same size force of men he had in his ships. They were a vicious force of killers—but with their numbers equally matched and the Volusians dead, Erec knew he at least had a chance.

As Erec's ship touched down at the edge of the harbor, Godfrey and his men throwing up ropes to help secure them, Erec leapt from the deck, not waiting for the ramp—the Knights had spotted them and were charging already, and Erec knew there was no time.

He landed below on the golden cobblestone. He was joined by Strom, and all around him his men did the same, jumping down, lowering the ramps, securing ropes and gathering their weapons, all hitting the ground running and ready for battle.

Even as the Knights charged, Erec scanned the faces, looking everywhere for Gwendolyn, wanting to free her; but not spotting her, he moved on, charging forward, leading his men, and bracing himself for battle.

There came a tremendous clash as the Knights of the Seven met his men. The clang of armor rang through the air as Erec led the way, the first in battle, blocking an ax blow with his shield, raising his sword and slashing, felling the first knight.

Erec felt ready for battle, especially after all that at sea. Joined by his brother, his men, and even Godfrey and the others, he let out a great battle cry as he threw himself into the thick of the sea of men, prepared to risk it all for freedom.

The Knights, well-trained, came at him swinging, and if he were a regular soldier, Erec surely would have fallen. But Erec was too well-trained for that; indeed, he had been trained since the time he could walk for battles such as this. He raised his shield as it glimmered beneath the sun and blocked blow after blow, dazzling his opponents. He also used it as a weapon when he chose to, smashing some knights in the head and others in the wrist, disarming them. He used his sword, slashing and jabbing—but he also used his feet and his hands, kicking other soldiers back and elbowing others. He was a one-man whirlwind of destruction.

The Knights focused on him and came at him in waves. He ducked and dodged and spun, slicing one in the stomach and stabbing another through the heart. He head-butted another, then thrust backwards and stabbed a soldier behind him, right before he could bring an ax down on the back of his head.

Erec moved like lightning, like a fish leaping in and out of water, defending and attacking, felling men and leading the way. Strom fought beside him, joined by other men from the Southern Isles, and they fought for their lives, spinning in every direction as the army closed in.

They killed men, yet some of Erec's men, he was pained to see, fell, too.

Erec's shoulders were tiring, and he, vastly outnumbered, was beginning to wonder how much longer his men could last—when suddenly he heard a great shout from behind the Knights. There was chaos in the crowd, and consternation in the soldiers' ranks, and Erec looked out, confused, to see them being attacked from behind. He heard a rattling of chains and couldn't understand what was happening—until he looked out and saw dozens of slaves, still shackled, rising up from the streets of Volusia and jumping the soldiers from behind. They descended on them with their shackles, strangling them, beating them, snatching away their swords—and the Knights were caught off guard. Sandwiched now between two forces, they did not know which way to fight.

The battle no longer theirs, the Knights fell in droves as Erec and his men, re-energized, made a final push forward, felling them left and right.

Those that remained soon tried to turn and flee—but Erec and the slaves did not let them. They surrounded them, cut off their escape, and killed every last one of them.

Soon, all fell silent. The air was filled with no sound but that of men groaning and writhing on the golden streets of Volusia. Erec, still breathing hard, heart pounding, looked everywhere for Gwendolyn, wondering about the fate of his people. But he saw no sign of her.

Godfrey came running over and Erec warmly embraced him.

"A face from the Ring," Godfrey said, in awe.

"Where is Gwendolyn?" Erec asked.

Alistair rushed forward and embraced Godfrey, too, and she studied him, wondering.

"Where is my brother?" she demanded. "Where is Thorgrin? Where are all the others from the Ring?"

"Are you all that remains?" Erec asked, cautious.

Godfrey shook his head sadly.

"I wish I knew," he replied. "Last I saw her, she was alive, with our people, and heading out into the Great Waste."

Erec processed the news, feeling dismayed. He had so hoped and expected to find and rescue Gwendolyn here. He realized his journey was far from over.

Suddenly, there came bursting forth from the crowd two people, a girl with fierce eyes and a man who resembled her, perhaps her brother, who ran with a limp. They ran right up to Godfrey, and he turned and faced them, seeming shocked.

"Loti?" he called out. "Loc?"

They embraced, and Erec wondered who they were.

"Is Darius here?" she asked, urgently.

He shook his head gravely.

"He is long gone, carted off to the Capital."

She looked dismayed.

"We have crossed the Waste. We saw the chaos in Volusia, and we awaited our chance to enter. And then we spotted you."

"Then join us," Godfrey said. "We shall embark from this place, and if there is any chance of finding Darius, we shall."

They nodded, satisfied.

"Perhaps we can still catch Volusia," Erec said, circling back to the topic at hand.

Godfrey shook his head.

"They departed moons ago," Godfrey added.

"But why?" he asked. "Where were they going?"

Godfrey sighed.

"They embarked for the second Ring," he said. "The Ridge. They thought it was our only hope."

Erec narrowed his eyes, thinking it through.

"And where is this Ridge?" Strom demanded.

Godfrey shook his head.

"I do not know if it even exists," he replied.

"If it does exist," said Silis, stepping forward, "it would be deep in the Great Waste. There are waterways that snake deep through the Empire that can take us there. It is a long way, and a roundabout way, and while it leads through the Waste, it might not ever lead us to your Ridge. But I can lead you there—if you and your ships are willing."

Erec sized up this woman and sensed that she was honest and true.

"I am willing," he said. "Whether this Ridge exists or not, I would go to the ends of the earth for Gwendolyn and the others."

"But how shall we make it out?" asked Godfrey, turning and facing the harbor.

Erec turned around and saw the Empire fleet, beyond the iron gates, blocking the entrance to the harbor.

Silis stepped forward and turned, scouring the city.

"This city has more than just one mere water exit," she said. "After all, this is the great Volusia, the city of water. I know waterways that can lead us out, through the back end of the city, and out into the northern harbor. That will take us out to open sea, and from there we can pick up the waterways that will take us into the Waste."

Erec looked her in the eyes and then surveyed the city, seeing the canals cut through it, leading from the harbor, just wide enough to hold his ships single file, and realized it might be the best plan they had.

"And what of us?" came a voice.

Erec turned to see dozens of slaves standing there, still shackled, men of all races, men whose faces were all etched with pain, men who had been abused their entire lives by the Empire.

Erec stepped forward solemnly, so grateful to these men for their help, raised his sword, and as he walked through their ranks, one at a time he slashed them, severing their bonds, setting them free.

"Your freedom is yours now," Erec said, "to do with as you wish. I, and all of my people, thank you."

One of the slaves, a tall man with broad shoulders and dark skin, stepped forward and looked him right in the eye.

"What we want with our freedom," he said, his voice deep and bold, "is vengeance. You sail for vengeance—we wish to join you. After all, your fight is our fight, too, and we can bolster your ranks."

Erec sized him up, and saw within him a great warrior's spirit. He could deny no man a chance for freedom, for battle, and Erec knew his ranks, too, needed replenishing, and that there was room on his ships.

He nodded back, solemnly, stepped forward and clasped his hand. His army had grown larger, Erec knew, and together, they would sail into this Waste, find Gwendolyn, and crush whatever Empire force stood in their way.

CHAPTER SIXTEEN

Thorgrin stood at the bow of the ship, gripping the rail, and looked out in anticipation as the tides pulled them deeper into the gloom of the Land of Blood. For the first time since he had begun this journey, he felt a sense of hope, felt closer to finding Guwayne than he'd ever had. On the horizon, before them, loomed the Blood Lord's castle, all black, appearing to be made of mud and to emerge from the blackened landscape all around it, as if an explosion of mud had hardened and settled into some awful form of a castle. A sinister glow came from its small windows, shaped like slits, and they did not make it feel more friendly, but rather more ominous. Thor could sense the evil of this castle even from here, and he felt without a doubt that Guwayne lay beyond its doors.

"I don't like this," came a voice.

Thor looked over to see Reece standing beside him, looking out, concerned. Angel stood on his other side, joined by Selese, O'Connor, Elden, Indra, and Matus, all of them lined up, studying the horizon, riveted by the sight.

"It is too easy," Reece said.

"The waters are too calm, the land too serene," Selese chimed in. "Something is wrong."

"Guwayne was taken by an army of creatures," Matus said. "There should be a battalion of gargoyles guarding this place, awaiting us. Or the Blood Lord himself. *Something*. But instead, there is nothing. Are we sailing into a trap?"

Thorgrin wondered the same thing. In spite of the quiet, the gentle breeze, he could not relax; a sense of gloom hung over them like a blanket, and the lapping of the blood-red water against the hull, bringing them ever closer to this place, only served to increase his wariness.

Before them the waters of the ocean forked. Straight ahead lay the black castle, while to the left, a strong current rushed, heading off into a horizon that was filled with breaking light, the waters turning increasingly light as they went.

"It seems like the way out," O'Connor said, turning, as they all looked to the left, to the breaking light. As Thor followed the waters, he saw the landscape, too, changed, from black to green; in the far distance, it appeared the waters widened back into ocean, demarcated by the waterfalls of blood. They were right: it certainly seemed like freedom lay that way.

Thor turned and looked straight ahead: freedom from the Land of Blood was not what he was seeking. He wanted Guwayne, whatever the cost. And Guwayne, he knew, lay straight ahead, in the very heart of the land of gloom.

They stuck to their course, continuing straight ahead.

Up ahead the waterway funneled to a long, narrow canal leading to the castle, and as the mist lifted, Thor peered ahead and saw, blocking the entrance to the canal, an arched stone drawbridge and a small gatehouse. With the entranceway blocked, they had no choice but to bring their ship to a stop before it, all of them puzzled by this entrance.

Thor spotted a sole figure standing on drawbridge, facing them. The gatekeeper was, oddly, a woman, unarmed, with long red hair the color of the sea spilling down the sides of her face, all the way until they touched the water. She stood there and stared back at Thorgrin with her large glowing blue eyes, perfectly still, barely clothed, and Thor stared back in wonder, mesmerized.

"I don't like this," Matus said softly. "One woman left alone to guard the castle? It must be a trick."

Slowly, their boat came to a stop before her, and as they floated there, she stared back, her eyes locking only on Thor's, and smiled back.

"I am no woman," she corrected, having clearly overheard them, "but a gatekeeper. The gatekeeper to the one and only gate there is, to the one and only Lord of all." She stared right at Thor, her eyes so intense they nearly burned through him. "The Lord who holds your son."

Thor flushed, filled with a sense of determination, of outrage.

"Stand out of my way, woman," he demanded, "or so help me God, I will kill anyone or anything that stands in the way of my son."

But she only smiled back in response, unmoving, and smiled wider.

"Come to me," she said. "Come to me and remove me from this bridge—and your son shall be yours."

Thor, determined, wasted no time. Without hesitating, he rushed forward on the deck, jumped up onto the rail, then leapt off of their ship, onto the stone drawbridge.

"Thor!" Angel called out, concern in her voice.

But he already stood on dry land, on the stone bridge, before the woman. He stood there scowling, one hand on the hilt of his sword, prepared to use it if need be.

But the strangest thing happened: as Thor stood there, facing her, slowly, he felt his heart melting inside. A numbing sensation took over his body, his mind, and as he stared back at her, he began to find it hard to concentrate. It was as if she were casting a spell, and he was slowly falling under it.

He blinked, trying to shake it off, but try as he did, he could no longer think of harming her.

"That's it," she said, her voice soft. "Kneel. Kneel before me."

Thor hardly realized what he was doing as his legs acted on their own accord and he knelt before her. She reached up, and he felt her soft hands running through his hair, her palms so smooth, her voice so comforting. He found it impossible to concentrate on anything else.

"Thorgrin!" Reece called out in alarm, as the other chimed in, too.

Thor heard the voices but he, still in a haze, felt unable to look away, unable to look anywhere but at this woman's eyes.

"You don't need them, Thorgrin," she said, her voice so soft, so hypnotizing. "Send them back home. Allow them to go. Back to their freedom. You don't need them now. You are with me now. You are home now—the only home you'll ever need. You will stay here with me. On this drawbridge. Forever."

Thor felt himself melting deeper into this woman's spell, believing everything she said and not wanting to be anywhere else. Everything she said made perfect sense. Why would he ever want to be anywhere else? He was home now. He felt it.

"Tell them, Thorgrin," she whispered, stroking his face. "Tell them to leave without you."

Thor turned to his shipmates, barely recognizing them through his haze.

"Go," he called out. "Leave me here."

"NO!" Angel shrieked. "THORGRIN!"

Suddenly a great tide came, and Thor watched as the ship started to be drawn away from him. It forked down to the river, to the path to freedom, out of the Land of Blood, its currents moving faster and faster. Within moments, it was getting smaller, disappearing, drifting off into the horizon, and as its currents picked up, Thorgrin knew it would never, ever return again.

But Thorgrin no longer cared. He wanted the ship to disappear. He wanted to be all alone. He was happy in this woman's arms, and he wanted to stay like this forever.

And ever.

"THORGRIN!" Angel cried, already so far away, a cry filled with despair, with longing, as they disappeared from view, their ship taken off to another world entirely.

CHAPTER SEVENTEEN

Volusia stood atop the parapets of the Empire capital, staring out at the vast desert before her, streaked scarlet by the breaking dawn, and took in the sight with awe. Surrounded by all her generals and advisors, she looked over to see all of them looking ashen. She could not blame them.

It was a magnificent sight before them: the world looked like one giant battlefield. The entire world seemed to be blanketed by the Knights of the Seven, their distinctive black banners flying high in the wind, their glistening black armor covering the desert like a plague, leaving not a single space free. This was unlike anything she had ever seen. It was not like the small force that had come before; rather, this was the entire army, all of the assets of the Empire unfurled before her. They were as numerous as grains of sand by the sea. It was as if the army had no end.

The banners alone, flying so high above the troops, were thick enough to blot out the sun. They rippled wildly, their sound audible even from here, though their front lines were several hundred yards away.

"Goddess?" asked one of her generals, panic in his voice. "They have the capital surrounded. There's no escape this time."

"Nor is there any chance we could withstand their attack," added another. "Not for long."

Volusia, wanting to see for herself, slowly turned in a wide circle, taking in the panorama. She saw the black army spread out as wide as could be, encircling them like a great ring. It was a greater army than she'd ever laid eyes upon—she did not know such force of numbers was possible. While she knew this might be the end of her, she felt grateful to be alive to see such a sight. There seemed no end to the number of soldiers that were alive in the world.

"Your sorcery won't help you now," added one of her advisors. "Not with the Volks gone. You will have no magic at your disposal—

just brute force. It will be us against them. It is a battle we could never win."

"To even attempt a defense would be suicide," added a general. "We have no choice—we must surrender."

"Raise the white flag," added an advisor, "and broker a truce. Perhaps they will show mercy."

Volusia stood there, a tense silence falling over them, as she studied the horizon.

"This is no mere army, Goddess," said a general. "This is the force of the entire Empire, the might of the world, descending upon our city. You have led us to ruin. Surrender. There is no other choice."

As Volusia stared out at the horizon, she tried to block out their voices. Their points were all true, she knew; with the Volks gone, she no longer had the power of sorcery. And yet, in a strange way, that made Volusia happy. All of this time, she had relied upon the external power of the sorcery of others. All along, she had secretly wanted to rely only on her own power. Because, deep down, she felt, she knew, that she was a goddess, that she was invincible. That she did not need the Volks. That she did not need anyone.

And now, finally, the time had come to prove herself, to show the world the power of the great Goddess Volusia. To show them that she, and she alone, could stop an army, had power enough within her to stop the entire world.

After a long silence, Volusia turned to her men and smiled.

"You are wrong," she said. "It is *they* who don't have a choice. They will all surrender to me, the great Goddess Volusia—or they will all pay the price."

They all stared at her, dumbfounded, speechless.

Volusia would waste no more time with them, these men who would never understand until they saw it for themselves.

"I alone will confront them," she added. "Now open the gates."

Her generals, faces frozen with fear, looked back at her as if she were mad.

Volusia turned and descended from the ramparts, down the stone steps, all of her men following hastily. She crossed through the golden courtyard of the Empire's capital, ceremoniously, all of her soldiers, all of her people, stopping what they were doing to watch her go. She walked alone toward the massive gates to the city, feeling her destiny bubbling up within her. Finally, the time had come. Finally, it was time to show the world who she truly was.

The huge, arched, golden gates opened slowly, creaking, as dozens of soldiers turned the cranks. She walked right for them, the first rays of sunlight pouring through between the gap, lighting her grotesque face.

Volusia continued walking, out of the safety of the capital, out into the desert, feeling the cobblestone beneath her feet give way to sand, crunching beneath her boots. Alone, outside, she continued to walk, slowly, one step at a time, never looking back.

Volusia could feel the eyes of thousands of her own soldiers upon her, watching her nervously from within the city capital—and could feel, even more so, the eyes of the millions of soldiers of the Knights of the Seven stopping and gazing at her. Still, she never stopped. She was a Goddess, after all, and she would stop for no one. She needed no one. She could take on the forces of the world all by herself.

Horns sounded throughout the enemy camp, and Volusia watched as all of the formations broke into action. Thousands of divisions rallied, charging forward with a great battle cry, eager for her head. Eager to tear her apart.

Still, she kept walking. She took another step, and another. Volusia closed her eyes, raised her palms to the sky, leaned back, and let out a great shriek. As she did, she willed for the world to bend to her will. She willed for the Earth to split before her, to swallow up this army. She commanded the heavens to strike down, the clouds to rush to her will, and lightning to kill their men. She willed for every power in the universe to rush to her aid. She *commanded* it.

Volusia stood there, bunching her fists, willing and waiting as the men rushed closer, the galloping of their horses shaking the ground, filling her ears.

And yet nothing happened.

There was no lightning, no earthquake; there were no clouds.

Instead, there was just the sound of silence.

Sickening, awful silence.

And she, alone, was about to be destroyed by an army.

CHAPTER EIGHTEEN

Darius knelt at his father's side, cradling his head in his hands, and felt overwhelmed with emotion as he watched him die. Blood poured from his chest where the elephant's tusk had speared him, and it trickled from his mouth as he looked up at Darius with the look of a man breathing his final breaths.

Darius felt wracked with despair as he watched his father die in his arms. Here lay this great man who had risked his life for him, who had saved his life, the greatest warrior by far Darius ever met. After his whole life of longing for him, finally, they had had a chance to meet, were reunited here, on the battlefield. And yet as kind as fate was, it was also cruel, as it had snatched this man away from him before they'd barely had a chance to know each other.

Darius would have given anything to have a chance to get to know his father, to find out how he had become such a skilled warrior, how life had taken him here, to the capital arena. He would have loved to get to the bottom of the mystery of his life, and of his absence in his own life.

But now, that would never be. Taking his father was the cruelest thing the Empire had ever done to him—crueler even than taking his own life.

"Father," Darius said, holding back tears as he held him in his arms. "You can't leave me. Not now."

Darius heard a great rumble as he waited for a response, and out of the corner of his eye he saw the elephants circling the stadium, their great footsteps rocking it, as they prepared to come back for him. Darius knew he didn't have much time. But he didn't care about that now. He was ready to die at his father's side.

His father reached up and grabbed his wrist, his grip surprisingly strong even as his life force began to ebb.

"I am proud that you're my son," he said, his voice raspy, fading. "So proud of all that you have done. You are a greater warrior than I

84

could have ever been. I see it in your eyes. I live on in you. Fight for me, Darius. Fight for me."

His eyes closed as he went limp in his arms.

Dead.

"NO!" Darius shrieked, leaning back, feeling waves of grief wash over him.

Darius wanted to take it away, to change the world, to go back and make everything happen differently. He wanted to curse at destiny, to curse at his life, which had been hard and cruel since the day he had been born. But he knew nothing could bring him back now, this man he had loved, and the only man left who had loved him.

Darius felt hot tears pouring down his cheeks as he held his father's head, feeling empty, feeling as if he had nothing left in the world to live for. He could feel the ground trembling as the elephants finished their circling and charged for him—but he no longer cared. Some part of him was already dead.

As Darius knelt there, laying his father on the ground, slowly the grief within him morphed to something else.

Rage.

Darius looked up, cold, calculating, and as he did, he tightened his grip on his sword. He thought of what they had done to his father, of his father's final words. They rang in his head like a mantra, like an order:

Fight for me.

Slowly, Darius stood. He faced off against these beasts, and he prepared to make his final stand. He burned, more than ever in his life, for vengeance. He would die trying—but he would not go down without taking somebody with him.

The ground shook as the two elephants neared, awesome, magnificent beasts, all black, being ridden by Empire soldiers. They gained speed, as if hoping to trample him, and as they did, Darius felt all the grief within him morph into cold, hard fury. All the rage he had ever had in his life—at the Empire, at his life, at his village, at his father's absence—it all bubbled up. It was a rage larger than the universe, a rage he could not control. A rage that turned his whole body hot.

Here Darius stood, a boy who had become a man, a man, finally, with nothing left to live for. His friends were dead, his father was dead—everything and everyone he had ever known or loved was lost and taken from him. And now, he was about to die too. He was a man with nothing left in the world to lose.

But there was one thing he still had, and he had that in abundance: a desire for vengeance. Vengeance for his father. Vengeance for his life.

Darius faced the elephants as they thundered down on him, feeling no fear for the first time in his life. Feeling free. He looked forward to taking them on.

As he stood there, time seemed to slow, and something happened to him he did not understand. The rage bubbled up, overtook him, became like a cancer in his body. It was so powerful, unlike anything he had ever felt. Waves of energy overwhelmed him, from head to toe, so intense he could barely feel his own skin. He felt his hair standing on end, felt as if he might explode.

And then, it happened.

For the second time in his life, Darius felt himself overwhelmed by a power, a power he had no control of, a power he had been terrified to acknowledge, and to embrace, up until now. It was a power he did not understand, and a power that had scared him.

Until now.

The power surged within him, and Darius found himself dropping his weapons. He knew instinctively he didn't need them anymore. He knew that the power within him, at his fingertips, was greater than any power, greater than anything forged of steel.

Instead, Darius raised his palms. As the elephants charged toward him, he raised them higher and higher in the air, aiming one at each elephant bearing down on him. They intended to kill him, Darius could see that.

But Darius had other plans.

As he raised his palms, Darius felt a searing ball of energy emanate from each palm. And as he raised his arms, the craziest thing happened: he felt the weight of each elephant in his palms. It was as if he were holding them.

And as he lifted his arms higher, he saw the most shocking sight in his life: the elephants, charging at him with fury, began to rise off the ground.

The elephants trumpeted as Darius lifted them higher and higher into the air. They rose five feet, then twenty feet, then thirty, then a hundred, their legs flailing. They hovered high in the air, helpless, at the mercy of Darius's power.

The crowd fell silent as they gasped, looking up at the sight, no one knowing what to make of it.

Darius did not give them time to react. As the rage coursed through his arms and shoulders, he quickly and decisively lowered his arms, thinking, as he did, of his father, of all his friends he had lost on the battlefield. He felt their blood calling out from the grave. Now it was their time. Now, it was time for vengeance.

Darius felt a power surge within them, a power that could move mountains, and he tapped that power for the first time in his life as he lowered his arms and hurled the elephants. He was amazed to watch them go flying through the air, end over end, trumpeting, flailing, as they headed, like comets, for the stone bleachers in the stadium.

The crowd realized, too late. A few rose, tried to run, but it all happened too quickly and there was nowhere for them to go.

The two beasts smashed into the stadium with a tremendous crash, shaking the arena as if it had been struck by a comet. The impact took out entire sections of stone, killing hundreds of people at once. The Empire cheers of cruelty and glee had now morphed into cries and shrieks of terror.

The crowd ran, trying desperately to get away, but the elephants tumbled through the bleachers, rolling and rolling, crushing thousands more.

The arena fell into chaos. People shrieked and ran as the weight of the elephants collapsed entire sections of stone, the avalanche killing hundreds more.

Darius stood there, the last one left on the battlefield, shocked at his power. The world, he felt, was his.

CHAPTER NINETEEN

Stara dug her heels into the horse's ribs, spurring it on, faster and faster, tearing across the Great Waste, determined not to stop until she crossed this desert, until she crossed the world and found Reece. He was somewhere out there on the horizon, she knew, beyond the Waste, beyond the sea, out there with Thorgrin, on the search for Guwayne. She knew her chances of finding him were remote, that she may very well die out here in the Waste. But she didn't care. As reckless as this was, she felt more joyful, more liberated, than she had in moons. She was free, finally, thrilled to be away from the Ridge, riding out under the open sky and following the desires of her own heart.

The safety of that Ridge, every moment she had been there, had been hell for her. She did not want safety: she wanted Reece. Danger meant nothing to her, if it stood between her and the man she loved most in the world. It was love, Stara finally realized, that mattered more than anything in the world—more than pleasures and riches and safety, more than any object she could want. It was love, and the freedom to pursue that love, that mattered. And that was what she had now.

Whether she died out here in this Waste, or somewhere at sea, none of that mattered—as long as she could be free to pursue her heart's desires.

Stara galloped on the horse, her skin still raw from having raced through the Sand Wall, her lips dry, her throat parched, her skin burnt from the sun, her turban having fallen off long ago. She hadn't stopped to get it, knowing that if she stopped moving for even one minute, she would never continue on through this Waste. The horse beneath her, too, was gasping, heaving, and Stara wondered how much longer they could go on. Somehow, she sensed, it understood the urgency of her mission, and without any prodding, raced forward on its own.

As the horse charged and charged, Stara tried to follow the general directions that Fithe had given her, going over them like a mantra again and again in her head: *cross the Sand Wall, then head north. Follow the North Star, which shines by day and night. If you live, you will reach the canals. There, you may find a hidden vessel in the harbor, stowed for times of escape, hidden beneath the branches of the willows that grow on its shores. If they are even still there. Your quest will be long and hard, and you likely will not make it.*

As Stara rode, she looked up time and again, looking for the North Star, knowing it was somewhere high overhead. Wispy clouds came in and out, and she no longer even knew if she was staying the course. She reached down instinctively and raised the sack of water to her mouth and squeezed—yet it was empty, dried out long ago. She chucked it, realizing she had nothing left.

Stara rode and rode, her legs aching, her back aching, her head beginning to droop, too tired to hang on. She felt herself slouching, felt that at any moment she might fall off her horse. She knew once she did, she would be finished. *Reece*, she thought, *I love you.*

Finally, when she thought she could not go no more, when she felt certain she might die out here, she felt the horse slowing, and she looked up. She felt them mounting a ridge, and as she looked up, she squinted, wondering if she were seeing things. She shook her head, realizing she was not, and her heart leapt within her: there, against the setting sun, was a shimmering body of water. The small rivers snaked every which way, ending in the desert.

The canals.

It was a startling sight, and as it came close into view, Stara was overcome with euphoria. Finally, the monotony of the Great Waste, the monotony she had never expected to finish, had come to an end.

Streams converged from a hundred rivers into a pool of water at the edge of the Waste, surrounded by a grove of willow trees, their branches hanging low, just as Fithe had said. Her heart beat faster at the sight. There was water. There was a path out, to the rivers, to the sea. There was the road to Reece. There was freedom.

Stara did not even need to kick the horse, which saw it, too, and increased its pace, racing down the ridge, not slowing until it reached the grove of trees at the edge of the water. Stara was so grateful for the shade, despite the sunset, and she dismounted as the horse bent over gratefully to lap the water. She fell down on her hands and knees beside it and began drinking, too.

Stara gulped the water, gasping; as she caught her breath, she splashed the cold water on her face, down her neck, in her hair, getting the dust of the desert off her. She knelt there for a moment, too tired to move, reveling in the sound of the willow branches as they stirred in the breeze off the water.

Finally the horse leaned over and licked her face, prodding her back up.

Stara regained her composure and as she sat up, she scanned the water, the branches, looking to see if there were any vessels still hidden. As she squinted, she thought she saw something hidden behind a clump of trees, as their branches swayed in the wind, and she hurried over and pushed back the branches.

There, she was elated to see, was a small vessel, rocking in the water, tied to shore, just large enough to hold her and one small sail. It had been well hidden beneath the trees and she thanked God for it, knowing that without it, she would die here.

Stara was about to get inside, to push off, when she remembered the horse. She turned, walked over to it, and stroked its face, looking into its eyes. It made a gesture as if to follow her into the boat, but she shook her head.

"It is a journey for me alone, my friend," she said.

It made a soft neighing sound.

"I shall never be able to thank you," she said. "You are free now. Roam the Waste, find a new home, answer to no man. You are free!"

The horse leaned in and licked her face and she kissed its head. It turned and ran off, never looking back.

Stara turned herself and slipped onto the boat. She extracted her small silver dagger, which she had carried with her from the Ring, and in one quick, decisive move, she severed the rope.

The currents caught her vessel, and as she raised her sail, she began to move into the widening river, gaining speed, into the sunset, out toward the open sea, and somewhere, she prayed, toward Reece.

CHAPTER TWENTY

Gwendolyn marched down the endless parapets of the castle, Krohn at her side and Steffen beside her, looking everywhere for Argon. She had been anxious to find him ever since she'd left the tower, since Eldof had told her what he knew. She was seeking Argon out even before reporting back to the King, as she felt a sense of urgency and desperation. Eldof, after all, had declared that the end of the Ridge was coming soon, and that there was nothing she could do to stop it. She felt in her heart that the only one who would truly understand, who might have any way of stopping it, would be Argon.

More importantly, Eldof's words hung in her ears, and she thought again and again about what he'd said, about Argon knowing how to find Thor, and about Argon's master. Why had Argon hidden these secrets from her? What was he hiding? Who was his master?

Gwendolyn burned with resolve to confront Argon, to not let him off the hook until he told her the truth. She had to know whatever he was hiding.

"Argon!" she yelled, calling out to the skies. "You cannot hide from me!"

She had been already to his chamber, to the spiral tower, and all throughout the castle, and he remained nowhere to be found. Had he left?

"My lady," Steffen said, after a long silence, Gwen leaning dejectedly on a rampart. "I checked everywhere, too. He's nowhere to be found. And no one has seen or heard anything of him."

Gwen turned and walked even faster, marching down the narrow stone walkways, scanning down below, across the city, her heart pounding with worry. Had he left for good this time? Could he really leave now, at this pivotal time, with all her unanswered questions?

Bells suddenly tolled, clanging throughout the city again and again, loud enough to drown out all else, and startling Gwen. She stopped and turned, hearing the collective gasp down below, and saw all the members of the Ridge stop and stare up, horrified, at the incessantly tolling bells. They rang again and again, ominously, and Gwen sensed right away that something was wrong.

"My lady," Steffen said, "those bells toll for death."

She knew it to be true the moment he said it, and she stood there motionless, looking down, watching as panic ensued across the capital of the Ridge.

"But for whom?" she asked, baffled.

Steffen shrugged in response, and she watched as she saw panic spread throughout the streets of the Ridge. She sensed dark things were coming.

"The King!" someone called out from down below. "Our King is dead!"

Gwen's heart went cold as she heard weeping erupt throughout the streets. She felt as if she had been stabbed in the gut. The King. Dead.

How could it be?

Gwen felt like running down there, grabbing someone, finding out what had happened; she wanted to run to the King's body, wherever he was, to see for herself. How could it be possible?

Gwen felt overwhelmed with conflicting emotions. If only she had gone straight to him after the tower, as she had promised, perhaps she could have saved his life. Now, it was all too late.

"GO!" she commanded Steffen. "Find out what has happened!"

"Yes, my lady," he said, turning and running off.

As Gwen looked down below, she could not help but feel that the chaos was already beginning to unfold, that the end of the Ridge was already arriving, just as Eldof, had prophesied. She was beginning to feel as if there were nothing left to stop it. It was if war had already arrived.

She felt an even greater urgency to find Argon now, before it was too late.

"Sometimes you find when you no longer search," came a dark, cryptic voice.

Gwen spun, and was at once startled and relieved to see Argon standing a few feet away, staring back. He wore his golden robe, held his staff, and he nearly shone in the sun, lighting up the gloomy day.

"I thought you'd left," she said. "To some other place, some other time."

92

He stared back, expressionless.

"Soon enough," he replied softly, "I will."

"Why didn't you tell me?" she demanded, indignant, stepping forward. "Why didn't you tell me about your master? That you knew of a way to find Thorgrin?"

Argon stared back, and for the first time, she could see real surprise in his eyes.

"Who told you of my master?" he asked.

"Why?" she pressed. "Why won't you tell me the secret you are holding? Why are you keeping me apart from Thorgrin? From Guwayne?"

Argon looked away, a pained expression across his face.

"Is it true?" she pressed, sensing she was onto something. "Do you have a master?"

"Yes," he finally replied.

She stared back at him, shocked.

"Just a simple yes? That frightens me."

"My master," Argon began, "is a creature of whom you should be frightened. I vowed to never lay eyes upon him again—and it is a vow I intend to keep."

"But he can lead me to Thorgrin?" Gwen pressed.

Argon slowly shook his head.

"You do not approach him unless you are prepared to lose your life. He is unpredictable—and very, very dangerous."

"I don't care if I lose my life," she pleaded, stepping forward. "Don't you see that? I have no life now without Thorgrin and Guwayne. How could you fail to see that all this time?"

Argon studied her for a long time, then slowly sighed.

"Yes, I do see," he finally replied. "You humans think differently than I do."

She breathed, hopeful.

"Then will you bring me to him?" she asked.

Argon turned and looked away, out at the sky.

"For you…"

As Argon's voice trailed off, Gwen heard a screech high in the sky, and she looked up and was shocked at what she saw. She could not believe her eyes.

A dragon.

She thought her mind was playing tricks on her, but there it was, a dragon, a small one, which looked shockingly like Ralibar, circling again and again, flapping its wings.

At first, as the dragon swooped toward them, Gwen felt an impulsive reaction of fear. But then, as she studied it carefully, she sensed that it was not out to harm her. It swooped down, then up, again and again, and she realized it could kill her if it wanted to.

But it did not want to kill her. It wanted something else. To warn her, perhaps. Or to give her a message.

The dragon circled around one last time, then finally swooped down, landing nearby, perhaps twenty feet away.

Gwen was shocked as she looked at it up close, sitting there, so proud. It screeched, looking right at her, as it flapped its wings once.

Gwen, in awe, stared back, breathless, in a state of shock. What could this mean?

"Go ahead," Argon said. "Touch it. It won't harm you. Dragons do not come randomly."

Gwen stepped forward, slowly, and she reached out tentatively and lay a hand on its neck. It was thrilling. She felt its ancient scales, so powerful, hard beneath her fingers, and it screeched.

Gwen jumped back as it flapped its wings; yet it stayed in place, and it lowered its head, and she sensed it wanted her to stroke it again. She stepped up, felt its bumpy scales, and she felt exhilarated to see a real dragon again. To be this close to one.

Even more so, as she touched it, she felt shocked that she could read its thoughts. She knew at once that it had been sent to her by Thorgrin.

She gasped.

"Thorgrin lives," she said, filled with hope. "He sent her to me."

Argon stepped forward with his staff.

"Yes," he replied.

"He wants her to help us," Gwen continued. "He wants to save me. To bring me to him."

Gwen turned to Argon.

"I cannot," she said. "Not with these people in jeopardy. I cannot abandon them. I made a vow to the King."

"Then where shall we take this dragon?" Argon asked.

"To your master," she replied, realizing at once it was meant to be. "You and I will ride it together. You will bring me to him. Now!" she commanded.

She looked at Argon, who hesitated, and Gwen knew this was a pivotal moment: he would either agree, or he would disappear forever.

Slowly, to her surprise, Argon stepped forward and leapt up onto the dragon.

He held out a hand for her.

She reached out and took it and she knew, as she did, that meeting his master, hearing his secrets, would change her life forever.

CHAPTER TWENTY ONE

Alistair stood at the rail of the ship, joined by Erec, Strom, and their men, and looked over all their new companions with a sense of joy: there stood Godfrey, Dray at his heels, a sight for sore eyes, one of the only familiar sights from the Ring, along with Akorth, Fulton, Merek, Ario, Loti and Loc, and her men, all those they had rescued from Volusia, joined by their dog, Dray. While they had not yet found Gwendolyn, seeing these people filled her with a sense of optimism, made her feel like, despite the staggering odds against them, they might actually find Gwendolyn and achieve their goal. For the first time, Alistair felt they were getting closer to finding all the others, whatever was left of the exiles of the Ring, and liberating them from wherever they might be in the Empire.

Alistair realized how lucky they were, too, to have found Godfrey and Silis; after all, she had helped navigate them out of Volusia, had shown them the back way out, and had led them where they were now, back on the open ocean, sailing north along the Empire coast. As Alistair reflected, the ocean breezes caressing her face, she realized their journey had been epic; at many points it had seemed they would not survive upriver, would never shake off the Empire fleet, would never reach Volusia. Yet they had made it, had managed to rescue Godfrey, and to escape—and to dam up the pursuit of the Empire fleet behind them.

Now, as she watched the ever-changing coastline, she saw it shift— the ocean turned into a deep harbor, and that harbor split into many waterways, all leading back into the Empire. She felt her ship slow and saw the men lowering the sails as they all came to a stop before the crossroads. Alistair peered out into the sun glaring on the water, concerned. Each of these waterways could take them anywhere—and if they chose the wrong one, they would never find Gwendolyn.

She could see the puzzled looks on all of their faces; none of them knew which way to go.

They all turned to Silis.

"And now which way?" Erec asked her.

She examined the waterways and shook her head.

"I wish I knew, my lord," she finally said to Erec. "I do not know which way Gwendolyn and the others went. I do not know if the famed Ridge even exists. These tributaries all will bring you deep into the Great Waste, and yet each in a different direction. The Waste, remember, is vast. Choose the wrong path, and you shall be a thousand miles from Gwendolyn."

Erec stood there, looking baffled as he stared out at the waters. A long silence fell over them, the only sound that of the waters rippling against the hull, the wind passing through.

"I'm sorry, my lord," she added. "This is as far as I know. I brought us here, and out of Volusia—but from this point on, the decision is as much yours as mine."

Erec stared for a long time, then finally turned to Alistair.

Alistair looked out at the water, wondering herself. Inside her, she could feel her baby girl, turning and kicking, and she felt comforted by her presence. She felt as if she were telling her something, urging her which way to go.

Alistair closed her eyes and searched deep within herself, summoning her own powers. She tried to visualize her brother Thorgrin, Gwendolyn, out there, somewhere.

Please, God, she prayed. *Send me the answer.*

Alistair heard a screech, high above, and she opened her eyes and searched the skies. High up, circling so high that she barely saw her, dipping in and out of clouds, she spotted Estopheles, Thorgrin's falcon, screeching. She swooped down, then up, and as she circled, Alistair felt the bird was trying to give her a message.

"Alistair?" Erec asked, breaking the silence.

Alistair knew that giving him advice was a sacred responsibility. The fate of this ship, of all these people with her, of all the exiles of the Ring, depended on her choosing correctly.

Alistair closed her eyes, feeling hundreds of eyes upon her, and stepped forward and placed both palms on the rail, feeling the energy. She breathed deeply and focused.

The world about her became very still; she heard the lapping waters against the ship's hull, the slight breeze in the air, the screech of Estopheles.

Gwendolyn, she thought, *where are you?*

As she stood there, Alistair began to feel her palms give off a warmth, and she slowly opened her eyes, looked at all the tributaries, and focused on one in particular: a winding river heading west, between three others.

Estopheles, she thought. *If this is the river, if this is our path, swoop down. Show me.*

Suddenly, Estopheles swooped down, to Alistair's shock, right over the same river she was staring at.

"There," Alistair said, pointing. "That shall lead us to Gwendolyn."

Erec studied her, his brow furrowed.

"Are you certain?" he asked.

Alistair nodded, feeling the certainty in every part of her body.

"That river shall lead us to what remains of the Ring. They need us now. More than ever. I can sense it. There is a terrific danger coming."

She turned to Erec, ashen, trying to blot out the hell she just saw.

"I do not know if they shall be alive by the time we reach them," she said.

Erec looked back in horror, then he turned and called out fresh orders, and his men burst into action, their ship immediately picking up speed, and the entire fleet falling in line.

Alistair turned and stared out at the looming river, and as she did, she prayed.

Please, Gwendolyn. Live. We're coming.

*

Godfrey sat at the stern of Erec's huge ship, leaning against the rail, legs dangling over the edge as they sailed, Dray lying beside him, his second sack of wine in his hand, and finally feeling good. Beside him sat Akorth and Fulton, already on their fourth sacks, Merek on his first, and Ario, who only stared out into the waters. All of them, finally, were relaxed, all of them, after the chaos, the whirlwind, with a chance to breathe.

Godfrey reflected as he looked out at the waters, trying to process it all. He could not believe they had escaped the horrors of Volusia, a city in which he was sure he was going to die—nor could he believe that he had run into Erec and Alistair—or that he had managed to help them escape, too. The fact that he was even sitting on their ship now, on the way to find Gwendolyn, was surreal. It was as if he had been given a second chance at life.

Finally, for the first time since arriving in the Empire, Godfrey was optimistic. He was back in motion, with an army of his own people—and an army of freed slaves—and on his way to save Gwendolyn and the others. He took another swig of ale, letting it all go to his head, not having realized how much he had missed it.

Yet on the other hand, as he looked out, Godfrey also felt trepidation; he knew they were still far from home, were sailing into even greater dangers, heading deeper into the Waste in their quest to find his sister, if she were even still alive. Surely they would soon be engulfed by hostile Empire armies, and the deeper they went, the harder it would be to get out. He did not know what the future held.

Yet for the first time in a while, he did not care. He was part of something greater than himself now, and he felt a driving sense of mission, of purpose. He would go wherever he had to, risk whatever he had to, to save his sister.

As Godfrey took another swig, he speculated on the future. What if they all made it back, safe, together again? What would he do with his life then? There was a part of himself, stirring deep inside, that he did not understand, that was giving him some sense of unrest. He felt himself changing. If they survived all this, would he go back to spending his days in a tavern? Or would he do something else? Would he become the responsible son his father had always wanted him to be?

It was an awful, boring sense of responsibility that was creeping over him, a sense that his life should be devoted to something greater, that he hated. He felt that perhaps, after all he had been through, he was changing, becoming someone else, someone who, as a boy in the taverns, he would make fun of. Someone too serious. Someone who did not want to devote his life to drink and games.

"If we ever find this Ridge, what do you think their taverns will be like?" came a drunken voice.

Godfrey turned to see Akorth seated beside him, staring back, eyes glazed from wine.

"I suspect, very much like ours," Fulton said.

"The taverns in Volusia were first rate," Akorth said.

"And their ale," Fulton added. "It was enough to make me want to stay and die there."

"Perhaps we should have," Akorth said. "We would have died, but at least we'd have a smile on our faces. Now we sail to who knows where?"

Godfrey stared out at the waters as they sailed, trying to shut out their voices; instead, he tried to reflect back on all the places he had been, all he had seen. What was it all for? He recalled the early days, when they'd all been in King's Court together, he and Gwendolyn, Kendrick and Gareth, Reece and Luanda. His father had seemed so invincible then, so almighty. How could such times of strength and glory, such an impermeable kingdom, have been reduced to this?

Godfrey felt the strong wine going to his head, and began to feel lightheaded. He knew there would be battles up ahead. Surely, there would be a battle to save Gwendolyn, wherever she was, and a battle to escape from this place. Battles in which he might very well die. The chances were still overwhelmingly against them; they were still a small fleet in the midst of a vast Empire.

A part of Godfrey, the old Godfrey, wanted to drink himself into oblivion, to forget all this. He wanted to be so drunk that, when battle came, it wouldn't even matter because he'd be so lost.

But the new Godfrey, the one he didn't understand, bubbling up inside him, was beginning to feel otherwise. It was prodding him to face his troubles, whatever lay ahead, clear-headed, with courage. With valor.

Slowly, Godfrey stood until he reached his full height. He stared out at the waters, reached back, and threw his still-full sack of wine.

He watched it land in the river with a satisfying splash and float away.

"What have you done?" asked an outraged Akorth, as if he had just killed a man.

"Are you mad?" cried Fulton. "I would have drunk that!"

But Godfrey turned to him, a smile on his face, feeling clarity for the first time in his life. There were troubles ahead—and he was going to face them.

"No," he replied. "I am not mad. I am awake. For the first time in my life, I am *awake*."

CHAPTER TWENTY TWO

Volusia stood before the open gates of the capital, palms held out uselessly before her, and watched, horrified, as the Knights of the Seven bore down on her, hardly fifty yards away. It was death, staring her in the face, galloping toward her, and she felt it coming with certainty. Finally, she was about to die.

But that was not what horrified her most. What filled her with a sense of cold dread, even more painful than the death to come, was her sudden realization. Was she not, after all, a goddess? She could not understand. She had tried to summon her powers and had failed. Why had the world not answered her?

Unless, Volusia realized, a pit in her stomach, it had all been a lie, one grand delusion. What if she was no goddess, after all? What if she were a mere mortal, like everyone else? What if all the statues she had erected to herself, all the services, the prayers, the incense, the holidays, the culture she had created—what if all of it had been false?

The idea that she was a mere mortal, a commoner like everyone else, was the most painful of her life. She was someone who could bleed and die. Someone who was not all-powerful. Someone whose life was about to come to an end.

To meet death in the face, and not be a goddess, what would that mean? Volusia considered all the people she had tortured and killed throughout her life; she had always thought she would not have to answer for it. But now, what if all of them were waiting to greet her on the other side? What if the cruel life she had led would not be waiting to face her? Would she be dragged down to the lowest hells?

She closed her eyes and willed one last time for the universe to answer her, willed for lightning to strike, the earth to move.

Yet nothing happened. With the Volks gone, she could not even move a grain of sand.

Volusia stood there, frozen in terror and fear as the army neared, half her face melted away, hating life, cursing that she was ever born. Flashbacks passed through her mind, and she was flooded with images of her life. She saw the day she murdered her mother; saw all the ways she had tortured people; saw herself as a child, being lashed by her mother, being told she would never amount to anything. She was sure she had proved her mother wrong, having become ruler, having taken the capital, having become far more powerful than her mother ever was.

But now, ultimately, she wondered if her mother was right. She had failed, as her mother had predicted. She was, after all, just another mortal, waiting to be killed like everyone else.

The cries of the men grew louder as they approached, so close now. In a panic, Volusia turned and looked back toward the city, wondering if she had time to make it back. But as she looked she heard a groaning noise and she watched in horror as all of her generals and advisors stood there, watching. They did not run out to save her, to protect her— but rather they stood there, leaving her unprotected, stranded out in the middle of the desert to face an army alone.

Worse, they began to close the door.

Volusia was horrified: the gates were not groaning to open, but to shut on her. To shut her out of the capital that she had vanquished. And to seal her out forever.

It was the final blow to her heart.

Volusia turned back and looked ahead of her to see the Knights of the Seven bearing down her, now hardly ten yards away, the horses thumping in her ears, the cries of men filling the air. They came right for her, lances extended. She wondered if maybe they would slow, take her as prisoner. Surely, someone as valuable as she would be much more valuable as a prisoner.

But as their faces neared, she saw them etched with bloodlust, and she realized there would be no prisoners on this day. They were not slowing, but rather speeding up, their sharpened lances lowered, aimed right for her chest.

A second later she felt it: the sharpened point of a lance pierced her, and she shrieked out, in more agony than ever in her life, as the lance went straight through, emerging from her back. To add insult to injury, it was just a commonplace soldier who had impaled her, and he sneered down, piercing her all the way to the hilt.

As forces closed in all around her, Volusia felt herself falling backwards, arms outstretched, still alive, wracked with pain, dying a cruel and merciless death as horses began to trample her. It was the death that never ended. She prayed for death, prayed for the pain to end, and soon, she knew, it would come. But not soon enough. For she was just a mortal now. A mortal, just like anyone else.

*

Darius stood in the center of the arena, watching the chaos unfold all around him, and wondered what he had just done. He stood there, feeling the heat still throbbing in his palms, feeling his veins throbbing with an unfamiliar power, and he wondered about himself. He looked out at the destruction all around him—the two elephants, dead, smashed into the bleachers, the thousands of Empire spectators dead, the arena cracked into pieces, people fleeing for their lives in every direction—and he could hardly believe he had just done all this.

Darius looked down, at the corpse of his father, and he felt a fresh wave of grief. This time, though, he felt spent. Summoning that energy had taken a great toll on him, and he sensed he needed time to recover. His arms and shoulders felt weak, and he did not feel he could summon it again.

He was just a normal human now, like any other soldier, and as he looked around at all the chaos, he knew time was of the essence. He reached down, snatched a sword off the corpse of an Empire soldier, and slashed his chains, freeing himself. It was now or never if he wanted to escape.

Darius disappeared into the chaos, melting into the fleeing crowd, weaving this way and that, no one paying attention as they were all running for their lives. He sprinted through the crowd and as he looked up ahead, he spotted a fissure in the stadium, a crack leading out to the Empire city, to freedom. He ran for it, merging with the throngs, getting bumped left and right and not caring.

He was nearly at the exit when an Empire soldier turned and looked his way, and his face fell in recognition.

"THE SLAVE!" he yelled, pointing at Darius. "He's—"

Darius didn't let him finish his sentence. He drew his sword, ran forward, and stabbed him before he could say another word.

Others began to turn and look at Darius, but he didn't wait. He rushed forward, entering the darkened tunnel, but thirty yards away from freedom, seeing the light at the end of it. He ran as fast as he could, shaking with adrenaline, and finally he burst through the opening, out into the open air and the bright light of the city.

Darius expected to see the orderly, open courtyards of the capital, but as he looked ahead, he saw something instead that was confusing. It appeared that people in the city were turning and running in panic. Soldiers ran every which way, crisscrossing the streets as if running from an enemy. It made no sense. Why would anyone be in a panic in the midst of the Empire capital, the most secure city in the world?

Darius heard a great commotion beyond the city walls, almost as if there were an army just beyond them, clamoring to get in. It all made no sense.

At the massive golden gates to the capital, Darius saw hundreds of soldiers lined up, as if bracing themselves from attack. Darius was puzzled. What force out there could be attacking the Empire capital itself? And where was Volusia?

Whoever it was, they clearly wanted all of these Empire soldiers within the capital destroyed—and ironically, that was a mission Darius shared. Whoever it was beyond those gates, Darius wanted to help them get in, to lay waste to this place. After all, there would be no better vengeance for his father, for his people. Darius knew at once that those gates were the key: he had to help open them, whatever the cost, even if it meant his life.

Darius rushed forward, sword held high, and set his sights on the group of Empire soldiers huddled before the great crank to the gates. There were a half-dozen of them, their backs to him, guarding the crank—and none expecting an attack from behind.

Darius let out a great battle cry as he charged and threw himself into the group. Darius slashed one, stabbed another, bashed another across the face with the hilt of his sword, kicked another, and elbowed another in the throat. A few tried to defend—but it was too little, too late. Darius was like a man on fire, throwing his life to the wind, a whirlwind, no longer caring. This crank was the key to opening the gates, to having this city destroyed. And for that, Darius, a man with nothing left to lose, would give anything.

105

As he finished off the last of the group of soldiers, Darius raised his sword high and slashed the heavy rope affixing the crank to the gate. He slashed again and again, but it was so thick, it took time.

Nearly done severing it, he was suddenly grabbed from behind by an Empire soldier. Darius reared back and elbowed him in the face, knocking him off. The soldier reached back and smashed Darius across the face with his shield, and Darius stumbled back and fell.

The soldier jumped on top of him, and soon Darius found himself wrestling with him. The soldier reached out and began to choke Darius. Darius, eyes bulging, felt himself losing air quickly.

Darius flailed about, grasping for anything, felt an object on the man's belt—then grabbed it, realizing it was a dagger. He pulled it back and stabbed the man in the ribs.

The soldier cried out and rolled off him, and Darius got to his knees and stabbed him in the heart.

Darius, breathing hard, wiped blood from his lip, and as he heard a great cry, he looked over to see that the other Empire soldiers had spotted him. They all began to turn and make for him, and given that they were only fifty yards away, Darius knew he had little time. It was now or never.

Darius leapt to his feet, reached up with his sword, and hacked at the rope again—and again. The soldiers neared, now but feet away, all with swords raised, ready to kill him.

Finally, there came a great snapping noise and the rope was severed. It went flying over the edge of the wall, and as it did, the crank went spinning, and the gates began to slowly open.

The gates opened wider and wider, and there rose up a huge cry—the cry of an army—from the other side. The Empire soldiers running for Darius stopped in their tracks and turned toward it, too, faces etched in panic.

There suddenly flooded through the open gates thousands of the Knights of the Seven, waving their black banners, donning their glistening black armor, coming in with a vengeance, as if they had been waiting to get in forever, like a thousand bats released from hell. They charged right for the Empire soldiers, never slowing, raising their flails and spears and lances and halberds, and cut their way through the ranks of men in one great clash of armor.

It was a wave of brute force and destruction, killing everything in its path, and the Empire did not stand a chance. Men fell left and right, their cries filling the air, and Darius felt a great sense of relief, of vindication. He had done it. He had helped topple the Empire capital. He felt his father looking down on him, smiling.

Darius, in the path of destruction, knew he had to turn and run. But just as he prepared to do so, suddenly, he looked up to see something coming for him, and he felt a tremendous pain in the side of his head. He heard a clang of metal, and he realized it was a club, and that he had been smashed in the side of the head by one of the Seven.

Darius went flying to the ground, and as he lay there, his world spinning, he felt himself beginning to lose consciousness. He felt several rough hands grabbing him from behind, and he was helpless to resist as he felt himself shackled, wrists and ankles bound behind his back. Before he lost consciousness all together, he heard a singular, dark voice call out through the crowd, and he knew his fate had been decided for him.

"Bring this slave to the ships."

CHAPTER TWENTY THREE

The Supreme Lords of the Knights of the Seven stood in their chamber, standing over the roundtable, lit up by the oculus high above that cast stark shadows on their faces as they emerged from the gloom. They entered the small circle of light in the otherwise blackened tower, something they would not do unless it was a momentous time.

Now was one of those times. The men stepped forward, aging faces pale and wrinkled, slowly removing the hoods from their faces, each face more hideous than the next as they revealed their cruel grins. They had each stared at each other's faces for a thousand years, and they each knew what the other was thinking. And on this day, they each knew that something had happened that would change the fate of the Empire forever.

"The blood moon has risen," said their leader, his ancient voice crackly, like a fire with no end. "The time that has been prophesied has come. Now is the time to end all times, the time when the Empire can be complete. Volusia has been destroyed. The Capital has been taken again. The exiles of the Ring have been found and are about to be obliterated. And, the biggest news of all."

A long silence descended on the group, as they waited anxiously.

"The Ridge has been discovered."

A gasp came from the others.

"The last bastion of rebellion in all the Empire has been found," he added. "And now it will be ours. We must send an army at once, the greatest army we can muster—and then the Empire will have complete control for all time."

The lord stepped back out of the circle, and as he did, another one of the lords stepped forward.

"The four horns and two spikes are behind you," he said. "We act as one."

The Master of Lords could feel them all looking to him, waiting for his final word. He stood there for a long time, breathing, feeling the ancient ones with him, urging him onto ultimate power. Soon, he knew, the Empire would have no foes left.

He smiled wide.

"It is time, my lords," he said slowly, his smile growing, "to obliterate the Ridge and everything in it. It is time for them to learn the true power of the Empire."

CHAPTER TWENTY FOUR

Angel grasped the rail as she stood at the stern of the ship, looking out at the fading Land of Blood as the currents pulled them downriver, away from Thorgrin. She was straining to see him as he faded from view, trapped in that woman's arms at the gatehouse to the castle. As she floated away, she knew, she just knew, that if she didn't stop this ship somehow, she would be taken away from him forever.

The currents carried them toward freedom, away, finally, from this land of gloom. But Angel did not want freedom—she wanted Thorgrin, alive, with them. She knew he would be trapped here, forever, along with his son, Guwayne. She could not turn her back on him. Thorgrin had saved her life, had rescued her from that island, and she never forgot a kindness. Life without loyalty meant nothing to Angel.

"Thorgrin!" she cried, again and again, determined to get him back.

She felt arms restraining her as she yelled, and she turned to see Reece and Selese holding her compassionately, out of concern for her.

"These currents are too strong," Reece said, his voice filled with anguish. "There is nothing we can do."

"NO!" Angel cried, refusing to accept it.

Without thinking, she tore free from their grip, jumped on the rail, and leapt, bounding off the edge, right for the waters below.

Angel felt the air rushing by her as she plunged, face first, into the sea of blood. Immersed in the thick liquid, she splashed back to the surface, fighting the currents with everything she had to make her way to Thorgrin.

She felt herself getting weaker, beginning to drown, and she closed her eyes as she flailed.

"Angel!" Selese yelled from behind her.

Angel heard a splash in the water beside her, and she saw that Selese had thrown a rope.

"Grab it!" Selese yelled. "We'll drag you back in!"

But Angel refused. She would not abandon Thorgrin.

Instead, she willed, with all her might and all her soul, that the currents take her to Thorgrin. Not for herself, but for him.

And then something strange happened. As she swam, she suddenly felt the currents reversing, taking her with them, back toward Thorgrin. It was as if her force of will had been strong enough to change the sea.

Angel swam and swam, feeling her love for Thorgrin, her determination to save him, carry her along the tides. It was so strong, there was nothing that could keep it back.

Angel reached the stone drawbridge, grabbed hold of the slippery stone, and scrambled her way up the surface, scraping her hands and knees.

She knelt there, breathing hard, covered in the sticky red waters of the sea of blood, and she looked up. Sitting there, perhaps ten feet away, was the enchantress, Thorgrin on her lap, eyes opened wide, as if in a trance. The woman looked over at Angel in shock, as if she had never expected her.

The woman slowly set Thorgrin down and stood, rising to her full height, as Angel gained her feet, too. The two stood there, facing off with each other.

"You dare trespass on the gatehouse of the Lord of the Dead," she seethed. "Thorgrin shall never leave here. What makes you think that you shall, too?"

But Angel, determined, stared back, unafraid. She had already faced death many times in her brief life, with her disease, and it had instilled her with fearlessness.

"I am immune to your charms," Angel replied. "I am no man. I am a woman. And your charms cannot work on me."

The woman scowled, as she must have realized that Angel, standing there, defiant, was right; clearly, her powers were useless against her. She must have been the first person in this woman's life, Angel realized, that she could not touch.

The woman let out a shriek of rage, as she rushed forward, claws out as if to tear Angel to shreds.

Angel could not react in time—and there was nowhere to run on the narrow stone drawbridge. She braced herself as she soon felt the woman tackling her, on top of her, grabbing her and driving her down to the stone. As the woman clawed for her face, Angel grabbed the woman's hair and yanked as hard as she could, until finally she cried out in pain and Angel was able to roll away.

Angel scrambled to her feet and kicked the woman hard, forcing her to roll out of her way, then she ran right for Thorgrin. He lay there, still bound by the invisible spell.

Angel reached his side and knelt down beside him, frantic, as the woman began to turn back.

"Thorgrin!" she yelled, shaking him. "It's me! Angel! Come back to me."

But, to her horror, Thorgrin just lay there, helpless, eyes glazed as he stared up at the sky of gloom.

Angel felt her heart sinking.

"Thorgrin, please!" she cried.

Suddenly she felt claws dig into her ankle, and she turned to see the woman grabbing her. The next thing she knew she was sliding backwards along the stone as the woman yanked her.

Angel managed to turn around, and as she did, she caught a good look at the woman's face, and she was horrified. No longer was there a beautiful woman there; instead, her true colors had come out with her rage. She was now an ugly demon, her face green, lined with warts. She pounced on Angel, landing on top of her, and put both hands on her throat. She squeezed, and began choking her for real.

Angel, gasping, reached up and grabbed her wrists and tried her best to get the grotesque woman off of her. But it was no use; she wasn't strong enough. This woman was a demon, and Angel knew she would die by her grasp.

"Thorgrin!" Angel called out weakly, gasping. "Help me! Please!"

Angel was losing air. She felt herself growing faint, knew that in moments she would be dead. But she did not regret it; at least she had died fighting for Thorgrin.

Suddenly, Angel could breathe again, as she saw the woman go flying backwards off of her. She blinked, confused, gasping, and her heart lifted to see Thorgrin rushing forward and throwing the woman off of her.

Angel jumped to her feet and Thor came running to her and embraced her.

"Angel," he said, clearly overcome. "You have brought me back. Your love brought me back."

They both turned and faced the woman who, as she stood, began to morph into something else. Her body stretched as she rose higher and higher, to a great height, thirty feet tall, her body green, slimy, with the face of a demon.

She raised one huge foot and brought it down, as if to crush them both.

Thor grabbed Angel and dove out of the way with her at the last moment. The demon's foot came down right beside them. Angel felt the wind rush by her air, and as it hit the stone, the world shook. Its foot hit with enough impact to crush the stone drawbridge, shattering it into pieces.

Angel felt herself falling, as she and Thor fell through the bridge, which collapsed around them in a great avalanche and rumbling of stone. She fell through the air, and a moment later, she found herself submerged again, back into the sea of blood, Thorgrin beside her.

They splashed and flailed, as this time, the currents, far stronger, took them in a rush downriver, away from the castle, back toward the ship. It was like being caught in rapids, and the two of them flailed end over end in the frothing waters, the sea clearly upset, wanting to eject them from this Land of Blood. In the distance, Angel could see the demon still standing on the bridge, roaring, infuriated, wanting its due.

They went gushing downriver and as she held onto Thorgrin, the two of them tried their best to stay afloat.

"Thorgrin, the rope!" called out a voice.

Angel turned to see a rope rushing by, and as she looked up, she saw their ship, Reece and the others standing at the rail and looking down in desperation.

Thorgrin reached out for it and just missed it—but Angel, closer to it, managed to grab it. She hung on for dear life, and Thor hung onto her, and the two of them were finally stopped, hanging on by the rope, bound to the ship.

She held on tight as she felt the others pulling them in, one hand at a time, and soon they got close enough for Reece and the others to reach down, grab them, and pull them back on deck.

113

Angel and Thorgrin knelt there, spitting out the waters of blood, breathing hard, as they were brought to their feet and embraced by the others.

Thor turned to Angel, a look of profound gratitude in his eyes— which, Angel was thrilled to see, were no longer glazed.

"I shall never be able to thank you," he said.

They embraced as the others joined them, and the roaring currents carried their ship away, toward a horizon of light, toward freedom, and away from Guwayne, from the Land of Blood.

CHAPTER TWENTY FIVE

Gwendolyn flew on Lycoples's back, Argon behind her, the two of them soaring over the Great Waste as they had been for hours, and she could hardly believe where she was. It seemed like just a moment ago she was trapped in the Ridge, that all had seemed hopeless; but now, flying on the back of a dragon again on the way to see Argon's master, to learn about Thorgrin, to discover the secret, she felt liberated again—and filled with hope. She felt as if the world were hers.

As Gwendolyn flew she looked down at the endless Waste spread out below, the ever-changing contours of the Empire lands, so deadly and yet so beautiful. From up here, the land seemed like a giant work of art, the sprawl of the red sands of the desert stretching in every direction, rising and falling, nothing but emptiness encasing the Ridge as far as the eye could see. Lit up by the two suns, it was breathtakingly beautiful, if desolate, the red sands reflecting and absorbing light, the terrain changing every so often to barren rock, cliffs, and reverting back to rock and sand. Every now and again, far below, she noticed small nomadic groups of slaves or creatures trekking through the desert, stopping and squinting up at them, probably, she figured, wondering what could be flying overhead.

Gwen had no idea where they were going, so she followed Argon's lead as he directed Lycoples north to the Northern Spike, to the land where he said his master resided. After so many hours of flying, covering so many thousands of miles, flying at such speed that she could barely catch her breath, Gwen could not help but wonder how far away the Northern Spike was, and whether Argon's master would truly be there. While she was excited to meet him, she also felt a sense of dread. After all, Argon had warned that meeting him would risk their lives.

Gwendolyn grabbed the dragon's scales tightly, holding on as the dragon flew in and out of the clouds, and as she did, she became lost in thought. A part of her wanted to take the reins and turn the dragon around and fly directly to Thorgrin, to Guwayne, wherever they were.

She wanted to fly away from all this, away from the Ridge's troubles, away from the Empire and its troubles, back over the open sea; she wanted to find her husband and her son, to live somewhere happily with them, in peace.

But she knew she could not. She had a responsibility. She had vowed to help the King, the people of the Ridge, and her exiles of the Ring were still back there, too. She still had the responsibilities of a Queen, and even if she were a Queen in exile, and she could not turn her back on her people.

As they flew, Gwen wondered with anticipation what Argon's master might be like. She could not even imagine how powerful he could be, someone powerful enough to train Argon. What would he have to say? Would he be able to help reunite her with Thorgrin? And what was the secret he was hiding? Gwen sensed that it was momentous, that it was the secret Argon had been withholding from her ever since she had met him. That it had to do with the very destiny of the Ring itself.

They slipped down beneath the clouds, and as they did, Gwen was afforded a view of something far below which made her heart beat faster. There, on the horizon, the desolation of the Great Waste gave way to a new landscape. It was a terrain unlike any she ever seen, water shimmering beneath the sun; it looked like the land had broken into pieces, looked like a thousand small isles floating in shallow waters, close to each other. It was as if the waste had shattered into a thousand tiny lakes, small islands of land between them connected by footbridges of sand and rock.

Lycoples dipped down low, circling, and as she did, Gwen's eyes were nearly blinded by the glare of the water. She saw this new terrain stretch forever, and she wondered: Could this be the place?

Lycoples suddenly shrieked and reared without warning, and swooped down low, Gwen's stomach dropping in surprise. She stopped right at the entrance to the islands, and set down on a large, flat rock.

"What is it, Lycoples?" she asked, as the dragon sat there and shrieked, but refused to lift off again.

Argon slowly dismounted, then turned and reached out and gestured for Gwendolyn's hand.

"This land is the domain of my master," he explained. "Dragons are not allowed here. This is as far she can go. I'm afraid we must cross the rest of it on foot."

Gwendolyn took his hand as she dismounted, and as she stood there, she turned and looked out at the vast landscape of interconnecting lakes and islands, seeming to stretch forever, as far as she could see, as if the world had been broken into a million little pieces. She looked down and saw that the water was shallow, hardly a foot deep, and she wondered at the nature of it. Here, she realized, one could truly walk on water.

"My master demands visitors be on foot," Argon said, as he turned and faced Gwendolyn, his face filled with concern, an expression she had never seen him wear before.

"This is a place of power, Gwendolyn," he added. "A place unlike any you've been. If my master still resides here, you may not survive the encounter. Are you sure this is a chance you are willing to take?"

Gwen felt a sense of apprehension as she looked back at him, realizing the finality of her decision—but having no doubts as she thought of Thorgrin, of Guwayne.

She nodded slowly, resolute.

Argon looked back at her earnestly, then finally nodded.

"Very well," he said. "Walk closely beside me. You are entering a land that is more magic than substance. Do not stray from the path. And you," he said, turning to Lycoples, "wait for us here. That is, if we return."

*

Gwendolyn hiked with Argon across the thousand isles, following him as he crossed the footbridges made of rock and sand, connecting the tiny islands like steppingstones in a vast lake, feeling as if she were walking into a dream. As she went, the small lakes each turned a different color, shifting from blue to yellow, to scarlet to pink, to white, making this entire place feel as if it were breathing, making it feel alive.

At one point, Gwen was going to step in the water, seeing that it was only a few inches deep, but Argon stopped her.

"That water seems shallow," he said, "but it is not. It is an illusion. Step into it, and you will plunge into the depths of eternity, and never be seen or heard from again."

117

Gwendolyn looked down at the clear water, the ground just inches below it, and was shocked. She was beginning to appreciate just how treacherous this place was.

They had been hiking for hours, all eerily silent except for the far-off cry of exotic birds and the sound of strange animals splashing in the water, which Gwendolyn could never see. The second sun was already beginning to set and a light mist began to fall, to spread over the entire place like a blanket. Strangely enough, it did not obscure the view, but rather made it more brilliant, making the very air seem as if it were sparkling, alive. The sky splintered into a million small rainbows, and as she walked, moisture heavy in the air, she could feel the intense energy here. It was as if she were entering a different realm, a different dimension of life, and she sensed it was the most powerful place she would ever be.

Gwendolyn, her legs aching, her heart thumping in anticipation of finding Argon's master, began to wonder what would happen if they did not. She was dying to ask Argon questions, but she held her tongue, knowing he would speak when he was ready.

"My master has lived here for a thousand centuries," Argon finally said, shattering the silence, his voice deep and somber. "It is a place of birth—and also of death. It is the place where the very world was formed."

Gwen wondered how much to ask.

"And who is your master?" she finally asked, dying to know.

Argon paused.

"He is of the very stuff the earth was formed of," he finally responded. "He is more creature than human. Less human even than me. He is something else, something far more powerful: he is a Paragon."

A Paragon. Gwen was shocked at the term, one which she had only heard of when reading the ancient books. She had never thought one really existed.

"I had only thought they were a rumor," she said. "The stuff of legend."

Argon shook his head.

"Most are dead," he acknowledged. "But one survives still."

Gwen reeled at the news. She remembered reading about the mythical Paragon, a race even more powerful than the Druids, said to be one of the pillars that formed and held up the world. They were supposed to have the power to see not only the past and the future, but also to control and shape time. They were rumored to be a step below God. She struggled to recall what the books had said.

"Cast out of the ranks of heaven by God himself, after they overreached their power," Argon said, reading her mind.

Gwen was startled as he dipped so easily into her mind.

"Is it true?" she asked.

He continued to walk, remaining silent, and she suspected he would never answer. Her sense of apprehension deepened. From all that she had read, an encounter with a Paragon meant a certain death.

Still, she hiked on, determined for Thor's sake, for Guwayne's sake, yet all the while wondering if this were a terrible idea. She hiked and hiked, crossing one island after the next, feeling as if she had been walking for years.

Gwen turned and glanced back as she went, and she could no longer see Lycoples, no longer see the place they had entered. It had all disappeared from the horizon what seemed like ages ago. She and Argon were alone, deep in this magical land, too far in to return. And as the sun set lower, she could not help but wonder as if she would *ever* return.

As they hiked, Gwen began to feel as if she were losing track of reality, and she was dying to break the monotony.

"Do you remember my father?" she finally asked Argon, getting lost in thoughts, in memories, and desperate for conversation. "Sometimes, I am ashamed to say, I don't. I try so hard to see his face, but I cannot. My past sometimes....feels like a distant world."

Argon remained silent for a long time, and Gwen did not know if he would even respond. After enough time passed, she began to wonder if she'd even asked the question.

"I remember him very well," Argon said. "He was a fine King, but a better man. He had a heart big enough for the Kingdom."

At his words, Gwendolyn missed her father more than she could say.

119

"Of all his children," Argon continued, some time later, "he was most fond of you."

Gwendolyn was surprised at his words.

"Me?" she echoed. "But I am a girl. Kendrick is the oldest and the leader of the Silver. Reece is a warrior with the Legion. Luanda was a Queen and the eldest daughter. Why would you say me?"

Argon shook his head.

"You speak of what your siblings did—not of who they *were*. The essence of a person is something else entirely. Yes, they were each fine in their own way, but you had all of their traits combined. You were more than a warrior—you were also a leader."

He walked in silence for a long time, as she contemplated his words.

"Your father was as close to a brother as I'd ever had," Argon said. "But there is a reason I do not miss him: because he lives on in you."

Gwendolyn felt touched by his words, and she had a sudden longing to be back in the Ring.

"Argon," she said, "do you ever wonder if—"

She suddenly stopped as Argon held his staff to her chest and stopped in his tracks. He looked out with caution, and Gwen looked out into the lakes and islands before them, wondering what was happening. Nothing appeared different to her.

Argon slowly lowered his staff, and as they stood there, listening, waiting, Gwen could see the genuine fear on his face. She peered into the sparkling mist, breathless, until finally, slowly, the waters began to ripple.

The waters rippled madly until soon there came a great splashing, and there emerged from the depths, like a volcano erupting, a creature that could only be a Paragon. Her heart stopped at the sight.

It looked like a man, but was twice as wide and tall, and it emerged looking like a pile of mud. Slowly, the mud fell away, sliding down its sides, and he grew taller as she watched, twice as tall again. Finally, he was all clear, looking like a skeleton with translucent flesh and huge, glowing white eyes that terrified her. He made an awful clicking noise from deep within, each time he breathed.

He craned his neck down to their eye level and stared at them, scowling, but inches from Gwendolyn's face—and her heart filled with fear.

He finally leaned back, standing upright and swaying in place, his arms and neck squirming like snakes, never static.

"You disturb me from the depths," he boomed, his voice as deep and loud as a hundred men, shaking the world as he spoke.

He turned to Argon, and his scowl deepened.

"You have come back to your master. But you are no longer welcome here."

Argon flushed.

"Forgive me, my master," he replied, and for the first time in her life, Gwen saw Argon kneel and lower his head. Gwendolyn followed his lead, kneeling and bowing her head, too.

Gwen heard its distinctive growling noise, saw the Paragon open his mouth and snarl, and for a moment, she felt they would be killed.

But then he seemed to pause, to reconsider.

"Rise," he said.

They rose, and as Gwen looked up at him, he seemed irate. He stood tall and looked down at Gwendolyn with such intensity that it nearly seared her eyes.

"Why have you come to me?" he asked Gwendolyn, his voice reverberating.

"I must find my husband," Gwen replied. "And my son."

The Paragon stood there for a long time, making a sound like a growling from deep within his chest, and she wondered if he would ever respond.

"Your son is lost," he said, "in the arms of the Blood Lord."

Gwendolyn felt like a knife had been plunged into her heart at his words, as she felt the certainty of them. She felt a horrific sense of loss and mourning.

"There must be a way to get him back!" she pleaded. "Please. I would give anything! Even my very own soul."

The Paragon paused for a long time, looking back and forth from Argon to her.

"There is always a way," he said. "After all, the world is a creation. And creation is not static."

Gwen pondered his words, feeling a sense of hope.

"What does that mean?" she asked, desperate.

But the Paragon turned to Argon, ignoring her.

"The end of days has arrived," he said to Argon. "Your time on this earth is nearly at an end. It was I who brought you forth, and I who must take you back. You knew this already to be true—which is why you did not want to see me."

Argon stared back, fear in his eyes.

"Do not worry," the Paragon continued. "I shall not take you now. But soon. Very, very soon. Choose your death carefully."

Argon nodded and looked down, humbled, and the Paragon turned back to Gwendolyn.

"You made a vow, did you not?" he asked her.

Gwen stared back, confused.

"A vow to the King of the Ridge. You vowed to save his people. Whatever the cost. To lead them out of the Ridge if his Kingdom was destroyed."

Gwendolyn nodded.

"I did," she said.

"The time has come. The King is dead, killed by his own son."

Gwendolyn gasped, horrified to hear it had been his son.

"The Ridge as you know it," the Paragon added, "will be no more. As we speak it is being invaded by hordes the likes of which the world has never seen."

He paused, leaning in close.

"You, Gwendolyn, are the last hope. You can save this people, lead them on their exodus. You think your destiny was the exodus of the Ring—but that was just a warm-up. Your true destiny is the exodus of the Ridge. You have not fulfilled your mission in life—you have not even begun it."

Gwen stared back, trying to understand.

"But where can I lead those people?" she asked. "The Ridge is surrounded by nothingness. I would only lead them through the Great Waste, to their deaths. And who am I to lead such a great nation?"

The Paragon leaned back his neck, twisted and turned and curved it upside down before turning back to her. Gwen did not understand this creature at all, and she felt terrific fear in his presence, a fear and dread she could not understand.

"Or," the Paragon continued, "you can choose not to save the Ridge. You can ride your dragon across the sea, all the way to Thorgrin. You can find him and be with him forever. The choice is yours."

Gwendolyn thought. Her heart leapt at the thought of seeing Thorgrin again, so easily within reach. But she considered her vow, and realized she could not break it.

"I made a vow," she said. "It was a sacred vow. That means more than my life. More, even, than Thorgrin."

The Paragon nodded back in approval.

"Good," he said. "That is what sets you apart. You are Queen because of merit, because your choices merit you to be one. That is why you shall lead this people."

"But I still don't understand," Gwen said. "Where can I lead them?"

The Paragon paused.

"Don't you know?" he asked. "It is the answer that has been sitting before you for all time."

She stared back blankly.

Then, suddenly, an image flashed in her mind. She was flabbergasted.

"The *Ring*!?" she asked, breathless.

It nodded back.

Gwen's mind raced with wonder.

"But how?" she asked. "The Ring is destroyed. And it lies across the sea, halfway around the world."

"And what of the Shield?" Argon chimed in, he, too, sounding surprised. "It, too, is no more."

"Without the Shield," Gwen added, "we could not hold back the hordes of the Empire."

The Paragon leaned back and laughed.

"It is even worse than that, I'm afraid," he said. "The millions of Empire soldiers waiting to attack you are the least of your dangers. There is a far greater force than them set on your destruction."

Gwendolyn waited, feeling a sense of dread.

"The dark ones," he said. "Led by the Blood Lord. By the creature that has your son. The great army is rising. An army greater even than the Empire has ever known. They are an unstoppable force."

"Then it is hopeless," Gwen said, resorting to fear. "We are all doomed to die."

"I took you to have more hope than that," the Paragon said, disapproving. "There is always hope."

"But how?" Gwen asked. "How can we return to the Ring with no Shield?"

The Paragon turned back to Argon.

"You were my greatest student," he said. "You know the answer. It lies deep within you. It has always been just beyond your grasp, always been the secret just out of your reach. It is the one thing that has been gnawing at you, the one secret I withheld from you for all these centuries. The one thing you could not be allowed to know until the time was right. But now, the time has come."

Argon stared back with trepidation and wonder.

"What is it, my master?" he asked. "What is the secret that I have yet to learn?"

The Paragon paused for a long time, its arms flailing like snakes, turning his neck this way and that—until finally he stopped and became very still. He stared at Argon.

"The Sorcerer's Ring," he said. "You have never fully understood what it means. You have always taken it only for the Shield. But the Sorcerer's Ring, my student, has two meanings. Yes, it is the Ring, the Shield about the Canyon. But there is another meaning. Another ring."

Argon squinted in wonder as the Paragon leaned forward and stared into his eyes.

"Another ring?" Argon asked.

The Paragon nodded.

"An actual ring," he said.

Gwen and Argon both gasped, blown away by the revelation.

"The Sorcerer's Ring is also an object. A magical ring, formed at the dawn of time. It is the only thing that can stop the Blood Lord, the only thing which can restore the Shield for all time, restore the Ring, restore the Kingdom you once had. This Ring is your only hope for salvation."

"And where can we find such a ring?" Gwendolyn asked. "I will go anywhere. Do anything."

The Paragon shook his head.

"It lies in the Land of the Ring," he said, "but is not for you to find. It is a quest which only one person in the world can take. It is a Ring which only one person in the world can wear."

Gwendolyn's eyes lit up with understanding.

"Thorgrin," she said.

The Paragon nodded.

"And how shall he know where it is?" she asked.

"He will know," he answered. "Deep inside, he will know."

Gwendolyn suddenly had another realization.

"The dragon," she said, piecing it all together. "She came so that I can send her back across the sea, to Thorgrin. So that I could deliver this message, tell Thorgrin of the Ring."

The Paragon nodded.

"But if I do so," Gwendolyn continued, "then I will have to let go of the dragon. Once it returns me to the Ridge, I will have no dragon to help me. I will have to lead the people out on foot."

The Paragon fell silent, and finally Gwendolyn understood. It all made sense: there was a supreme test ahead for her, and for Thorgrin. Two sides of the same coin, both needed to restore the Ring.

"And my son?" she asked.

"The Ring is the only thing that can save him now," the Paragon replied. "If Thorgrin fails to find it—and most likely he will fail—all of you will be nothing."

The Paragon suddenly lifted his arms up to the sky, let out a shriek which split the earth, then just as quickly sank back down beneath the waters, the water bubbling and hissing all about him, leaving nothing but smoke and mist.

Gwendolyn and Argon stared at each other, each realizing that before them lay their greatest trials yet.

CHAPTER TWENTY SIX

Kendrick galloped through the Great Waste, alongside Brandt, Atme, Koldo, Ludvig—and now Kaden—the six of them charging back, after their confrontation with the Sand Walkers, back toward the safety of the Ridge. Kendrick was elated, as were the others, all of them so relieved they had found Kaden in time, and were bringing him home unscathed. They had been riding hard all day and all night ever since retrieving him, and Kendrick felt the urgency, as did the others, to make it back to the Ridge.

Finally, after hours of monotony, the landscape began to change, and Kendrick, to his relief, saw the Sand Wall looming on the horizon, and he knew the Ridge wouldn't be far behind it.

"I still don't see them," Ludvig called out.

Kendrick peered into the horizon and he, too, saw no sign of Naten and the others; he was surprised. Those knights of the Ridge had vowed to come back for them, with horses. Kendrick knew the knights of the Ridge to be honorable, and he suspected Naten was behind it. Perhaps he hadn't wanted Kendrick to return, and he knew that if hadn't come for them, they likely would not. But little did he know that they had found their own horses, had found their own way back. He suspected they would have hell to pay when they returned.

As they rode, Kendrick noticed the expressions on Koldo's and Ludvig's faces, and it seemed that they were more hurt by the betrayal of their people than Kendrick.

"Then they did not come for us," Koldo replied, disappointment in his voice.

Ludvig snorted.

"Should we be surprised?" he replied. "Naten talks big, and he threatens others. But when it comes down to it, he is a coward."

"When we get back, he shall be disciplined," Koldo replied. "He left us out there to die, and justice shall be done."

Koldo turned to Kendrick.

126

"You were gracious to put up with him," he said. "I am sorry he gave you such a hard time. We owe you for joining us on this mission, a mission that was not even yours. We cannot thank you enough."

Kendrick nodded back, his respect and admiration for Koldo and Ludvig mutual.

"Not all members of a court hold to the same values," he replied. "The same holds true in the Ring. It was an honor to join you on this mission. After all, what makes a brother is equal honor, courage—and you two are my brothers today."

They rode and rode, and the sound grew deafening as they approached the Sand Wall, Kendrick squinting as the sand began to hit him even from here. Kendrick covered himself in the wrap that Koldo had given them, wrapping himself again and again, until finally, as they entered it, he wrapped his face, too. He remembered, from having ridden through it once, how rough this Sand Wall could be, and he was not looking forward to entering it again.

The noise hit a fever pitch, drowning out all else, as Kendrick suddenly found himself immersed in a wall of sand, a stationary tornado. Sand scraped him from every possible angle. It was almost impossible to see, and Kendrick gasped for breath, the air and sand so intense as he galloped through with the others. He did not feel as if it would ever end.

Kendrick finally burst out the other side, along with the others, charging back out into the open sky, the open desert, and he gasped with relief. The blinding sunlight bore down on him, and he didn't care—he was just happy to be out in the open again. And as he looked to his sides, he saw the others unwrapping, too, and could see the joy and relief on their faces, all of them, and their horses, scratched up, but still alive.

But Kendrick also noted the startled expressions on their faces as they stared straight ahead, and he turned himself, looking back ahead, wondering what they were seeing.

As he did, Kendrick's mouth fell open in shock. There, up ahead, were the peaks of the ridge, sitting on the horizon—and at first he was relieved to see them. But before them, between their group and home, was a sight that filled him with dread, a sight that he had never expected to see in his lifetime. It was a sight which made them all come to an abrupt stop on their horses.

They all sat there, breathing hard, staring, speechless.

"It is not possible," said Koldo.

Kendrick was thinking the same thing. Because there, before them, was the largest army he had ever seen, millions of soldiers, wearing glistening black armor, spreading out in every direction, their backs to Kendrick. They were all, Kendrick cold see, preparing to invade the Ridge from every side. They swarmed like ants in a massive circle, closing in on the peaks.

Kendrick heard a noise, and he turned and saw bursting through the Sand Wall, thousands more of these soldiers, more pouring in every second. They flew distinctive banners, and he struggled to understand who they were, who could be mobilizing to attack the ridge.

"The Knights of the Seven," announced Koldo, his voice grave.

"They bear all the weight of the Empire armies," Ludvig said, dismay in his voice. "If they have discovered the Ridge, we're finished."

Kendrick sat there, his heart pounding, realizing they were right.

Kendrick also realized that they were in an unusual position now, being able to witness this from behind, their presence still undetected from the Empire. They could not, of course, whatever the odds, turn around and leave, not with their brothers inside, not with Gwendolyn there.

They all exchanged looks, and silently they were all thinking the same thing. They would have to find a way to attack.

"We must find a way back in," Koldo said, "and help them defend. Even if it means our lives."

"Our brothers will all die in there," Kendrick said. "And we shall die defending them."

"And how shall we get in?" Brandt asked. "They have the Ridge surrounded."

Kendrick saw Koldo and Ludvig scrutinizing the landscape, the contours of the Ridge, and they then exchanged a knowing look.

"Behind that rock formation, far from the ranks of the soldiers," Koldo said, pointing, "there lies a tunnel, concealed. It leads underneath the Ridge. It was built for times like this. We can reach it undetected. Let us go quickly and join our brothers, before the soldiers detect us."

Koldo kicked his horse and they all joined him, racing under the desert sky, for the Ridge, for their brothers, for the greatest battle of their lives—for valor.

CHAPTER TWENTY SEVEN

Thorgrin sat on the deck of the ship, head in his hands, elbows on his knees, utterly despondent. After the currents had taken them out from the Land of Blood, out from under the gloom, through the waterfall of blood and back into the open sea, they now drifted aimlessly in the vast open ocean, Thor feeling as if his whole life were drifting away from him. The sun shone down, illuminating everything, and Thor knew that he should be happy to be back out under an open sky, away from the darkness of the Land of Blood.

But Thorgrin felt nothing like joy; instead he felt as if, for the first time in his life, he had failed a quest. He had endeavored to rescue his son, and he had failed his mission. He had failed to reach his most prized possession in the world, had failed to overcome a foe, a land, more powerful than he. He had, in fact, been meant to die there, he knew, and if it were not for Angel, he would still be there now, trapped forever.

Now here he was, drifting at sea with the rest of the Legion, too despondent to move even though all of them were looking to him for leadership. For the first time in his life he felt paralyzed, felt purposeless, felt like he could provide none. He had failed his son, and didn't see the point of going on. He knew there was no way back into the Land of Blood, knew that it was an insurmountable place for him. He was not strong enough yet—just as Ragon had warned.

It was humbling for Thor to realize there were foes out there stronger than he, that there were limits to his power—even when his own son was at stake. And, most of all, it tormented Thorgrin to think of Guwayne stuck there, in the clutches of the Blood Lord and his dark beings, to be molded to whatever evil purpose they had for him. His own boy, snatched away from him; a father unable to save his son.

Thorgrin sat there holding his head, hating himself.

As he sat there, Thor went over and over in his head what went wrong, how he could've done it all differently. As their ship rocked on the rolling waves, he felt aimless, as if there were no reason to go on without Guwayne. He could not return to Gwendolyn without him, a failure—he could not even live with himself as a failure. And yet he saw no other way.

He felt hopeless for the first time in his life.

"Thorgrin," came a soft voice.

Thor felt a reassuring hand on his shoulder and he glanced up to see Reece standing over him. Reece sat beside him, good-naturedly, clearly trying to console him.

"You did all you could," he said.

"You got further than anyone else," came another voice.

Thor turned to see Elden come over and sit on his other side. He heard the wood creaking on the deck, and he looked up to also see O'Connor, Matus, Selese, Indra, and Angel, all of them gathering around him, and he could see in their eyes their concern, how much they cared for him. He felt ashamed; they had always seen him as being so strong, as being so sure of himself, being a leader. They had never seen him like this. He no longer knew how to act; he no longer knew how to be with himself.

Thor shook his head.

"My son still lies beyond my grasp," he said, his voice that of a broken man.

"True," Matus replied. "But look around you. We are all alive. You have survived. Not all is lost. We shall all live to fight another day. We shall achieve some other mission."

Thorgrin shook his head.

"There is no mission without my son. All is meaningless."

"And what of Gwendolyn?" Reece asked. "What of the exiles of the Ring? They need us, too. We must find them and save them, wherever they may be."

But Thor could not bear the thought of facing Gwendolyn, of returning to them all as a failure.

Slowly, he shook his head.

"Leave me," he said to them all, being harsher than he'd wanted.

He could sense them all staring back at him, all clearly surprised that he would talk to them that way. He had never spoken to them that way before, and he could see the hurt in their faces. He immediately felt guilty, but he was too numb within himself, and too ashamed, to face any of them.

Thor looked down, unable to look at them, and he heard the groaning and creaking of the deck. Out of the corner of his eye he watched them all leave him, crossing to the far side of the ship, leaving him be.

Thor felt a pit in his stomach; he wished he could have acted otherwise. He wished he could have rebounded, regained his leadership, gotten over this. But this failed quest hurt him too deeply.

Thor heard a distant screech, and he searched the skies, wondering if he were imagining it. It sounded like the cry of a dragon. Could it be? Was it Lycoples?

As he looked up, searching, Thor's heart suddenly skipped a beat to see Lycoples swoop down, break through the clouds, and circle the ship, screeching, flapping her wings. He could see something dangling from her claws, and as he looked up into the sun, shielding his eyes, he struggled to figure out what it was. It appeared to be a scroll.

Moments later Lycoples dove down and landed on the deck before him, opening her wings slowly. She stared right at him and he could see the fierceness, the power in them, staring back defiantly, with a sense of purpose. He wanted to go and embrace her, to check the scroll, but he felt too listless to do so.

The others, though, all crowded around the dragon on deck, keeping their distance.

"What is on the scroll?" Angel asked.

Thorgrin shook his head.

Angel, impatient, jumped up and ran over to Lycoples, reached out tentatively, and took the scroll from her claws. Lycoples screeched softly, but did not resist.

Angel unrolled it and looked inside.

"It is from Gwendolyn," she said, turning to Thorgrin and thrusting it into his hands.

Thor felt it in his fingers, the tough parchment, and it felt so brittle; he could hardly believe it had crossed the world. Holding it somehow broke him out of his reverie, and despite himself, he began to read:

My Dearest Thorgrin:

If the scroll finds you, know that I still live, and that I think of you with every breathing moment. I have met Argon's master, and he has told me of a Ring. The Sorcerer's Ring. It is this Ring that we need to be reunited again, to save Guwayne, to restore our homeland and return all of us to the Ring. It is only you who can find this Ring. Thorgrin, we need you now. I need you now. Lycoples will lead you to the Ring. Join her. Do it for me. For our son.

Thorgrin lowered the scroll, his eyes bleary, overcome with emotion at having received an object from Gwendolyn, at hearing her voice, her message, in his head.

Thor looked up at Lycoples, who stood there, waiting, and a part of him felt energized, renewed with a new sense of purpose, ready to depart.

But another part of him still felt too crushed, too exhausted to go on. What was the point, when the Blood Lord still existed, someone out there whom he could never vanquish?

"Well?" Angel pressed, staring at him, waiting for a response.

Angel took the scroll and read it herself impatiently, then she stared back at Thor.

"What are you waiting for?" she demanded.

Thorgrin sat there, listless, depressed. A long silence fell over them, and finally, he just shook his head.

"I cannot go on," he said, his voice broken.

All the others looked at him in shock.

"But they *need* you," Angel insisted.

"I am sorry," Thorgrin said. "I have let everyone down. I'm sorry."

He felt terrible even as he said the words, and he couldn't bear to see the look of disappointment in Angel's eyes.

The others crossed the deck, again giving him space, but Angel stayed by his side and took a step closer. He saw her looking down at him with her soulful eyes, and he felt overcome with shame.

"Do you remember when I told you of the Land of the Giants?" she asked. "The place that might hold the cure for my leprosy?"

Thorgrin nodded, remembering.

"The Land of the Giants is a metaphor," she said. "It is not an actual land. It is a place where the great ones live. This is the place that

133

Gwendolyn speaks of. I know, because I have heard of it my whole life—the place rumored to hold not only the cure for leprosy, but the Sorcerer's Ring."

Thor looked back, perplexed.

"Don't you understand?" she pressed. "If you find this Ring, it could not only save the others—it could save me, too. Can't you do it for me?"

As Thor looked back at her, he wanted to help her, wanted to help them all—but something inside him felt weighed down, felt like he could not go on.

Despite himself, he looked down.

Angel turned, a look of betrayal in her eyes, and stormed across to the far side of the deck.

Thor closed his eyes, suffering, feeling a pain in his chest. Then, for some reason, he thought of his mother.

Why, Mother? Why have I failed? Why have my powers met their limits? Why have I let you down?

He closed his eyes, trying to picture his mother's face, waiting for an answer. But there came none.

He focused with all his might.

I've never asked for anything, Mother. I ask you now. Help me. Help me save my son.

This time, as Thorgrin closed his eyes, he saw his mother as she stood at the end of her skywalk, a smile on her face, looking back at him with compassion.

Thorgrin, she said, *you have not failed. You cannot fail. What you see as a failure is just a delusion. Don't you see? A failure is what you define it to be.*

Thorgrin shook his head in his mind's eye, grappling with her words.

No. I have failed. My son is without me.

Is he? asked his mother.

I shall never find him again.

Shall you not? she asked. *Never is a long time. In life, we fail. Life would not be life without failure. Loss. Defeat. But it is not the defeat that defines us. It is what we do* after *the defeat. Will you crumble and fall, Thorgrin? That is failure. Or will you stand and rise? Will you be brave enough to get back on your feet? Will you have the courage to fight again? That is victory.*

Something stirred within Thorgrin, and he realized she was right. Courage, chivalry, honor, valor—it had nothing to do with victory or defeat. It had to do with the courage to try, to stand up for what you believed in, the courage to face your enemy, however formidable he was.

Thorgrin suddenly felt a fresh wave of energy overcome him, and suddenly, he felt himself casting off the wave of gloom that had oppressed him ever since leaving the Land of Blood. He stood, rising to his full height, and felt himself getting stronger, bolder, until he was standing tall and proud.

Thor began to cross the deck, to walk toward Angel, and as he went, the others in the Legion must have sensed it, because they all turned and watched him go, and this time, their eyes were filled with joy as they saw him standing tall and proud. He was back to the old Thorgrin.

Thor walked over to Angel, tapped her on the shoulder, and she turned, and her eyes lit up, too.

He knelt down and embraced her, and he leaned back and looked her in the eyes.

"I shall find the Sorcerer's Ring," he said. "Or I shall die trying."

She hugged him, and he hugged her back. Then he stood, turned, and solemnly, one by one, embraced each member of the Legion.

Thor turned and his eyes met Lycoples, two warriors, eyes gleaming. He could see the resolve on her face, and it was a resolve that he himself now felt. They would ride, gladly, to the ends of the earth together.

Thor turned to the others, as they all stood there, ready to see him off, and as they all looked to him hopefully, for leadership.

"Set sail for the Ring, all of you," he said, his voice filled once again with confidence. "Meet me there. I shall find this Sorcerer's Ring, I shall return to the Ring, and there, we shall be united for all time. I shall find this Ring, or I shall die trying."

The group stared back solemnly, a long silence falling over them.

"And if you do not return?" Matus asked.

Thor looked at him gravely.

"I shall," he replied. "This time, no matter what, I shall."

CHAPTER TWENTY EIGHT

Naten stood resentfully on the platform as it rose higher and higher alongside the peak of the Ridge, his men yanking the ropes as the rickety wood swayed and creaked. The horses pranced beside them, all of them anxious to descend the other side and venture on into the Great Waste to search for their brothers in arms, for Koldo, Ludvig, Kendrick, and the others. Naten bitterly resented it.

Naten stood there, and he brooded. He had done everything in his power to convince the soldiers *not* to go back out there, to abandon his brothers, and especially Kendrick and his men, and to remain behind here, in the safety of the Ridge. Naten despised Kendrick and the others; he did not want these exiles from the Ring here. He loathed outsiders, and he wanted things to be the way they had been before they arrived. He wouldn't mind Koldo and Ludvig's not returning, either—that would only give him greater power in the ranks of the Ridge's army.

"It is their grave, they dug it," Naten said bitterly, trying to convince his men one final time.

They all—the six other soldiers—stood there solemnly, unmoved.

"For us to go out there now, it is foolishness," Naten continued. "We shall never find them. It took too long to regroup. And even if we do, by this point they shall certainly already be dead. Shall we all kill ourselves too? Will that benefit the Ridge? The Ridge needs us here now. You know this."

But his men stared silently, glum, unwilling to budge.

Finally, one of them shrugged.

"We have orders," one said. "We cannot abandon the mission. If they return, we'd be imprisoned."

"We do not abandon our brothers," added another.

Naten was silent, burning, hating this mission. He should have killed them all himself earlier when he'd had the chance. Now he was stuck, doomed to go back out there.

As the platform rose higher and higher, Naten racked his brain, desperate to come up with a scheme, some way out of this. As he thought and thought, an idea came to him: when they reached the desert floor, when the others weren't looking, he would stab the horses in their underbellies. No one would know it was him. And with the horses dying, they would have no choice; they would have to turn back.

Naten smiled at the thought; it was the perfect strategy. As the platform continued to rise, he longer dreaded it, but looked forward to implementing his plan. As they neared the peak of the ridge, Naten had a smile on his face—he would outsmart them all. He always did.

The platform finally came to a stop at the peak of the Ridge, shaking as the wooden doors opened, and out went all the horses and men. Nathan led them, the first out, making sure he was out front and assuming command of the mission, not letting any of the others take it from him. He marched with a bounce in his step as he considered his new plan. The others, beside him, all held onto the group of extra horses they were taking back to Koldo, Ludvig, Kendrick, and the others—and Naten smirked inwardly, knowing they would never have the chance to use them.

Naten kept up the pretense, though, marching across the wide platform at the peak of the Ridge and heading for the far side, where they would board the next platform and descend. He looked out as he went, enjoying the vista from the other side of the Ridge, the vast, open sky, the sense of eternity. From up here, he felt like he ruled the world.

Naten finally reached the far side, and as he did, he stopped, looking forward to enjoying it. He had always loved this spot more than any in the world, where he could stand on the edge of the cliff and feel as if he were looking out into eternity.

But this time, as he stood there, Naten knew immediately that something was wrong. He looked out and saw no platform waiting for them. For the first time ever, it was missing.

He looked down, perplexed, and as he did, he was even more baffled to see the platform rising, making its way up to greet him. It made no sense—there was no patrol due to be headed up now. Who could be riding it up?

Before Naten could make sense of it, before he could understand what was happening, the platform stopped at the top. And before he could register what was happening, its doors opened, and he saw staring back at him faces he did not recognize. Faces that he realized, a moment too late, were not even human. Faces that were the enemy.

Naten's mouth dropped open in shock and horror as he realized, standing before him, was a platform packed with Empire soldiers, Knights of the Seven, all armed and deadly—the first invaders ever to reach the soil of the Ridge. The harbinger of a vast army to come.

Before he could react, Naten watched, as time slowed down, one of them raise a long spear and thrust it through his belly, its blade piercing his chest, he in agony as the pain rippled through him. How ironic, he thought: it was the same death he had envisioned for his horses.

Naten began to fall, silently, wordlessly, over the edge of the cliff, plummeting down below toward his death, the first casualty of war. As he did, he saw below, waiting to greet his corpse, the final sight of his life: millions and millions of Empire soldiers, preparing to ascend, preparing to destroy the Ridge once and for all.

CHAPTER TWENTY NINE

Gwendolyn stood on the peak of the Ridge, on the broad, stone platform she had once toured with the King, and searched the sky. Argon stood beside her, Steffen at her other side and Krohn at her heels, as she searched the horizon, watching Lycoples disappear. After Lycoples had flown them back from Argon's master and had dropped her and Argon off here, atop the Ridge, Gwen had commanded Lycoples to depart, to go and find Thorgrin and give him her message. His finding the Sorcerer's Ring was their last hope, and Gwendolyn, as much as she wanted to for selfish reasons, could not keep Lycoples here with her. So she had let go of her one chance to escape, and instead had chosen to make a stand here, with the Ring, to not abandon her people, her vow, whatever dangers would come.

Gwen had no regrets. It was not in Gwendolyn's makeup to abandon her people, and she had vowed to the King to help his people, and she intended to keep it. She could have had Lycoples drop her down below, in the safety of the capital, across the lake, far away from the front lines of the invasion to come—but that was not who she was. If a war was coming, this was where she wanted to be, on the frontlines, rallying the troops, preparing.

Gwen felt her heart fluttering, felt a familiar tingling sensation in her hands, her arms, as she steeled herself for battle, as she entered the mental mindset. As she had flown over the Great Waste, she had watched in awe, terror, and fascination the endless number of troops of the Empire, all marching for the Ridge—it had looked as if the entire world were rallying to destroy the place. It was a surreal feeling to be flying right into the heart of trouble, and not away from it. It was as if Lycoples had dropped them down right in the eye of the storm.

And she knew, if Argon's master's prophecies were true, that nothing would hold the Empire back, that the Ridge would soon be destroyed.

But Gwen was not one to give up easily, or to heed prophecies. Since arriving, she had, on the contrary, done everything in her power to rally the troops of the Ridge, all of the King's knights, to help defend it. She had at first tried to get them to heed her words and evacuate the Ridge, but they would not hear of it, and she knew she would never be able to force this people to evacuate their home of centuries and head out into the unknown. Especially when there was no enemy yet in sight. Many of them still lived in denial that the Empire would attack.

So Gwen did the next best thing. She sounded all the horns, which continued to sound even now as she stood there, all of them sounding in a chorus, again and again, rallying all the knights in the King's name, commanding them all to gather at the peak of the Ridge. The people, still in shock at the news of the King's death, had listened, looking for leadership, especially with the King's eldest sons still gone and knowing that Gwendolyn was acting with the former King's will. At least he had made that much clear to his commanders before he'd died.

Now all the brave knights of the Ridge stood atop this broad plateau, lining up as far as she could see, their armor glistening in the sun, all awaiting her command. It was the entire strength of the Ridge, all standing at attention in the silence, as they had been for hours.

Yet now they were all beginning to look to her with skepticism, as the horns sounded again and again, and as yet another set of reinforcements arrived up the platform.

Standing before them all was Ruth, the King's eldest daughter, more proud and fierce than them all, and holding, in her brother's absence, the respect of all the men. She stepped forward, finally, and looked at Gwendolyn fiercely.

"My father is dead," she said, her voice deep, strong. "This is no time to rally our men to the peaks of the Ridge for a fantasy invasion."

Gwen looked back at her steadily, admiring her courage.

"The invasion is real," Gwen said.

Ruth frowned.

"Then where is this army? Show them to me and I shall kill them. No army, even if they found us, can scale the peaks of the Ridge. We have every advantage in the world. But there is none—you follow a fantasy. You have wasted our men's time up here. It is time to return back to the capital and to bury my father. My brothers shall return soon, and it is Koldo, the eldest born, who shall be in command. Along with your Kendrick. You are a dreamer."

Gwendolyn sighed; she could not blame her. She could sense how antsy the men were, all for her assurances, and she knew she could not keep an army waiting up here forever—especially with no enemy. She thought of Mardig, down below in the capital, his refusal to join the knights, and she wondered what evil he was plotting down below, after murdering his father. Surely if they returned he would try to seize power and prevent any defense of the Ridge.

The mention of Kendrick, too, made Gwen think of him, the battles they had fought in together, and more than ever, she wished he were here, by her side, wished he had returned from the Waste already. She could use him to help lead this battle. More than anything, she was concerned for him: would he die out there?

"My lady is no dreamer," Steffen snapped, tensing up, defending her. "If my lady says there will be an invasion, then there shall be. You should learn to respect—"

Gwen laid out a hand, though, on Steffen's shoulder and stopped him. She appreciated his loyalty, but she did not want to inflame the situation further.

Just then another platform of men stopped at the top from the Ridge side, and as it did, Gwen's stomach dropped to see Mardig appear, flanked already by several of the former King's advisors. He scowled at Gwen as he marched right for her.

"What is this?" he called out, disapprovingly. "I did not approve this. You have no right and no authority to assemble my father's men."

"I have every right," she countered, feeling sick at the sight of this murderer. "Your father gave me that right."

Mardig stopped before her and scowled.

"My father gave you nothing," he said. "I am in command now. With my brothers gone, I am the King's eldest. And I command all of you," he said, turning to his men, "to return back to the capital." He turned back to Gwen. "And to arrest this woman!" he added, pointing at her.

The men stood there, a great tension filling the air, all clearly unsure what to do. Krohn snarled, stepping between Gwen and Mardig, and Steffen lay his hand on his hilt—and Gwen knew that she would not be imprisoned without a fight.

Suddenly, Gwendolyn heard a sound, like an arrow whizzing by, and she looked up to see one of Mardig's entourage standing there, face frozen in shock, with an arrow through his throat.

It was followed by a thunderous battle cry, a commotion like a hundred claps of thunder—and suddenly, all was chaos.

Gwen turned and was utterly shocked to see the platform rise on the far side of the Ridge, and dozens of soldiers appeared, dressed in the black armor of the Empire. Barely had they set foot on the ground when dozens more men appeared, scaling over the sides of the walls with grappling hooks. They all let out a shout, drew their swords, and charged her men.

And barely had they begun when dozens more soldiers appeared behind them—in wave after wave.

Gwen saw her knights standing there, stunned; clearly, they had not expected this. How could they? Not once in their history had they been invaded.

"CHARGE!" Gwen shouted, stirring them out of their daze and leading them forward, as she drew her sword, to meet the attackers.

The horns sounded, more urgently now, and her men met her command, snapping out of it and rushing to stop the invaders.

A great clash of armor ensued. It was an all-out war, fierce, bloody, hand-to-hand battle, as men fought with swords and shields, axes and hammers, felling each other on both sides. Gwen hurled a spear, killing a fierce soldier before he could bring an ax down for her head, and then she raised her shield as another soldier attacked her with a hammer. The strength of the blow shook her arm, sent her down to her knees, and as her attacker raised his hammer again, she did not think she could resist another blow.

There came a snarl, and Gwen looked up gratefully to see Krohn charge forward, leap into the air, and clamp his jaws on her attacker's throat, pinning him down on his back.

But barely had Gwen a chance to get her wits, when another soldier appeared, raising a sword and lowering it for her face. She braced herself, unable to block it in time—and there came yet another clang of metal. She rolled out of the way and looked over, gratefully, to see

Steffen blocking with his sword, sparing her from the fatal blow. Steffen then swung his sword around and chopped off the soldier's legs.

Back and forth the battle went, the stunned knights of the Ridge slowly getting over their shock and fighting for their lives.

"FIGHT FOR YOUR HOMELAND!" Ruth called out.

Ruth fought more fiercely than most of the men, and she led a contingent of knights at they cut through the crowd, swinging and slashing left and right, felling attackers in all directions. She did not stop slashing, cutting through their ranks like a whirlwind, until she reached the last soldier, just climbing the cliff, and kicked him hard—sending the first Empire soldier, shrieking, back over the side they had come from.

Gwen, catching her breath, noticed movement out of the corner of her eye, and she flanked back to see Mardig fleeing. She could hardly believe her eyes—there he went, the coward, turning and running, panic in his eyes, back to the safety of the Ridge side. Even worse, once he reached it, he took the only empty platform for himself, boarding it and preparing to descend alone, to escape.

"STOP HIM!" Gwen shrieked.

Several of her soldiers turned to chase him—but it was too late. He was already lowering the ropes, and already out of their reach, descending quickly, alone, leaving them all abandoned up there and fleeing the battle like the coward he was.

Gwen was filled with hatred and loathing. There was nothing she hated more than cowardice.

Gwendolyn turned and looked for Argon, hoping for his help. But he was nowhere to be found. Somehow, he had disappeared.

Gwen realized she was alone now, and alone for a reason—she had to win this fight on her own merits. She looked back and saw her knights beginning to take back ground, to hold the line of Empire ranks scaling the walls like ants. She surveyed the battlefield and realized immediately their weak point: the Empire was using the platform, depositing one cart after another filled with soldiers, reinforcing their ranks. She knew they had to put a stop to it.

"THE PLATFORM!" Gwen cried.

She steeled herself, grabbed a bloody sword off a corpse, and rushed into the battlefield, raising her shield. She ran right into the thick of men, and she raised her shield as soldier slashed at her left and right. Krohn and Steffen accompanied her, guarding her on each side, and thanks to them she was darting through the ranks unscathed, save for several bruises and scratches.

Gwen finally neared the far side of the plateau, heading for the platform, arriving yet again with more soldiers, and as she did, Ruth saw what she was doing and joined her with several men. They attacked, fighting the new crop of soldiers hand to hand as they exited the platform, and Gwen knew this was her chance. While they were all distracted, she had to put an end to that platform, delivering more soldiers to them by the second.

Gwen charged forward recklessly, putting caution to the wind, forgoing the protection of the others. A terrific sword slash knocked the shield from her hand and bruised her wrist; yet still she kept running. Another soldier came at her, slashing down at her, and she dodged—but not before he could slash her arm. She cried out in pain but kept running, grasping her wound to staunch the bleeding.

Gwen ran single-mindedly until she reached the platform, then in one last desperate move, she raised her sword, lunged forward, and cut the ropes.

She felt the satisfying feeling of cutting rope, then there came the sound of wood groaning, followed by wood bouncing off the stone and crashing through the air, like a meteor about to hit earth.

Gwen inched up to the edge and looked over the side, hardly believe what she had just done. She saw the platform tumbling, hurling down over the side, still filled with dozens of Empire soldiers, all of them shrieking. It fell down like a boulder and it landed below with an explosion, killing dozens of men as it landed on them, crushing them.

At first Gwen was elated, feeling that she made a huge difference in the battle; but then, standing there, breathing hard, she looked over the edge and saw exactly what the platform had landed on, what was down below—and her heart stopped.

There, spread out below as far as the eye could see, was the largest army, the largest force of assembled men, she had ever seen. It stretched to the horizon in every direction. It was a sea of swarming black. She could not even see the ground. There must have been a million men. Perhaps more.

And as she leaned back and looked over the cliffs, looked down the steep Ridge, she saw thousands more, all in black, climbing with hooks one step at a time, scaling the cliffs and spreading over the stone like ivy. It was an army in motion, all coming up to kill them. It was unstoppable. Limitless.

Gwen realized now what was happening: the Empire, with so many men at its disposal, could afford to use these men as fodder. They would never stop. If they killed a thousand, they would merely send at thousand more. These men were expendable. Gwen realized at once, with a deepening pit in her stomach, that this was a battle they could never win.

Still, that did not mean she would give up. She was her father's daughter, and she had never seen him back down from a battle.

Gwen watched yet another soldier climb over the ridge, pulling himself up on his rope, and as he did, she was the first to step forward, raise her boot, and kick him in the chest, sending him backwards, falling, flailing, down hundreds of feet to his army below.

All around her, her men followed her example, finding inspiration in her leadership. Her ranks were joined by Steffen and Ruth and her dozens of knights, even Krohn, all of them fighting their way right for the edge, and as they made it, kicking and stabbing and punching men back over the side.

Some of her men raised rocks and threw them down, crushing men's skulls as they climbed the ridge, while others hurled spears. Gwen found a discarded bow, took aim, and fired several arrows straight down the cliff, taking out dozens more.

They pushed back row after row of Empire soldiers—but that also left their flanks exposed to the soldiers who had already managed to make it up to the ridge. Gwen cried out as an Empire soldier slashed her other arm, and she wheeled to him as he was about to stab her in the chest—and then Krohn leapt forward and sank his fangs into the man's wrist, severing his hand.

All around her, though, her men were not so lucky, and many fell, stabbed from behind, while they fought off the ranks of newly approaching soldiers. That left openings for many Empire soldiers to successfully scale onto the plateau and join their ranks. Everywhere, Gwen saw grappling hooks appearing over the edge, digging into rock, launched by arrows from down below, from the other side of the ridge. Dozens of hooks landed with each passing moment, an Empire soldier behind each one, climbing his way up.

Gwen's men fought gloriously for hours, never retreating, killing more men than armies could, sending thousands of Empire soldiers back over the edge. But even so, they were only human, and they began to tire beneath the suns, overwhelmed by the fresh Empire ranks. Gwen's ranks of Ridge knights began to thin out—and her ranks were much more precious than the Empire's. A dozen of her man fell—and that turned into two dozen, then three. On and on the fighting went, hundreds of Empire falling, dying, being pushed back—but hundreds more appearing behind them. Gwen fought until her ribs hurt from trying to catch her breath—but always there were more men. They were like a tide that could not be stopped.

More and more Empire made headway, scaling the cliffs, taking over the plateau and beginning to push her men further back on the platform, creeping back toward the Ridge side. Soon, so many Empire had scaled their side that Gwen and her men could no longer reach the far edge, no longer have the advantage of kicking them over as they arrived, or fighting straight down.

And their buffer from the edge deepened—first five feet, then ten, then twenty, then thirty—a buffer that became so deep that soon the halfway point was crossed, and Gwen and her men found themselves in the position of creeping back toward their own edge, their own plunge, their own death. Gwen, heart pounding, sweating beneath the fading suns, realized they were losing.

All around her, more and more of her men were dropping, the Empire's black filling the world. The platform was slick, running red with blood, and they were losing.

A soldier kicked Krohn, sending him tumbling, whining, while Steffen was locked up fighting two soldiers at once. That left Gwen alone, and she raised her shield and blocked a fierce below from a huge Empire soldier, but it was so strong, she lost her shield. He was so quick, he stepped forward and kicked her in the chest, and his large boot sent her flying back, winded, landing on her back on the hard rock. She felt as if her ribs were cracked.

Gwen looked up and saw him standing over her, scowling, raising his sword high, about to kill her.

As he brought down his sword, Gwen saw her life flashing before her, and she knew she was about to die. She saw her father's face, urging her on, urging her to be strong. And she was not ready to die yet.

Gwen lifted her foot and at the last second, kicked the soldier hard between the legs. He groaned and dropped his sword, and she jumped to her feet and grabbed him by the back of the head and kneed him in the face.

He fell to his side, unmoving, and Gwen felt born again. She was not down yet.

Just then, Gwen sensed motion out of the corner of her eye, and she turned, too late, to see a sword slash coming for her face. She braced herself for the blow—when suddenly, there came a distinctive clang of sword stopping sword, but inches from her face.

Gwen looked over and was shocked to see, standing a few feet away, Kendrick, blocking the blow, spinning the sword around, then stabbing the soldier in the heart.

She looked over and saw he had just arrived from the Ridge side— and along with him, Brandt, Atme, Koldo, Ludvig and Kaden.

"You must retreat!" Kendrick yelled. "All of you! There is no time! Come with us!"

Gwen watched in shock as Kendrick and the others threw themselves into the battle with fresh strength, blocking and slashing, saving many of her men and sending scores of Empire back. They brought a fresh energy into the battle and allowed her men to catch their breath—and more importantly, to be reinvigorated. Gwen was overjoyed with relief to see them back from the Waste, to know they were still alive.

Gwendolyn heard a scream, and she turned and looked out in horror to see the first of her own men had been pushed backwards, over their own side of the Ridge, hurling to his death. Only a few feet remained now between her people and the edge, and their time was running short.

"We must evacuate!" Kendrick called out. "We must go, Gwendolyn! We cannot win up here!"

"We cannot!" Gwendolyn yelled. "I vowed to the King to defend the Ridge and his people!"

"We cannot defend them up here!" Koldo yelled. "It is defensible no longer!"

Gwen knew they were right, and she finally nodded back.

"MEN, WE MUST RETREAT!" Koldo called out to his father's knights.

Gwen could see them all look at him with great respect, and she was relieved he was here, to lead the men of the Ridge in battle, just as his father would have wanted. Immediately, his men began to mobilize.

His presence alone inspired them, and as they retreated slowly, one step at a time, they all also made a terrific push, fighting with renewed energy, felling soldiers on every side. They fought gloriously, killing dozens, rallying as horns sounded all around them.

As they were backed up nearly to the edge, Gwen saw there was no platform left—Mardig had taken it, had left them all without a means back down. All that was left were the ropes, still dangling on the beams that had born it. She looked down and saw them swinging there, dangling hundreds of feet.

"JUMP!" Koldo commanded.

All around her, their men turned and jumped, grabbing ropes, sliding all the way down, far, far, hundreds of feet below.

Gwen reached down and picked up Krohn. Then she stood there, hesitating.

"WE MUST, my lady!" Kendrick called out.

She suddenly felt Kendrick's strong arm around her waist, and he jumped.

The next thing she knew they were flying through the air, over the Ridge, plummeting, flailing, aiming for a rope, a final lifeline before falling into oblivion.

CHAPTER THIRTY

Thorgrin raced through the air on the back of Lycoples, clutching her scales, willing her onward, and for the first time in a long time, he felt alive again. He felt a driving sense of purpose, unleashed from the Land of Gloom, knowing that Lycoples was taking him to the Land of the Ring, knowing that soon enough he would have a chance to find the sacred object that could change the fate of mankind forever.

Thorgrin could feel the excitement in the dragon's body, this ancient beast who carried the blood of Ralibar and Mycoples, whose ancient power told her exactly where to go. As they flew, passing over vast stretches of sea, feeling as if they were flying to the end of the world, Thor felt Lycoples's power coursing through him, and he felt his own skin tingling, knowing, with each passing cloud, that they were getting ever closer to the place that would yield him the Sorcerer's Ring.

Thor knew it would not be easy; he knew that whatever lay before him would be the greatest trial of his life. His head swam as he thought of it. The Sorcerer's Ring. The one needed to restore the Ring for all time. The ring that only he, the chosen one, could wear.

And yet he knew it would come with a price. He knew it would be fiercely guarded, and he prayed that he was up to the test. He also knew that, somehow, finding this ring would increase his power, would be his final trial in becoming a Master Druid. In becoming King of the Druids.

Thor closed his eyes as he went, breathed deeply, and pictured his mother's face. He could feel her with him, and he knew that he would need her powers, her help, to get him through this.

Lycoples screeched, jolting Thor from his thoughts, and as she dipped out of the clouds, Thor looked down and was amazed by what he saw: far below, amidst a sea of clouds, he saw a series of cliffs, shaped in a circle. Their walls were jagged, protruding up into the air, but at their top was a narrow, smooth circle, like the lip of a volcano. From up here, it looked like a ring, perhaps a mile in diameter, with mist and fog and clouds on the inside, and fog all around them. The circular walkway at the top was narrow, wide enough to hold Thorgrin and not much else. Thor sensed immediately that this was the place that held the Ring.

It was the most unusual landscape he had ever seen, and Thor sensed he'd have to walk along it, in a circle, in a ring.

Immediately, he felt a sense of apprehension. What sort of ring was this? There was no sign of a sacred object, of the Sorcerer's Ring. It was but a ring of rock emerging from the clouds, a narrow walkway that wound around a huge, perfect circle, with no person, no destination, in sight. Thor saw no creatures to defend against, no sorcerer waiting to greet him. He saw no weapons or shields, no structures of any sort. Nothing but this massive ring of rock, tempting him to land below, and to walk it.

But why? Why walk in a huge circle?

What was this place?

Lycoples suddenly dove downward, screeching, flapping her wings, aiming for the platform atop the rock, and Thor knew he had found the place. He sensed the power in the air, a vibration that coursed through him.

Slowly, it began to dawn on Thor that this place was only partially real—and that it partially existed in another dimension, deep within the canals of his own mind. In some ways, it was like the Land of the Druids, a land created partially by his own mind. Yet, it was partially real, too. He sensed he was entering another realm, a realm much more dangerous than reality. It was a realm of magic. It felt like a trap.

It would demand his greatest battle, he knew, because he would not be battling an outside opponent. He would be battling for the inside of his mind. He would be battling himself.

Lycoples set them down on the edge of the rock and Thor quickly dismounted, warily standing on the narrow platform atop the cliffs. Looking about, he saw the jagged cliffs disappearing into the clouds, and saw only clouds in the center. The walkway was narrow—but a few feet wide—and he knew that if he took a wrong step in either direction, he would plummet into nothingness for eternity.

Thor turned back to face Lycoples, and she looked at him, craning her neck forward, her intense eyes staring at him.

This is where I leave you, he heard her saying in his mind's eye. *This is a warrior's journey. A journey for you alone.*

Thor looked back at her, feeling a deepening sense of apprehension.

"Old friend," Thor said, "where will you go?"

Thor reached out to touch the scales on her face, but as he did, he was shocked to see she had disappeared.

Thorgrin turned, looking all around, wondering where she was, wondering what this place was exactly. He had a deep feeling of dread here, stronger than any other place he'd been. The enemy here, he sensed, was invisible. He would have preferred to face a den of monsters, a Blood Lord, even the gates of hell, over this place. Because this was a place, he feared, that would make him confront himself.

"Your training is nearly complete, young Thorgrin," came Argon's voice suddenly.

Thor spun, shocked, looking all around for Argon, but saw him nowhere.

"Argon?" Thor called out, his voice echoing. "Where are you?"

"I am everywhere and nowhere," Argon replied. "The question is: where are *you*?"

"Where is the Ring?" Thor called out. "Where is the Sorcerer's Ring?"

There came a long silence, then finally Argon's voice echoed again.

"The Ring can only be found, only be worn, by one who deserves it. One who has become a Master Druid. The King of the Druids. That is what it means to be King. You must pass your final step, your final test."

"And what is that test?" Thor asked.

"If you can win," Argon called out, "if you can defeat yourself, then the Ring shall be yours."

Thor frowned.

"But how can I defeat myself?" he asked.

All fell silent, and Thor looked around, but there came no more sound. There was only the sound of the clouds, of the vapor drifting in and out on the wind.

Suddenly, there came a clang of armor, and Thor jumped, startled. He spun, shocked to see a warrior standing a few feet away, appearing out of the mist, facing him. His silver armor shone in the fog, and as this fine knight raised his visor, Thor was breathless to see it was himself he was facing.

Thor gripped the hilt of the Sword of the Dead, drew it slowly, and raised his shield. He then braced himself, as his double charged him.

His double brought his sword down, a blow meant to kill, and Thor raised the Sword of the Dead and blocked, sparks flying—and he was surprised at how powerful the blow was. Thor was shocked to see that his double, too, wielded the Sword of the Dead.

His double brought his sword down further, nearly touching his neck, and Thor, struggling, finally spun and knocked his sword of the way. As he did, Thor lost his balance and stopped himself before falling over the edge.

Thor's double took advantage of it and rushed forward before Thor could regain his footing, and kicked Thor in the ribs.

Thor let out a cry as he slipped off the side and began sliding down the rock. He reached out with one hand, flailing, managed to grab the edge, and he held on, dangling. He looked down over his shoulder and saw he was about to slip down into nothingness.

Thorgrin pulled himself up with all his might, straining, as his double appeared before him and raised his sword, preparing to finish him off. Thor knew his life hung in the balance and that he had to act fast. In one quick motion, he yanked himself up, swung his legs around, and with all his might, kicked his double behind the knee, causing him to fall.

His double fell backwards, over the side of the cliffs, tumbling into the mist, his armor clanking as he fell and fell, disappearing into the clouds.

Thorgrin knelt there, gasping for breath, rubbing his ribs where he had been kicked. It had been a quick and fierce and unexpected confrontation, and it had caught him off guard. Had he really beaten him? Was it himself he had beaten?

Thor looked left and right, wary, looking for more enemies—but there were none.

He slowly gained his feet, and as he stood there, alone, baffled, he felt instinctively that in order to find the answers he was looking for, he had to walk this ring, walk the entire circle. Complete it.

Thor began to walk, one step at a time, in and out of the mist that blocked his view at times. He looked down, searching everywhere for a ring, for any sacred object—but there was none. He wondered if he would ever find it, and where it could be hidden.

As Thor walked, wary, he heard a faint clanging of armor, growing stronger. He peered into the mist, and was shocked to see several more of his doubles charging for him, single file, each raising battle-axes. They charged out of the mist, and Thor knew he could not avoid them—and that they would pose the fight of his life.

As they charged, Thor had a sudden realization: by trying to oppose them, he was opposing himself. He would lose. He suddenly had the insight that these doubles were, in part, his creation. This place was his creation. The more power he endowed to them in his mind, the more power they would have. The only way to defeat them, he realized, would be not to acknowledge them. Not to give them power. To realize that they were his own creation—and to stop creating them.

So Thorgrin, instead of attacking, instead of defending, stood very still. He did not even confront them. He closed his eyes and stood very still as he raised palms to his side, and felt the heat throbbing within them. In his mind's eye, he chose to create a different reality: he did not see hostile warriors charging him; instead, he saw nothingness. Mist. Silence. He saw the warriors fall off the side of the cliff and disappear forever. He replaced violence with peace, harmony.

Thor opened his eyes, but, feeling his power searing within him, he no longer braced himself as the first soldier reached him, bringing the ax down for his head. He knew he was stronger than that. Stronger than believing what was before him was real. Thor forced himself to stay focused, centered, and to see a different reality up until even the last second. It was the hardest effort of his life, as every ounce of him screamed out to defend. But he knew he had to keep his mind strong. He knew that if his mind was not strong enough, he would be killed by this opponent.

Thor stood there calmly and stared, believing in himself, in the power of his mind, and at the last second, the double leading the charge leaned sideways and fell off the cliff, tumbling in a loud clanging of armor. Behind him, one by one, all the other doubles fell, too, disappearing down the sides of the cliff, into the mist.

Thor kept walking boldly forth, and as he circled the ring, dozens more of these doubles appeared out of the mist. But Thor walked right into them, keeping himself centered, feeling the heat in his palms, having faith in himself, and as he continued, taking one step after another in a walk of faith, he walked right down the middle, the knights parting ways, falling off on either side of the cliffs.

Finally, they stopped coming. Finally, as he walked, there was peace. Silence.

He had defeated them. He had defeated himself.

Thor was slowly realizing that the only power left to overcome in the universe was the power in his mind. He was coming to realize the greatest source of power in the universe was not outside somewhere, but within himself. It was the final, and the greatest frontier, the infinite well which he had barely begun to tap. It was the scariest thing in the world—and the most inspiring.

As Thorgrin continued walking, going fearlessly forth, halfway around the circle, the mist lifted. The sun began to appear, shafts of light coming down on him in scarlet, and as the walkway lit up, he stopped short. He saw that before him, there was a gap of about twenty feet in the walkway before it picked up again.

This, too, Thorgrin realized, was a test. It was a test of faith, faith to cross this. Was his faith strong enough? Was his belief in himself, in his mind, strong enough? Was it strong enough to step into nothingness?

Thorgrin realized that it needed to be. That was what it meant to pass the final test. That was what it meant to master himself. That was what it meant to become the King of the Druids.

And what was what was required to be worthy of the Sorcerer's Ring.

Thorgrin closed his eyes, took a deep breath, and walked forth. He took the final, fateful step off the edge, into nothingness. As he did, he willed himself to imagine a different outcome. He refused to see himself falling, but instead saw himself standing on air, walking.

Thor's visualization become so strong in his mind's eyes that he was no longer surprised when he took that fateful step into air and instead felt himself standing on what felt like solid ground. He looked down and saw that it was air, mist—and yet he was standing on it.

Thor continued walking, crossing the gap, walking on air, continuing around the ring, one foot after the next, until finally he had reached stone again.

He had done it.

He continued walking, feeling buoyed by a power he had never felt before, a power overwhelming him completely. He felt stronger than he'd ever had, no longer fearing any opponents, but welcoming them. No longer fearing himself—but welcoming it.

And as he finished walking the circle, he felt a sense of completion, felt as if he had completed something within himself. Finally, after all these years and all these battles and all these conquests, he was no longer afraid. Finally, he had supreme faith in himself.

Suddenly, the mist lifted completely and the sun broke through, sparkling in a haze, a million colors, like a rainbow all around him. Thorgrin felt the world opening up before him as he stood at the completion of the circle, and as he realized he was right in the place where he had begun.

Thor looked out to see a skyway suddenly appearing, an arched walkway made of stone, forking off from the circle, curving, rising, higher and higher out of the mist. At the end of it, there sat a castle made of stone, perched at the edge of a cliff. He could sense the power coming off of it even from here. It was the castle that had haunted his dreams ever since he could remember. It felt like his mother's castle—but different.

He saw a single object shining in the sun, gleaming, waiting for him before the shining castle door.

And as he took the first step, he knew, he just knew, that at the end of the walkway, as he completed this final path of his final test, there would be waiting for him the Sorcerer's Ring.

156

CHAPTER THIRTY ONE

Darius opened his eyes slowly, his head splitting, and he looked all around in the blackness, trying to get his bearings. He lay face down, his face planted on a floor made of hard wood. It smelled like ocean water. His world bobbed up and down, and he saw streaks of sunlight pouring in through slats, and he realized, with a start, that he must be below deck on a ship.

Darius tried to sit up, alarmed, yet as he moved his arms and legs, he felt them restrained by thick iron shackles, their chains scarping against the wood. His head pounding, his eyes hurting even in the dim light, he tried to sit up and put his head in his hands, tried to understand where he was. What had last happened. It was so hard to remember.

The creaking of wood filled the air, and as his world slowly bobbed up and down, Darius realized he was out at sea, riding the massive ocean waves, being taken God knows where. He was someone's captive. But whose?

Darius heard groaning all around him, and as he looked around, slowly adjusting to the dim light, he was surprised to see hundreds of others, like he, shackled to the deck, their noise filling the air in a soft rattling of chains. As he tried to move, to get a better look, his body wracked in pain, he realized that he was a slave now—that they were all slaves. That could only mean one thing: they were prisoners to the Empire.

Darius rubbed his head and tried to think. Somehow, he had ended up here, in the holds of this ship. Somehow, he had been captured.

Darius closed his eyes, trying to numb the pain, and forced himself to remember. He saw his father's face, and he remembered being in the arena…in the Empire capital…his father dying in his arms…. He remembered, with a jolt, his rush of power, the exhilarating feeling that Darius would never forget. He remembered seeing those elephants hurling through the air, destroying the arena…. He remembered escaping, opening the city gates and allowing the Knights of the Seven to pour in, to destroy the capital.

Then he, himself, being clubbed.

Darius rubbed his face, realizing he had been knocked unconscious, chained, during the invasion of the capital. Given the size of that army, though, he was lucky to be alive.

He was a slave again, ironically. An Empire slave. But this time, a slave to the Knights of the Seven.

But where were they taking him?

"SLAVES! ON YOUR FEET!" suddenly boomed a voice.

The hold flooded with harsh ocean sunlight as two huge wooden doors were suddenly opened high above, and in marched dozens of Empire soldiers.

Darius heard the crack of a whip and he suddenly jumped in pain as he felt the lash of a whip across his back, his skin feeling as if it were being torn off him. He turned to see rows of Empire soldiers storming the hold. Several stepped forward, raised swords, and brought them down.

Darius braced himself, expecting to be killed; but instead, he heard a clang and felt his shackles being severed.

Rough hands grabbed him and dragged him to his feet. He immediately felt weak, nauseous, dizzy, and he wondered when was the last time he ate.

Kicked in the back, Darius stumbled forward, falling in with hundreds of other prisoners, as dozens of soldiers escorted them roughly, leading them out of the dark hold and up toward the light of the upper deck.

As Darius stumbled with the others, he remembered his power, and he tried to summon it again.

But for some reason he could not understand, he was unable to. Whatever it was he had, he had lost it once again. Perhaps, he realized, he needed time for it to recharge.

Darius squinted and held his hands to his face as he stumbled up the stairs into the harsh sunlight, and he collapsed on the deck as a soldier shoved him and he tripped over others.

Another soldier grabbed him and dragged him roughly to his feet, and he looked around, trying to get his bearings. He scanned the ship and saw hundreds of Empire soldiers patrolling the decks of a massive warship, commanding hundreds of galley slaves chained to benches and forced to row. Dozens more slaves were chained to cannons alongside the ship, while dozens more were forced to do hard labor, scrubbing the decks, hoisting sails, or doing whatever the soldiers, whips in hand, commanded.

Darius looked out, beyond the rail, and saw that this warship was but a speck in a vast fleet of Empire warships, thousands of them filling the horizon, all sailing somewhere together. He wondered where.

"Move it, slave!" commanded an Empire soldier, then elbowed him in the ribs.

Darius stumbled forward with a group of slaves and found himself grabbed roughly and ushered over to a bench filled with slaves, all slumped over their oars—none of them moving. Darius looked closely and saw the lashes on their exposed backs, burnt from the sun, and wondered why none of them were moving. Had they fallen asleep at the oars?

His question was answered as a soldier stepped forward, severed the chains one by one, grabbed each one, and pushed back each slave.

Darius was shocked to see each fall backwards, limp, landing flat on their backs on the deck.

Dead.

More soldiers stepped forward and hoisted the corpses in the air, one by one, then walked them to the rail and hurled them over the edge. Darius saw the bodies splash in the water below, and watched as the currents carried them away quickly. Before they submerged, he saw several sharks surface and snatch them, dragging them beneath the surface.

Darius looked down at the empty bench, covered in blood where the dead slaves had just sat, with a sense of dread. He wondered how long they had been here, how long it had taken them to be worked to death

Before he could think it through, he was shoved down to a vacant seat and re-shackled, his chains locked to the bench where the dead slaves had just been. His wrists were chained to the oars, as were the other fresh slaves seated beside him, and he was suddenly lashed across the back, feeling an awful pain rip through his body.

"ROW!" a commander shouted.

All the other slaves began to row, and Darius joined them, lashed sporadically and wanting to make it all go away. One hell, he knew, had been replaced with another. Soon enough, he would die here.

Darius looked out to sea and studied the horizon, studied the angle of the suns, and he realized they were heading east. And then suddenly it struck him: that could only mean one thing. They, this vast fleet, all of the Empire, could only be heading to one place:

The Ring.

A war was coming. The greatest war of all time. And he, Darius, fighting for the wrong side, would be stuck right in the middle of it.

CHAPTER THIRTY TWO

Gwendolyn shouted as she went flying through the air, off the side of the Ridge, reaching for the rope dangling before her as she gripped Krohn in her other arm. Gwen managed to just barely grab hold of it, as Kendrick grabbed hold of the rope beside her. As she did, she swayed wildly, grabbing on for dear life, her palms burning as she began to slip at full speed down the side of the Ridge, Krohn clutching her with his paws.

All around her, Gwen saw the survivors sliding down ropes, too, among them, Kendrick, Brandt, Atme, Koldo, Ludvig, Kaden, Brandt, Atme, Kaden and Ruth, along with dozens of soldiers of the Ridge, all descending at dizzying speed, all that was left of the fighting force that had made a stand against the Empire invasion. They descended so quickly that Gwen could barely catch her breath, and as she looked down, she saw they still had hundreds of feet to go. She was feeling optimistic, when suddenly she heard shouts all around her.

Gwen looked over to see one of her men cry out, and she was shocked to see an arrow in his shoulder; he lost his grip and plunged down below, flailing, all the way to his death.

She looked up to see Empire soldiers standing at the edge of the cliffs, firing arrows straight down at them. She watched one whiz by her head, then heard another cry and looked over to see another of her people fall several hundred feet, down to his death below.

Gwen slid faster, her heart pounding as spears, too, were being hurled down at her, flinching each time as they just missed, praying one did not hit her. All around her, her men were being picked off as they went, their numbers diminishing. Her stomach plunged as she forced herself to slide faster, almost in a free-fall.

As they neared the bottom, still a good fifty feet away, Gwen heard more shouts, and she looked over in horror to see the Empire were now chopping the ropes. Several of her men clutched onto their ropes, now useless, as they tumbled and fell to their deaths.

161

Gwen looked down and saw the ground fast approaching, littered with corpses. She tightened her grip on the rope, trying to slow her descent, despite the pain in her palms, not wanting to break her legs. She began to slow, and was about twenty feet from the bottom—when suddenly, she felt her rope cut out from under her.

The rope lost all tension, and Gwen went flying, flailing with Krohn, right for the ground. As she did, she took aim for a heap of corpses, hoping to cushion her fall.

Gwen landed on the bodies, the wind knocked out of her, feeling again as if she'd cracked her ribs. She tumbled, rolling over them and onto the hard ground, stirring up a cloud of dust and dirt, and finally coming to a stop on her back, Krohn whining nearby.

All around, she saw the others landing, too, their armor clanging as they rolled.

Gwendolyn slowly came to her hands and knees, feeling as if her ribs were broken, and she knelt there, breathing hard. Krohn came over and licked her face, and she reached up and petted him.

A spear suddenly landed in the ground beside her, and as Gwen looked up, she saw the rain of weapons had not ceased.

She quickly gained her feet and began to run, scrambling to help Kendrick and the others up, back on their feet, and to get them to run with her. Slowly, they all rallied, and hobbled, then jogged, away from the deadly cliffs. It pained her to leave behind so many dead comrades, but they had no choice.

Gwen looked up and saw the lake before them, and she and the others ran for the boats. They jumped in, all of them still covered in dirt, piling into several boats, and disembarked.

They all began to row, to distance themselves from the cliffs and from the Empire soldiers, some of whom were already beginning to follow them down on the ropes. Gwen looked about at the shore, saw all the empty boats, and suddenly, she realized.

"Wait!" Gwen called out. "The other boats!"

Kendrick, in the closest boat, turned with the others and realized, and he stopped his boat, turned it around, then stood. He hurled a spear, and Brandt, Atme, Koldo, Ludvig, Kaden and Ruth stood beside him and hurled their spears, too. They punctured the boats, one at a time, and their soldiers followed suit; some hurled spears, while others rowed next to the boats and wielded flails, smashing holes in them until they began to sink. Gwen watched in satisfaction as they sank.

They turned and they all rowed faster, gaining distance from shore, the Empire arrows still falling in the water all around them. Soon, though, they were a good hundred yards from shore, and the enemy arrows and spears fell fruitlessly in the water behind them.

Gwen turned and saw the Empire soldiers already reaching the beach—but standing there, stranded, all the boats sinking. She had, at least, bought them some time, time enough, she prayed, to rally the survivors in the capital and to try to convince them to evacuate.

Yet evacuate to where, and how, Gwen still had no idea. After all, the city was surrounded by this lake, and while that deterred attackers, it also made escape impossible. And even if they did, there was the Waste beyond it. It seemed impossible.

As they rowed and rowed, Krohn at her feet, her mind whirling with flashbacks of the battle, Gwen began to see the capital city of the Ridge ahead. She could hear the bells tolling, could see the people milling about in the harbor, and she realized there would be a tough road ahead for them all—if they even survived.

Koldo rowed up beside her, with Kendrick and the others, and as he did, Gwen turned to him.

"Your father once asked me to help evacuate his people," Gwen told him, "if that day should ever come. But he is dead now, and you are firstborn, and that leaves you in command. These are your people. I do not wish to step on your toes."

Koldo looked back, serious, with a look of respect.

"My father was a great man," he replied, "and I respect his wishes. He knew it was you who was meant to lead us out, and it is you who shall. I can lead my men, and you can lead the people. We can lead together."

Gwendolyn nodded back, relieved; she had always had a great deal of respect for Koldo.

"And yet, where can we go?" she asked. "Did your father have a route in mind?"

Koldo studied the shore as they all approached, getting closer to the city, and he sighed.

"There has always been an escape plan for the Ridge," he said, "for the day that we were discovered. There lies a tunnel, concealed beneath the castle. It leads beneath the water, beneath these lakes, beneath the Ridge itself, and all the way out to the other side of the cliffs, into the Waste. From there, we would head north, through the Waste, for the rivers, which lead, if we are not discovered, out to the open sea. From there—it is anyone's guess. But at least we can escape—assuming we can rally all of our people in time. And assuming they are willing."

Gwendolyn nodded, satisfied with the idea.

"Show me," she said.

*

Gwen raced through the chaotic capital of the Ridge, bells tolling, horns sounding, its citizens screaming, running in every direction. It was outright pandemonium. With the Ridge never invaded before, its citizens had no idea what to do. Many were hoarding food, carrying it with both arms, while they brought it home, barred doors, and locked themselves into their homes. Gwen shook her head. If they really thought a few simple locks could keep out the Empire, they had no idea what was coming for them on the other side of the Ridge.

Gwen had already spotted Empire soldiers crossing the water, having constructed two makeshift barges. They were slow moving, wide, flat boats made of planks of wood tied together, carrying tons of soldiers—they were moving, though, pushed by long poles, and soon enough, they would be here. Soon enough, all that she saw here in the Ridge would be wiped out forever.

Gwen continued to run, crisscrossing the city with Kendrick, Brandt, Atme, Koldo, Ludvig, Kaden, Ruth, Steffen, and Krohn, all of them splitting up and trying to corral people toward the castle—beneath which, Koldo had told her, the tunnel lay. Some of the citizens had listened to her—yet Gwen was distressed to see that most did not. They ignored her, some in denial, refusing to believe that the Ridge could ever be discovered, invaded; while others thought they could defend, or wait it out. Still others gave up all hope, seeing no way out, and sat where they were on the streets, refusing to budge. How differently people reacted in times of distress, Gwen realized, was an endless wonder to her.

Having finished corralling a group of several hundred citizens, the best she could do, Gwen led them toward the castle. As she reached the entrance, though, meeting up with Kendrick and his group of citizens, she stopped at the door, remembering.

"What is it?" Kendrick asked.

Gwen realized she had one mission left before she could leave.

"Jasmine," she explained.

Gwen knew she would find Jasmine deep in the bowels of the library, oblivious to all that was going on here; she probably had no idea. Gwen could not leave without her.

"I shall return," she told Kendrick.

Kendrick looked back with concern.

"Where are you going? We have no time."

Gwen shook her head, hurrying off.

"There's one more left I need to save."

Gwen bolted, having no time to explain, and she ran across the royal courtyard, burst through the streets, set her eyes on the library, and ran for it.

Suddenly Gwen felt herself jolted, and she turned to see a citizen in a panic, an oversized man, desperation on his face, stopping Gwendolyn and trying to grab the purse of coins off her belt. He held a dagger out and scowled at her, showing missing teeth.

"Give me what you got before I slice your throat!" he ordered.

Gwen was too horrified to react, realizing she had been caught off guard, as she felt the blade pressing against her. A moment later she heard a growling noise, and Krohn appeared, launching himself on the man and sinking his teeth into the man's cheek.

The man screamed and cried as Krohn pinned him down to the ground, shaking him until he finally stopped moving.

Gwen stroked Krohn's back, his hair still sticking up.

"I owe you," she said, as grateful to him as ever.

Gwen continued running, Krohn at her side, blood dripping from his fangs, until they finally reached the royal library and burst inside.

It was dark and still here, catching Gwen off guard, shutting out the worries of the world. It was deceptively peaceful, and a part of Gwen felt she could just close the doors, forget her worries, and pretend the world outside was peaceful.

But she knew it was an illusion. There was death and war outside these doors, even if one could not hear it in here, and it was coming for them all.

"Jasmine!" she shrieked.

Her voice echoed in the empty halls of this solemn place. Gwen looked up and down the aisles, at all the books stretching forever, and saw no sign of her. Her heart momentarily fluttered in panic: what if she didn't find her?

"Jasmine!" she yelled again, and began to run through the halls. She could not leave her behind—whatever the cost.

Gwen barely turned a corner when she suddenly stopped short, running into Jasmine, who stood there looking up at her in surprise, a book in her hand.

"I heard you," she said. "I was reading. What is all the panic anyway? I was just in the middle of a volume on—"

Gwen grabbed her arm, turned, and began to run with her.

"There's no time," she said, "we're under attack."

"Attack?" Jasmine echoed, surprise in her voice.

Gwen continued running, dragging Jasmine with her—when Jasmine suddenly pulled away from her grip and ran over to a stack of books.

"Where are you going!?" Gwen asked, exasperated.

"Those are my favorite books," she called out. "I cannot leave without them!"

Gwen sighed.

"This is your *life*," Gwen exclaimed, exasperated.

Jasmine ignored her, running down the hall while Gwen waited impatiently, until she finally snatched two small leather-bound books and turned and ran back.

"*Books* are my life," Jasmine countered, as the two turned and began to run again.

"I'm sorry," Jasmine added, as they ran. "But I'd rather be dead than without them."

Together the two of them burst out of the library doors and into the bright, noisy, chaotic streets. Gwen saw Jasmine's face fall as she saw the chaos all around her.

"What has happened to my city?" Jasmine asked. "Could a people really be this scared?"

Gwen took her hand and the two of them continued running, weaving their way in and out of the crowds, Krohn keeping pace with them as they ran toward the castle.

As they neared it, Gwen saw its massive doors already halfway closed, kept open only by Kendrick and Steffen, who stood there, looking out, waiting impatiently for her return. Their faces lit up at the sight of her, and as she burst through the doors with Jasmine, they quickly closed them, slamming them behind her with a reverberating thud.

Gwen found herself in a huge mob of people crowded inside, and she cut through the crowd and reunited with Koldo in the huge castle corridors.

"I didn't think you'd make it," Koldo grinned. "We couldn't have waited much longer."

Gwen grinned back.

"Nor would I want you to," she replied.

"Where's Mother?" Jasmine demanded of Koldo.

Koldo looked at her and blinked, as if just realizing.

Gwendolyn, too, suddenly remembered the Queen, and her heart lurched in panic.

"We can't leave without her," Jasmine declared. "She must be in her chamber. She would never leave her chamber, especially in times of distress."

Jasmine suddenly turned, bolted through the crowd, and made her way for the grand staircase.

"Jasmine!" Koldo called out.

But she was already gone.

Gwen knew she could not leave her, or the Queen, and without thinking, she took off after her—Krohn joining at her heels.

Gwen bolted with her up the marble steps, taking them three at a time, down twisting corridors, until finally they burst, breathless, into the Queen's chamber. Gwen was surprised at first to see that no one was standing guard, the door ajar—but then again, she knew she shouldn't be: everyone else had already evacuated by now.

Gwen was shocked as she burst in and found the Queen sitting there, her touched daughter in her lap, by the window, stroking her hair. The Queen had tears in her eyes.

"Mother!" Jasmine called out.

"My Queen!" Gwen chimed in. "You must come now! The Empire advances!"

But the Queen merely sat there as they rushed for her.

"My husband," she said, softly, her voice filled with grief. "He is dead. Killed by my son's hand."

Gwen felt her grief, understanding too well, from one Queen to another.

"I am sorry," Gwen said. "I truly am. But you must come with us now. You will die here."

But the Queen merely shook her head.

"This is my home," she replied. "This is where my husband died. And this is where I shall die."

Gwen stood there, shocked. Yet strangely, she understood. This was the only home the Queen had ever known, and with her husband's body here, she could not go on.

"Mother!" Jasmine cried, clutching her arm, inconsolable.

But her mother merely stared back, blankly.

"There is no life for me without my husband," she said. "This was my life. It was a good one. Go on without me. Save yourselves."

"Mother," Jasmine cried, hugging her tight. "You can't!"

The Queen hugged her too, as she stroked her other daughter's hair, and wept as she did.

"Go on, Jasmine. I love you. Stay with Gwendolyn. She will be a mother to you now."

Jasmine cried, clutching her mother, unwilling to let go. She even dropped her books to hold her.

Finally, though, the Queen shook her off and placed her books back in her hands.

"Take your books. Go with Gwendolyn. And remember me. Remember this place not for what it is now, but for what it was. Go!" she commanded firmly.

Jasmine, stung, stood there, and Gwen stepped forward and took her arm. She turned with her and ran, after taking one long last look at the Queen. They nodded to each other, Queen to Queen, and Gwendolyn, as much as she wished she didn't, understood.

*

Gwendolyn, holding Jasmine's hand, burst down the corridors, Krohn at their heels, twisting and turning, then raced down the steps several at a time, hoping to catch up with the others. As they reached the bottom she saw the main corridors of the castle were empty now, the people having already moved through the castle for the tunnel, and Gwen turned down the corridors, hearing their din in the distance, and raced to catch up with them, Krohn running with them.

Finally, she and Jasmine caught up with Kendrick, Steffen, Koldo, and the other knights, alone with the several hundred remaining exiles of the Ridge, all of them following Koldo into a vast chamber, down the end of a long corridor in the castle.

"Women and children first!" Koldo yelled, as the mob pressed forward, anxious, rushing to follow. In the distance, outside the castle walls, Gwen could hear the chaos in the city streets worsening. She wondered if the Empire were getting closer. She knew their time was short.

Several of Koldo's men turned cranks and opened a huge steel door, creaking as it went, and the women and children rushed forward. But before they could enter it, there suddenly came a man sprinting through the crowd, pushing past them.

A gasp spread through the crowd, and Gwen was horrified to see it was Mardig, rushing to beat them all into the tunnel, rushing to be first.

Mardig burst past them all, into the crack of the open door—then just as quickly he reached up and began to pull the doors, in an attempt to seal them behind him and keep all of the others trapped outside.

Gwen was outraged at his cowardice, at his cruelty, as were all the others. Kendrick, closest to him, was first to react. He lunged forward, throwing himself between the doors before they closed, clearly knowing that if he did not, the doors would be closed forever, and that all of them would be trapped here to die, leaving only Mardig to escape.

Kendrick stood between the doors, but they were closing on him, and for a moment it looked as if he would be crushed.

169

Suddenly, Krohn snarled and raced forward, leaping through the air and pouncing on Mardig, forcing him to loosen his grip.

Kendrick's brothers then stepped forward and helped, all prying back the doors.

Koldo reached in, grabbed Mardig by the shirt, and yanked him out, sending him tumbling to the ground. He lay there, hands up, shaking.

"Don't kill me!" he yelled out, his voice cracking.

Koldo sneered down.

"You don't deserve death," he replied. "You deserve worse."

"You betrayed us," Ludvig said, shock in his voice. "Your brothers."

Mardig sneered back.

"You were never my brothers. We hail from the same father—that is all. That does not make you my brother."

"He killed the King," Gwen said, stepping forward.

A gasp spread through the crowd.

She looked down at him.

"Tell them," she said down to him. "Tell them what you've done."

Mardig sneered back.

"What does one more death matter now?" he asked.

Koldo sneered and stepped forward and placed his boot on Mardig's chest, looking down at him with disgust.

"Death would be too good for you," he seethed. "You wanted power, wanted this castle, and you should have it. You shall stay here in this castle, while all of us leave, while the Empire invades. It shall be yours—all yours. They shall decide what to do with you," he grinned. "I am sure they will have many ideas."

Several soldiers stepped forward and pulled Mardig to his feet, shackling him to a stone wall. He was made to stand there and watch as the steel doors opened wider, revealing a stone staircase, and women and children, grabbing torches, filtered down, deeper and deeper.

"NO!" Mardig cried out. "You can't leave me here! Please!"

But all ignored him as they continued filtering into the tunnel.

Gwen waited until the last of them entered, Kendrick, Steffen, Illepra and her baby and the others beside her, and she paused and turned and looked out one last time at the castle. The noise was deafening now, the Empire breaking through. They were at their gates, and soon, Gwen knew, all would be destroyed.

She shared a look with the others, the last remaining few, they all nodded solemnly to one another, then they all entered through the steel doors just before it slammed and locked behind them. And the last thing she heard, before being sealed in for good, was Mardig's screams, echoing throughout the empty castle.

CHAPTER THIRTY THREE

Thorgrin walked slowly up the skywalk, the mist evaporating all around him as the sun broke through, its rays streaking down, a shaft of light illuminating him as he went—and he looked out in awe at the castle ahead of him. Its door and windows were burning with light, and before it, at its doorstep, lay the Sorcerer's Ring.

After having completed the circle, Thor felt like a changed man. For the first time in his life, he no longer felt a need for a weapon, realizing the power that lay within him was far greater than that. He held within him the power to create reality—and the power to refuse the reality he saw. He had the power to realize that everything and everyone he saw before him—all friends, all enemies, all brothers, and all foes—were creations of his own mind. It was deep within his mind, he knew, that the most powerful lands lay.

As he walked on the skywalk, he knew it was real—and yet he also knew that this land lay within his own mind. The walls between what was real and what was in his mind were blurring—and for the first time, he was realizing how thin those walls were. They were two sides of the same coin, each inextricable from one another. And with every step he took, he was walking deeper into his own mind, he knew, like a waking dream.

As he reached the end of the walkway and looked up, he saw his mother standing there, arms outstretched, smiling, and he felt as if he were home. He knew he had completed a sacred journey, that he was ready for the next and final level. He realized now that his first trip to the Land of the Druids was just an introduction, not a completion; he had left something unfinished. This time, though, it was a final return. The return of a victorious warrior. A warrior who had mastered himself.

Thor stopped before the castle as he finished crossing the skywalk and stood on the stone platform, just feet away from her, from the ring that lay at her feet, and he stopped and stared. The light shining off of her was intense, and he could feel her love and approval pouring through.

"Thorgrin, my child," she said, her voice immediately setting him at ease. "You have passed every test. You have gained for yourself what I could not give you."

She held out her arms and he stepped forward and embraced her, and she embraced him back. He felt the power of the world coursing through him, and as he stood back and looked up at her, she smiled down.

"When I first saw you, I so badly wanted to warn you of all the dangers and tribulations that lay ahead of you," she said. "The losses you would suffer, the victories you would achieve. But I could not. It was for you to learn, and you to discover."

She took a deep breath

"I have watched you achieve splendor. You are a true warrior. Do you understand now the secret?" she asked. "Do you understand the essence of power?"

Thor thought it through carefully, sensing the answer to the riddle.

"The essence of power lies within ourselves," he replied.

She nodded back approvingly.

"It does not lie in weapons," he continued. "Weapons require someone else to craft them—and true power comes from within. True power requires we lean on no one else."

She smiled down, her eyes shining, and nodded.

"You have learned more than I could ever teach you," she responded. "Now, my son, you are ready. Now, you are a master. Now, you are King of the Druids."

She raised a long, thin, golden sword from her side and raised it high, shining in the sun.

"Kneel," she commanded.

Thorgrin knelt and lowered his head before her, his heart pounding.

She lowered the sword point, touching each of his shoulders lightly.

"Now rise, Thorgrin," she said. "Rise, King of the Druids."

Thor stood again, and as he did, he felt different. Older. Stronger. Unstoppable, filled with the energy of the world.

She stepped to the side and gestured, and Thor's eyes opened wide as he saw, lying on a small golden pedestal behind her, the Sorcerer's Ring.

"It is time for you to complete your destiny," she said, "and accept the ring that will change your life."

She gestured for him to step forward.

"It is a walk you can take alone," she said. "It is a ring meant for you, and you alone."

Thor stepped forward, breathless, as he approached the Ring, but feet away. A light shone from it, so bright that he at first had to raise his hands to his eyes. As he neared, he saw it was crafted of a metal he could not discern, appearing to be platinum, streaked with a single thin black ring in its middle, looking to be made of black diamonds. It shone so intensely, it made the sun seem dark.

Thor stopped before it and reached out with a trembling hand, fearing the power coming off of it, sensing that wearing it would change his life forever.

"You must wear it on your right hand, Thorgrin," his mother said. "On your index finger."

Thorgrin reached out and slipped it over his finger.

The second it touched his hand, he felt alive, truly alive, for the first time. He felt a tremendous heat pouring through it, through his finger, through his veins, through his arm, his shoulder, and spreading through his chest, to his heart. It was like a warmth filling him, a fire in his veins, a power he did not recognize. It was like the energy of the sun, filling him to capacity, making him feel so powerful, making him feel as if he could lift the sky.

It was like the power of a thousand dragons.

His mother looked back at him, and he could see in her face that she saw him differently. He knew it himself: he was different now. He no longer felt like a boy, or even a man. He felt greater than a knight, greater than a warrior, greater than a Druid. He felt like a master. He felt like a king. He felt like the King of the Druids.

As he stood there, Thor felt ready to take on the Blood Lord. He felt ready to take on his entire army.

"You are the chosen one, Thorgrin," his mother said. "Your people look to you now. Fulfill your destiny. And fulfill theirs, too."

Thorgrin reached out to embrace her, but suddenly she was gone.

Thor stood there, blinking, confused, and as he looked all around, the castle was gone. The walkway, too, was gone. He stood instead atop a single, empty cliff, on the edge of the world, the edge of nothingness, nothing but a sea of clouds all around him.

Thor heard a screech and he looked over to see Lycoples sitting but feet before him, staring back with her intense yellow eyes, waiting. She looked at him, at the ring on his finger, and he could see the new respect in her eyes.

Thor stared back, feeling his power on par with hers.

With a single bound, he leapt onto her back, feeling a power equal to that of the dragon—and even greater.

"Let us go," he commanded, "and retrieve my son."

As she flapped her wings and lifted into the air, Thor felt the thrill of battle before him. This time, he was ready.

Finally, he was ready.

CHAPTER THIRTY FOUR

Reece stood at the bow of the ship, joined by O'Connor, Elden, Indra, Matus, Angel, and Selese, leading his Legion brothers in Thor's absence, and as they sailed heading east, he focused on the destination that lay before them: the Ring. It was somewhere out there on the horizon, and as they sailed closer with each passing moment, his heart beast faster just to think of it. Finally, after all this time away, he was returning home. *Home.* It was a word which had long ago lost its meaning.

Reece felt a great deal of pressure to reach the Ring before it was too late. He knew that Thorgrin would return, would be meeting them there, and would need their help. After all, the Ring was not back in their hands yet, and that meant they would be heading into battle—indeed, the greatest battle of their lives—just as they had when leaving it. It was likely that the entire Empire would descend on it, and Reece knew it was likely that it was battle they could not survive—even with Thorgrin and his dragon.

And yet still, the thought of fighting for his homeland thrilled Reece, however bleak the odds. The idea of having a chance to inhabit it again, to rebuild it, to start life over once again in this place where he had been raised, where he had all of his memories, made him feel complete, made him feel alive again. Even if he died in the battle, it was a cause he would gladly lay down his life for. After all, what else did one have in the world if they did not have a home?

As they sailed and sailed, their ship felt empty without Thorgrin there, without his dragon, their presence missed. Now they all looked to Reece for leadership, and he knew he had big shoes to fill. He had always headed into battle with his best friend by his side, and not having him there made him feel more alone.

Yet Selese stood beside him, having barely left his side since she had joined them on the ship. Reece had grown used to her as a constant presence, so grateful he'd had a second chance with her. The two of them had sailed nearly halfway around the world together, ever since she had emerged from the Land of the Dead, and Reece now couldn't imagine life without her. He had been so grateful to have her back, to have a chance to rectify his errors, to have a second chance at love with her.

Reese turned to see Selese looking at him, her light blue eyes angelic, looking more beautiful in the morning light than he'd ever seen her. She stared back, so serene as she always was, an ethereal quality to her. Indeed, since she had left the Land of the Dead, it was as if a part of her were not really here.

When she looked at him this time, her eyes were watering, and Reece could sense a special intensity to her gaze; he sensed right away that something was wrong.

"What is it, my love?" he asked, concerned, as he reached for her hand.

She stared into his eyes.

"This time we have had together has made my life," she said, holding his hand.

Reece felt a pang of concern at her words, at their finality.

"What do you mean?" he asked, struggling to understand.

"We were given a second chance, don't you see?" she said. "I was meant to stay below, in the Land of the Dead, and you brought me back. Your love brought me back."

She paused, and in the silence that followed, he wondered where she was going with this.

"But there was a deal I made," she finally continued, "a price I had to pay. I knew I was not meant to be with you again forever. It was always meant to be fleeting. Just a chance for us to rectify what we had lost."

Reece stared at her, his heart pounding, feeling a sinking sense of foreboding.

"What are you speaking of, my love?" he asked.

She looked off into the horizon, and her eyes, so light, filled with tears, nearly glowed.

"Our time together has come to an end," she said as she turned and faced him, her eyes watering. She reached up and touched his cheek, caressing it, her skin so soft.

"But I want you to know that I've always loved you," she added, as his heart broke. "And I will always love you. I shall be looking down on you, always. And always with you."

Reece grasped her hand as hard as he could, not wanting to let go.

"You can't leave now," he pleaded, a wave of desperation washing over him. "It's not fair. I won't let you."

He clasped even harder, trying to hold on, but even as he did, he felt her hand disappearing, ebbing away, as if there were nothing left to hold onto.

She smiled through her tears.

"You can never let go of me," she said. "Nor I of you. We shall always be together."

Selese leaned in and kissed him, and he kissed her back, feeling his own eyes watering, as he felt her fading from him.

"I must go, my love," she said softly, crying. "Life is coming for you. A new life. But for new life to come, sometimes, death must come first."

Selese pulled away from him, Reece feeling her slipping through his fingers, and she backed up until she was at the rail. Then she gently fell backwards, over the railing, falling overboard and into the water.

Strangely, Reece never heard a splash.

"Selese!" Reese called out.

Reece rushed to the rail, the others, alarmed at his voice, went rushing over, too. He reached it and looked over, prepared to jump in after her.

But he spotted her already impossibly far from the ship, floating on her back, arms spread out, a smile on her face. A mist rolled in, rainbow-colored, embracing her, obscuring her.

Moments later, she disappeared beneath the surface, and he knew, he just knew, that she was gone from him forever.

"SELESE!" he called out in anguish, gripping the rail so hard his knuckles turned white.

He peered into the mist, wondering how the universe could take her away from him, and as he did, out of the mist, he was shocked to see something else appearing, floating toward the ship.

Reece did a double-take, wondering if he were seeing this. Out of the mist there approached a small vessel, a tiny boat with a single, tattered sail. Inside there lay a body, unmoving.

The current carried it out of the mist and right for their ship, until it finally smacked against the hull. Reece stared down, baffled—and as he did, his heart stopped in astonishment.

Death brings forth life.

Reece's breath caught in his throat. He looked down and saw lying there, unmoving, a woman he had once loved.

There, alone in the vast sea, unconscious, was Stara.

CHAPTER THIRTY FIVE

Gwendolyn hurried through the tunnel with the others, hundreds of them jogging through the dark, cavernous passageway, the only light cast from the bouncing torches held in soldiers' hands. Gwen led the pack beside Koldo, fleeing for her life with the rest of the Ridge, leading them deeper and deeper through a tunnel which she only prayed led to freedom.

Kendrick and his men ran beside her, along with Steffen and several others, Krohn at her heels, and as they twisted and turned down the endless tunnel, voices of fear echoing in the darkness, she realized how dangerous this was. Right now, she and hundreds of others ran deep below the lakes, in a tunnel not used for centuries, one that could collapse at any moment. The tunnel echoed eerily with the sound of chaos, of panic, of people running from their homeland into a dark unknown, only torches to light the way, hoping that somehow it would lead to freedom. And rising above their sounds, even more ominous, was the distant sound of something else: a slamming on the metal doors. The Empire was trying to crash them down, to get in, to follow them, and they pounded relentlessly. It was like a pounding on Gwen's heart.

Gwendolyn looked up ahead, saw nothing but more blackness, and she wondered if they would escape in time—or if this tunnel even led to freedom.

"Are you certain it is not stopped up?" she asked Koldo, who was jogging beside her.

He shook his head grimly.

"I am not certain of anything," he replied darkly. "The tunnel was built before my father's time. My father never had occasion to use it. None of us had. It is an escape route—and we have never had to escape."

Gwen felt a sense of foreboding.

"Are you saying it could lead to death?" Kendrick asked.

180

"It may," he replied. "But behind us, don't forget, is certain death."

They all continued running, picking up their pace, and as they did, there came a horrendous crash from far behind them, enough to make Gwen jump. It echoed and boomed off the walls, and it sounded as if the metal doors had been not only bashed in, but destroyed.

Worse, this was soon followed by a cheer—the cheer of thousands of soldiers out for blood, inside the tunnel.

Gwen's heart dropped; she knew they had broken through. Already, they were closing in fast. She could hear their voices, too close. They, after all, had a professional army, had horses. Gwen, on the other hand, had a huge, unwieldy crowd of civilians, moving along too slowly despite her best efforts.

As they turned another corner, Gwen strained to see into blackness—but still, there was nothing but more tunnel.

"We must stand and fight!" Koldo cried out, reaching for his sword, determination in his face.

But Gwen was equally determined; she had been in evacuations before.

"No!" she countered. "If we fight, we shall all die in here. Behind us is certain death. Up ahead lies the only path to freedom."

Koldo looked hesitant, deliberating.

"You are a leader now, Koldo," she added. "You must decide as your father would—not as a warrior would. These people are yours. They are your responsibility. They don't have the luxury of valorous decisions. You must think of the general good. We must not stop."

She could see Koldo would consent, though unhappily. Behind them, the Empire voices grew louder.

"I shall give it one more bend in the tunnel," he said. "If the exit does not appear, then we shall turn and face them. And we will die as men—not as dogs with our backs to them."

Gwendolyn ran with the group, her heart pounding in her mouth, praying that as they made the turn there would be a change in the tunnel, something, any sign of hope, up ahead. She knew if they stopped and fought the Empire, they would all die down here, trapped underground. She did not mind dying—but she hated to see all these innocents die, and she felt a responsibility to them.

Gwen was all for valor; and yet, she knew great leaders had to pick their battles. As a Queen, she had been in that position many a time. Koldo might be a great commander, but he had never before had to think as a ruler. And being a ruler, sometimes, was humbling.

They turned the corner, Gwen gasping for air, her lungs killing her, not sure how much further she could go on, and as they did, her heart lifted with relief to see, in the distance, a shaft of light. Up ahead there was a small opening in the tunnel, leading back up to the desert floor. It was but a hundred yards away.

Koldo looked at her, and she could see the relief on his face, too. He nodded at her in respect.

"A wise decision, my lady," he admitted.

With the cacophony of the Empire growing ever louder behind them, they ran for their lives, all of them picking up the pace for the final stretch, and soon they reached the exit. Gwen stepped aside with the other warriors and let the women and children pass, followed by all the citizens.

When everyone had passed through Gwen prepared to leave—when Koldo raised a hand and gestured.

Gwen looked up and followed his finger and saw, high up on the wall, a huge iron wheel, rusted with age.

"Before we go," Koldo said, "why don't we leave them a little parting present?"

Gwen looked at him questioningly.

"What did you have in mind?" she asked.

She heard a shout and looked back over her shoulder and her heart dropped to see the Empire army turn the corner, now in sight and racing right for them.

"The tunnel lies beneath the lakes," he said, "and that wheel opens the valves."

He looked at her with a serious expression.

"We can flood this place," he added.

Gwen looked up at the wheel in awe.

"It will not keep them back forever," he said, "but it will buy us time."

Gwendolyn nodded in approval, and as she did, their men broke into action. They followed Koldo's lead as a dozen of their best warriors, including Koldo's brothers and Kendrick, jumped for the wheel, yanking at its rusted iron crank.

They pulled with all their might, and at first nothing happened.

Gwen turned and looked with apprehension at the army closing in on them, now less than a hundred yards away, then turned and looked back to the tunnel exit. A part of her wanted them all to leave it be and dash to freedom—but another part knew they had to do this to assure their safety.

The man yanked again, straining and groaning with the effort—and this time there came a creaking noise, and Gwen's heart leapt to see the wheel start to move. At first it moved a few inches—then a lot more.

The men gave one huge pull, shouting, and suddenly the wheel spun in a full circle.

There came the sound of a steel valve opening, followed by rushing water, and Gwen turned and watched, amazed, as water began pouring out from pipes on either side of the cave.

The men pulled and turned the wheel, spinning it in several circles, and water suddenly came gushing in, flooding the tunnel.

It swooshed and swelled in every direction, and Gwen yanked on Koldo's and Kendrick's arms, realizing their exit would soon be blocked.

"IT'S ENOUGH!" she cried.

They all turned and ran with her as they scrambled to get up and out of the tunnel, barely making it through the exit as the water level rose, and as more valves opened and more water gushed through.

Outside, in the safety of the Waste with all the other survivors, Gwen stopped with the warriors at the entrance to the tunnel and looked behind her one last time. Inside, water gushed like a river through the tunnel, and the Empire soldiers stopped, faces frozen in fear, and turned to flee. But it was too late. Their shrieks rose up, echoing, as they were swallowed by the water like a tide.

Gwen turned and looked at Koldo, Kendrick, and the others, and they looked back at her, all sharing a look of satisfaction as they turned, mounted their horses with the others, and all began the journey away from here, away from the Ridge, and somewhere north, toward freedom.

*

Gwendolyn kicked her horse, urging it to go faster, excited at the sight before her as she crossed with the great throng through the Waste. They had been riding all day, and now, before them, was the sight that Koldo had promised would come: there, on the horizon, were the Crystal Lakes, the pools of water that branched out to the all the rivers of the Empire. It was a vast body of water, nearly translucent, shining, reflecting the desert suns, and now, finally, it lay several hundred yards away. She was so grateful it did; she did not know how much longer this throng could have tolerated the Waste.

Gwen was in awe at how meticulously the King had planned this escape route from the Ridge, prepared for a contingency like this. She looked out and saw all the ships on the horizon, hidden at the shores behind the branches of willow trees, and she realized that the King had planned for it all. He knew it would not be enough for his people to only exit the tunnel into Waste. He knew that, in the event of an invasion, his people would have to flee somewhere far away, across the Empire. And those dozens of ships at the water's edge represented their lifeline, their ticket out.

Gwendolyn looked out at the sight with relief; they would finally have a way out of here, back out of the Empire, away from the Ridge. They would have ships and rivers that led to open water, to the open sea, to a chance for freedom. She could not help but think of Argon's master's words, of her leading this people back to the Ring, and her heart quickened at the thought. It was all happening. It felt surreal.

And the idea of embarking on a journey to return *home*, after all this time, made her ecstatic. It filled her with a new sense of purpose— especially if it meant a chance to be reunited with Thorgrin and Guwayne again.

They all came to a stop beneath the grove of trees beside the ships, they and their horses all winded. The suns hung low in the sky, now, and Gwen watched the hundreds of people dismounting, kneeling at the water, rinsing their faces and necks, drinking, and making their way to the ships, in awe.

The ships remained concealed, as the King must have planned in his wisdom, perfectly sheltered behind trees and in large caves filled with water. Unless one knew they were there, they would never be found. There were dozens of ships, enough to transport all of these people. Gwen could feel the King looking down, and she was in awe at his foresight.

Gwen glanced back over her shoulder, out at the great Waste, and she thought of the thousands of Empire soldiers somewhere out there, surely pursuing them. For now all was empty and still, but she wondered how long it would be until they all caught up. She knew there wasn't much time.

"Do you think the flood killed them all?" she asked Koldo, who came up beside her.

He shook his head, glancing back gravely.

"Those valves only run so long," he said. "The first wave of water will kill the frontline. But the rest will make it through soon enough. They are probably halfway across the Waste by now."

"But they have no ships," Ludvig said, stepping up beside them.

Koldo gave him a look.

"The Empire's unstoppable," he replied. "They will find a way. They have one million men; they have tools. They can build ships."

He sighed and studied the landscape.

"They are perhaps half a day behind us. With a day without wind, without our sails at full mast, they can catch us."

"Then there's no time to waste," Kendrick said, joining them and walking for the ships. They all fell in beside him.

"Let us each take command of a different ship," Koldo suggested, looking at Gwen and Kendrick and Ludvig and Kaden. "We need strong leaders on each one."

They all agreed and they broke up, each heading in different directions as they boarded the sailing ships, each large enough to hold perhaps a hundred men. As Gwen reached hers, Steffen beside her and Krohn at her heels, she reached up, grabbed hold of the long rope ladder dangling down, and pulled herself up. As she reached the top, she turned, and Steffen reached up and handed Krohn to her, and soon they were both up over the rail and onto the deck.

They were followed by dozens of soldiers and citizens of the Ridge, all filling up the ships, one at a time. They all pitched in, realizing the urgency, each of them setting to work to immediately raise sails or grab oars. They were all wordlessly a fine-tuned machine, each united in their desire to flee as far from the Empire as possible, each of them determined to find a new shore, to make another life.

"And where shall we go now?" came a voice.

Gwen turned and looked over to see a citizen of the Ridge, a woman holding a small child, looking back at her with a hopeful face. She saw behind her a small crowd, all looking to her with hope, for answers. Gwen felt a great responsibility to lead them well.

She glanced over at the other ships, and she saw Koldo and the others looking to her, too, all falling silent. Gwen knew the time had come to tell them.

"We sail to the Ring!" she announced definitively, the sound of authority carrying in her voice impressing even her. It was her father's voice.

She could see the look of surprise in their faces—especially in those of Kendrick, Brandt, and Atme, of her people.

"It was your father's wish," Gwendolyn said to Koldo, "for me to lead your people to safety. The Ring is the only place I know."

"But it is destroyed!" Brandt called out.

Gwen shook her head.

"It can be rebuilt," she replied. "The Empire has vacated. It is ours for the taking."

"But the Shield is down!" Atme called.

Gwen sighed.

"It will not be easy," she said. "But it has been prophesied. The Ring, one day, will rise again."

Gwen wished, more than ever, that Argon were here now, with her, to explain. But as usual, he was nowhere to be found.

"There is a sacred Ring," she continued. "The Sorcerer's Ring. Thorgrin even now quests for it. We must sail forth. If he finds it in time, he shall meet us there, and can help us restore the Ring."

"And if your prophecy is wrong?" Ludvig asked. "If Thor does not find this Ring?"

Gwendolyn felt a heavy silence as they all looked to her.

"It is a leap of faith we must take," she said. "Yet life is always a leap of faith."

They all fell silent, realizing the challenges that lay ahead, and Koldo nodded back, gravely.

"I respect the Queen's decision!" he called out, and Gwen appreciated his using that title. It made her fell as if she were, indeed, a Queen again. And if they were returning to the Ring, perhaps, indeed, she was.

The people, satisfied, all continued on, breaking back into motion, hoisting sails and shoving off. Soon their ship was moving, Gwen feeling the currents catching, carrying it. She looked back and saw, with relief, the shoreline of the Waste grow further and further.

Gwendolyn made her way to the bow of the ship, looking out at the waters ahead, thrilled to feel motion beneath her, the gentle rising and falling of the ship, and as she did, her new people congregated around her hopefully. She felt like a messiah, leading her people for a new horizon, a new home, for a place to finally be free.

CHAPTER THIRTY SIX

Thorgrin cut through the air on the back of Lycoples, returning from the Land of the Ring, and feeling the power radiating off of the Sorcerer's Ring as he wore it on his finger, clutching the dragon's scales. Thor felt like a different person since wearing it, like a bigger version of himself, stronger, more powerful—able to do anything. He felt the energy of the Ring throbbing on his finger, and was in awe of the bright light that it cast off. He had never encountered an object more powerful in his life. Wearing it felt all-consuming, as if he were lost in its universe.

He also felt empowered, as he if understood for the first time what it meant to be alive. He knew that the ring represented a great victory, the culmination of all the tests and trials and training he'd ever had, all the obstacles he'd overcome, all the setbacks he had not backed down from. It was more than a ring of power: it was a ring of destiny. A ring of completion.

Thorgrin raced through the skies, knowing that anything was possible now. He knew that any foes that had been too strong, any places too dark, he now had the power to confront. And his trials were not yet done. They were, in fact, just beginning.

The Sorcerer's Ring, he realized, demanded a price: it demanded the best of whoever wore it, demanded them to climb to ever higher heights, face ever greater foes, greater trials. For Thorgrin, he knew that meant facing his worst enemy, facing the one place that had defeated him, the one place he'd had to flee: the Land of Blood. It meant returning, facing the Blood Lord again, trying once again to save Guwayne. It meant returning to the place of his defeat, and having the courage to confront it one more time, now that he was a different person.

And if he lived, Thor knew the Ring would then demand of him one more sacred responsibility: to return to the Ring itself, to the land of its birth, to fight to take it back, to save Gwendolyn and the exiles. He felt the Sorcerer's Ring calling him there, demanding it of him.

But first he had to save Guwayne.

"Faster, Lycoples!" Thorgrin called out to his friend, his heart pounding with anticipation as the horizon began to shift.

Lycoples, empowered by the presence of the Ring, flew faster than Thorgrin could remember, and she lowered her head, Thor gripping her scales, and burst through the clouds. Up ahead, Thor saw the landscape change: the bright skies overhead came to an abrupt end as they met the waterfalls of blood, the chilling entrance to the Land of Blood.

Thor felt a moment of apprehension, recalling his past failures in this place. He remembered what it was like to enter a world too strong for him, to be besieged by bouts of madness, by a seductress. It was a place of darkness that knew no bounds, a place he had not been strong enough to face.

But that was the old Thorgrin. Now, having passed his final tests, and wearing the Sorcerer's Ring, he was stronger. It was time to put himself to the test, to face his demons. And most importantly, his son lay beyond that wall—he could not abandon him. He would retrieve him, or die trying.

Lycoples screeched as they approached the waterfalls of blood, hesitant, and Thorgrin recalled her being unable to enter before. But this time, he knew, it would be different. This time, they had the Ring.

"Onward, Lycoples," Thor whispered. "You are untouchable now."

Thor held out his hand with the Ring on it, and as he did, an aura of red light slowly spread and encased them, like a bubble.

Lycoples stretched out her great wings and screeched, and Thor could sense her hesitation; but she trusted him, lowered her head, and flew forward in faith.

Thor felt himself encased in blood as they both entered the waterfalls. They were immersed in the deafening waters gushing down, splashing all around them. But the aura spread over them, and the water bounced off of it harmlessly, keeping them safe and dry, flying through it as they would a cloud.

Soon, they emerged on the other side, to Thor's relief.

Lycoples screeched with joy, with victory, as they did, bursting out into the Land of Blood. It was a stark contrast. Here, the clouds hung low, were thick and heavy, black, ominous. There was no sun to speak of, and the land below was grim, covered in ash, as Thor remembered it. Thor felt himself tensing up at the sight of it, remembering all that had happened—but he forced himself to fly on.

They flew over the sea of blood, racing by landscapes of dead trees, of dried lava, the entire land looking charred and desolate, as if nothing could live here. They flew and flew, so fast Thor could hardly catch his breath, covering more ground in a minute than they had in days with the ship. Down below, every now and again, Thor spotted a lone monster on the landscape, looking up and roaring at them, and he knew that if they were down there, it would like nothing more than to tear them to shreds.

Finally, Thor spotted the place that had haunted his nightmares: the castle of the Blood Lord. He tensed up at the sight of it. There it sat on the horizon, like mud that had risen from the earth and hardened, its sinister glowing lights within it. Thor could feel the gloom of it even from here. And yet his heart quickened, every fiber of his being on fire, as he knew his son lay beyond its walls.

Lycoples flew and flew, over the shattered gatehouse, over the winding canals leading to it. He was further now than he'd ever been in the Land of Blood, past the Straits of Madness, past the Enchantress, and he knew there was nothing left now between him and the castle.

Thor expected her to fly right to the castle gate—but she surprised him by coming to a stop several hundred yards before it, as if she'd hit an invisible wall, and diving down low. It was some sort of sorcerer's bubble, he realized, even more powerful than the bubble cast by the Ring.

As she prepared to land, Lycoples, Thorgrin realized, could go no further.

Thor dismounted as Lycoples set them down on the road leading to the castle, and he looked over at the road before them. It was a long approach, the road made of smooth, blackened brick, its gleaming pathway lined with torches and with pikes, each impaled by a severed head.

Thor looked at Lycoples and she stared back, and he sensed that she wanted to go on—but she could not.

I shall wait for you here, she said in his mind's eye. *You shall return, warrior. With your son.*

Thorgrin reached up and stroked her head and turned toward the castle. He drew the Sword of the Dead from its scabbard with its distinctive ring, turned, and took the first step onto the road, knowing he would have to go it alone.

Thor walked, then jogged, then ran down the path, passing all the impaled heads of others who had been foolish enough to come here. He sprinted with all he had, knowing his son was in that tower, desperate to lay eyes on him again.

As he ran, approaching the stone drawbridge spanning a moat, Thor looked down to see the floor of the drawbridge was lined with spikes, and the moat's blackened waters were teaming with snapping alligators and hideous creatures he did not recognize. He saw them gorging on human flesh, body parts floating in the water.

As he looked up, approaching the bridge, he saw two guards standing before it, in all-black armor, twice as tall as he, each holding long halberds as they guarded the entrance.

Thor never slowed; he continued sprinting, sword drawn, and as they broke into action, raising their halberds and swinging for him, he felt the power of the Ring propelling him forward. Faster than he'd ever been, stronger than he'd ever been, Thor leapt into the air—higher than ever—flying over the heads of the soldiers. With one clean slash, he chopped off one of their heads, then leapt across the bridge and chopped off the other.

Their halberds fell harmlessly to the ground as they each collapsed, dead.

Thor looked down at the spikes before him, and he took a running leap. In a single bound he leapt over the drawbridge, over all the spikes, and landed before the door to the castle.

Thor examined it. It was an immense door, thirty feet high, shaped in a huge arch, made of iron and wood—but Thor did not feel intimidated by it. Instead, he reached up, grabbed the knocker, and with one pull, with the strength of a giant, he tore the door off it hinges, the power of the Ring coursing through him as he did.

It was time for payback.

As Thor tore off the door, he faced a grim blackness, the inside lit only by the faint orange glow of torches. A freezing cold gale rushed out at him, damp and cold, feeling like souls being released from hell. There was a faint moaning and howling in the air, as if Thorgrin were entering another realm of hell.

Thor rushed inside, refusing to give in to his fears, thinking only of his son. He ran through the gloom and blackness, sword drawn, ready for anything, and as he did, he suddenly heard the screech of what sounded like a gargoyle.

Thor suddenly detected motion, and he looked up to see one of the hideous creatures from Ragon's isle, one that had snatched Guwayne, hanging upside down from the ceiling. Its glowing yellow eyes fixed on him, startled by his presence, and its face suddenly contorted in a sneer of rage as it released its claws, swooped down from the ceiling, and plunged right for him, screeching.

Thor reacted, the Ring increasing his speed and reflexes. He stepped forward and met it, slashing the Sword of the Dead and cutting the creature in half.

Thor sprinted through the castle, barely slowing to get his bearings, realizing dimly that this place was made of mud and stone, its walls warped. He ran through vast open chambers, his footsteps echoing, and down narrow, twisting and turning corridors, the floor made of mud; he jumped over lava streams and ran through empty rooms with walls made of ancient black granite. He ran through a huge arch and found himself in a chamber with a ceiling so high, he could not even find it.

Thor heard a great cacophony, louder than the sound of his own breathing, his own pounding heart, and he realized he'd run into a nest of these gargoyles. The chamber lit up with their glowing yellow eyes, and they all screeched and began swooping down at him. It was as if he'd disturbed their nest.

Thor slashed one after another, like huge bats coming for him. He was in the zone as he fought, feeling the Ring propelling him, slashing each one expertly, ducking and dodging the claws that came for his face. He slashed one, severing its wings, stabbed another, ducked, then jabbed backwards and knocked down yet another with the hilt of the sword. He felt more dexterous than he ever had, the Ring giving him a buoyancy, a power unlike any he'd ever known. It was almost as if it were telling him when to strike before he did.

Thor continued sprinting through this cave, running blindly forward, not knowing where he was going, where his son was, but feeling the Ring urging him on. He was like a wild animal racing through, able to see and hear and react ten times faster than he'd ever had. He fought as he ran, until finally he was out of the chamber.

Thor burst into another cavernous room, and he was shocked by what he saw. This room was lit up, streams of lava running along its edge, letting off enough light to see by as they sparked and hissed—and as he saw, Thor wished he didn't. The screeching of the gargoyles was intensified in here, and as he looked up, he saw thousands of them blackening the ceiling, their wings fluttering, filling his ears, like a den of bats crisscrossing the room.

Thor knew he should be afraid—but he was not. He did not feel fear. He felt focus. Intensity. He knew he was facing his worst enemies, and instead of wanting to flee, he felt privileged to be able to have the chance to stand against them.

Thor moved faster than he could ever imagine, faster than even he himself could control. The Sword of the Dead was like a live being in his hand, directing him to slash and turn and spin and stab, allowing him to fell creatures left and right as he cut through the room, a single wave of destruction, felling gargoyles in every direction. Sharp fangs protruded from the Sword's hilt, and they extended and killed creatures, too.

But it was the Ring, Thorgrin knew, that propelled him to fight on another level. As Thor's shoulders began to weaken, to tire, exhausted from spinning, slashing, reacting, hacking down so many of these things, he felt the Ring shoot a wave of energy up his arm, refreshing him, renewing his strained shoulder, as if he had just arrived to battle. When several gargoyles attacked him from behind and Thor could not turn to react in time, he felt the Ring turn and direct his arm, and he watched in awe as the Ring shot out an orb of light that knocked the gargoyles back across the room.

Their carcasses piling up all around them, the gargoyles began to realize the inevitable. They backed off, dozens of them, all that was left of the thousands, retreating to the far corners of the cavern, now scared of Thorgrin.

Thorgrin finally stopped fighting, breathing hard, and he surveyed the chamber in the stillness. Straight ahead, in the distance, on the far side of the chamber, he noticed a series of black granite steps leading upward, carved into a mountain. And as he looked up, at its top he saw an immense throne, twenty feet wide, covered in black diamonds, and he knew it was the throne of the Blood Lord.

Yet it sat vacant.

Thor was baffled, wondering why the Blood Lord was not here. Perhaps he had not been expecting Thor, had never thought he could arrive here, to his inner chamber.

And as Thorgrin heard a sudden cry, he looked back up again, his body on high alert, and studied the chamber closely—and he was even more shocked by what he saw: there, sitting beside the throne, hiding in the shadows, was a shining golden bassinet.

Guwayne.

There came another cry, and Thorgrin's heart lifted at the sound. Guwayne. He was really here, alive, unharmed, at the side of the throne.

Thor did not hesitate. He broke into a dash, sprinting up the steps, taking them three, four, five, six at a time, until he reached the top. And as Thor raced by the throne, he suddenly stopped, feeling the strangest thing happen. It was as if the throne were magnetic. It was as if it wanted Thor to sit in it. To rule. To become King of the Dead.

Thor stopped before it, shaking, barely able to fend off its power. He looked back and forth between it and Guwayne, knowing he should snatch Guwayne and leave.

But as he stood there, his knees grew weak. He felt the Ring vibrating on his finger, trying to help him, and he knew he was caught in a supreme test of will. It was an ever harder test than confronting the Blood Lord: he was confronting himself. His own deepest, darkest impulses.

You, Thorgrin, are meant to be here, a voice rang out. *You are meant to be King. The Dark King. Sit, and feel the seat of power. Embrace us, rule here, and you can have powers beyond your wildest dreams. Sit, and finally be King.*

The Ring burned hotter and hotter on Thor's finger as he leaned forward, barely able to contain his desires, about to sit on the throne.

But then, at the last moment, Thor felt a searing flash of power course through the Ring and through his body, pushing him away, as if stung. He turned away from it.

"NO!" he shouted.

Thor instead turned to Guwayne, just feet away. His heart pounded as he lunged forward to embrace him, bracing himself, fearing that he might, like last time, find it empty. He could not take another disappointment.

But as Thor reached down he was elated to see Guwayne in the bassinet—and he reached down and scooped him up and held him, feeling overwhelmed with emotion.

Guwayne cried as Thorgrin held him, and Thor felt the tears running down his own cheeks, elated to hold him again, to see him alive, healthy, unharmed. Thorgrin held him tight, feeling Guwayne's power course through him as he stood there. He felt that he was a very powerful child, more powerful even than Thor would ever be. He felt within Guwayne a power for good or for evil, and he shuddered, recalling the prophecy that his son would turn to darkness. He prayed it was not true. As long as he was alive, Thorgrin would do everything he could to shelter him, to prevent that.

As Thorgrin lifted Guwayne from the bassinet, as he turned his back on the throne, suddenly, the entire castle, as if furious, began to shake. The walls began to crumble, to shake and collapse, as if Thorgrin had stolen from them their most precious possession. The gargoyles began to drop down from the ceiling, to fly away, to flee the room, as boulders began to drop and the ground began quaked.

Thor realized they had little time. He clutched Guwayne tight, turned, and fled from the chamber, rushing down the steps four at a time, racing back through the cavernous room, dodging falling boulders as he went, all of them crashing beside him in a cacophony of dust.

Thor twisted and turned his way in the darkness, back down the tunnels, racing for his life as the castle began to collapse all around him, Guwayne screaming in his arms. But as long as he held on tight to Guwayne, nothing mattered to him anymore.

Thor saw the exit to the castle up ahead, and he saw the walls collapsing all around it, leaving but a sliver through which to escape. He gave it one last sprint to the finish.

A moment later, Thor burst out of the castle, bumped roughly by a boulder that smashed his shoulder, sending him stumbling. But he kept running, never stopping, and as soon as he burst through, the entire castle crumbled in one huge avalanche of rock.

Thorgrin ran and ran, escaping the spreading avalanche, the mound of rubble, sprinting for his life. He leapt back over the bridge of spikes, ran back down the pathway, the long trail leading back to Lycoples. The ground shook, as if the whole Land of Blood were collapsing, and a fissure in the ground began to open right behind Thor. It spread wider and wider, chasing after him as he went, a great chasm opening to the bowels of the earth, and Thor ran for his life, knowing he was but a step away from death.

Thor looked up, saw Lycoples waiting, and as reached her, leaping onto her back, never slowing, she screeched and lifted off, as anxious to go as he was.

The second she did the fissure spread on the ground right beneath where they had just been, and Thor knew that if they had waited just one more second, they would have all been finished.

Thor held onto Lycoples, clutching Guwayne, who finally fell silent in his arms. Flying in the air, holding his son, lifting off, away from this place, he felt restored again. He could hardly believe it. He had made it. This time, he had won.

They sped through the air, and Thorgrin and Lycoples both knew where they were going. There was one place left for them to go in the world. A place that would be the scene of an epic war. A place where, Thor knew, the Blood Lord and all his hosts would follow. The place where Gwendolyn, his Legion brothers, and all his people awaited him.

It was time to return home.

It was time, finally, to fight for the Ring.

CHAPTER THIRTY SEVEN

The Blood Lord arose from his ancient slumber, disoriented, in complete shock. He had felt his castle shaking all around him, rousing him from his sleep, had felt a great disruption in the force, had felt instantly that someone had intruded in his sacred space.

It was impossible. No one had ever before approached his castle—much less broken inside it. Not in a thousand millennia.

At first, the Blood Lord assumed it had been a nightmare. But as the walls continued to shake and crumble all around him, deep underground, he soon realize that it was not. It was a disruption unlike anything he had ever felt. And as he sat up, at attention, he sensed immediately that the boy was gone.

Guwayne.

The Blood Lord let out a horrific shriek as he jumped to his feet then jumped straight up, raising a fist and shattering the stone. He flew up, through the floor, bursting out of the rock into the chambers above.

As he stood there, in a room now filled with rubble, he was distraught. Around him, nearly all of his precious gargoyles lay dead, crushed, writhing. The few who remained were screeching and circling high above.

He turned immediately and looked up, for his throne, for the bassinet—and with a sense of horror and dread, he saw that his throne was crushed, and that the bassinet lay empty. Someone had snatched the child.

The Blood Lord seethed, as he realized immediately who it was: Thorgrin. He had snatched away his child. He had taken away his most precious jewel, this power child whom he'd hoped to raise as his own, whom he'd groom to become greatest darkest Lord of them all. Whom he would use to rule the world—just as the prophecies had proclaimed.

197

Yet he did not understand how it was possible. He was more powerful than Thorgrin; he had already defeated him once. Thorgrin did not have that kind of power—unless, he suddenly realized, he had retrieved the sacred Sorcerer's Ring. Had he?

The Blood Lord shrieked in agony, seeing his whole life's mission destroyed, feeling his veins burning with fury, with a desire for vengeance. He knew instantly what he had to do: find Thorgrin. Crush him. Retrieve the child.

And he knew instantly that there was only one place that Thorgrin could have taken him: the Ring.

He leapt up, as the walls continued to collapse, and this time he burst right through, out the other side of his castle, into daylight, smashing through rock with his fist. He emerged on the ground, outside his castle, and immediately he looked up and searched the skies. There, in the distance, on the far horizon, he spotted Thorgrin. He was flying away on the back of a dragon, and holding something.

Guwayne. His child.

The Blood Lord howled in fury, his face contorted in agony, and he knew there was only one thing he could do: muster his army.

He put his palms out to his side, turned them, and slowly raised them, higher and higher. As he did, all around him the landscape of ash and mud began to crawl, to squirm, to come alive. There slowly emerged from the black soil an army. An army of undead, emerging as if from a field of eggs, reaching up out of the soil with their long, hideous red claws and pulling themselves up. They looked like gargoyles, but were five times the size, with blackened scales, hairy bodies, and long, slimy fangs. They had wings as long as their bodies, and tails just as long, which flopped against the soil. They stared back at the Blood Lord with their glowing orange eyes, thousands of them, awaiting his command, drooling, shrieking. Wanting to kill something. Anything.

Thorgrin had made a grave mistake. The Blood Lord was no primitive sorcerer. No local king. He was the Lord of all Lords, the one who could raise an army from dust, the one that no one had ever defeated. The one who had punished anyone who had dared defy him.

Thorgrin had provoked a nest the likes of which the world had never known. He would follow him to the ends of the earth, until the earth was scorched with his creatures, and tear him—and his son—to pieces.

The time had come to destroy the world.

And the first stop on his mission could be but one place:

The Ring.

CHAPTER THIRTY EIGHT

Gwen and her people sailed at a good speed downriver, the wind picking up, the currents getting stronger, sailing further and further east, the suns low in the sky, the shores of the Waste not even visible anymore on the horizon. Gwen looked down at Krohn at her feet, looked over at Steffen at her side, Koldo, Ludvig, Kaden, Ruth and Kendrick manning the ships beside her, and she felt fortunate. The reality of their situation was starting to sink in: they had escaped. Despite all odds, they had fled the Ridge, had saved hundreds, and had made it out to open water.

They made good speed, the sails full, the river tides pulling them out toward the sea, which she knew lay somewhere on the horizon. She knew that once they reached the open sea, they would be far from the mainland of the Empire, farther from their clutches, and closer and closer to the Ring.

Yet for now, as they still navigated these narrow rivers, Empire land on either side of them, other rivers still feeding into this one from all directions, Gwen was still very much on guard. They twisted and turned through the landscape of the Empire, and Gwendolyn knew they could not relax yet; they were still deep in hostile territory. They were still vulnerable to attack from all sides. And if the Empire blocked their way, or caught up with them before they made it out to open sea, they would die here, in this land.

Gwen heard a gushing of water up ahead, and she looked out in the dim light and saw the river currents changing. They were approaching an intersection, several major rivers of the Empire merging in this spot, widening the river and strengthening the current. She was relieved to see the tides grow stronger, knowing they would gain momentum—yet she was anxious to see this river being fed into by dozens of rivers. Empire ships could arrive from any direction in the Empire.

As they merged into this new river, the ship bobbing wildly as the currents picked up, Gwen suddenly heard a distant horn sound, and her heart dropped. It was a sound she recognized well: the war horn of the Empire.

Gwendolyn looked back over her shoulder, and she saw another sight that made her blood run cold: a thousand arrows blackened the sky, like a flock of bats, soaring in a high arc, then dropping down right for them.

"GET DOWN!" she yelled.

They all took cover as the arrows all dropped in the waters behind them, splashing like a school of fish. Gwen looked up and sighed with relief to see the arrows land just short of their fleet.

But then her heart stopped to see dozens of Empire ships sailing after them, catching up from all the different rivers, now pursuing them and nearly in range. Their ships were sleeker, faster, and she could see in an instant that they would soon overtake them.

Gwen realized their chances had just dwindled to almost none. They could not fight off this fleet—not with their meager numbers, weapons, and ships. And yet the thought of being captured again by the Empire was something she could not tolerate.

She looked over at the other ships, at Koldo, Kaden, Ludvig, and Kendrick, and saw the same disconsolate look on their faces. They were all prepared to fight—and yet they all knew this meant defeat.

Before they could call out commands, Gwen flinched as there came another sudden sound of arrows soaring through the air—yet this time, when she looked up, she was confused: the arrows came from in front of them, sailing over their ship in the other direction. Had they been surrounded, flanked in both directions?

Gwen turned, expecting to see more Empire ships—and was shocked and elated to see it was something else entirely. She could hardly believe to see these were people she knew, recognized, loved. People from the Ring.

Erec smiled back, beside him, Alistair—and Godfrey on his other side, Dray at his heels. They all stood at the bow, as Erec commanded a fleet of soldiers from the Southern Isles, along with a fleet of freed slaves of the Empire. She watched with admiration and hope as Erec sailed forward, right for her, and commanded his fleet to fire arrows back at the Empire. The arrows sailed through the air, over her fleet, and toward the distant Empire ships. They pierced dozens of Empire soldiers, who cried out and began to fall—and Gwendolyn's heart leapt with joy.

Now they had a battle.

*

Erec stood at the bow of the ship, his heart racing with joy to see Gwendolyn and the other exiles from the Ring again, along with Kendrick and his other fellow Silver members, each at the heads of their own ship, along with several hundred people he could only imagine were exiles from the Ridge. He had never thought he'd lay eyes upon members of the Ring again, especially here, so far from home, and he was beyond elated to see that Gwendolyn was still alive. He had been battling to find her for longer than he could remember, and after missing her in Volusia, he was beginning to wonder if he would ever see her again.

But Erec was already focused, in battle mode, as his eyes locked on the Empire fleet bearing down on his brothers in arms.

He wasted no time instructing his men:

"FIRE!" he yelled again.

His men fired another volley of arrows, using their long-range crossbows designed for situations like this, and he watched in satisfaction as they sailed through the air, over Gwen's fleet, higher and higher in a great arc, all the way to the Empire fleet. He watched in satisfaction as he saw them bombard a deck and distract the soldiers from attacking Gwendolyn.

Yet Erec knew this was not enough—there were hundreds of Empire ships, and he knew he needed to make a bold move if he were to rescue Gwendolyn and the others in time.

Erec immediately scanned the landscape with a professional soldier's eye, and as he did, he noticed how the Great Waste rose in elevation alongside the river, rising up in steep cliffs along the river's edge. As he scanned the slopes, he spotted massive boulders perched precariously amidst them, and he was struck with an idea: if he could shoot out those boulders, he might be able to get them to tumble down into the river and smash the Empire fleet. They would take out dozens of ships, and, if he loosened enough of them, clog the river and dam it up behind Gwendolyn.

Erec turned to his men.

202

"Aim for the rocks!" he commanded, pointing.

To demonstrate his point, Erec rushed across the deck, snatched a crossbow from one of his men's hands, aimed high, and fired—as his men watched, confused.

The arrow lodged beneath a small boulder. Erec watched with satisfaction as the rock loosened and tumbled down the cliff, gaining momentum as it went, bouncing and finally smashing against the hull of an Empire ship. The ship rocked, a hole in its side, and moments later, it began to list and sink.

Erec's men, realizing, all took aim and fired at the cliffs. Many arrows bounced harmlessly off of them—but enough of them made an impact. Soon, many small boulders went rolling down the hillside, taking out others, creating small avalanches. Bit by bit, they were damming up the river.

But while the small boulders were clearly a nuisance for the Empire, the big boulders were untouched. Erec realized that without dislodging them, they would never dam up the river and take out the ships.

While he watched, Erec saw the Empire ships close in on Gwen and the others; they put up a glorious fight, not flinching from the attack, and firing back volley after volley of arrows for each round that came at them. Despite their smaller numbers, they were fending them off— for now.

But Erec saw hundreds more ships closing in, saw the sky blacken with more Empire arrows, saw more of their people fall, and he knew that soon Gwen and her men would all be vanquished. He felt an urgency.

Standing there, desperate, Alistair stepped up beside him. He saw that serene, confident look in her eyes, and he knew she was summoning her powers. Her eyes closed, her palms turned upward, and Erec saw her getting strength, a slight halo appearing all around her. He could feel her power emanating from here.

Suddenly, Alistair opened her eyes, raised her palms, and threw them forward, one palm in each direction. Erec watched as a ball of light shot forth from each palm, each to a different side of the river, heading for the huge boulders on the cliffs.

There came a great rumbling sound, the cliffs shook, and Erec watched in awe as the boulders were dislodged. They began to roll, faster and faster, speeding down the cliffs, taking tons of rock with them as they created an avalanche.

All Empire eyes turned and looked up, seeing the devastation coming for them, rolling down the cliffs. They tried to flee, to turn back, but their ships were too big, too unwieldy. They had nowhere to go as boulder after boulder rolled right for them, a massive avalanche thundering toward the river.

Shrieks filled the air as the boulders smashed into the ships, their wood cracking, splintering, as one at a time, their ships were shattered. Hundreds of soldiers flailed as they fell overboard into the currents.

The Empire ships that were spared still could not escape the dam. Hundreds more boulders poured down before them, stopping up the river in a huge mound, preventing any more ships from passing as they settled in a great cloud of dust. Within moments, the river closed up behind Gwendolyn, and the Empire was unable to pursue them.

Erec sailed up to Gwendolyn's fleet, the two fleets meeting, each beaming with smiles, and as their ships met he ran and jumped up onto her ship. They embraced, followed by all their men, leaping onto each other's ships, the two fleets blending, all of them now one unified power. He watched Gwendolyn embraced her brother Godfrey, and he stepped forward and embraced Kendrick, Brandt, and Atme, his Silver brothers in arms. He met Koldo and the others, and he watched as Alistair embraced Gwendolyn.

He could hardly believe it. After all this time searching, it felt surreal. They were together again. Together, he knew, as one force, they could do it—they could snake their way out of this Empire, into the open sea, and make their way back home. As they all embraced, tears of joy in their eyes, these fractured elements of the Ring back together, Erec slowly felt their past returning to them. He felt optimistic for the first time in as long as he could remember, and he knew that nothing would stop them now. Now they would all make for the Ring, for Thorgrin, for their homeland—or die trying.

CHAPTER THIRTY NINE

Reece sat on the deck of the ship, back against the rail, and holding Stara in his arms, as he had been all night, still feeling as if he were in a surreal state. So much had happened to him in the last twenty-four hours, he could barely process it.

He looked up, bleary-eyed, at the rising sun, having been awake all night with dreams of Selese reaching out to him from the water, melding with dreams of Stara. He looked down now in the first light, feeling someone in his arms, and was still amazed to see it was Stara and not Selese. Selese had truly left him.

And just as shocking, Stara had truly appeared.

Their ship sailed along at a steady clip, its sails full as they caught the morning wind, bobbing up and down on the huge rolling waves of the open ocean, and as Reece smelled the ocean air, he marveled at how mysterious life was. His mind spun with the events of the last day. On the one hand, Reece knew, from the day Selese had emerged from the Land of the Dead, that her time with him was limited. She had always had an ethereal quality, and in the back of his mind he knew that she would leave him one day. Yet he had allowed himself to slip into denial, and had somehow believed that he could hold onto her forever. His time with her was too short; he had not seen the ending coming so soon. It left him with a feeling of sadness in his stomach.

It had all left him even more confused when he had seen Stara appear. It was as if Selese had sacrificed herself for Stara, as if each had taken some time from the other, in some karmic cycle of destiny. It was an act of selflessness on Selese's part, Reece knew, the final act of selflessness from a girl who had loved him entirely from the day they'd met. Selese had known she could not be with him forever—so before she'd left this world, she had found him someone who could.

Stara, unconscious when he found her, still lay unconscious in his arms, as she had all night long. He wondered if she'd ever wake. It felt good to hold her again, to keep her warm, to keep her alive. He held her limp body tight, a part of him imagining it was still Selese. And yet he knew that this was what Selese wanted: to love Stara now was to love Selese.

Holding Stara, Reece slowly began to realize how much he had missed her, too, all this time. Was it wrong to love two people at once? He wished it were otherwise, but he had to admit he did. And now that Selese was gone, all Reece had left was Stara, and he was determined to keep her alive, whatever the cost. And to learn to love her once again. As much as he ached for Selese, Reece knew, after all, that this was what she wanted.

Reece leaned down and kissed Stara's forehead, holding her, silently willing for her to come back to him. He could not believe she had come for him, had crossed the world for him, alone; he could not fathom the dangers she had faced, the sacrifices she had made. He was beyond touched. He saw how much she loved him, how she would literally cross the world for him.

"I love you, Stara," he whispered to her. "Come back to me, please."

It was a sentiment he had repeated often throughout the night, staring back at her eyes, beautiful even while closed, and wondering, hoping.

But now, as he stared in the early morning light, Reece for the first time thought he saw them flutter. And as he sat there and watched, he was shocked to see her slowly open her eyes.

Stara's watery, light-blue eyes stared up at him, shining, so filled with life, with love—and as they did, he remembered how much he loved her. They were as beautiful, as mesmerizing, as he remembered, those eyes that had haunted his dreams ever since they were children—and he fell in love with her all over again.

Reece, his own eyes tearing up, felt reborn again, and couldn't believe how elated he was to see her alive, back in his arms.

"Reece?" she asked softly, her voice hoarse. "Did I make it?"

Reece smiled with joy and a tear fell from his eye as he leaned down and kissed her on the lips.

She lifted her head and kissed him back, and he could feel her love for him.

"You did, my love," he said.

206

She reached out and clasped his hand, and he held hers.

"Did you cross the sea alone?" he asked in wonder.

She smiled and nodded, tears rolling down her cheeks.

"I did," she replied. "I searched the world for you. I prayed to God that if I did not, then to let the waters take me."

Reece pushed back his tears, overwhelmed by her words, that she would love him that much. He felt once again the connection that they'd had since they were children. It had never completely left. And though so much time had passed, it was as if it were yesterday.

As Reece looked into her eyes, it was the strangest thing—he watched something shift within them, and for a fleeting moment, it was as if Selese's spirit lay within her, as though Selese looked through Stara's eyes too. He felt Selese's spirit strongly, living through Stara, and no longer did he feel the conflict. He felt to love Stara would be to love Selese, too.

"I love you, Reece," she said, sitting up, looking into his eyes and holding his cheek. "And I always will."

They kissed, her warmth returning, and for the first time since Selese's death, Reece's heart was restored again.

As they sailed for the Ring, ever closer, he knew a great war lay ahead of them, perhaps the greatest battle in his life. He hoped and prayed they could rebuild the Ring, that he could start life over again in his homeland, with Stara by his side. That they could one day have a family of their own.

But whether they lived or died, for now, at least, being together with Stara once again, he had truly lived.

CHAPTER FORTY

Erec stood at the stern of his ship, Alistair by his side and Strom nearby, looking out as the two suns began to fall on the open sea, and feeling alive with a greater sense of purpose than he could remember. Not since his days in the Silver, in the court of King MacGil, had he felt this way. He didn't realize how much of a sense of loss he had been feeling ever since he left his home, left the Ring, left the company of his brothers, the Silver, left King's Court and King MacGil. Since then, he realized, a piece of his heart, of his soul, had always been missing.

But now he had a chance to have it all back again, to restore the life he once knew and loved. Now, finally, he could see a future for himself, a place in the world that felt like home. His future was not in the Southern Isles; he realized that now. That may have been where he was born, where his people were—but that was not *home*. Home, he realized now, was where he had been raised; where he had learned to fight, where he had met his brothers and fought side by side with them; where he had met and fallen in love with Alistair. Home was the land which he had risked his life defending. It was his adopted land, perhaps—but it was *home*.

The thought of returning there now, of having a chance to take it back, made him feel alive again like nothing else had. Erec would risk it all just for a chance to return to the Ring again.

The Southern Isles, Erec felt, was no place for his people now. The Ring needed to be rebuilt and the Ring needed men and women to populate it. It needed warriors. And he could think of no finer warriors than his people of the Southern Isles. The time had come, he knew, as King of the Southern Isles, to merge their peoples. The Ring, anyway, would need them to take it back. They could help fight for their new home. They had no option to remain isolationists now, anyway; if the Ring was lost, they would all be lost. If the Empire defeated the Ring, they would turn, with all their might, to the Southern Isles next, the last bastion of freedom in the world. To lose the Ring would be to lose it all.

Which was why he would sail there first, rally his people, and convince them to sail to the Ring with him, to join the battle with him and his people and help reinforce Gwendolyn. It was why he had split off from Gwendolyn's fleet—so that he could return with an even greater army.

"Are we not sailing north?" Strom asked, coming up alongside him.

Erec turned to see Strom standing beside him, Alistair on his other side, very much pregnant, and he could see the look of confusion in Strom's face.

"But we must sail south to reach the Southern Isles by morning," Strom added.

Erec nodded.

"I know, my brother. But we are not turning to the Southern Isles just yet."

Strom blinked, confused, and Erec looked out at to the waters ahead. In the distance, he saw the Dragon's Spine. It brought back memories he'd rather forget.

"Then where do we sail?" Strom asked.

Erec gestured to the horizon.

"An injustice was performed here that must be rectified," Erec said.

Erec gestured to a remote outcropping of rocks on the horizon, shooting out from the ocean, with dozens of ships anchored in its harbor. He could slowly see the look of recognition in his brother's face.

Krov's isle.

"Those ships once had to cower in the cover of darkness," Erec said. "Now Krov anchors them openly, with impunity, with no fear from anyone. That is because of the deal he struck with the Empire."

Erec raised a looking glass to his eye and could see the ships, even from here, overflowing with treasure. He handed the glass to Alistair, who looked, then handed it to Strom, who peered through and whistled.

"Krov's reward," Erec said, "for selling us out. Not only does he have Empire protection, but he now has more riches than he could ever dream."

Strom looked through the glass, his mouth open in shock.

"And to think we trusted him," Strom said.

Erec sighed.

"All wrongs come back to you, eventually," he said. "The time has come for him to pay for his betrayal. I never forget a friend—and I never forget an enemy."

Strom's look changed to one of admiration, and slowly his smile broadened. He stepped up and clasped Erec on the shoulder.

"I'm beginning to remember why I like you, brother."

Erec turned to Alistair, whom he now consulted on all things.

"I know it takes us out of our way," he said, "and I know our time is short. But I feel strongly," he said.

He expected her to try to dissuade him, to talk him into abandoning the idea, to going straight to the Southern Isles, then to the Ring, to leave vengeance alone.

But instead, she turned to him with a look of determination, a look of agreement that surprised him.

"We live in an unjust world, my lord," she said. "And every wrong you set right, every small piece of justice, can help set the world right."

"Then you agree?" he asked, surprised.

She nodded.

"You would be wrong to turn away."

He looked at her, loving her more in that moment than he ever had, and he knew he had married the right woman. A warrior, like he.

Erec nodded, satisfied.

"We shall wait for the cover of darkness," he said. "Tonight, we attack."

*

Erec sailed in the dark ocean, lit only by the full moon, leading his fleet in stealth as they cut silently through the water. His entire fleet disciplined, silent as he'd commanded, the only sound that hung in the air was that of the lapping waves against his boat, the wind at night, the occasional cry of a gull. And, of course, of the waves crashing against the sharp rocks of Krov's isle, looming closer and closer as Erec approached it.

As Erec approached Krov's fleet, anchored in the harbor, his heart beat quicker and he had the familiar feeling he had before entering battle. His senses were heightened; he grew more focused, more intense. He blocked out all else but the strategy before him.

As Erec neared Krov's half-dozen ships, bobbing unsuspectingly, he got a good glimpse: sailors lounged on deck, asleep, drunk, feet up, as undisciplined as their commander. Sailors sat slumped against the deck, empty sacks of wine in their hands, not suspecting anything. The decks themselves were filled to overflowing with loot and ransom, and no one bothered standing guard. They had no reason to; they had the protection of the Empire now.

Erec burned with indignation. These men had sold him and his people into captivity, had left them all for dead—and all for a few piles of gold.

Erec directed his ships right alongside Krov's, his heart pounding as he stayed silent, hoping they weren't discovered. Each gust of wind brought them closer, and as they neared, he could feel his men, feel his brother Strom beside him, getting antsy.

"Not yet," Erec whispered.

His men obeyed, waiting, getting so close they could see the whites of the sailors' eyes, the tension so thick one could cut it with a knife.

They sailed closer and closer still, until they were but feet away, all awaiting Erec's command.

"Now!" Erec called out in a harsh whisper.

Erec's men threw their ropes, hooks at the end, quickly and expertly over the rails of the other ships, and as their hooks latched onto the rails of the other ships, they all yanked, pulling their ships next to each other. When they were close enough, Erec led the way, leaping over the railing and onto Krov's ship.

As they ran through the deck, slowly, Krov's men roused, seeing the invaders, but Erec did not give them time to react. The moment they did, he raced for them and bashed them with the hilt of his dagger, smashing them on the skull and knocking them out. He did not want them to tip them off to his presence—and he did not want them dead, either, even if these traitors were deserving of death. His men did the same, as Erec had instructed, knocking out men left and right.

Erec's men, led by Strom, fanned throughout the other ships in the fleet, striking other men, knocking them out quickly and silently, overwhelming the ships before they knew what had hit them.

Erec had chosen the ship which he knew to be Krov's, and sure enough, he found him where he knew he would—sleeping by the bow next to an empty cask of wine, two naked women lying asleep in his arms.

With all Krov's sailors contained, Erec walked slowly, confidently, right for Krov, his boots echoing across the deck, until he stood over him.

Erec drew his sword and lowered it until the tip was touching the base of his throat. He stood there, waiting, smiling down with great satisfaction, as Krov suddenly opened his eyes, feeling the tip of the metal at his throat—and looked up at Erec in panic.

Erec smiled down with great satisfaction, finally feeling vindicated.

"We meet again, old friend," Erec said.

Krov tried to sit up, to reach for his sword, but Erec pushed the blade harder and stepped on his wrist, and Krov lay back down. He raised his hands, trembling, while the two women woke, cried out, and ran off.

"How did you get free?" Krov asked. "I was certain you were dead."

Erec smiled wider.

"That has always been your downfall," Erec replied. "You're too certain of everything. The valiant do not die, my friend. Only traitors do."

Krov gulped, terror in his face. He licked his lips.

"Don't kill me!" he called out, his voice shaking. "I'll give you everything I have!"

Erec grinned.

"Will you?" he replied. "We've already taken all of your gold, your weapons, all that is yours. What is there left for you to give?"

Krov gulped, at a loss for words.

"As far as killing you," Erec continued, "I believe that would be too civil. I have quite something else in mind. On your feet, old friend."

Krov rose to his feet, self-conscious, wearing only shorts, shivering in the cold, his fat, hairy belly exposed.

"Please!" Krov whined, whimpering, looking pathetic in the moonlight.

"You are spared," Erec said. "You can return to your home. You and all your men. We'll be taking your ships, though. Now go!"

Erec prodded him with the sword, and Krov, up against the rail, looked out at the sea, shocked.

"You want me to swim?" Krov asked, terrified.

He turned and looked out at his isle, hundreds of yards away, the ocean black and cold.

"I have no clothes," Krov said. "Those waters are freezing. I would freeze to death. So will my men. And there are sharks! We won't make it back."

Erec grinned.

"I'd say you're right," Erec said. "The chances of your making it are remote. Practically none. Just about the same chances you gave us when you sold us out. Now go!"

Erec stepped forward and kicked Krov as he turned, and Krov went flying over the side of ship, shrieking, splashing into the icy water, wearing just shorts and boots. All up and down his ship, Erec's men shoved Krov's men overboard, stripping them of their arms first, and their splashes filled the sea all around them.

Erec watched with great satisfaction as Krov and his men started to swim clumsily, heading back toward their isle, already shivering, barely able to catch their breath in the huge rolling waves. Justice had been served.

Erec turned and surveyed with pride all the new ships he had taken captive, all the loot, the gold, the weapons, the armor…. He knew it would serve the Ring, their new army, their new homeland, well. Very well indeed.

It was time now to retrieve his men, to turn to the Ring, and to prepare for the greatest battle of his life.

CHAPTER FORTY ONE

Darius cried out in pain as yet another whip lashed him across his back, feeling as if it were tearing off his skin. He gripped the oar before him until his knuckles turned white, trying to reach around and fight back, but stopped by his shackles. He sucked in his breath, trying to control his pain—while the whip cracked again, aimed at the slave chained beside him. Darius expected the slave to cry out, and was shocked that he was silent. He did not know how a man could withstand such pain silently.

Until he looked over at him and saw the man slumped beside him. Dead.

Darius looked on either side of him and saw all the other slaves chained, all of them now dead. He had somehow outlasted them all, and hadn't realized that they had all long ago stopped moving, making his rowing even harder. Whether the heat killed them, or the sun, or the labor, or the whip, or the lack of food and, water, or the exhaustion, Darius would never know. But dying, in these conditions, would be a relief.

Darius, however, was determined not to die. He thought of where this Empire fleet was sailing—east, for the Ring, to kill Gwendolyn and the others—and he was determined to stay alive. He would stay alive long enough, he decided, to do whatever he could to sabotage the Empire's efforts.

As Darius pulled at the oar, his palms chafed, his back covered in sweat and blood, an Empire taskmaster lifted his whip to lash him again. Darius braced himself, not knowing how many more lashes he could endure—when suddenly, the taskmaster stopped in mid-lash, holding the whip high overhead, frozen. The soldier stared out onto the horizon, as if surprised by the sight, and Darius turned, too, and looked out.

Darius squinted into the sun, sweat stinging his eyes, and in the distance he was shocked to make out a small fleet of ships on the horizon. As he looked more closely, he was even more surprised to see them flying a banner not of the Empire. It flew proudly, flapping in the wind, and Darius's heart lifted with pride to it was Gwendolyn's banner. The colors of the Ring.

Empire horns suddenly sounded up and down the fleet, and the ship broke out in commotion as Empire soldiers barked commands and soldiers took positions up and down the decks. The sails rose higher, the ship gained speed, and Darius's heart pounded as he saw them closing in on Gwendolyn's unsuspecting fleet.

With perhaps a hundred yards to go, Darius's ship suddenly shook with the sound of cannon fire; Darius looked over to see a huge cannon, manned by soldiers near the bow of his ship, was smoking, having just fired. He watched with trepidation as the cannonball flew through the air, right for Gwendolyn's ship, and was relieved to see it land short, splashing in the water.

But they adjusted the cannons, and he knew the next time Gwen might not be so lucky.

"This is your lucky day, slave!" snapped a taskmaster.

Darius felt rough Empire soldier hands grab him from behind, yank back his wrists, and unlock the shackles on his wrists and ankles.

"To the cannons!" he yelled.

The soldier shoved Darius, sending him flying forward until he landed face-first on the deck, painfully.

He then picked him up and shoved him again, merging him with a group of other slaves all being rushed to different battle stations. Darius was shuffled down the deck, and the next thing he knew, he was shoved into a cannon station.

At the station were several Empire soldiers and one other slave, all of them kneeling, looking out. One of the soldiers grabbed him roughly and made him kneel before the cannon.

"Try anything, slave," he seethed, "and you'll feel my sword through your heart."

Another soldier leaned forward.

"See those balls, slave?" the soldier demanded. "You will stock the cannon with them. Now move!"

He smacked Darius on the side of the head, and Darius reached down and hoisted a cannonball with shaking arms. It was so heavy, and his palms so sweaty, he could barely hold it, especially in his weakened state—and the other slave, seeing him struggling, leaned over and helped him. This slave had pale, white skin, and he looked back at Darius with eyes filled with fear.

As the Empire soldiers turned back to scanning the sea, Darius, kneeling there, looked surreptitiously out at his ship, at the Empire fleet, and he began to formulate an idea. He knew this was his chance—it was now or never.

He turned to the other slave and gave him a look of confidence.

"On my signal, do as I say," he whispered.

The other slave's eyes widened, and he shook his head frantically.

"They'll kill us," he said.

Darius grabbed the man's wrist hard, realizing he needed to assure him.

"We will die otherwise," he said. "Do you want to die coward? Or a warrior?"

He held the man's wrist until finally he relaxed. His eyes gradually narrowed, and Darius could see a growing confidence emerging in him—and then he nodded back quickly.

"Get moving, slave!" yelled a soldier, smacking Darius on the back of the head.

Darius, with the help of the other slave, reached up and placed the ball into the open cannon, and as they did, an Empire soldier quickly slammed closed the lid. Another soldier lit a torch and began to lower it for the long fuse.

Darius felt the other slave looking at him for direction, and he shook his head.

"Not yet," he whispered.

The torch came closer, and Darius knew he could not allow the fuse to be lit.

Finally Darius nodded.

"Now!"

Darius reached out and snatched the dagger hanging from the belt of the Empire soldier, then thrust it into his heart. He then spun and slashed the throat of the other Empire soldier behind him, before he could react, and he collapsed, dropping the torch.

As the other Empire soldier lunged for him, the other slave, Darius was proud to see, jumped in his way, wrestling him down, and as they rolled, Darius leaned over and stabbed the soldier in the heart.

Another Empire soldier appeared, raising a whip, and the other slave snatched it from his hands, wrestled him down, and jumped on top of him, putting his hand over his mouth, strangling him.

The Empire soldier was strong, though, and as he writhed, Darius came over and helped—until finally the man stopped moving.

Darius spun and grabbed the torch, then he turned and looked everywhere, hiding in the shelter of the cannon station, making sure no one had seen them. The other slave huddled close, frantically, and wiped sweat from his forehead.

"Hold the torch," Darius said.

The slave took the torch with a shaking hand, and as he did, Darius, with all his might, turned the heavy cannon. He put his shoulder into it, groaning with the effort, until finally he managed to turn it away from Gwendolyn's ship, now but twenty yards away; instead, he managed to point it inward, toward his own ship.

The slave's eyes widened as he realized.

"Do you want to live forever!?" Darius called out, with a crazed grin.

"Hey you!" shouted a voice.

Darius turned to see a group of Empire soldiers had spotted them, and were charging for them as they held the torch.

"Do it!" Darius yelled.

The slave lowered the torch with shaking hands and lit the fuse, as the Empire soldiers bore down on them.

"STOP THEM!" the soldier cried.

But it was too late—a huge explosion rocked the ship, Darius flying back as the cannon roared beside him, smashing into the rail. The cannonball fired straight down into the deck, the sound of splintering wood filling the air as the ball went through one side and out the other, splashing into the water.

The ship lurched and began to list immediately, dozens of its soldiers killed from the impact of the ball and the wood shrapnel.

As the ship delved into chaos, the soldiers bearing down on them slowly set their sights on them again, and began to charge. Darius knew this was his final chance.

"Come on!" he yelled to the slave, and without waiting, he turned, ran across the deck, and jumped onto the rail. He paused, seeing the twenty-foot drop below into the rolling waves.

But then the other slave joined him, and he felt a renewed sense of courage.

"Do you want to live forever?" the slave echoed, and with a crazed grin of his own, he leapt overboard, grabbing Darius's arm and bringing him with him.

As they landed in the freezing waters, Darius bobbing beside the slave, gasping for air, Darius looked up and saw Gwen's ship ahead— and he swam for his life. It lay perhaps twenty yards away now, and Darius only prayed that Gwen spotted them, and realized they were friendly.

"Stop those slaves!" yelled an Empire soldier from behind.

Darius glanced back to see several Empire soldiers huddling on the deck of the sinking ship, raising their bows and firing. Several arrows landed close to Darius in the water, and he flinched as they grew closer.

But suddenly the ship turned upside down, sinking, and the arrows stopped coming. Soldiers shrieked behind them.

At the same time, Darius reached the hull of Gwendolyn's ship. He floated beside it, the slave with him, and he looked straight up the twenty-foot hull, hoping and praying Gwen would see him. He was losing strength, the other ships were closing in, and there was no way he could climb it.

"Gwendolyn!" he called out.

As the ship continued to sail, leaving him floating there in its wake, Darius began to despair. After all that, he realized, he would die out here.

But as he floated there, thinking all was lost, he suddenly saw Kendrick's face at the stern, and saw it light up with recognition.

"Darius!" he called out.

Immediately, a rope was thrown down to them, and Darius and the slave reached out and grabbed it, holding on tight as they were pulled up, one rope length at a time.

Darius, with one final pull, landed on deck, the slave beside him, and he gasped for breath, coughing out water, feeling exhausted but a great feeling of satisfaction. He could hardly believe it: he had escaped. He was really here.

Finally, freedom was his once again.

As he lay there, coughing up seawater, the slave beside him doing the same, he felt a tongue on his face, heard a whining, and he looked over, elated, to see his old friend Dray again. He kissed him and stroked his head, as Dray jumped on him, and he wondered how on earth he got here.

Darius looked up to see Gwendolyn and Kendrick gather around with all the others. Strong hands reached down and pulled him up, and he embraced Kendrick, dripping wet, and then Gwendolyn.

"The last I saw you," Gwendolyn said, "you were marching to Volusia to protect your people. It was a daring raid."

Darius lowered his head, overwhelmed with sadness as he remembered.

"My friends did not make it, my lady," he said.

"No," she said. "But you did."

He examined her; she seemed older, stronger, than when he'd last seen her.

"And last I saw you, my lady," he said, "you were venturing into the Waste to find us help."

He smiled.

"You found it, after all," he added. "A bit late—but just when I needed it."

They all grinned and embraced.

"And who is this?" Gwen asked.

They all turned to the other slave, and he grinned back.

"I honestly don't know," Darius said. "We never met. But he saved my life."

"As you saved mine," he replied. "Tinitius is my name. Mind if I join you?"

He shook hands, and Kendrick grinned.

"You are most welcome to join our cause," he replied.

Darius's face fell, serious again.

"My people are all gone, my lady," he said.

Gwen paused.

"Not all of them," she replied, cryptically.

He looked back at her, not understanding, when suddenly, the crowd parted and up stepped a girl who made his heart melt. Darius's eyes opened wide in shock and joy, as she rushed forward, past all the others, and embraced him.

"Darius," she said in his ear, hugging him tight, her hot tears pouring down his neck.

He held her tight, hardly believing it was possible.

"I thought you were dead," he said.

Loti shook her head.

"No," she replied. "I lived for you."

As Darius held her tight and Gwen's ship picked up speed, sailing further away from Empire assault, he felt that everything was right in the world again. For the first time in as long as he could remember, he was with people he loved, back to the closest thing to home he had—and on a mission that meant everything to him. For he would give his life to defend Gwendolyn, Kendrick, all of these people—his adopted brothers—and most of all, to help them take back the Ring.

He thanked God for one thing most of all: that, live or die, he would be there to fight another war.

CHAPTER FORTY TWO

Gwendolyn crossed the deck of her ship, joined by Kendrick, Steffen, and now Darius, whom she was thrilled to have back with them, as she headed for the bow. Their last encounter with the Empire fleet had been too close, and she knew that if it hadn't been for Darius and his ingenuity with the cannon, they might all not be alive right now.

She reached the rail and scanned the horizon, the others at her side, hundreds of members of the Ridge behind her, filling her ship and filling the other three ships of her fleet, each manned by Koldo, Ludvig, and Kaden—and her heart leapt as she spotted, on the horizon, the outline of a landmass, one she knew like the back of her hand:

The Ring.

Gwen's heart slammed and her throat went dry, and she felt a wave of jubilance rush through her unlike any she'd ever experienced. Her homeland. Even destroyed, it was still her home, and now, finally, it lay within reach again. It restored her heart, made her feel as if there were a purpose to life again, a chance for all of them to be together and to build a life again.

Gwen saw the gleam in Kendrick's eyes, too, in Brandt's and Atme's, and she could see that they felt the same way. She also saw the looks of wonder in the eyes of Koldo and Ludvig and Kaden and Darius—and all those of the Empire and the Ridge who had never laid eyes upon the Ring before. Its shores, even from here, were so beautiful, so mysterious, with cliffs that rose high in the air, framed by jagged rocks, a lush green forest behind it, and a mist that hung over it all. Its circular shoreline, most of all, caught the eye, making it feel, even from here, like very special place, like a magical land that rose from the sea.

"So it is not just a myth," Koldo called out, studying it in awe. "The famed Sorcerer's Ring truly does exist."

Gwendolyn smiled back at Koldo.

"Finally," Ludvig called out, "the two sides of the MacGil family, the Ridge and the Ring, shall be united in one homeland!"

Gwendolyn was feeling the same sentiment, and wanted more than anything to celebrate, especially as she knew that being here, in the Ring, meant that she might see Thorgrin again. She prayed that Lycoples had delivered the message, that he had found the Ring and their son, and would meet her here. She prayed with all her heart—nothing else would make her joy so complete.

But suddenly Gwen's reverie was shattered as horns sounded on the horizon behind her. She turned and looked back, and her heart stopped to see that the horizon was filled, once again, with Empire ships, all of them having rallied, having pursued her here. There were hundreds of them this time, a massive black fleet covering the horizon, waving the black banners of the Empire, and closing in fast—too fast.

The Empire ships were superior to theirs, and Gwendolyn knew they would reach them soon. She glanced back and forth, gauging how far away the Ring was, and how far away the Empire was, and she wondered if they would make it in time. It would be close, down to the wire.

"And if they overtake us before we reach it?" Kendrick asked, studying the horizon with her.

"They outnumber us ten to one, my lady," Darius said. "We must reach the Ring before they do."

Kendrick turned back and studied the horizon critically.

"And even if we do," he said, "we will be but on the edge of the Ring, at the Wilds. We will still have to cross them—and more so, cross the Canyon."

"And what good will it do to cross the Canyon without a shield?" Steffen asked. "This is not the Ring we once knew. This land lies unprotected. The Empire will be on our heels. We will not be able to outrun them. At some point, we will have to stand and fight."

Gwen, thinking the same thing, looked up and searched the skies, waiting, watching, hoping more than anything to hear the screech of a dragon, to see Thorgrin return to her.

Thorgrin, please. We need you now. More than ever. Please return to us, for one last battle. For old times' sake.

222

But her heart fell as she saw and heard nothing. Just dark, rolling clouds growing darker by the moment, as if the heavens were angry, as if they knew the bloodshed that was about to happen.

Gwen turned back to the others, resolute. She was alone, as always, and she would find a way to fight alone.

"If we must fight the whole of the Empire," she said, her voice firm, "then we shall fight. And if we shall die, then we shall die. The battle before us is a battle for our homeland, for ourselves, for our freedom. Whether we win or lose matters little: it is the chance for battle that is the gift.

"Raise the sails!" she yelled, turning to her men. "Take up the oars!"

Steffen and the others scrambled to follow her command, carrying it up and down the ships, as the men rushed to further hoist the sails, to pull harder on the oars. They all redoubled their efforts, their fleet gaining speed as they sailed for the Ring, trying to make land. As Gwen stood there, looking out, she watched, desperate, as the Empire fleet crept toward them like a plague, knowing there was little she could do. She turned and looked back at the Ring, studying the shoreline, and she had an idea.

"Head northeast!" she cried. "For the Shallow Bay!"

They altered their direction, and as they did, Kendrick came up beside her, studying the looming shoreline of the Ring.

"The Shallow Bay is shaped like a horseshoe, my Queen," he said. "If we enter, if we even make it, we shall be trapped inside."

She nodded.

"And so will the Empire," she replied.

He looked back, confused.

"It will force them to funnel in," she replied. "It is a bottleneck. One million ships cannot fit in at once. A few dozen, perhaps—and these will narrow the odds."

Kendrick nodded back, clearly pleased.

"That is why Father chose you," he said approvingly.

Gwen's heart raced as the land of the Ring loomed but several hundred yards away, the strong coastal winds bringing them closer. The Shallow Bay jutted out, two long peninsulas on either side, like a

223

horseshoe, with a narrow opening of less than fifty yards, and she sailed her ship, leading her fleet right inside it.

As they entered its calm waters, sheltered here from the wind and ocean currents, the other ships sailed up beside her, Koldo and Ludvig and Kaden staring back, awaiting direction in what was, for them, a new land.

Gwendolyn studied the topography of the Ring, and she was shocked to see how much it had changed since they had left. The Wilds were now overgrown, their thick, dark wood leaning over, growing into the water, thicker and blacker than she had ever seen it. Of course, it made sense; the patrols of the Silver had not been here in moons to clear it out, and the Wilds, she knew, were likely filled with savage beasts again. This would not make their trek to the Canyon any easier.

Another horn sounded, and Gwen turned to see the Empire fleet closing in, entering the bay, trapping them in here, the forefront of their fleet, a dozen ships, entering at once. She turned back and saw the shore still a hundred yards away, and she knew they would not make it in time.

She felt torn. Here they were, so close to home after all this time, and she wanted more than anything to disembark. Why could the Empire have not given her but an hour's more lead? Just an hour to touch down on her homeland, to feel it beneath her feet once again? It broke her heart.

She knew that, at this point, it would take a miracle, and she searched the skies again, hoping for any sign of Thorgrin.

But, again, there was none. Her heart fell. Had he made it? Was he, too, lost to her?

Gwen gritted her teeth and resigned herself to the battle before her. They would have to make a stand; they had no choice. They would all die here, she knew—and yet there was no place she'd rather die than fighting for the Ring. At least they would not die a foreign death, a lonely death in a strange land, in the waste of Empire, in lands unknown, so far from home. She would die here, where her father had died, and his father before him.

"We fight!" she yelled, turning to her commanders.

They all could see the seriousness of her expression, and as a somber air fell over them, they all knew the time had come. It was time to put their battle faces on.

Hardly had she issued the command than the first shot appeared across the bow. Gwen looked up as she heard the whistling of a thousand arrows, and she saw the sky blacken with the Empire's first volley.

"Shields!" she cried.

All of her men, prepared for this, raised their shields and took a knee in tight formations, huddling close together. Gwen joined them, pulling Krohn in tight beside her, raised her oversized shield, and took a knee with the wall of soldiers.

The thump of arrows hitting wood sounded all around her, as arrows landed on the deck like rain, some splashing into the water, not enough distance to reach them—but most hitting wood. Gwen felt her arm jolt as more than one hit her shield. She was surprised at the force with which the arrows hit, even from so far away.

Finally, all fell silent, the volley ended, and she and all her men slowly stood and looked out.

"ARCHERS!" she commanded.

Dozens of her archers stepped forward, raising their bows in neat lines.

"AIM FOR THE SAILS!"

Her men did as she commanded, firing back, and the sky blackened again—this time with her own arrows, flying back across the harbor. Her men aimed high, something the Empire was clearly not expecting, as they all took cover down below and the arrows sailed harmlessly over their heads.

Nor were they expecting the damage it did: thousands of arrows punctured the sails, filling them with holes, leaving them in tatters; soon, the sails flapped wildly in the wind, useless. Their ships immediately lost speed, and while they continued to advance, it was not nearly as quickly.

Gwen's ships, on the other hand, continued to sail at full speed, and as another volley of Empire arrows came back at them, this time they were mostly out of range, most arrows landing harmlessly in the sea.

But a few of her men cried out, pierced by arrows despite their shields, too many slipping through. She knew time was short.

Gwendolyn looked back to the shore, closer, but still far enough away. She knew she had to take this fight to the land; out here, in the open sea, they were sitting ducks. But as she turned and looked, she saw more and more Empire ships filing into the harbor, and she knew the odds were not good.

"FIRE!" she yelled.

Her men unleashed another volley of arrows, these into the soldiers, Gwen taking up a bow and firing along with them, and she watched in satisfaction as more than one Empire soldier was hit and fell.

But an Empire volley came right back at them, and Gwen and the others took cover once again.

Back and forth the volleys went, the Empire ships slipping ever closer, until Gwen finally looked back and saw the shore but twenty yards away. Her men were dying, and she knew they had to make it. They were so close now. She could almost feel the land beneath her feet, and if the water wasn't still so deep, she would have had her men jump.

Suddenly, Gwen heard a noise which made her heart sink. It was a sparking noise, the sound of a fuse being lit. She turned, and her heart stopped to see an Empire cannon being turned and aimed right for them.

"GET DOWN!" she yelled.

But it was too late: there came a terrific boom cutting through the air, followed by an echo, and suddenly, an explosion of wood.

All was chaos, as the ship beside Gwen was smashed to bits, dozens of her men dying, shrieking as they fell overboard, some in flames. The boat, Kaden's, immediately began to sink, half the men sliding down the deck, falling over the edge and into the water.

Kaden fell with them, and he helped rally them, keep them afloat, as Gwen and her men immediately threw them ropes and helped them climb onto her ship, saving those who were not too wounded to climb.

The Empire took advantage of their weakness and fired another volley of arrows, taking aim at those climbing the ship, and as men were being pulled back up, more than one of them, impaled by an Empire arrowhead, slipped back into the water, dead.

Gwen turned and saw the situation getting desperate, more and more Empire ships sailing into the harbor, and many with cannons. She saw a soldier with a torch leaning to light another fuse—and she knew that in a moment, another one of her ships would be taken out.

As Gwen watched, wanting to take action but knowing there was no time, she was shocked to see a spear go through his back and out the other end. The soldier stood there, stunned, and suddenly fell face first, dropping his torch harmlessly on the deck.

Gwen could not fathom what had possibly happened and she wondered if she were seeing things—when suddenly she spotted a single ship, what appeared to be a commandeered pirate ship, flying a banner she recognized, cutting through the Empire ranks. Her heart raced to recognize the people on board—there, at the bow, was Reece, joined by O'Connor, Elden, Indra, Matus, Stara and Angel. They sailed solo, cutting through the ranks of Empire ships from behind, clearly none of the massive fleet of the Empire expecting to be attacked from behind by a sole ship.

Reece and the others sailed headlong into danger, hurling spears left and right, taking out dozens of Empire soldiers before they even realized what was happening. They aimed for those manning cannons, sparing Gwendolyn, and they cut a path right through, between ships, as they broke through the ranks and entered the bay.

They never slowed, even as the Empire caught wind and fired arrows at them. They fired back and continued sailing, their commandeered pirate ship sleeker and faster than all the others, sailing all the way to Gwendolyn's ship.

Gwendolyn realized at once that this was the diversion that she and her men so desperately needed; she could no longer afford to sit there, trading volleys with the Empire, which was still closing in. Nor could they afford to race for the shore—which they would never make in time—and which would leave Reece and the others alone in the harbor, vulnerable to attack.

Instead, they had to do what was counterintuitive, what the Empire would never possibly expect: they had to attack.

"TURN ABOUT!" Gwen yelled, "AND ATTACK!"

Her men glanced back with stunned expressions—but none hesitated to execute her command. All of her ships slowly turned around and sailed headlong, straight for the Empire fleet.

The Empire commanders of the dozen or so ships before her stared back, baffled, clearly not expecting this; they immediately scrambled to man their cannons.

And that was exactly what Gwen wanted them to do. She knew that if she came close enough, it would render their cannons useless, the angle too steep to maneuver for firing. It would give Gwen and her people the advantage, forcing their ships to battle each other one on one, cause a backlog, and allow her men to fight hand-to-hand. They could board the Empire ships and kill them in close range—and once they boarded Empire ships, the greater fleet would be stymied, as Empire could not fire upon Empire.

Gwen saw the looks of wonder and consternation on the Empire faces as her fleet approached theirs. They turned their cannons frantically, and she could see their look of dismay as they realized the angle was too tight.

"FIRE!" she yelled.

Her rows of archers fired volley after volley, killing the stunned Empire at close range, while Kendrick and the others hurled spear after spear.

Moments later her ships reached theirs, bumping into them roughly with a jolt—and the second they did, dozens of her men threw their ropes and hooks and tied the ships together, while dozens more, swords drawn, let out a great battle cry and followed Kendrick, Koldo, Ludvig, Kaden, Ruth, Darius—and even, Gwen was surprised to see, Godfrey—as they all threw caution to the wind and leapt overboard onto the Empire ships, Dray following Darius.

At the same time, Reece's ship reached theirs, and Reece and the Legion joined in, leaping onto Empire ships from the side.

The stunned Empire soldiers barely knew how to react—and it was clear that the last thing in the world they were prepared for was a direct attack.

Gwen's men sprinted all throughout the Empire ship, up and down the decks, each zeroing in on another Empire soldier, and fighting them one on one. They slashed and stabbed as they ran, spreading through the unprepared ship like a storm. Darius shouted and tackled two soldiers, knocking them to the ground and punching them before wresting their swords away and stabbing them. Gwen could see the vendetta against the taskmasters in his eyes. He was a one-man killing machine as he gained his feet and tore through the ship, killing Empire left and right, Dray at his heels, killing all those that dared come too close.

The men of the Ridge were no slouches either. Led by Koldo, Ludvig, Kaden and Ruth, they landed on the Empire decks with a great battle cry and never slowed, stabbing the stunned Empire left and right, darting through their ranks and meeting soldiers as they charged for them. Kendrick, Brandt, and Atme led the remainder of the Silver, along with more soldiers from the Ridge, and Godfrey, Gwen was proud to see, joined them as they fought brilliantly, wielding swords, axes, flails, and spears, catching Empire soldiers by surprise and hunting them down. The soldiers outnumbered them and fought back intensely—but they were no match for the superior fighting skills of the Silver.

Even Godfrey managed to do well, ducking beneath a sword slash and raising his shield and bashing an Empire soldier in the head. He then grabbed the disoriented soldier from behind and threw him overboard.

Reece and the Legion attacked the Empire ships from the other side, fighting to meet up with Kendrick in the middle. Reece fought like a man on fire, like a man fighting for his homeland, as he ducked and rolled from several slashes, and wielded his halberd brilliantly, it flashing beneath the sun as the stabbed several men. Indra threw her spear, killing two soldiers at once, then ran and extracted it and threw it again. Elden swung his battle-ax sideways and, with a great blow, knocked two Empire soldiers over the rail and into the sea. Matus swung his flail, knocking swords from hands before they could do damage, and then impaling soldiers in their chest. And O'Connor wielded his bow as if it were alive, firing up and down the ship and saving his brothers before they were struck.

Gwendolyn joined in, leaping onto the ship with the others and leading the remnants of her men, Krohn at her side, snarling and killing several soldiers as they approached. Whomever Krohn did not kill,

Steffen did, the clanging of swords all around her as he blocked blows on all sides. Gwen ran before her people, raising her bow and firing three arrows, killing three Empire soldiers who charged her from three sides.

Now that Gwen's men had boarded the Empire ship, she figured they would be safe from the sea of Empire arrows firing down from the fleet. But she was shocked as she heard their distinctive whistling, and as another volley landed on the ship all around her.

Shrieks rang out as soldiers all around her were shot—not only hers, but Empire soldiers, too, killed by their own people, their own arrows, shot in the back. Gwen ducked, barely missing an arrow as it sailed past her and found a target in a soldier's throat. Another volley came, and Gwen could not believe that the Empire would keep firing on their own people, killing as many of their own men as hers. They were ruthless; they didn't care about their own men, as long as they killed her.

More volleys came, more shrieks rose out, with nowhere to hide; the Empire ranks began to thin out, and so did hers. Even with her men fighting brilliantly, all of them hand-to-hand, all of them taking the battle to the Empire, even with her having taken control of several Empire ships, still, with all of these arrows, the tide was turning against them. More and more Empire ships were entering the harbor, and as more arrows sailed down, Gwen realized they had taken this fight as far as they could. They had gotten farther, had done more than anyone could have expected of them, but now it seemed, there were no moves left to make.

Gwen cried out as an arrow pierced her arm, grazing it, and she reached over and felt the blood trickling down—and as she let down her guard, two Empire soldiers came charging for her, raising their swords and bringing them down before she had time to react.

The sound of metal rang out and she was showered with sparks as Steffen stepped forward and blocked the blow of one soldier, then wheeled around and stabbed him in the gut. At the same time, Krohn, beside her, snarled and leapt and sank his teeth into the other soldier's throat, forcing him to drop his sword and pinning him to the ground.

Gwen, her arm bleeding and in terrific pain, many of her men dead or wounded, looked out at the harbor, filled with more and more black, and knew this was a lost cause. They had come so close—and yet they remained so far. They would die here, in this harbor; she knew that for sure.

She looked up and searched the skies, saw no sign of Thorgrin, of the dragon, and her heart sank. She searched everywhere for Argon, but saw no sign of him.

It was all over now.

Then suddenly, scanning the horizon one last time, Gwen saw something that filled her with hope, with possibility. There, gleaming on the horizon, came a fleet of golden ships, approaching the Empire from behind. There must have been hundreds of them, and their banner, she was elated to see, was one that she recognized: the Southern Isles.

She knew instantly that there could be only one person leading this fleet, and as she looked, she saw that he was, indeed, standing at the bow of the lead ship.

There, shining beneath the sun in his golden armor, was Erec.

And he had brought an army with him.

*

Erec rushed forward on the deck of his ship, his veins pumping with adrenaline, flanked by Strom and his men as he led the fleet from the Southern Isles, dozens of ships, thousands of the finest warriors in the world, all ready to lay down their lives to take back the Ring. All ready to leave the Southern Isles behind and make the Ring their new home—or die trying in the process.

As Erec sailed into the Shallow Bay, he expected conflict—yet he had not expected her to be in such dire straits. His heart fell to see her trapped, surrounded, to see thousands of Empire ships blocking their way. He had hoped to reach her sooner.

His fleet moved quickly now as they hoisted the sails to full mast, his men rowing for their lives, rowing to save Gwendolyn. The one advantage they had was that the Empire did not expect an attack from behind; Erec hoped they wouldn't spot them coming until was too late.

Erec sailed his fleet into the bay, attacking the rear of the Empire fleet like a sudden storm, and as they bore down on them, he shouted out his first command.

"FIRE!"

Up and down his ships, his men fired arrows and hurled spears, turning the sky black with their weapons as they whistled through the air.

They landed with a deadly precision, and hundreds of Empire soldiers fell. So preoccupied were they with attacking Gwendolyn before them, they were woefully unprepared to handle an attack from behind.

Erec did not give them a chance to collect themselves. He put his ships into full battering mode, directing them all to follow him single file, and to ram a path through the Empire blockade. He led the way, and with his iron-tipped hull, he smashed into the first Empire ship, creating a hole in its side and sending dozens of its men overboard with the collision.

The Empire ship listed and bobbed out of the way, and as Erec's ship sailed past, all of his men fired arrows and hurled spears, killing all of its soldiers at close range before they could mount a defense.

With an opening created in the Empire fleet, Erec continued to smash through the blockade, his ships falling in behind him, until finally he burst through the other side, into the Shallow Bay. As they passed, Empire soldiers, their ships in close proximity, fired back; some tried to leap onto Erec's ship, but Erec and Strom led their men in a defense, stepping forward and stabbing and slashing the attackers, kicking them backwards over the rail, back into the sea. The soldiers of the Southern Isles were too hardened, had seen too much battle, for them to be deterred by any foe, and to ever back down. Days like this, battles like this, were what they lived for, what they dreamt about as small children. Erec's men fought like men with their lives to lose, and soon the Empire soldiers realized what a mistake they made in trying to board. The waters were filled with flailing and wounded Empire soldiers, their ubiquitous splashes filling the air.

Alistair stood on the deck, near Erec, and as more than one Empire soldier broke through the ranks and charged for her, assuming he had found low-hanging fruit, she, standing there poised, calmly raised a palm and aimed it at the men. As she did, the soldiers stopped in their tracks, falling backwards and landing flat on their backs, dead.

Erec glanced over in the thick of battle, and he had no worry for her; he could see her power had been restored, and that she was stronger than ever. The Empire men could not get within ten feet of her.

As Erec's fleet progressed further into the Shallow Bay, he directed ships to the Empire ships that were surrounding Gwendolyn and her men. He rammed these, breaking through the blockade and finally freeing her and closing the gap, so that he and his ships now joined up with hers, all of them one unified force, facing the Empire together.

Erec saw the thrilled look on Gwendolyn's face, on the faces of all her men, Kendrick, Brandt, Atme, all his Silver brothers. He could hear the shouts of joy from their men at their having broken through and joined the battle just in time.

Yet they had no time to celebrate. The Empire fleet was regrouping quickly, and bearing down again. Erec turned and saw hundreds more ships filtering into the bay.

"What now, Queen?" he asked Gwendolyn, knowing her next decision would decide the outcome of this battle—and trusting her, as he would her father, to decide well. To pay her respect, after all, was like paying respect to King MacGil, a man whom Erec had dearly loved.

All the commanders looked to Gwendolyn and as she looked back and forth from the Empire fleet to the shores of the Ring, Erec could see she had come to a decision.

"Bring all of our ships close together," she announced, "and set them on fire."

Erec was, at first, shocked at her command; but as he watched the Empire ships filling the harbor, he realized it was brilliant. A great conflagration would create a bottleneck, stop up the harbor for a while and keep the Empire forces at bay; it would give them enough time to disembark and swim for shore, and gain them some time, even, to enter into the Ring. They could not possibly win this battle on land, either; but on foot, at least, in the homeland they knew, they could put up the fight of their lives.

Burning the ships was a bold act. It was the bold decision of a fine leader.

"My Queen," Koldo said, "if we burn our ships, we have nothing left. We have only the Ring, and no other choice."

Gwendolyn nodded.

"And that is exactly why we should," she replied. "The Ring is our home now. For life or for death. There can be no other option."

Erec heard the horns, saw the Empire regrouping, and watched them positioning the cannons on their ships; he knew it would only be a matter of time until they fired.

Gwen nodded, and Erec gestured to his men, as did all the other commanders, and they quickly lit and passed out torches. They all touched them to the sails, to the deck, to any surface they could find. And soon, the ships were all aflame.

A massive wall of flame spread their way, and Gwen joined the others as they all leapt from the ship, jumping out into the sea, thousands of their people entering the waters, swimming for shore, for their new and final home.

Now, they had no choice.

*

Reece cut and hacked his way through the Wilds, elated to be back in the Ring, his heart pumping as he ran alongside his brothers, all of them making their way as fast as they could from the shore. Not far behind, in the Shallow Bay, the Empire, he knew, was regrouping, pursuing, and making its way closer with each passing moment. Reece and the others did not have a second to lose.

As Reece ran alongside his Legion brothers and Stara, Gwendolyn, Kendrick, and all the others, he hacked at the brush and was amazed at how overgrown the Ring had become since they had left. Huge branches blocked the path, scratching them every which way, and as he went, he held onto Stara's hand with his free hand; she still weak from her journey.

It was surreal to be back in the Ring again, and it was surreal, after all this time, to be back at his sister's side, to be reunited with his brothers, Kendrick and Godfrey, with the Silver members, Erec, Brandt, and Atme. He was anxious to spend time with them—but now, there was no time. They were all too busy running for their lives, trying to distance themselves from the Empire and reach the Canyon.

He knew they were in a desperate situation; as he checked back over his shoulder, he saw great plumes of black smoke rising on the horizon, what remained of their burning fleet. He could already hear the shouts and horns in the distance, and he suspected the Empire had already gotten around the burning ships and reached the shore. He suspected that soon enough they would reach them, and that it would only be a matter of time until they were vastly outnumbered on land.

Reece looked ahead, already running for what felt like hours, covered in sweat, and he knew that soon they would arrive at the Canyon. But then what? The Shield was no more; they had nothing to protect them from the hoards of the Empire. Even if they managed to cross the Canyon, they would all be killed inside the Ring, or forced to flee it again. He wondered what Gwendolyn had in store.

As he ran, Reece sensed motion out of the corner of his eye, and suddenly he spotted a beast, tall, the size of a gorilla, with smooth, green skin, long claws, and glowing red eyes, leap out of the woods. It leapt right for Stara, and Reece reacted. He approached, swung his sword, and sliced it in half before its claws tore her apart. It had been the tenth such beast he had killed in the last hour, the road littered with the carcasses of these things. As if their people didn't have enough to worry about, they now also had to consider the thousands of beasts that roamed the Wilds.

Through the thick trees, Reece caught glimpses of the sky, and he searched it, hoping for a sign of Thor, of Lycoples. He missed his best friend dearly.

But he was nowhere to be found. Reece missed his friend, but he was resigned they would have to fight this final battle on their own.

They turned a corner, and as they broke through the dark woods, Reece looked out and was awestruck at the vista before them: the Canyon. The sight left him breathless, as it had always done. Looking at it now, it was like the first time he'd ever laid eyes upon it—a huge chasm in the earth, stretching nearly as far as the eye could see, mist swirling inside it. It made him feel tiny in the scope of the universe.

They ran for the Eastern Crossing, an endless bridge spanning the Canyon. In the past, the idea of crossing to the other side would have made him feel safe and secure, knowing that when they crossed, they would be protected by the Shield. But now, with the Shield down, it was like any other bridge, leaving them as vulnerable to attack as anywhere else.

They all came to a stop, congregating at the base of the bridge, Gwendolyn out front as they all looked to her. It was a huge group of people, comprising Kendrick and the former Silver; Erec and the men of the Southern Isles; Gwendolyn and Koldo and the exiles of the Ridge; and, of course, Reece himself and his Legion brothers. It was an entire nation ready to start life again, bent on re-entering the Ring.

"Women and children first!" Gwendolyn called out. "The elderly, the young, and all citizens who cannot fight—all of you cross now, enter the Ring. The rest of us, all those who can fight, will stay here and guard your way until you have crossed."

"You must not!" a citizen yelled out. "Come with us! The Empire advances with a million men, while there are but hundreds of you. How can we cross and leave you here, to your death?"

Gwendolyn shook her head firmly.

"Cross!" she commanded. "Go deep into the Ring, find refuge. We will kill as many of them as we can. Perhaps they will stop with us."

"And if you do not succeed?" asked another citizen.

Gwen looked back, somber, serious in the silent day, the only sound that of the howling wind. Reece could see the resolve in his sister's face.

"Then we shall die together in one last act of valor," she replied. "Now go." Gwen gave a command to her men, and they stepped forward and prodded the people onto the bridge; but the people stood there, clearly not wanting to leave Gwen's side, devoted to her as a leader.

Koldo stepped forward and faced them.

"By the authority of my father," he boomed, "King of the Ridge, I command my people to go! Cross that bridge!"

Yet his people stood there too, unmoving.

"And all of you of the Southern Isles," Ere called out. "Go!"

Yet his people stood there, too, none willing to budge.

"If you die here, then we shall die here with you!" someone yelled back, and there came a shout of approval amongst the people.

Yet suddenly Reece heard a noise behind him, one that raised the hair on the back of his neck, and he turned to see, breaking out of the woods, into the clearing, the Empire army. It was an awe-inspiring sight—thousands of them broke through the Wilds, letting out a great

236

battle cry, swords raised high, and closing in on them. Behind them, there emerged thousands more; it seemed as if the entire forest were filled with them, row after of soldiers marching ahead, looking like death itself had appeared for them.

With their backs to the Canyon, the exiles of the Ring, the Ridge, and the Southern Isles—all of them—were trapped. They had nowhere left to run.

"GO!" Gwen shrieked, facing her people.

This time, her voice carried a great authority, and this time, they listened. The women and children, the elderly, the crippled, all those citizens unable to fight, finally turned and began to run across the bridge, heading for the mainland of the Ring.

"Close positions!" Gwendolyn yelled out to her soldiers who remained behind.

Kendrick and his knights, Erec and his warriors, Alistair, Koldo, Ludvig, Kaden and their knights, Reece and his Legion, her brother Godfrey and his friends, Darius, Steffen—and all the warriors who could fight—all of them came in close, hardening in a tight wall around Gwendolyn, all of them blocking the entrance to the bridge, bracing for an attack.

Reece, standing beside his sister, turned to Stara and Angel, who still remained by his side.

"Go," he urged Angel. "Go with the others!"

But she stood there and shook her head.

"Never!" she said.

Reece turned to Stara.

"Go," he said. "I beg you."

But she looked at him as if he were crazy—and with a distinctive ring, she drew her sword.

"You forget who I am," she said. "My father was a warrior; my brothers were warriors. I was reared on the Upper Isles, a nation of warriors. I am a greater warrior than you. You can run if you wish—but I am staying here."

Reece grinned back, remembering why he liked her.

As the Empire thundered closer, all of them stood there, all of them united, all of them prepared to make one last stand together. They all knew they wouldn't make it—and yet none of them cared, and none of them lost resolve. Just being able to stand here on this battlefield today, Reece knew, was a gift. Win or lose, they had been granted the gift of battle.

Only one person, Reece realized, was missing; only one other person would make this all complete. It was the man his heart ached for dearly, his best friend, his partner in battle: Thorgrin. Reece glance up at the skies, hoping, wishing—and yet still, there was nothing.

The Empire shouts grew louder, their running shaking the ground, as they came closer, closer... Soon they were but feet away, charging at full speed, so close that Reece could see the whites of their eyes. He braced himself, anticipating a terrific blow to come as several Empire raised their sword and zeroed in on him.

Stara stepped forward, drew her bow, took aim, and fired—killing a soldier but a few feet away, the first to draw blood in the battle.

The first Empire blows came like a wall, like an avalanche. Reece raised sword and shield, blocking multiple blows at once from all sides. He spun around with his shield and smashed one in the head, then continued spinning and stabbed one in the gut. But that left his flank exposed, and another soldier smashed him in the ribcage with his shield, sending him down to the ground, his head already ringing from the blow.

The battlefield filled with the clang of armor, of swords, the cacophony of two walls of metal smashing into each other, as men fought men up and down the ranks, brutal, bloody, hand to hand, neither giving in an inch. The air was quickly filled with the sound of men's shrieks, as bodies fell and blood stained the ground.

Under Koldo, Ludvig, and Kaden's command, the brilliant soldiers of the Ridge did not wait for the Empire, but charged themselves, leading with swords and axes, felling a dozen men before the Empire could regroup. As Empire soldiers reached them, swinging for their heads, they ducked and let them fly right by—then spun around and slashed, letting their momentum send them falling face-first in the mud. Kaden was especially impressive, blocking a soldier's blow before it killed his brother Ludvig, then stabbing the man in the gut. Ludvig looked at his younger brother with surprise and gratitude.

"You saved me," Kaden said. "You didn't forget me in the desert. Did you think I really would not pay you back?"

Erec led his men of the Southern Isles with a different strategy, all of them lined up in their golden armor, perfectly disciplined, one fine-tuned unit as they stepped forward and, on Erec's command, all hurled spears together. A wall of spears sailed through the air, felling dozens of approaching Empire—and causing the Empire soldiers behind them to trip and fall on their corpses.

Barely had they regrouped when Erec's soldiers hurled another round of spears—then another.

When they ran out of spears, Erec and his men rushed forward with a shout, drawing their swords, and stabbed the wounded where they fell—before turning to the next wave of attackers. Erec ducked and dodged several blows, then kicked one soldier, knocking him back, then spun around and chopped off another's head. He used his shield as a weapon, too, smashing and stunning his opponents before following up with his blade. He was an unstoppable force, a one-man army. And his men, Strom in the forefront, were nearly as good as he.

Gwendolyn, standing in the middle of it all, raised her bow and dropped one soldier after the next before they got close to her. Around her were Kendrick, Brandt, and Atme standing guard, watching over her. When Gwen ran out of arrows and the Empire soldiers got too close, Kendrick stepped forward, slashing them, keeping them at bay, Brandt and Atme and the rest of the Silver joining, rallying around their Queen. Steffen stood right beside them, guarding Gwendolyn from all directions, slashing and tackling any man who came too close. And if anyone slipped through the cracks, Krohn leapt up again and again, taking down one soldier after the next, as he hovered around Gwendolyn.

Alistair stood close to Gwen, and she reached up with her palms, aimed them at the soldiers, and shot out red balls of light. They felled soldiers left and right, knocking them down from ten feet away.

Godfrey did his best to fight, wielding a sword awkwardly beside Akorth, Fulton, Ario, and Merek. But he was no warrior, and after a few clumsy blows, he soon found himself off-balance, staggering, exposed. A particularly large soldier stepped forward, grimaced, and raised a battle-ax high—and Godfrey knew he was about to die.

There came a clang of metal, and Godfrey looked over gratefully to see Darius holding out his sword, blocking it, sparing his life. Merek rushed forward, too, and stabbed the soldier in the gut. And when another soldier lunged for Darius's exposed back, Dray rushed forward and bit off his ankle.

Ario wielded his sling, as did Angel, and the two of them took out dozens of soldiers. Akorth and Fulton tried to fight, but within moments their shields were stripped from them, and they, too, were on the verge of death. But Dray spotted it, and rushed forward, and spared them, snarling as he bit their attackers, giving Akorth and Fulton a chance to scurry to their feet and flee.

From Koldo to Erec to Kendrick to Darius to Alistair to Gwendolyn, they all stood and fought together, shoulder to shoulder, a wall of warriors united in will, united in love for their homeland, none giving up, none backing down. They all fought for the Ring, for the last place they had left in the world, this land that was more than just a place.

But as the suns sank lower and hour blended with hour, Reece, exhausted, sweat stinging his eyes, covered in blood, heaps of corpses at his feet, felt his shoulders getting tired. He was slowing, getting sloppy; his response time was not as fast and he began to swing lackadaisically. As he looked around, he noticed all his men were tiring. More and more death shouts rang out—and not on the Empire side. His ranks were thinning.

Reece cried out as he received a slash wound on his neck, but he forced himself to drive it from his mind. Stara stepped forward and stabbed his attacker in the gut with her spear.

It was small consolation. Knowing he was going to die, a part of Reece, despite himself, hoped this wound would finish him, that this would all finally be over—while another part of him hoped this day would never end. He wanted to kill as many men as he could before he went, to die with honor, to fight up to his very last sword slash in this, the greatest battle he knew he would ever fight in his life.

But as yet another wave of fresh Empire soldiers emerged from the wood, he did not know how much longer he could last.

Please, God, he prayed, *lend my shoulders strength. Allow me to raise my sword one last time. Give me the strength to die with honor.*

*

Godfrey held his sword with two shaking hands, Akorth, Fulton, Merek, and Ario beside him, Darius close by with Loti, and Dray at his heels, and he willed himself to hold his ground, to overcome his fears. The Empire kept advancing in endless waves, as if there were no end to the soldiers in the world, a fresh wall of men coming to kill him. He knew this was the end, and a part of him, shaking with fear, wanted to get it over with, to turn and run.

But another part of him forced himself to stay strong, to throw caution to the wind. He was tired of running, of being afraid, as he had his entire life. Something had been changing inside him, and now that he was back in his homeland especially, this place where his family had fought so bravely, for so many generations, he was having a realization. He realized he had been *resisting* his entire life: resisting his father, resisting his brothers, resisting his role in the royal family, resisting the life of a warrior. Resisting responsibility. Resisting valor.

For the first time in his life, he realized how much energy all of this resisting took. For the first time, staring death in the face, he no longer wished to resist—he wished to join in. To embrace his family. To embrace his lineage. To become a hero like his father, like his brothers. He wanted honor. *Honor*, he realized, had always been lingering right in front of him, just out of reach. He had always been afraid to reach out and grasp it, to embrace it. But now, finally, he realized how easy it was. To achieve honor, one merely had to act with honor, to act in an honorable way. One could embrace honor at any time; it was always waiting for you, like a parent that never stopped believing in you.

Godfrey stepped forward with a great battle cry, and he released all of his pent-up fear, his rage, his desire to protect himself. He raised his sword high and brought it straight down on an Empire soldier who went to stab him, and as he did, he sliced through the soldier's armor and slashed him across the chest. He was surprised by his own strength, his own speed. That soldier had been twice his size, and surely had killed many men.

Godfrey looked down, shocked, as the soldier fell before him. He couldn't believe what he had just done; he was a stranger to himself. And he liked this stranger.

Beside him, Darius fought brilliantly, weaving in and out of the soldiers, killing the Empire with a vengeance, two, three, four at a time, while on his other side, Loti threw spears and her brother Loc, even with his limp, wielded, with his one good hand, a long machete, felling soldiers all around him.

Merek and Ario fought like men possessed, Merek slashing men with his dagger and Ario hurling with his sling and disarming soldiers. Akorth and Fulton at one point seemed to lose their courage and begin to retreat to the bridge with all the other citizens and women and children. But Godfrey was surprised and elated to see them have a change of heart, to see them turn back and throw themselves into the battle. They were overweight, awkward, off-balance, but they used their weight well, managing to tackle several soldiers down to the ground. Rolling on the ground, they used found large rocks and used them to bash their attackers unconscious.

Godfrey, veins pumping with adrenaline, with the thrill of battle, with the sense of purpose of defending his family, his only homeland, finally felt a sense of purpose in the world. He felt closer to his father than he'd ever had, closer to his people, to Kendrick and the knights. For the first time, he felt like one of them. For the first time he understood, finally, what chivalry meant. It meant not giving into your fears; it meant losing yourself in battle; it meant giving up your life for those you loved. For the first time, Godfrey was gasping for air, covered in wounds—and not caring.

He would die today, he knew that for sure—especially as fresh waves of Empire soldiers burst through the wood—and yet he no longer cared. He would die, at least, with valor.

*

Gwendolyn stood by the edge of the Canyon, pushed back all the way to the edge, as were all her men, all fighting for their lives but no longer able to hold back the Empire tide. The two suns nearly setting, they had been fighting the entire day, had put up a more heroic defense than she could have ever dreamt, and for that, she was so grateful.

But now, the tide had turned. She heard a whine, and she looked over to see several Empire soldiers kicking Krohn and bashing him with their shields; she saw Kendrick stabbed in the arm as a half dozen Empire soldiers surrounded him; she saw Darius drop to his knees, smashed by a war hammer on his shoulder; she saw Dray take an arrow in his paw, collapsing; and she saw Erec and his men, Koldo and his men, all of her people being pushed back in an unstoppable wave.

Soon, she knew, there would be nowhere left to back up to. In but a few feet, they would all be pushed over the edge of the Canyon, to their deaths below.

Gwendolyn, in one final act of desperation, looked up, searched the skies, and prayed.

Thorgrin, my love. Where are you? I need you now. I need you more than ever.

Gwen watched, eyes fixed on the sky, as an Empire soldier stepped forward, raised a shield, and smashed the bow and arrow from her hand, then bashed her on the head.

She stumbled and fell on her back, too numb to even feel the pain anymore. She looked up from this vantage point, searching the skies, her ears ringing, all the world seeming to be a daze. She tried to focus, her vision blurry, as she saw an Empire soldier stand over her and raise a sword with both hands. She knew her time had come.

But as she continued to look up, beyond him, over his shoulder, Gwen was sure she saw something. At first she thought it was her eyes playing tricks on her.

But then, as she looked closely, her heart leapt with joy. She felt like weeping.

Because there, bursting through the clouds, diving down low with a look of vengeance, of fury—of utter confidence—came a man she loved and knew as she loved herself. He was the sum of all her hopes and dreams, of everything she'd ever wanted, and he was here. Finally, here.

There, flying down for her, was Thorgrin.

CHAPTER FORTY THREE

Thor raced on the back of Lycoples faster than he'd ever had, gripping her scales with one hand and holding Guwayne in the other, and as he urged her faster, he prayed it was not too late. He had crossed half the world since fleeing from the Land of Blood with Guwayne, ecstatic to be able to hold his son again—and desperate to reach Gwendolyn and the others in time to take back the Ring. Indeed, as he flew, the Sorcerer's Ring throbbed on his finger, and he knew it was pulling him to his homeland, as if it were anxious to return there itself.

They flew and flew all night long beneath the light of a full moon, through the breaking dawn, through another day and now, finally, through the setting suns. All along, he had sensed the Blood Lord and his army just behind him, pursuing. He knew he would have to confront them soon enough.

But the time was not now. Now, first, he had to reach the Ring at all costs. He raced east, knowing his beloved Ring was somewhere on the horizon, anxious to lay eyes on it again, this place to which he never thought he would return. He thought of seeing Gwendolyn and Reece and Kendrick and the Legion and all his brothers in arms again, all of them waiting for him, needing him—and he felt an urgency beyond any he'd ever felt. He only hoped it was not too late, and that they were not already dead.

Guwayne cried in his arms, and Thor imagined Gwendolyn's joy at seeing him again, at finally being reunited. He felt a sense of pride that he had accomplished the mission—that he had not only retrieved the Sorcerer's Ring but had retrieved their son. He had promised, so many moons ago, that he would not return to her empty-handed, without their child—and he did not.

Thor heard behind him, somewhere on the horizon, the awful shrieks of the Blood Lord's creatures, raised from the depths of hell, howling as they had all throughout the night. He knew he had provoked a force even stronger than the Empire, and he knew there would be a price to pay. Their army would follow him anywhere, and Thor assumed they would find him, would all converge on the Ring. It would make an epic battle with the Empire even more so. Thor could feel the fate of the Ring hanging in the balance, and he knew that it could go either way. He had a great power now, with the Sorcerer's Ring and Lycoples beneath him—but the Empire had vast numbers, and the Blood Lord's reach was beyond all power.

Thor felt that he was flying into his destiny, the day he was chosen for, the battle he was born to fight. His whole life, everything he had learned, all of his training, it all led up to this final moment. This would be the deciding battle for himself, and for his people.

As Lycoples dipped through the clouds, suddenly the land mass of the Ring came into view, and Thor's heart beat faster at the sight of his old home, perfectly round with its jagged shores and high cliffs, from high above. He flew past its long shore, with its serrated edges of rock, rising high above the ocean, flew over the Wilds, the long stretch of dark woods beyond it, so fast he could hardly breathe. Then finally, the landscape opened beyond it, and Thor was breathless, as he always was, to see the chasm of the Canyon open up, the most mystical place on earth, with the long bridge leading across and into the mainland of the Ring.

As he looked down, Thor was even more shocked to see what appeared to be a million men, Empire soldiers bursting through the Wilds, a sea of black approaching the Canyon. And his heart fell as he saw what they were attacking. There, their backs to the Canyon, stood everyone he loved in the world, putting up a heroic defense. There was Reece, the Legion, Kendrick, Erec, his sister, Alistair—and most of all, in the middle, his heart leapt to see, was Gwendolyn. She was on her back, looking up, an Empire soldier standing over her and about to kill her.

"DOWN, LYCOPLES!" Thor shouted.

Lycoples needing no prodding. She screeched, as if she had seen it, too, and dove nearly straight down, Thor's stomach dropping as he held Guwayne tight, clutching onto Lycoples with his free hand. They plunged closer and closer to the earth, Thor willing Lycoples to go faster, and as they nearly reached the ground, they were so close now that Thor could see the terrified faces on all those below, looking up and looking death in the face.

And Thor was even more shocked as Lycoples suddenly opened her mouth and, for the first time since he had known her, roared.

Suddenly, there followed a stream of fire, as Lycoples craned back her neck and breathed with all her fury. The fire rained down like the hand of God—and everything changed on the battlefield below.

She aimed for the enemy, careful to avoid Gwen and her people, and hundreds of Empire soldiers were suddenly aflame, shrieking, flailing. She flew up and down their ranks, breathing fire again and again, decimating one wave of Empire soldiers after the next. Thor was especially relieved to see Gwendolyn rise back to her feet, spared from the fatal sword thrust just in time. He could see her looking up at him with love and hope—especially as she saw him clutching Guwayne—and more than anything, he wanted to be with her, too.

But they had more work to do first. Lycoples, after decimating the thousands of Empire soldiers before the Canyon, now one huge wall of flame, turned to the Wilds, to the Empire ranks pouring out of it and now trying to turn around, take cover in the trees, and hide. There would be no hiding, though.

Lycoples dove down low, flying over the treetops, Thor's stomach dropping as they came so low he could nearly touch them. Below, running beneath the trees, he saw the divisions of Empire soldiers, moments before so confident, ready to destroy the Ring, and now running for cover.

Lycoples opened her jaws and let loose a stream of flame, setting the Wilds on fire.

Great shrieks arose as she killed Empire soldiers by the thousands, setting the entire forest on fire. The blaze shot up to the sky, spreading out all the way to the base of the Canyon.

A few Empire soldiers tried lamely to resist, firing arrows, hurling spears, or raising shields to their faces.

But Lycoples was moving too fast—and her flames melted them all. Human weapons were harmless against her. Thor, never having seen her like this, was amazed at how powerful she had become.

Soon, though, there came a rasping noise, and Thor looked down and realized that as Lycoples opened her mouth, she was unable to breathe any more flame. She tried again and again, but no more flames appeared. She was still young, Thor realized, a baby dragon, and she needed time to recover. Thor looked down and saw, with dismay, tens of thousands more Empire troops on their way, marching through the Wilds. It was beyond belief; after all that destruction, the waves of men just kept on coming.

Thor circled back with her, realizing he needed to get Gwendolyn and the others to safety before the next wave of soldiers arrived. As they flew back into the clearing, along the edge of the Canyon, Thor felt the Sorcerer's Ring vibrating in his hand. He knew that this ring was supposed to be able to restore the Shield—and as he flew over it, he expected to see it come back, as in old days.

But it did not. Thor was baffled. He circled the Canyon again and again, feeling the Sorcerer's Ring vibrating, expecting the Shield to go up. For some reason he didn't understand, it did not. He realized something was still missing; there was something more he needed to complete.

Thor turned back to his people with a deepening sense of apprehension. With no Shield, and with more Empire on the way—and the Blood Lord's army—and with Lycoples unable to breathe fire, his people were all left in a precarious position. He would have to get them to safety fast.

Lycoples descended, Thor directing her to land before Gwendolyn, and as soon as they did, dozens crowded around them. Her people all stood there, stunned survivors, looking out at a wall of flame, saved by Thorgrin and Lycoples and eyes filled with gratitude. They all had been given a second life.

Thor dismounted and, holding Guwayne, ran and embraced Gwendolyn. He held her tight, a momentary reprieve amidst the carnage and smoldering flames, and he could feel Gwen sobbing over his shoulder as she held him tight.

She leaned back and kissed Thorgrin as she looked deep into his eyes, in a kiss that felt like it lasted forever. It was surreal to hold her in his arms again, to be standing next to her, on the same side of the world, after so much time, after so much had happened—after it had seemed so certain that they would never lay eyes on each other again. She embraced him again, clutching him as if afraid she would lose him again.

She finally looked down, and Thor reached out and handed her Guwayne, all bundled up. She slowly unraveled his blanket, then she burst into sobs again at the sight of him, taking him and clutching him tight. She held him as if she would never let go again.

The others came rushing forward—Reece, Kendrick, Erec, his sister, Alistair, the Legion—and one by one he embraced them all. Krohn rushed forward, too, jumping on him, licking him, and Thor embraced him like a brother. It lifted his heart to see them all here, together, all in one place—and on the verge of taking back their homeland. More than anything he wanted to speak to each and every one of them.

But Thor suddenly heard a rustling, and he turned and looked out and his heart dropped to see, emerging from the smoldering woods, thousands more Empire soldiers—the next wave of recruits, ready for blood. They were unstoppable.

Thor felt the Sorcerer's Ring vibrating on his finger and the Sword of the Dead vibrating in his grip, and he knew that Lycoples had taken it as far as she could—the rest was up to him now.

Thor turned and grabbed Gwen's shoulders urgently. He could see her and all the others looking to the Wilds in shock, as if amazed that more soldiers could still be coming. As if they had all celebrated too soon.

"The Shield," Thor said urgently. "It is not restored."

Gwen looked back at him and he could see the fear in her eyes—she knew what that meant.

"I don't understand," she said. "The Ring. The Sorcerer's Ring. It was supposed to—"

Thor shook his head.

"It did not work," he said. "Something is missing."

She looked back, shocked.

"You have no time," Thor continued. "You and all the others—you must cross now, to the far side of the Canyon. This battle, what's left of it, is mine now. Take our son, take these people, and cross."

She looked at him, terror and longing in her eyes.

248

"I vowed to never be apart from you again," she said. "Whatever the cost."

He shook his head.

"I can only fight this battle alone," he said. "If you want to help me, cross. Protect those on the other side. Allow me to fight here. This is my war now. And take Lycoples with you. The Sword of the Dead summons me, and I can't have you near me when it does."

She looked at him and her expression slowly shifted to one of understanding. Another battle cry filled the air, and the Empire soldiers, seeing Lycoples grounded, unable to breathe fire, were emboldened. They sprinted now for them.

"GO!" Thor yelled.

Gwendolyn finally seemed to understand, and she led the others as they all turned and finally heeded his request, crossing quickly over the Canyon to protect those on the other side, Lycoples joining them.

Thorgrin, standing there alone, facing the incoming army, looked forward to it. He felt the Sorcerer's Ring throbbing on his finger, felt the Sword of the Dead throbbing in his hand, and as he drew it, it rang with a sharp sound that seemed to cut through the world. It was ready—desperate—for a fight.

High above, he heard a screech, and Thor looked up to see Estopheles, his old friend, circling, and felt her with him, felt the presence of King MacGil with him, of all those who fought and died for the Ring.

And as thousands of soldiers charged, Thor felt the sword come to life in his hand, urging him on.

You are a warrior, it urged. *You never defend. You never wait for your enemies! You attack!*

Thor suddenly charged, letting out a great battle cry of his own, and he dove into the crowd, swinging the Sword like a thing possessed. He had never felt himself so powerful, never felt himself move with such speed. With each blow, he killed twenty Empire soldiers. He struck again, and again, and again, moving like a whirlwind, killing them by the dozens, feeling his sword come alive, like an extension of his arm. This was the battle he knew he, and the Sword, were meant for.

Thorgrin felt bigger than himself, bigger than he had ever been. Buoyed by the power of the Ring, and of the Sword, he was like a channel for their energies. He let them take over his body, and as light shone forth from the Ring, he felt himself darting about the battlefield like lightning, felling hundreds of soldiers at a time. He moved so fast, even he did not understand what he was doing, none of the Empire soldiers, despite their greater numbers, standing a chance. It was as if they had all walked into a tsunami.

Whereas before there was noise, shouts, chaos, now there came peace, quiet, stillness. Thor blinked several times as he stood there, breathing hard, covered in blood, trying to understand what had just happened. He looked around, and he saw all around him, in circles, heaps of corpses.

All the Empire divisions that had come for him. All of them, dead.

Thorgrin slowly came back to himself, in a dim haze. He turned and looked back over the bridge and saw, on the far side, Gwendolyn's and the others' shocked expressions, all looking to him as if he were a god. He had single-handedly killed an entire division of Empire troops, ten thousand men, at least. The Empire waves, finally, had come to a stop. Finally, they were no longer being pursued.

But as soon as he had the thought, Thor suddenly heard an awful noise in the skies, like a rumbling of thunder, and as he looked up, his stomach fell. He knew immediately that he had won the most epic battle of his life—only for it to be replaced by one even more epic to come.

For as he looked up, Thor saw an army of creatures from hell—and at their head, the Blood Lord, face contorted in fury.

Tens of thousands of his creatures, larger than gargoyles, smaller than dragons, black, hairy, screeching, were converging behind him, plunging down, right for Thor. Finally, they had caught up with him. Finally, he would have to pay the price for stealing back Guwayne.

They came at him as one army of death, claws extended, and Thor knew that he was in for the battle of his life.

Thor stood there, watching them come for him, and felt the Sword of the Dead buzzing in his hands, willing him to fight.

There is no foe too great for you, young warrior! it urged.

And in his hand, holding the Sword, he felt the Sorcerer's Ring, throbbing, sending a heat up his arm that urged him to fight.

The first gargoyle descended and Thor slashed, again and again. He did not stop slashing as one wave of gargoyles after the next plummeted, claws out, aiming for his face, slashing them down as he spun left and right. He chopped off claws, heads, arms; he stabbed them, swirled, feeling the power of the Sorcerer's Ring emboldening him as he felled them by the dozens.

They fell all around him, piling up in heaps, none able to touch him.

But Thorgrin suddenly heard awful cries rise up behind him, and he turned and looked out to see Gwendolyn and all of their people on the far side of the Canyon, bracing themselves as the gargoyles descended for them, too. Thousands more gargoyles emerged, encircling them on every side, leaving nowhere to run. Thorgrin did not fear for himself— but he feared for his people, especially as he watched them begin to fall.

Thorgrin knew that, despite everything, despite the powers of the Sword of the Dead, of the Sorcerer's Ring, he was losing this battle. He would not be able to save his people in time.

What he needed, he knew, was the Shield restored. It was the only way to protect them. But there was something he was missing, some final riddle, some final piece of the puzzle.

"ARGON!" Thor called out, turning to the skies. "Where are you!? I need you now!"

There came no response, and Thor turned and searched in every direction.

"ARGON!" he persisted. "What is it I am missing? What is it that I need to be worthy?"

Thorgrin suddenly sensed a presence behind him, and he turned and saw Argon appearing, standing alone in the center of the bridge. He stood there, facing him, holding his staff, staring back at him, eyes so bright they outshone the suns.

As he stood there, mesmerized, Thor suddenly felt himself get scratched by a gargoyle—and then felt a tug at his hand. He was horrified to feel another snatch the Sword of the Dead from his hands, to watch it carry it away, farther and farther from him, flying up until it disappeared in the skies.

Thor stood there, now defenseless, knowing he was failing. He would lose this epic battle for all time.

He ran to Argon, across the bridge, rushing to meet him, and he watched as Argon slowly closed his eyes, turned his palms, and raised them to the sky. As he did, a shaft of sunlight shot down from the heavens, illuminating him.

"Thorgrin," he boomed, his voice so powerful it resonated like thunder, echoing throughout the Canyon, rolling even above the sound of the gargoyles. "The Sorcerer's Ring can bring back the Shield—but it cannot do it alone. You are still missing one piece of the puzzle. One piece of yourself, which you have forgotten."

He opened his eyes and looked right at Thorgrin, now just feet away, his eyes so intense, they were more fearful than the hordes of the earth. And then he said:

"The Destiny Sword."

Thor stared back at Argon in shock.

"I thought it was destroyed," Thor said.

"It was," Argon said. "But the Sorcerer's Ring can bring it back. The weapon of the Chosen One will always be yours. What protected this Canyon must be returned. Only the Sorcerer's Ring can raise it up—and a sacrifice."

Thor stared back, puzzled.

"A sacrifice?" he asked. "I will do anything."

Argon shook his head.

"It is not for *you* to do."

Thor stare back, baffled.

"It is my sacrifice, Thorgrin," Argon said. "I can raise the Sword—if I give up my life."

Thor began to realize what he was saying, and he felt overcome with a sense of dread, of loss. Argon. His mentor. His teacher. The one he respected more than anyone in the world. He had been with him on his journey since the beginning, before he had even ventured to King's Court. The one he had met when just a boy, a boy who did not know his power. The one who had encouraged him to follow his destiny, who had told him he could be something, someone, greater. The only one who had been a real father to him.

"NO!" Thor yelled, realizing.

Thor ran for him, the last few feet, trying to grab him to save him in time.

But it was too late.

Argon walked to the rail, and slowly, gracefully, dove off of it, arms out wide by his side.

Thor watched in horror as he plummeted. As he did, the shaft of light followed him, swirling all different colors.

"ARGON!" Thorgrin shrieked.

Argon fell straight down in a swan dive, right into the mists of the Canyon, and disappeared from Thorgrin's eyes forever.

Thorgrin felt his heart torn to pieces as he watched, knowing this time Argon was truly gone forever.

And Thor was equally shocked to see there rise out of the mist, right where Argon had fell, a single weapon, illuminated in the shaft of light.

It rose higher and higher, then floated right to him, right into his palm. It was a perfect fit.

The Destiny Sword.

It was his, once again.

CHAPTER FORTY FOUR

The Destiny Sword vibrated and pulsed in Thor's hand, and as the Sorcerer's Ring shone, Thor felt himself having a power unlike any he'd ever known. He felt a driving vengeance to end this war, for himself, for Gwendolyn, for the Ring, for Argon.

Thor turned and, facing the gargoyles with a new energy, leapt into action. He leapt up into the air, slashing wildly, meeting them on their own terms, and cut through them like butter, their screeches filling the air as he felled them in every direction. They dropped all around him in heaps, until the surviving gargoyles finally turned and flew off in fear.

Thorgrin stood there in the center of the bridge, his people still being attacked in the Ring, and he sensed that the Shield was almost ready to rise again. But there was still one last task he had left to perform.

The skies thundered and all the remaining gargoyles quickly parted, as plunging down there appeared Thor's nemesis: The Blood Lord. He landed before Thorgrin in the center of the bridge, holding a massive halberd, sneering back, twice Thor's size, all muscle. Thor stood his ground, facing him, wielding the Destiny Sword, and he knew that this would the most important battle he'd ever fought. The one that defined him for all time. The one that decided the fate of his people.

Thor could see the armies lined up on both sides, watching this epic fight, knowing the results would dictate the future for them both.

As the Blood Lord approached, Thor was on guard, remembering he had been defeated by him once, and sensing within him an energy more evil than any he had ever known.

As Thor faced him, examined him, he sensed something—and suddenly had a realization.

"You are my father, reborn," Thor said, realizing. "You are Andronicus."

The Blood Lord grinned down at him with an evil grin.

"I warned you I would haunt you," he replied, "that my spirit would live on. That you would have to face me one last time. Now I shall kill you for good, and take back what is mine—my bloodline—Guwayne."

Thor, filled with fury at the thought, felt the Destiny Sword itching in his palm. He threw it back and forth, from palm to palm, ready.

"Let us meet then, Father," he said. "Finally, let father and son embrace!"

Thorgrin raised his sword and the Blood Lord raised his halberd, and the two of them rushed each other, meeting in the center of the bridge like rams, in a clash of arms, a clang of metal, that echoed throughout the Canyon.

Back and forth they went, Thor slashing and the Blood Lord blocking, each with a weapon powerful enough to destroy the world, and each well matched against the other. Thor sensed this was an epic battle between light and darkness, one which held the very fate of the world in the balance. He was facing off, he knew, with the most powerful demon in the world, more powerful even than all the Empire. Thor sensed that the Blood Lord was an amalgamation of dark forces, all released from the darkest corners of the world and coming together in one being.

As they fought, slashing and blocking, Thor ducking and whirling, he knew the Shield would never be restored until the Blood Lord was finished, until he defeated this final, and worst, enemy. He would also be defeating his father, and a piece of himself.

"You cannot defeat me," the Blood Lord said, as he blocked a blow from the Destiny Sword, turning his halberd sideways, then shoved Thor, sending him stumbling back. "Because I am you. Search deep inside, and you can feel it. I am the darkness within you."

He rushed forward, swinging the halberd, and Thor was amazed at how fast it came down, slicing through the air even though it was so huge, so unwieldy in his hands. If he had been anyone else, Thor knew, that blow would have sliced him in half.

But some instinct kicked in Thor, propelled by the Sorcerer's Ring, that allowed him to jump out of the way at the last second. The halberd just missed, Thor feeling the wind of it.

The Blood Lord's eyes widened in surprise, as if he had not expected this. He then swung around, raised the halberd high, and brought it down with both hands, as if to chop Thor in half.

Thor jumped back, and the halberd lodged itself into the stone of the bridge, embedding itself almost a foot deep as it cut through the stone, the sound of it echoing off the Canyon walls as if thunder had just struck.

The Blood Lord growled, infuriated; Thor was certain his weapon was stuck, but the Blood Lord surprised him by yanking it out smoothly, as if it were nothing, and charging again.

As the halberd came down again for his head, this time Thor raised the Destiny Sword and blocked the blow with a clang, sparks flying everywhere, holding it in place overhead. The clang was so loud it, it echoed throughout the cliffs of the Canyon.

The Blood Lord swung the halberd around again and again, from side to side, each time Thor blocking. Thor was surprised to realize that it was difficult to block each blow, so powerful, even with the Sorcerer's Ring, even with the Destiny Sword. He realized that any of these blows would have cut an army in half. They were two titanic forces, two titanic weapons smashing into each other.

Thor, after being backed up by dozens of blows, felt a heat beginning to rise in his palms, felt the power of the Destiny Sword beginning to well up within him. It forced him to raise his arms in one quick gesture, swing the Destiny Sword around and down, both arms above his head, and bring it straight down for the Blood Lord. It came down with more power and strength than he had ever felt, and with a greater speed, and he felt certain it would slice the Blood Lord in two.

But he turned his halberd and blocked, and Thor was amazed to see him able to stop the blow, albeit with shaking hands. Thor saw the shocked expression on the Blood Lord's face, and knew he was surprised, did not expect a blow of such force.

Back and forth they went, swinging and blocking, parrying and ducking and dodging and slashing and stabbing. Neither could land a blow. They were perfectly matched, their great clangs ringing out again and again, like two mountains colliding with each other, as they pushed each other back and forth the Canyon bridge.

As Thor blocked a blow overhead, his arms shaking, beginning to tire, the Blood Lord surprised him by immediately swinging around for a second blow. Thor blocked, but it threw him off balance, and he found himself stumbling to the side, to the edge of the stone railing lining the bridge.

Before he could regroup, Thor suddenly felt rough hands grab him from behind, felt himself hoisted high in the air, and found himself weightless, up high, and looking down over the edge of the Canyon.

Thor could hear his people gasp, thousands of them, as his life hung in the balance.

And a moment later, Thor felt himself go flying over the edge, hurling into the abyss.

CHAPTER FORTY FIVE

As he flew through the air, Thor suddenly felt the Sorcerer's Ring throbbing on his finger. He felt an incredible power radiate from it, control his hand, his arm, and guide him. It forced him to swing his arm around, impossibly fast, to reach out and grab the stone railing with one hand.

Thor was amazed to find himself grabbing holding of the stone and, in the same motion, swinging himself back up and around onto the bridge. As he did, he kicked the Blood Lord in the chest, and he, clearly not expecting this, went stumbling back, landing on the ground.

Thor could hear his people cheer.

Thor charged and slashed, ready to finish him off, but the Blood Lord surprised him by rolling and blocking. He then swung his halberd around for Thor's feet. Thor jumped, it barely missing.

The Blood Lord gained his feet and the two of them faced off, once again slashing and blocking, weapons sparking, as they drove each other back and forth.

"I am stronger than you, Thorgrin," the Blood Lord said, between blows. "Darkness is stronger than light!"

He brought his halberd down and Thorgrin blocked it. But the blow was stronger this time, and as he pushed, it came closer and closer to Thor's face. With shaking hands, Thor barely held it back.

"Give in," the Blood Lord snarled. "Give in to the sweet darkness and join me for all time!"

Thor managed to push back the blow, sending him back.

But at the same time, the Blood Lord surprised Thor by immediately swinging up with his halberd, straight up with lightning speed, coming underneath Thor's sword and managing to smash it out from his hands, disarming him.

Thor watched in horror as the Destiny Sword went flying up in the air, spinning end over end, then skidded across the stone floor of the Canyon bridge.

Thorgrin stood there, facing him, unarmed, the Blood Lord between he and his sword, grinning back an evil grin. Thor realized he did not need the Sword. He did not need any weapon; he had all the power he needed within himself.

Thor lunged forward, unafraid, and tackled the Blood Lord, driving him down to the ground. The Blood Lord was caught off guard by the sudden move, and his halberd went flying as he fell, clanging on the stone.

The two of them rolled on the stone, Thor trying to pin him down; but the Blood Lord was twice his size, and all-muscle, and as Thor final pinned him, the Blood Lord managed to roll and then pin Thor.

The Blood Lord held him down, choking him, and as Thor reached up and grabbed his wrists, holding him back, his huge, sharp claws came down right for his throat.

Thor, losing air, weaved in and out of consciousness. He struggled back with all that he had, but he realized he was losing. The dark force was prevailing. The Sorcerer's Ring was shining less brightly, as if it, too, were dying.

As Thor felt himself go weaker, images passed through his mind. He saw his mother, her castle, the skywalk. He saw himself kneeling before her, asking forgiveness.

"Forgive me, Mother," he said. "I have failed. I have lost for all time."

She placed a hand upon his forehead.

"You have not failed, Thorgrin. Not until you admit failure."

"He is too strong for me," Thorgrin said. "I have lost the secret. I do not know how to vanquish darkness. My faith does not match his."

She smiled down.

"It is your final lesson, Thorgrin," she said. "It is the final secret you have been missing all this time. The one you need to win for all time."

Thorgrin stared back, in and out of consciousness as he was choked.

"Tell me, Mother," he said.

"It is not power," she said. "It is not power that makes a warrior great."

Thor blinked, feeling his life force ebbing away.

"But what is it, Mother?"

She smiled.

"It is *love*, Thorgrin. It is *love* that makes us powerful. Love for your family. Love for your people. Love for your country. Love for honor. And most of all, love for yourself. That is the power you are missing. It is a power greater even than hate."

Thor blinked, several times, realizing, and as he did, he felt his body grow warm.

Thor suddenly opened his eyes, feeling the Ring throbbing on his finger, seeing its light shine more brightly. He looked up at the Blood Lord's face, saw him scowling down, and finally, Thorgrin understood. He understood the secret to battle. The secret to power. And he suddenly felt an insurmountable power.

Thor swung his arms around, knocked the Blood Lord's arms' grip from his throat and threw him off of him, sending him tumbling back on the stone.

The Blood Lord turned and looked back in shock. He scrambled to his feet, and for the first time, Thor could spot real fear in his face.

The Blood Lord scrambled for his halberd, running to it and gripping it with both hands as he faced Thor.

Thor, feeling all-powerful, walked to the Destiny Sword, reached down and picked it up, knowing that nothing could stop him now.

The two of them stood there, facing each other, and the Blood Lord let out a fierce battle cry, raised his halberd high, and charged Thor.

He swung down at Thor, and this time, Thor blocked it easily with the Destiny Sword. Their weapons clanged and sparked as he came at Thor again and again, swinging left and right. But this time, something had changed: Thor reacted more quickly, blocking the blows easily. Thor felt more powerful than ever, and he blocked each blow as if it were nothing.

The Blood Lord noticed, too, as he stared back at Thor with increasing fear in his face.

Finally, the Blood Lord stood there, breathing hard, spent.

Thor, though, was not tired at all. He stepped forward, slashing again and again, his blows more powerful than ever, the Blood Lord raising his halberd and blocking them, but barely in time, weakly. With each sword slash, his reaction time became slower, Thor pushed him back further, and it was getting harder for him to even lift his halberd.

Finally, Thor came up and around with a great slash, and as he did, he knocked the halberd from the Blood Lord's grip.

It went flying, end over end through the air, over the side of the railing, and plunging down into the Canyon.

The blow had also managed to knock the Blood Lord down onto his back. He lay there, staring up at Thorgrin, shocked. Terrified. Clearly, he had never expected this.

Thor stood over him, calm, relaxed, stronger than he'd ever been. He had conquered something within himself, and for the first time in his life, he felt free. Fearless. Invincible.

The Blood Lord must have sensed it, because he looked back at Thor as if he knew something had shifted within him. He raised his hands weakly.

"You cannot defeat me, Thorgrin!" he yelled. "Lay down your sword and accept me!"

But Thor stepped forward, drew back the Destiny Sword, and with one definitive thrust, he plunged it into the Blood Lord's heart. The thrust kept going, the sword lodging in the stone with a tremendous noise, like an earthquake, the entire bridge, the entire Canyon, shaking as it did, as if Thor had plunged the Sword into the spine of the world itself.

The crowds on both sides of the Canyon gasped as the Blood Lord lay there, flat on his back, staring up at the sky with a look of surprise.

Dead.

Suddenly, the dark clouds above parted and there appeared a black funnel cloud, whirling down from the sky like a tornado. It came down right for the body of the Blood Lord, scooped him up, and carried him away, spinning, into nothingness.

As he died, suddenly, all of his creatures, on both sides of the Canyon, even those attacking Thor's people, burst into flames, dying, too. His entire army, wiped out with him.

Thor felt the Sorcerer's Ring throbbing in his hand, and he reached out and slowly raised his ring finger, knowing the time had come. He aimed it down at the Canyon, and slowly, it began to shake.

A wall of red and purple light rose up from the mist, swirling, climbing higher and higher; as it increased in velocity, it spread, all the way through the Canyon, aglow with all different colors as it grew more and more solid. Thor's heart lifted as he realized: the Shield. It was, after all this time, restored.

Thor watched as on the far side of the Canyon fresh hordes of Empire soldiers tried to cross the bridge, to attack him and his people. But he watched with joy as they bounced into the Shield and were killed on the spot.

His people, finally safe, let out a great cheer.

And Thor could not help smiling himself.

The Ring, finally, was protected. It was one again.

TWELVE MOONS LATER

CHAPTER FORTY SIX

Gwendolyn stood at the window of her chamber, atop the newly built castle in the center of the newly built King's Court, and as she, holding Guwayne, looked out at the splendor of the city being erected, her heart swelled with joy. Down below, stone by stone, brick by brick, building by building, King's Court was being rebuilt on its foundations, whatever remained, restored, and whatever did not, built from memory. Even more, they had spread out its original foundations, so the capital was now twice the size it had been in her father's time. The streets were bustling, joyous people roaming them, hard at work, filled with industry, with purpose. An air of peace, of comfort, spread over the city.

Endless groups of newly minted knights strolled the newly paved cobblestone streets in their shining armor, making their way to and fro from the newly built training grounds, jousting lanes, and the Hall of the Silver. They also bustled to and fro at the new Hall of Arms, choosing from an endless array of newly forged weapons and armor. She spotted Erec, Kendrick, Brandt, and Atme amongst them, joined by the new ranks of Silver and by scores of knights from the Southern Isles, all laughing, jostling with each other, true joy on their faces.

Across the new marble courtyard, replete with a golden fountain in its center, Gwen examined the new Hall of the Ridge, hundreds more knights swarming outside it. Koldo, Ludvig, Kaden, Ruth and the remnants of the elite fighting force of the Ridge lingered outside it, the two sides of the MacGil family united from the two ends of the earth. Two armies, now one, and stronger than they had ever been. Gwen thought of her father, of the pride he would take to see them all like this, to see King's Court like this again.

The boom in building and prosperity had spread to every corner of the Ring, slowly being re-inhabited over these past twelve moons—even across the Highlands. With the McClouds gone, no longer was there tension on the two sides of the mountains, but harmony and peace, all of them one nation, flying the same banner. Citizens, every day, spread out to new towns, rebuilding old ones, or starting new ones. The sound of hammers and anvils were everywhere, as new life spread, like a force which could not be stopped. Even all the vineyards and orchards, burnt to the ground but a year ago, were now, under Godfrey's watchful eye, in bloom again, and bore more fruit and wine than ever. The Ring, Gwen was surprised to realize, was more magnificent than it had ever been.

But all of that was not even what made Gwendolyn as happy as she was. What filled her heart to overflowing was not only being back home, but more importantly, being back at Thorgrin's side again—and having Guwayne back in her arms. She held him tight and looked down into his glowing gray eyes, his blond hair, and she could hardly believe that he was one year old today. He was a strikingly beautiful child, and not a day went by when she did not spend all the time with him that she could, taking more joy from him than just about anything else. After all they had been through, she could appreciate, more than ever, what it meant to be apart from him, and vowed that should never happen again.

Bells tolled in the distance, harmonious, soothing, and Gwen remembered why she was even happier on this day than most. For today, after so much turmoil, so many obstacles, so much time apart, she would officially be wed to her love, to Thorgrin. Gwen's heart beat faster at the thought, and she looked down and saw the city resplendent on this day, people hurrying in all directions as wedding preparations filled the city. Doors were being draped with roses, streets lined with petals, casks of wine being rolled out onto fields as benches were set before them. Jugglers and musicians and bards were gathering in bands, preparing, while cooks were toiling over vats of meat. And in the center of it all, countless chairs were being lined up before the most beautiful altar Gwen had ever seen, ten feet high and draped with white roses.

Thousands of people, all dressed in their finest, were pouring through the half-built city gates, all eagerly awaiting the big moment. It was a wedding befitting a Queen—and much more than that. Today was a very special day, indeed the most special day in the history of the Ring—for on this day, not only would she and Thorgrin wed, but six other couples would join them: Erec and Alistair, Reece and Stara, Kendrick and Sandara, Godfrey and Illepra, Elden and Indra, and

Darius and Loti. It was already being dubbed the historic Day of Seven Weddings, one that was sure to be famed in the annals of the Ring forever. It made Gwen recall, many moons ago, Argon's prophecy: *You will experience a darkness, followed by a joy, a joy so great that it will make all the darkness seem light.*

"My Queen?" came a voice.

Gwendolyn turned and looked across her chamber, and her heart skipped a beat to see Thorgrin standing there, dressed in his finest, wearing a long, black velvet robe atop his armor, looking more gorgeous than she'd ever seen him. He looked her up and down, and his eyes shone with pride and joy.

"Your dress," he said. "It is the most beautiful I have ever laid eyes upon."

Gwen beamed, remembering her wedding dress, forgetting she'd even had it on, and as he approached, she walked to him, holding Guwayne, and they leaned in and kissed.

"May I escort you to the altar?" he asked, a smile on his face, his eyes shining.

She beamed back.

"There is nothing I would like more."

*

As Thor walked with Gwendolyn, the two holding hands as they strolled, he relished their alone time together. Gwendolyn had given Guwayne to Illepra to hold during the ceremonies, and the two of them, always so busy with a million affairs of court, of rebuilding, finally had a quiet moment before the big ceremony. Thor wanted to spend the time alone with her, before they were back in the limelight.

"Where are we going, my lord?" she asked with a smile, as he led her away from the wedding grounds.

He smiled back mischievously.

"I wanted to steal some alone time with my Queen. I hope that's OK?"

She smiled back and squeezed his hand.

"Nothing would make me happier," she replied.

They walked, weaving their way through court, past throngs of people who smiled and half-bowed as they went, removing their caps, all grinning ear to ear, all ecstatic for the big day. Thor could see all the trumpeters lining up, all the boys preparing the fireworks for the big night to come. He could see the torches being lit up and down the aisle, even though it was still sunset, and he could see thousands of people taking their seats. Bells continued to toll lightly, as if to signify festivities that would never end.

"Thor, look!" cried out an excited girl's voice.

Thor turned at the familiar voice, and was thrilled, as he always was, to see Angel, running up him, beaming, her new friend Jasmine at her side. Thor was especially happy to see Angel perfectly healthy, healed from her leprosy, as she had been ever since he had retrieved the Sorcerer's Ring and raised the Shield. Happy, beaming, healthy, she was like a different kid.

Especially now, that she had a new best friend in Jasmine—who seemed equally delighted to have her. Jasmine never stopped carrying her books, and Angel, book-starved from all her years on an island, could never get enough of hearing Jasmine's long, scholarly monologues.

"Do you like my dress?" she asked, excited.

"Will we make the perfect flower girls?" Jasmine echoed.

Thor grinned as he looked down and saw them both in beautiful, white silk dresses, white roses in their hair, each so excited.

"You couldn't be more perfect," he said.

"I shall get married just to see the two of you walk down the aisle looking the way you do!" Gwen added.

They both giggled with delight and pride.

"Krohn is trying to get your attention!" Angel added.

Thor heard a whining and he looked down to see Krohn at his heels, struggling to catch up. He clearly wanted Thor's attention, and he turned and saw not far away, Krohn's five new cubs, with their mother, a female leopard. Thor smiled wide, realizing how proud Krohn was, and patted him on the head, leaned down, and kissed him.

As he did, Thor heard a jealous screech, and he looked up to see Lycoples suddenly swoop down, much bigger now than ever, land before them, and lower his head, waiting. Thor and Gwen stepped forward, stroking it, and Thor laughed.

"Don't be jealous," he said to Lycoples.

Lycoples screeched, flapped her wings, then took off, circling high in the sky.

"Let's chase her!" Angel cried out in delight, and the two of them ran off, giggling, trying to chase after Lycoples' trail in the sky.

Thor took Gwen's hand again and they continued walking, Thor leading Gwen to a spot that was sacred to him. The Kolvian Cliffs. This place had survived the war, the great invasion, and was much like it had always been, giving Thor a peaceful feeling. This had always been a special place for him, the place they had buried King MacGil, a place he could get away, have peace, solace, and look out, from the highest point, over the Kingdom. Thor held Gwen's hand as the two of them stood there, looking out together, at the vast empty sky, the setting suns, both red now, the sky streaked with a million colors, so perfect for their wedding day. Looking out, it was as if the world were being born anew. As if hope were springing up again.

As they stood there, far from the throngs, alone, peaceful, just the two of them, Thor could feel Gwen's palm in his, and he reflected. He was flooded with memories. He remembered his first appearance in King's Court, arriving here as just a boy, being so intimidated by this place; he remembered the first time he had lain eyes upon Gwendolyn, how tongue-tied he had been; he remembered the first time he had met Reece, remembered his joining the Legion. He remembered The Hundred, his training, all the men he had learned from, fought with. He remembered Argon's lessons, his counsel, and it was a presence he missed dearly.

He thought of his journey, how he had started out as just another boy with big dreams, a boy with no riches, no connections, no special skills. A boy who had been laughed at when he had arrived here—and yet who now, somehow, had achieved it all. He felt, most of all, a deep sense of gratitude. He knew that he had been very blessed.

Thor remembered, too, all the darkness. He remembered the trials, the assassinations, the demons, the destruction. The long, cold exile. He remembered all the times when he was sure he would not make it, sure that he could go no further. He thought back on all the hardship, and despite it all, he realized that if given the chance, he would not hesitate to choose to do it all over again. Because his quests were never for the sake of riches, or gain, or titles, or fame, or power—they were always

268

for the sake of honor. It was honor that drove him, and that always would.

Most of all, he remembered how much he loved Gwendolyn. She had been with him from the start, had taken a chance on him, just a boy, despite his position, despite his rank—and her love had never wavered. She had continued to love him all the way through their separation, had never given up hope, had survived, he was sure of it, so that they could be together again. It was her love, he realized, that sustained him most of all, that kept him going through all those hard times, that had given him a reason to live. Somehow he had always known they were destined to be together, and that nothing, no armies, no exile, no war, would ever keep them apart.

Now, as he stood there, holding her hand, watching the sun set, Thor marveled at how it all had come full circle, at how mysterious life was.

"What is it, my lord?" Gwen asked, squeezing his hand.

Thor shook his head and smiled, turning to her.

"I'm just remembering, my love."

She looked out at the sunset, too, and she nodded, understanding.

"I think of my father in this place," she said sadly. "So much we have lost. And yet so much gained."

Thor could feel King MacGil's spirit hovering over them in approval, along with Argon's. He thought of everyone he had loved and lost, and he felt his mother with them too. Finally, his quests were over.

Yet he also wondered. He knew the Shield was strong, knew that all those Empire forces out there could never penetrate it again. He knew he had nothing to fear, outside or inside the Ring. They were safer than they had been even in King MacGil's time.

Yet he also could not help but think of the prophecies, of the price he would have to pay for his sacrifice. Of the prophecy about his son, Guwayne, that he would one day rise to become a dark lord, more powerful even than Thorgrin. Thor looked down at the Sorcerer's Ring on his finger, at the Destiny Sword on his belt, and he wondered if that could be possible. He shuddered, thinking of the day. He pictured Guwayne, so pure, so innocent, thought of his intense love for him, and he could not imagine how it could be possible.

Just sorcerer's words, he thought.

Thor shook the prophecy from his mind, shook all dark thoughts from his mind. Now was not a time for brooding. Now was a time for joy. Unequivocal joy.

"Thorgrin! Gwendolyn!"

Thor turned with Gwen, and he was thrilled to see a group of men and a group of women, all dressed in their finest, approach: the grooms and brides. Kendrick, Erec, Reece, Darius, Elden, and Godfrey walked in one group, Dray at their heels, while Sandara, Alistair, Stara, Loti, Indra, and Illepra walked in the other. The six other couples, all set to be married with them today.

Illepra held Guwayne, and Alistair held her baby girl, now nearly one year old, the most beautiful baby girl Thor had ever seen, her eyes light blue, shining like her mother's. Thor knew she would grow up with Guwayne, that she, his sister's child, would have a fate inextricably linked with his son's. He could not help but wonder what would become of the next generation.

Godfrey held out a sack of wine for Thorgrin, while Illepra held one out for Gwendolyn, and Thor could see all the brides- and grooms-to-be were each already holding one. As the sun began to set, they all had such joy on their faces, faces filled with the expectation of the glorious wedding to come.

Godfrey raised his sack for a toast, and as all the others leaned in; Thorgrin did, too. They stood there against the setting sun, and Thor looked out at their faces, illuminated in the last light of day, these people he loved and respected the most. It was a privilege, he realized, to be able to fight by their side.

"What is best in life?" Godfrey asked, posing the question to all of them.

They all fell silent, and as they all pondered the question, one after another called out:

"Truth!"

"Sacrifice!"

"Duty!"

"Valor!"

"Courage!"

"Honor!" Thor chimed in.

270

There suddenly came a lone screech, high above, and Thor looked up to see Lycoples circling, joined by Estopheles, the two spreading their wings.

"It is settled, then!" Godfrey said.

They all nodded and raised their sacks higher.

"To honor!" Thorgrin called out.

"TO HONOR!" they all replied, their toast echoing off the cliffs of the Ring—and echoing in eternity.

AUTHOR NOTE

I am honored that you have read all 17 books in the Sorcerer's Ring. For those of you who wonder what the future holds for Guwayne, that epic tale will be told one day, in its own series, THE SORCERER'S SON. But that series is not planned for anytime soon.

Now it is time for me to focus on a new series, with new characters, new settings, a new world, and a brand new plot. Please allow me to be the first to invite you to my new epic fantasy series: KINGS AND SORCERERS.

NOW AVAILABLE!

RISE OF THE DRAGONS
(KINGS AND SORCERERS—BOOK 1)

"All the ingredients are here for an instant success: plots, counterplots, mystery, valiant knights, and blossoming relationships replete with broken hearts, deception and betrayal. It will keep you entertained for hours, and will satisfy all ages. Recommended for the permanent library of all fantasy readers."
—*Books and Movie Reviews*, Roberto Mattos *(regarding A Quest of Heroes)*

From #1 Bestselling author Morgan Rice comes a sweeping new epic fantasy series: RISE OF THE DRAGONS (KINGS AND SORCERERS—Book 1). Kyra, a 14 year old girl who dreams of following in her father's footsteps and becoming a famed warrior, is a finer archer than all the others. As she grapples to understand her skills, her mysterious inner power, and what secret is being kept from her about her birth, she comes to realize that she is different than the others, and that hers is a special destiny.

But her people live under the thumb of oppressive noblemen, and when she comes of age and the local lord comes for her, her father weds her off to save her. Kyra, though, refuses, and she journeys out on her own, into the dangerous wood—where she encounters a wounded dragon and ignites a series of events that will change the course of the kingdom forever.

15 year old Alec, meanwhile, sacrifices for his brother, taking his place in the draft, and is carted off to The Flames, a wall of flames a hundred feet high that keeps back the army of Trolls to the north. On the other side of the kingdom, Merk, a mercenary striving to leave behind his dark past, quests through the wood to become a Keeper of the Towers and help guard the Sword of Fire, the magical source of the kingdom's power. But the Trolls want the Sword, too—and they have other plans, preparing for a massive invasion that could destroy the kingdoms forever.

With its strong atmosphere and complex characters, RISE OF THE DRAGONS is a sweeping saga of knights and warriors, of kings and lords, of honor and valor, of magic, destiny, monsters and dragons. It is a story of love and broken hearts, of deception, of ambition and betrayal. It is fantasy at its finest, inviting us into a world that will live with us forever, one that will appeal to all ages and genders.

"[An] entertaining epic fantasy."
—Kirkus Reviews *(regarding A Quest of Heroes)*

"The beginnings of something remarkable are there."
--San Francisco Book Review *(regarding A Quest of Heroes)*

"Action-packed .... Rice's writing is solid and the premise intriguing."
--Publishers Weekly *(regarding A Quest of Heroes)*

"A spirited fantasy ....Only the beginning of what promises to be epic young adult series."
--Midwest Book Review *(regarding A Quest of Heroes)*

Books by Morgan Rice

KINGS AND SORCERERS
RISE OF THE DRAGONS (Book #1)
RISE OF THE VALIANT (Book #2)
THE WEIGHT OF HONOR (Book #3)
A FORGE OF VALOR (Book #4)
A REALM OF SHADOWS (Book #5)
NIGHT OF THE BOLD (Book #6)

THE SORCERER'S RING
A QUEST OF HEROES (Book #1)
A MARCH OF KINGS (Book #2)
A FATE OF DRAGONS (Book #3)
A CRY OF HONOR (Book #4)
A VOW OF GLORY (Book #5)
A CHARGE OF VALOR (Book #6)
A RITE OF SWORDS (Book #7)
A GRANT OF ARMS (Book #8)
A SKY OF SPELLS (Book #9)
A SEA OF SHIELDS (Book #10)
A REIGN OF STEEL (Book #11)
A LAND OF FIRE (Book #12)
A RULE OF QUEENS (Book #13)
AN OATH OF BROTHERS (Book #14)
A DREAM OF MORTALS (Book #15)
A JOUST OF KNIGHTS (Book #16)
THE GIFT OF BATTLE (Book #17)

THE SURVIVAL TRILOGY
ARENA ONE: SLAVERSUNNERS (Book #1)
ARENA TWO (Book #2)

THE VAMPIRE JOURNALS
TURNED (Book #1)
LOVED (Book #2)
BETRAYED (Book #3)

About Morgan Rice

Morgan Rice is the #1 bestselling and USA Today bestselling author of the epic fantasy series THE SORCERER'S RING, comprising seventeen books; of the #1 bestselling series THE VAMPIRE JOURNALS, comprising eleven books (and counting); of the #1 bestselling series THE SURVIVAL TRILOGY, a post-apocalyptic thriller comprising two books (and counting); and of the new epic fantasy series KINGS AND SORCERERS, comprising six books. Morgan's books are available in audio and print editions, and translations are available in over 25 languages.

TURNED (Book #1 in the Vampire Journals), ARENA ONE (Book #1 of the Survival Trilogy) and A QUEST OF HEROES (Book #1 in the Sorcerer's Ring) and RISE OF THE DRAGONS (Kings and Sorcerers—Book #1) are each available as a free download!

Morgan loves to hear from you, so please feel free to visit www.morganricebooks.com to join the email list, receive a free book, receive free giveaways, download the free app, get the latest exclusive news, connect on Facebook and Twitter, and stay in touch!

Made in the USA
Monee, IL
30 September 2021